Shepherdess
of the
Sumertun Ranch

A novel by
J.B. Wallace

This novel is dedicated to Lloyd Keene, a friend and fellow teacher, whose experience as a
youth gave me the idea for the novel.

The characters in this novel and the events of the summer are fictional. The trek is based
on an annual occurrence that occurred each summer, until after World War II, when loss of
Federal grazing lands and trucking made the annual drive obsolete. Photographs verify that
sheep did cross the Columbia River on the Grand Coulee Dam.

ISBN-10: 1479175870
EAN-13: 9781479175871

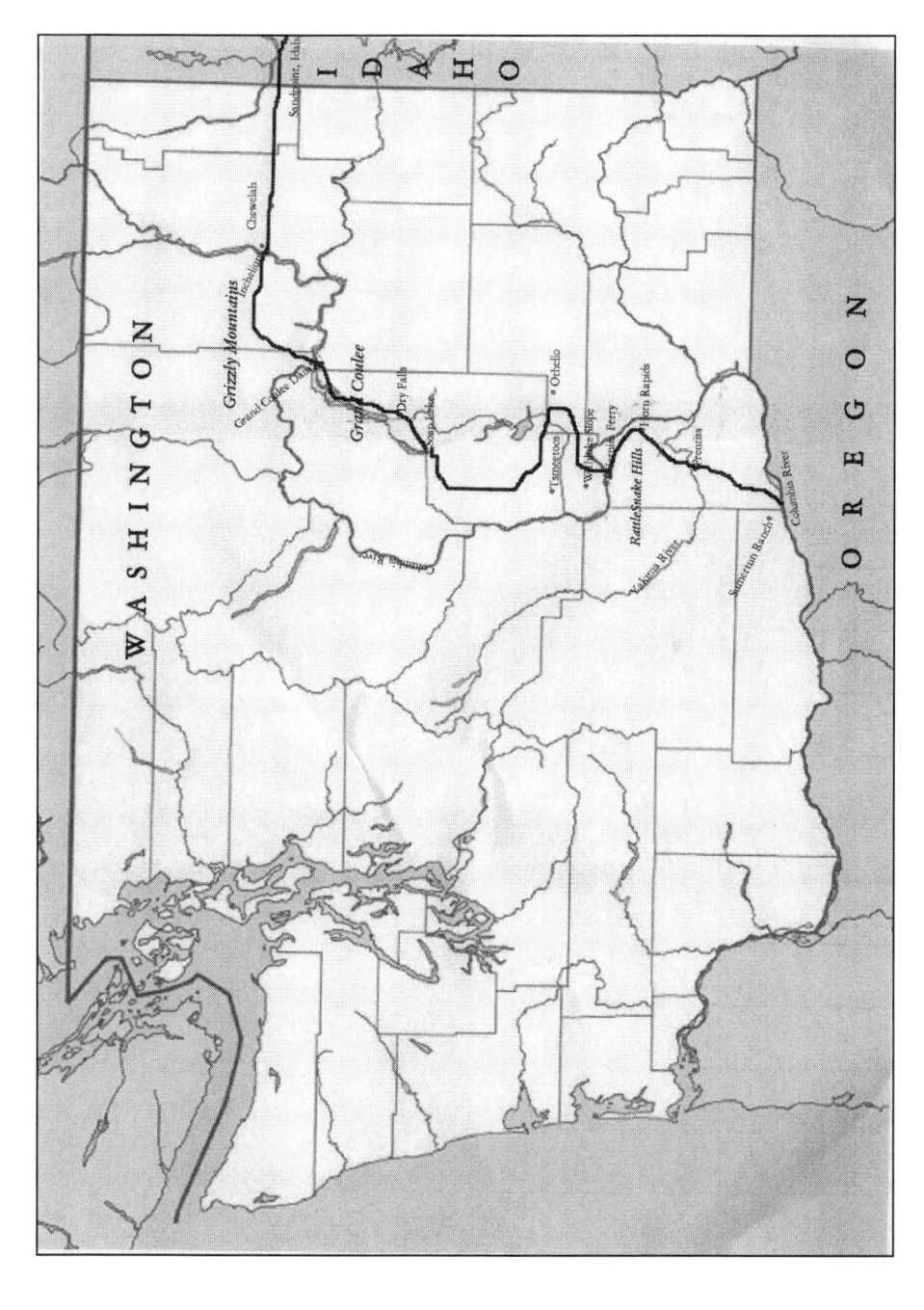

1
Home, February 4, 1940

Catherine Sumertun had wasted little time in catching the 1:45 pm. train for the three hour ride from Portland, Oregon to Pasco, Washington. Her stepfather, Corwin Turnoch, had called her home from the Western College for Women in Portland to care for her flu stricken mother. It had been a frustrating ride for the twenty year old Catherine. She had no idea how sick her mother was. When she had returned to college three weeks ago her mother had been cheerful, well and happy. Anyone who lived on the isolated Horse Heavens bench of southeastern Washington knew how serious flu could be and how difficult it was to get medical help. The closest medical facility was thirty miles away and any doctor had to travel that far over gravel roads from Prentiss, Washington to get to the Sumertun Ranch.

༄

Amidst hissing steam condensing in the frigid winter air and screeching brakes the locomotive slowed to a stop at the Pasco train station. Corwin and Alex, her sixteen year old brother, met her as she walked into the train station. Alex dutifully carried her suitcase to the waiting family four-door, Chevrolet sedan. The fifty mile ride to the ranch house overlooking the Columbia River gave her time to find out about her mother's illness. She learned her mother's had been sick a week before her desperate stepfather called and asked her to come home. That meant he didn't know what else to do. That worried her even more.

When Catherine arrived home she immediately went to see her ailing mother. She lay in bed supported by a myriad of large soft pillows. A woolen Pendleton blanket draped over her shoulders and the light-blue, flannel nightgown she wore. Her arms lay outside of the blanket, free to reach out and extend a feeble welcome home greeting to her daughter. Catherine sat on the edge of the bed and tenderly hugged her mother, cheek to hot cheek.

Dampness darkened Sarah's light brown hair. The faint smell of sickness and tussled bedding hung in the air. She certainly didn't resemble the five foot, three inch dynamo she left after Christmas to return to Portland and Western. Catherine pulled away to stroke her mother's forehead, which felt hot to the touch. She touched her mother's cheek before blurting out, "After Corwin's call this morning, I didn't know to what expect. Mother, you look awful."

Sarah laughed weakly and reached up to her daughter's face and tenderly caressed her cheek. "Catherine, don't ever change. Stay straightforward and bluntly honest. That's the young woman we all love." She patted her daughter's hand before she slumped back onto the pillows. Catherine leaned closer to hear, "I'm glad you're here."

"Me too. Now let's take your temperature so I'll know where we are."

She gently squeezed her mother's hand before she escaped to the bathroom for a tissue to dry her misty eyes. She returned with the thermometer from the medicine cabinet, shook it to get the mercury to the bottom of the bulb and then placed it under her mother's tongue.

∽

Alex quietly followed Corwin into the bedroom to find Sarah resting comfortably amid the pillows with the thermometer sticking out of her mouth.

Corwin protested. "What are you doing? She's has a slight fever. That's all."

"How high has it been?"

Corwin mumbled, "I don't know." The tension in the room increased. "Her forehead was warm to the hand, but that's not high." For that instant, his slender, apologetic posture took Catherine back to the summer her mother hired him.

Catherine reached over, removed the thermometer from under her mother's tongue and held it to the light. She gasped, "104.5°."

If looks could freeze Corwin would have been one giant icicle. Catherine coldly informed him. "No wonder she feels like she does. Don't you realize she's on the verge of something very dangerous? You let her lay here this sick for over a week and never made any attempt to get her to a doctor?" Corwin couldn't escape the caustic wrath that only an outspoken, twenty-year old college student could bestow. "What the hell would you have done if Alex hadn't called Dr. Hobson? Let her lay there and die?"

Corwin paled. He defiantly protested, "That's not fair," His eyes hardened, "And don't you dare yell at me like that! Of course I wouldn't just watch and let her die. I didn't know what to do, so I asked Merigold Andreason to come over and help." He angrily stepped toward his stepdaughter. "Alex called Dr. Hobson again yesterday and he will be here in two days, so you can ask him anything you want. I drove to Prentiss for the new anti-biotic pills he prescribed. Don't forget that!" He snarled, "Make sure she takes them." He failed miserably to mask his cold fury as he left.

Catherine's knew her mother had to be upset by this little to-do. She held her hand and quietly sat on the side of the bed to think about the moment. It was time to cool down and help, not hinder.

In the bathroom Catherine washed her face clean of any angry tears before soaking a clean washcloth in cold water. She read the prescription and the directions. She returned to her mother's bedside with a glass of cool water and the prescribed pill. Next she gently cooled her mother's face and forehead with the moist washcloth. Then she brushed and smoothed her hair before sitting contentedly with her mother until she drifted off. A slight grimace crossed her mother's normally serene face as she drifted into sleep. It was hard to imagine this woman as the "Queen of the Sumertun Ranch", who ruled with an iron hand and had done so since Catherine's eighth birthday.

2

A Secret Revealed

A rare house call to the 3000 acre dry land wheat, barley and sheep ranch amid the isolated Horse Heaven Hills emphasized the seriousness of the illness. After her mother's light breakfast and short nap Catherine gently washed her mother's face, hands and arms with a warm wash cloth and brushed her hair in preparation for Dr. Hobson's visit. She read the prescription and gave her mother the prescribed morning pill.

For her own satisfaction Catherine prepared to take her mother's temperature before Dr. Hobson arrived. She shook the mercury to the bottom of the thermometer, and then under her mother's tongue it went. After a few minutes she removed the thermometer, held it up against the light and announced to no one. "Good! It's almost down to 102.5° degrees." Sarah gave her daughter a faint smile.

Catherine took both as good signs.

In spite of her good intentions to stay politely in the background Catherine eagerly rushed ahead to greet Dr. Hobson the moment she heard his car coming into the lane from the county road. She was there to greet him when his car stopped. As always he was dressed impeccably in a dark blue suit, a bright red vest, blue tie, and shined shoes. His suit fit his slender frame like it was tailored. Somehow his impression gave Catherine added confidence. She accompanied him to her mother's bedroom and stayed when her stepfather left.

Sarah reclined against the fluffed pillows with her light brown hair combed and brushed. The dullness in her dark blue eyes had given way to a slight sparkle. She extended her hand to Dr. Hobson.

Dr. Hobson gently took his patient's hand in both of his, "I see you have someone to care for you, Sarah. That's good." He immediately became serious and began his examination. He put the stethoscope on Sarah's chest and listened. He concentrated intently. The only sounds were "umms" and "aahs" at each stop around her chest. When he finished he turned to Catherine and smiled and nodded, "Much better." When he straightened up he seemed satisfied. "Her chest sounds much, much clearer, not so congested."

He withdrew the thermometer from under her tongue and checked the reading. He had more encouraging words. He looked at Catherine. "I see her temperature has dropped a little... it's down to 102.5 degrees. You took her temperature the day you came home and it was 104.5? Right? "

Catherine nodded.

He reread the prescription and counted the pills. "Make sure she takes these anti-biotic pills with a full glass of water; one in the morning and one in the evening. Sulfa is new, very new, and holds great potential." Catherine stifled her giggle. Dr. Hobson looked like a mother hen ready to cluck "tsk, tsk, tsk" at any moment. He carefully recounted the pills again. "Catherine, it looks like someone hasn't been real faithful about giving her the pills. Not good. Make sure she takes her medicine as directed."

He paused then told Catherine, "This may be your most important job."

Dr. Hobson immediately poured a glass of cold water from the pitcher, which stood on the nightstand, and gave his patient another sulfa pill. She swallowed the pill and greedily gulped down the glass of cold water.

He grimaced, his voice almost a whisper. "Yes, yes ... your most important job." He straightened up. "However, what she has taken has helped. She's somewhat better. I came here today prepared to put her in the hospital if her temperature stayed above 104 degrees, but with love, constant care and proper medication this may not be needed." He put his hand on Catherine's shoulder. Concern radiated from those kind eyes. "If for any reason her temperature rises, give me a call, and get her to Prentiss. Now let's go to the kitchen. We can talk over a cup of hot coffee."

His eyes twinkled, "Is there any of Mrs. Andreason apple pie left in the fridge?"

Catherine gave silent thanks that she had not wolfed it all down last night.

⁓

Dr. Hobson was savoring the hot coffee and apple pie when Corwin rejoined them at the kitchen table to hear the results of his examination. Catherine discretely listened while he made his point very clear to Corwin, "She's better. Her temperature is down." He paused. "However, the medicine hasn't been given as prescribed. Sulfa must be given twice a day with plenty of water, once in the morning and once at again at night until the medicine is gone. That hasn't been done!"

Catherine thought Corwin shrunk down a little into his chair.

Dr. Hobson turned his attention to cutting another bite from the pie with his fork, and continued, "She seems to have improved some, but the medicine must be given as prescribed.

I've already told Catherine if there is any change for the worse I'll make arrangements to admit her into the hospital."

For a brief hostile moment Corwin centered his fierce glare on Catherine.

After the farewells Dr. Hobson got in his car, backed up, turned toward the lane, waved good-bye through his open window, and drove away.

Her stepfather immediately grabbed Catherine's shoulder and spun her around toward him. His eyes burned with a fury. "I hope you're happy. He made me feel like an ass because of those pills."

Catherine angrily shoved his hand off her shoulder. They stood toe to toe, face to face. "If you feel like an ass there must be a reason. You refused to put her in the hospital when it became too much for you. You didn't call me until you were desperate. She could have died because you didn't give her the sulfa pills as directed. Now keep your hands off me." Angry tears ran down her cheeks. She screeched, "All you had to do was read."

He raised his hand to deliver a blow.

Catherine matched him, angry glare for angry glare. "Go ahead and hit me. It won't change one thing."

A hopelessness she couldn't read crossed his face. He slowly dropped his hand. "Alex and I will care for her." His voice was resigned. "Why don't you just go back to Western?"

Puzzled, Catherine remained angry. She pointed to the house. "Because that's my sick mother in there and this is my home. You called me because you couldn't handle it. Remember?" She defiantly added, "I plan to stay until she's well, and I'll go back to Western when I'm damn good and ready. Got that?"

Corwin swelled up like a toad.

Catherine braced herself for another onslaught.

Her step father simply turned away and wandered, slump shouldered, back into the house. He stood five foot, eight inches, but at the moment seemed much shorter. She expected something, but not what she witnessed. She watched him wipe the back of his hand across his eyes. Tears?

What just happened? Why was he so helpless, so apologetic? He should have been madder than hell. Nothing had prepared her for that kind of reaction.

༄

In the clear western sky the wintery chill had the desired cooling effect on her fiery temper. Catherine pondered on her own lack of control. She hung her head a little and then laughed. That temper had caused trouble before. She knew it had to be controlled, but damn it, the misread prescription could've cost her mother her life. Just thinking about it made the flush of anger creep back into her cheeks. It was time to calm down and start thinking in a more rational manner.

A quiet walk around the farmyard restored some of Catherine's normal good spirits, but her active imagination let her explore the worst of circumstances. What would have happened if she hadn't come home? What if Corwin had kept on not giving the sulfa as prescribed? She shuddered at the thought. Her mother could have died.

What would happen then? Did Corwin think he could acquire land through the death of her mother? She cursed herself for even thinking like that. She knew the Sumertun Trust wouldn't let that happen, but what if Corwin didn't know?

She looked up and spotted Alex waiting in the small backyard. He didn't look happy.

"Sis, what the devil did you say to him? He's not handling Mom's sickness well as it is. You storming around didn't help anyone."

"You heard what the doctor said. She was given only half her pills. Thank heavens it was only three days. Whose fault is that?"

"It may be mine." He mumbled, "I didn't step up and help him."

That remark puzzled Catherine. She carefully studied her brother. Alex seemed reluctant to say any more.

"Come on, Alex. How could you have helped?"

"I could have read the directions for him."

"Why would you do that? Tell me what's bothering you!"

Before his impatient sister exploded Alex raised his eyes from the ground and delivered his bombshell. "I think Corwin can't read."

3
Alex

Catherine's stomach churned. No tell-tale swoosh of air followed, but it felt like someone had hit her in the stomach. It just wasn't possible! Catherine plopped down on the porch bench and stared with unseeing eyes at the morning sky. Alex's news explained a lot. Still, it seemed impossible. Everyone could read and write. "Alex, what did you just say?"

He put his hand on her shoulder and leaned down to face his sister. His voice became low and confidential. "You heard me, Sis. I think Corwin can't read."

Catherine's mind remained confused by a thousand images, none of which made the picture any clearer. Since her eighth birthday her mother had controlled everything with an iron hand. After she married Corwin nothing changed, but she must have seen some clues.

Catherine followed her own logic. Ask questions if you want to know something. She asked Alex, "How did you find out?"

"There was no magic moment. Corwin only had to follow directions when he first came to the ranch. Granddad Carter probably gave him all the work instructions and he did as he was told. Casual observations over time just added up."

Catherine could understand how Corwin got along under those conditions, but she wanted more. "What observations?"

"I kept noticing the little things." Alex stood a little taller. He had surprised his sister. That didn't happen very often. A self-satisfied smile appeared.

Catherine listened carefully to her sixteen year-old brother as he confided, "There were some things I didn't understand as I got older. Maybe it's a male thing. Corwin isn't dumb, but how could he let a woman run every part of his life? He worked every day, and was bossed every day. Constant bossing would bug you and it bothered me, but it didn't seem to bother him."

Alex enjoyed this moment. Somebody actually listened to him. He told her his theory. "I wondered why he made me read directions on fertilizer bags and tools, so I read the directions wrong a few times to see if he caught them. He didn't."

There was more to explain to his sister. "He's figured out how to survive by avoiding situations that would expose him. People help him and they don't even know it." Alex watched his sister absorb these facts.

She asked, "What about the sheep? I find it hard to believe Pete could be fooled."

"Don't worry, Sis. Nothing has changed down there. Even Mother doesn't boss Pete Alzola. He's the best sheep man around and she knows it. She confers with him on matters that involve the sheep." He scratched his ear lobe and chuckled before he spoke again. "So now you know."

Alex knew one more serious problem had to be agreed to, or all hell would break loose. His sister was smart, but she had to know everything. What would she do with this new discovery? Would she cause problems? He hoped not. He had to say something. "Corwin makes sure he isn't put in the position where he has to read. You can see he has no confidence and the medicine slip-up shows you why. He makes sure everyone else does the reading. He has been here long enough to know the ranch routines, and he's a steady worker, so everything runs smoothly. The only thing that has changed is he dresses better, looks better and is much smoother. Mother still does all the book work and he seems to enjoy my mother taking charge of his life." He looked at her sternly and warned her. "You couldn't live like that and neither could I, but he can, so leave it at that. Okay?

How good was this? His sister actually agreed. He made his expression serious and his voice strong, but above all he prayed his voice wouldn't crack. This had been an annoying factor lately. Everyone told him he was just growing up. He made every effort to keep his voice on the same level as he told her, "You're pushier than mother, so be careful. Don't get the idea you should teach him to read and write. He's okay for now. Can you do this?"

Catherine nodded. She wondered how many younger brothers had suddenly grown up unnoticed by their families. Catherine put her hand on his shoulder.

He drew back. Was she going to argue with him?

She smiled and laughed and threatened to hug him. "Alex you're a revelation. Remind me to never take you for granted again. I think you are becoming quite the young man." She pulled him close and hugged him. "Thanks for sharing, Alex. I appreciate what you have observed and that you told me. I love you."

Alex rewarded his sister with a wide grin and a deepening pink-to-red blush that blazed up his cheeks. Arm in arm the two strolled into their mother's bedroom to the amazed looks of their stepfather and mother.

Alex knew it was time for Catherine to check on her mother before preparing Merigold Andreason's fresh chicken noodle soup for lunch. Alex stood on cloud nine. His sister's compliments had done that. His pretense at adulthood faltered when he cheerfully hailed his mother. "You're looking much better, moth—."

His voice trembled between being a baritone or a tenor at that exact moment. Mutual smiles lasted until the high pitch sank back to his normal speaking tone. He felt engulfed by a giant squeeze and a quick smooch on the cheek from his sister. He couldn't stop the blush that heated his face.

4
The Lambing Shed Beckons

W hen her temperature dropped to 100° the next day a
smile blossomed on every face in the bedroom. Sarah
Turnoch seemed well on the road to recovery.

Her stepfather surprised Catherine. Perhaps he appreciated
not having his secret exposed. Perhaps he was glad to see his
wife's recovering. Whatever the reason, Corwin Turnoch put his
best foot forward, "Looks like you're a good nurse, Catherine.
Your mother's much better." This was a far cry from the anger
he displayed after Dr. Hobson left.

Catherine didn't let the opportunity for peace pass. "I'm glad
you called me to come home. Thank you." She quickly excused
herself to go to the kitchen and prepare a lunch tray with more
of Mrs. Andreason's home-made chicken noodle soup, the star
attraction. She sat with her mother while she finished her lunch.
When she comfortably dozed off Catherine felt free to visit the
lambing sheds, one of her favorite places in the world.

She went to her room to change clothes. She slipped on
heavier socks and shoved her feet into older, weather-beaten

boots, wiggled her toes until they felt comfortable, and laced up the worn leather shoestrings. Next the fleece-lined jacket came out of the closet. She began the brisk walk to the part of the ranch she loved, but which college seemed to be distancing from her.

From the ranch house near the top of the ridge overlooking the Columbia River and Oregon on the other side to the lambing sheds on the flood plain was a half mile walk. The sheds and lambing pens were further out when her father lived. Her mother and Pete Alzola thought the best location was closer to the ranch house and barn. That's when Catherine learned "The Queen of the Sumertun Ranch" viewed Pete Alzola as an equal, well almost.

As a teen-ager she had come down to the lambing shed every chance she got. Taking care of bum lambs had been her sacred duty. Her father had started this. Happy memories of these nurturings returned on the walk down the hill to the sheds.

Sheep were not known as smart animals. She never understood why a ewe couldn't bond immediately with her lamb or lost that bond if separated. This happened often with twins. One bonded. One was neglected. The motherless bum lamb had to be fed and saved. It had been immensely satisfying to Catherine to hold the large bottle of prepared milk while the little critter sucked on it. The bum lambs weren't gentle when they butted her for attention or food. They had to be fed and cared for until they were old enough and strong enough to exist on grain, hay and then grass. This was vital if they were to survive the long summer drive to Montana.

The warm thoughts stayed with Catherine and time disappeared on her walk. She returned to the present when she walked between the rows of pens that held the expectant ewes. The cacophony of bleating ewes and their new lambs became a constant. The ever present need to exchange fresh straw for old lingered. It was a smell she understood and loved.

The lambing shed was nothing more than a large wooden framework covered with canvas. When the lambing season was over the canvas would be removed, folded and stored. The spring winds would blow part of the straw away from the pens. The present arena of beehive activity would become an abandoned derelict until the next year.

The adjacent rows of pens were utile in nature and cheaply made. The fences were four feet high and made of straw tamped down between two sides of woven wire. The straw came from the wheat fields on the ranch. Each small ten foot by ten foot enclosure was easy to make and cheap to maintain.

She spied Pete Alzola leaning over the fence to check on an expectant ewe. It was a familiar, pleasing sight. His decision on the urgency of the inspected ewe came from years of experience. He beckoned to the young man hovering nearby. He opened the gate and the two of them ushered the ewe toward the lambing shed.

Catherine couldn't hide a slight smile. The young man was a handsome son-of-a-gun. A small wisp of brown hair stuck out from his black, knitted watch cap. Brown eyes complimented the hair. He wore the customary pair of Levi pants and a red-black plaid, flannel shirt. Urging the ewe forward he passed Catherine and smiled and then ... he winked.

She couldn't stop her sparkling smile from appearing.

Pete barked, "Okay, Romeo, get your mind back on the sheep. You have work to do."

She watched the two men hustle the expecting ewe inside where she disappeared into the maze of activity. The winker stood several inches taller than Pete. His muscular shoulders matched Pete's. Impressive! Catherine followed them into the lambing shed. The familiar sight greeted her. This part hadn't changed since she was a little girl.

The plaintive sound of hard labor, the small bleats of new life and the splashing of cleansing water was a symphony unlike no other on earth. It fascinated Catherine, always had; probably always would. Sheep were a large part of the ranch's success. The upcoming summer trek with free grazing across state and federal lands to Montana was vital to the economic success of the Sumertun ranch.

～

The familiar sight of Pete moving around the lambing stations reassured her. As a small girl it was always Mr. Alzola, but over the years it became Peter Alzola, then Peter and finally Pete. Her love and respect grew with each shortening. His dark hair sported a few gray streaks, but the muscular shoulders and stocky build on a five foot, nine inch frame never changed. After her father died he had become a second father, an encourager and wise counsel.

Pete walked forward to greet her. He wore the same familiar uniform; Levis and a plaid flannel shirt worn over a white tee shirt. It was a wonderful sight. A smile played on Catherine's lips. He opened strong arms to engulf her, lift her and swing her around. "Ah, Catherine it's good to see you." His dark eyes sparkled as he gently pushed her away to arm's length to look. "You look great. College agrees with you." Pete could always spare a few minutes for her. They talked about Sarah's progress in her battle with the flu, about college and finally about the upcoming summer drive to Montana.

Pete confided, "This year's mystery is almost solved. The young man with the rakish smile and the winking eye looks like he will replace Ed Carrisetta." He noticed the question in her eyes. "I guess you wouldn't know. Ed's been pretty sick this winter. He doesn't want to go again." He squeezed her shoulders and joked, "I bet you still have that dream."

The dream had started in the first grade after her father brought home the first bum lamb for her to care for until it could make the summer drive. She jealously watched the sheep leave the ranch each spring and every year she dreamed of taking them to Montana.

The dream faded some as she realized her stepfather pushed her into Western Women's College for two reasons; to find a husband and to get her away from the ranch. Many times he had let her know young ladies didn't do outdoor ranch work.

That hadn't stopped her from getting home during spring breaks to watch the sheep start up the grade from the meadow along the Columbia, past the horse barn, the ranch house above the ridge, and out into the open range. Her mother's illness insured her presence at the beginning of this year's drive.

Before there were any more questions a worker called for Pete. Nothing different here; someone always needed Pete. She stepped outside the lambing shed for some fresh air.

She froze at the sight.

5
A Burning Question

A thin wisp of smoke drifted up from the lambing pen. Catherizne wasted no time. She darted back inside to the nearest water barrel, grabbed a bucket, scooped it full of water, and sprinted back toward the smoke. Any fire in the straw pens was a catastrophe waiting to happen. She opened the gate and darted inside.

Some idiot squatted low in the corner of the pen puffing on a cigarette. Who would be stupid enough to hide behind a straw wall to sneak a smoke? Catherine didn't wait to find out. She threw the water at the cigarette dangling from a half-open mouth.

Surprised, then angry, the young man sputtered and struggled to rise from his sudden drenching. Water dripped from his uncut, stringy dark-brown hair. His face was contorted with rage, but the soggy cigarette still hung in his mouth. He stammered, "What the hell is the matter with you? You can't go around throwing water on people."

"I'll throw water on anyone who is dumb to smoke around all this straw. You should be horsewhipped for putting everyone in such danger."

He defiantly dared her, "I suppose you think you're the one to do it."

Others came running toward them, but Catherine was too mad to notice. She glared at the stupid dolt and yelled, "If I have to, yes. Don't think for one minute I wouldn't do it." She was ready to fire the belligerent little clod.

His face registered shock again as a second torrent of water followed. Catherine dived for the falling roll-your-own cigarette. She caught it before it hit the straw floor. The man, who had winked at her, stood beside her. He never took his eyes off of the offender. "Art, you know better than this. Smokers go outside the area. Now get out of here and get some dry clothes." His stare turned icy. "You know Pete has to hear of this, don't you?"

The entire scene mesmerized Catherine.

The smoker had been caught in the worst of circumstances. He would have to face Pete. If Catherine had her way he would be fired. The narrow face with a receding chin reminded Catherine of a rat.

"Don't worry about it, Hank." His voice became defiant. "Nothing's going to happen." He turned to Catherine, "I don't know who you are, and I don't care, but what's a good looker like you doing here where you have no business; slumming?"

She stepped toward rat face, ready to deliver some very unlady-like words at this small, slender snippet of a man. A restraining arm reached around her waist, held her tight and lifted her off the straw floor. The man who had winked at her was equal to the task. There was a great deal of pleasure in his voice. "Art, I'd like you to meet Miss Catherine Sumertun."

It pleased her to see the first glint of fear creep into those watery, pale blue eyes.

Her savior's bright, glistening smile replaced his familiar wink. "Catherine, meet Art Wheeler. I'm sure he won't forget you." His eyes twinkled. "I know I won't."

The two of them watched the sopping wet man slink away, but he wasn't home free. Pete met him halfway. He placed a fatherly arm around Art Wheeler's shoulder.

Catherine smiled. That wouldn't be a sympathetic father-son conversation.

⁓

The handsome winker's smile brightened Catherine's world. She almost lost her breath when he said, "Catherine Sumertun, let me introduce myself. I'm Henry Hirsch Jr. I go by Hank."

She managed to keep her voice steady. "I'm very glad to meet you Hank. I'm Catherine." Her voice dropped to sugar sweet, "Now that we have been introduced, don't you think it's time to take your arm from around my waist and put me down?"

"You're right Catherine." He gently lowered her to the ground and gallantly added, "It did feel awfully good, though."

Catherine smiled. This guy was smooth. She took a deep breath. Her pleasure couldn't be completely masked, but she did have the luxury of a serious question. "You certainly got here fast enough. How did you know?"

"Anytime some runs out of the lambing shed carrying a bucket of water, the only thought is fire. You'll notice several others were following me."

"Yeah, I noticed afterwards, but you got here first. That second bucketful splashing on the cigarette was a very welcome sight." She laughed. "He damn well deserved it."

Art Wheeler's last defiant declaration nagged at her. Nothing about him seemed right. This man in front of her, who had held her around the waist, was a stranger. At this point, everything about him seemed right. His heart-grabbing smile certainly impressed her. Had he been a knight riding a white charger the caption would read, "Sir Hank to the rescue."

It seemed natural to ask, "Did you hear Art Wheeler when he said, 'Don't worry, nothing will happen.' I was ready to fire his smart mouth when you arrived."

"I haven't had time to think about it, but it did seem he thought no one would bother him." He turned those beguiling dark eyes loose on her.

That wasn't fair. Her weakened knees didn't want to function.

He quizzed her, "What do you know about him?"

"Until today I didn't know he existed and now that I've seen him, that's enough." She looked up the lane between the pens. Close to the lambing shed Pete still held the smoker captive with a strong arm around his shoulders.

"Hank, maybe it's time to ask some questions."

"It wouldn't hurt. Let me know if you learn anything. I'll do the same." He looked toward the beckoning Pete, and then at Catherine. "Looks like it's time for work." Smoothly he took her hand, raised it to his lips and kissed the back of her hand. "It's been a pleasure, Catherine of Sumertun. I hope to see you again while you're home." He released her hand and left before she recovered.

She watched the lean, hard muscled Hank walk away. Thanks to the water being tossed about his cotton shirt clung tightly to his chest and shoulders. A smile crossed her lips. He would see her again. She would make sure of that.

6
The Lambing Shed

Her mother enjoyed another restful night. Her temperature had crept steadily down toward normal. She sat up most of the morning and enjoyed the rare February sun. This allowed Catherine to go down to the lambing sheds again. She thought of Hank. A wink or a smile wasn't much to go on, but it was better than nothing.

The lambing season was winding down, but she found him with Pete in their usual place, leaning over a straw fence deciding which ewes were ready to deliver their lambs. Catherine followed them inside.

She watched men and sheep working together to bring the new lambs into the world. If the mother paid little attention to her new, wobbly lamb it was up to Hank to push them into the sheltered pens to bond, feed and recuperate. This was a crucial time. Sometimes several ewes and their lambs were pushed out together toward the pens and became separated. If the two didn't bond at that crucial time the mother wouldn't accept her lamb. Hank and several others tried to make sure this didn't happen.

She wandered around the big canvas-covered framework while they worked. She thought of April 1; the start of the summer trek with three bands of 1,500 sheep each to Montana would soon be here.

"Why so sad, Catherine?"

She turned to the welcome voice. "Just thinking. Did you know I cried the first time my father brought me to the old pens?"

Hank's eyes danced mischievously at this question.

He must think I'm a nut.

He surprised her by simply asking, "Why would you cry here?" After a moment's pause he cautiously probed for an answer. "Care to tell me?"

Catherine was glad for the opening. "I was five years old when my father brought me here to watch the sheep sheared. The barns were further out then. They brought the sheep into this same type of canvass covered shed to shear them. I watched the men cradle the sheep's back into their legs to hold them tight while they sheared them. They used hand shears then. The long fleeces fairly flew off the sheep. It scared me.

"I thought cutting their wool hurt them and without their wool the sheep would get cold. I still remember Pete and my father talking to me. They very carefully explained that the sheep felt no pain, and that they would grow enough wool before the next winter to keep them warm." She sighed at the memory.

"Why the sigh, Catherine?"

"My father died in the field a year and a half after that."

Hank reached over and took her hand. "I'm sorry. That's always hard; no matter how it happens."

Catherine wondered what that meant, but she needed something to distract her from the increasing warmth she felt. She pointed to the lambing process going on. "It was two years before I came down here again. This was where the lambs were delivered and wiped dry before their first nursing. They were herded out of the lambing shed to bond again in the pens. Those lambs looked so pitiful."

Catherine kept wondering how one man could be so pleasant by just being there. There was not a tinge of impatience, not even a hint of a laugh as he listened to her thoughts from childhood. He made her feel those thoughts were the most natural thing in the world

Oh! That's great Catherine. How long have you known him?"

She told Hank, "Here is where I developed my real love for the sheep."

"Oh, that's right. I've heard you were 'The Bum Lamb Princess'."

She searched his face for any obnoxious man-putting-down-woman thing. Did he really understand how she must have felt, or was he just teasing? An unexplained relief flooded her senses when he didn't make fun of her. She said, "As long as you were there to give them their bottle they were warm, cuddly and loving. If they weren't satisfied they would butt you. Believe me those little buggers could butt pretty hard." She noticed Hank's little half-smile.

That's better. I could really get to like this guy.

"Did you know when each bum lamb became self-sufficient and left for Montana I wrote a "1" in my notebook. Over the years I took care of 263 bum lambs." She watched him do the mental arithmetic. Catherine could see his amazement. Did he believe her numbers? Did he think saving the bum lambs was important? She hoped he had been impressed.

He had been. He pushed his knitted cap further upon his head. "Catherine. I'd say you made the ranch a ton of money over the years." He shook his head in wonderment, smiled that golden smile, and reached to congratulate her.

Catherine wanted to obey the urge to walk into those arms, but Hank had another question. "I was here for harvest last summer and I heard the title "Queen of the Sumertun Ranch" given to your mother. How did that come about? What did she do to earn that title?"

"She saved the ranch."

"And just how did she do that?" Catherine heard doubt in Hank's voice.

"Would you like to hear the story of my eighth birthday and how fate intervened?"

"You're making this sound mysterious, but yes."

"Okay. Here goes.

❧

"July fifteenth was a perfect day for my eighth birthday party. The normally hot July sun stayed hidden behind drifting clouds and the temperature remained cool. The guests were several neighboring schoolmates and their parents. After the three-legged race and a game of tag it was time to open the presents. I joyfully ripped away the colored tissue paper and the bright ribbons. After the oohs and aahs it was time to light the candles on the cake.

"Everyone eagerly waited for me to blow out the candles. I heard my mother whisper, 'If your wish is to come true, you must blow out all the candles.' I took a deep breath, stood on my toes, and blew out all eight candles. The birthday cake and ice cream was served.

"When my mother asked me what I wished for, I haughtily said, 'If I tell you, my wish won't come true.'

"Harvest usually followed my birthday by ten days to two weeks. With all the wisdom of an eight year old I had wished for needed help. I glanced past mother into the large, weather-beaten, faded red machine shed. The unmaintained combines spoke volumes.

"I looked so sad my mother asked what was wrong. I couldn't tell her harvest would be like the rest of the ranch work since daddy died ... late and not good.

"Fate entered our life after my birthday party. Lily Andreason, who helped my mother with the party, couldn't get her car started, so mother had to drive her home. This move became a turning point in my mother's life. Driving on the lane to the county road the summer fallow fields should have been harrowed clean, weeded and ready for the fall seeding of winter wheat. Instead my mother saw fields covered with two to three foot tall, moisture-sucking weeds. Total disaster loomed. Next year's crop would never survive. The neglect she had allowed shocked her. Fate had played her trump card.

"The next day I stood just outside the parlor and listened as my mother ranted at my Grandfather Carter. I'll never forget what my mother said. 'Carter Sumertun, I've literally let this place go to hell.'

"I put my hand over my mouth to keep quiet. My mother paced about like a caged tiger. She told my grandfather, 'I couldn't believe what I saw. There'll be no winter wheat crop this fall, unless things change. Believe me, Carter, I'll be out there every day to make sure there is a change. Burke deserves more than a weed clogged ranch, and so do you! Enough is enough.'

"I watched my grandfather smile."

"My mother reacted to his smile. 'That must sound funny coming from me.'"

"No, no Sarah, not funny, just human."

"My grandfather gently embraced my mother. 'Welcome back, Sarah. I know the ranch will be in good hands again, and I know my son would be proud of you.' He carefully wiped away her tears.

"From that fateful revelation, my mother gradually took control of every facet of the ranch operation. She checked every order, paid every bill, and hired, fired and paid the help. She oversaw the operation of the ranch. 'The Queen of the Sumertun Ranch' was on her way. The one exception was Pete Alzola. My father always claimed he was the best sheep man in the country.

Sheep became more of a partnership, but both knew who had the final word."

"Okay you two, playtime is over." A familiar voice interrupted. Pete walked purposefully toward them. That infectious smile never changed, but neither did the solid, no nonsense aura.

Amused, Catherine said. "Hank, if you are going back to work, you have to let go of my hand."

"You're right again, Catherine. It's becoming a habit. Maybe another time?"

There was no doubt in her mind.

‌ ❧

While Hank guided another expectant ewe into the shed Pete waited to talk to Catherine about Art Wheeler. A flicker of amusement sparkled in his dark eyes. "I hear you weren't very polite to him."

"He deserved everything he got. Just the thought of someone smoking in the pens scares everyone to death." Catherine's anger started rising. "Neither Hank nor I wasted any time being polite. He was smoking in a straw pen. Even though it wasn't my call, I almost fired him on the spot, but you were already on your way to see about the problem. I saw you talking to him with your arm around his shoulder. You were probably far more diplomatic than I would have been."

She asked, "Why did you ever hire him?"

"I didn't really hire him. Corwin insisted I take him on."

"Do you know anything about him?"

"No. He's here because of Corwin."

"Would you hire him if it was up to you?"

"Frankly, no!" Catherine thought it a very emphatic no. Pete continued, "He doesn't know anything about sheep and he's worthless as a worker. You have to watch him every minute."

The incessant bleating of another expectant ewe got Pete's full attention. Their chat ended. She watched him nudge another expecting ewe toward the lambing shed.

Why Art Wheeler knew he wouldn't be fired remained unanswered.

ᏇᎧ

Art stopped cleaning the pen to watch the three of them talking. How cozy can it get? Disgusted and angry he watched Hank and then Pete leave. She had no call to throw the bucket of water in my face. I was just enjoying a quick, but careful smoke. She screeched at me and shamed me. People like her never stop blaming someone. Even that damned Hank tossed water on me. No one should be allowed to make me feel like she did. Someday--someday I'll get even. In that instant he looked at Catherine and vowed revenge. Nobody can do what she did to me and get away with it.

Art Wheeler brightened some at the prospect of leaving the ranch with the Sumertun sheep to Montana. Corwin had told him he could.

ᏇᎧ

Catherine's idle gaze drifted across the shed and found Art. Pure hatred stared at her.

7
Inspection

Since the day she arrived home Catherine had marked each passing day on the calendar with a big, black X. February had come and gone. She marked March 10 with a big red X. It marked the day her mother walked out of the ranch house onto the open porch. She pulled the sky blue and pale yellow shawl tight around her shoulders and walked far enough into the farmyard area to see the Columbia River, her favorite ribbon of water. The river flowed serenely west until it became the energetic, white foamed Umatilla Rapids. She deeply inhaled the mild March air and declared she was ready to live again.

෴

Dr. Hobson stood with Corwin and smiled. It had been a slow recovery, but the new antibiotics had done their job. "Catherine, your mother has certainly benefited from having you home. Maybe you should look into becoming a nurse."

Catherine looked at Corwin and wondered what this was all about.

"Your studies at Western could easily be adjusted to utilize the training facilities in Portland. Compared to office jobs it's easier for a nurse to get a good paying job than it is to get a good paying office position."

Catherine noticed Corwin exchanged glances with Dr. Hobson. It looked like Corwin was still trying to get rid of her. She laughed. She knew he would be glad to see her go. "Mrs. Welsh has already assured me Western will be glad to have me back and I plan on being there for the spring quarter. That lets me stay and help my mother for a while. The last of my winter class assignments were sent last week, so I can still salvage the winter quarter." She shrugged her shoulders. "My grades will drop some, but that's all."

She was sure the delay didn't please Corwin, but this was a minor concern. A friendly closeness, which had developed with her mother, was a major bonus.

e~

The lengthening days allowed Catherine plenty of time to walk to the lambing shed after Dr. Hobson left. She couldn't help singing the lilting melodies that kept popping into her head. At the lambing sheds her smile still played around the edge of her lips as she and Pete set the time for Hank's morning's meeting with Sarah at eleven o'clock the next day. When Pete learned the real reason for the meeting he put his arm around Catherine's shoulders and beamed that enormous smile. He knew this meeting would not be sedate. Exuberance, suspicion and smiling would be the rule. How wrong could he be?

She sneaked several casual glances around the shed.

"There's no use looking for him here, Catherine."

Pete knew. She didn't fool him one bit. While enjoying her obvious embarrassment he pointed toward the three wagons, which resembled the old covered wagons that once rolled westward. "He's working on his Shepherd wagon every time he gets a chance. April isn't very far away." Pete mischievously chided her, "Maybe you should personally deliver this news about meeting with your mother tomorrow morning."

Catherine demurely kissed him on the cheek. "Thanks Pete. I'll try not to keep him from his work too long."

He watched her alternately skip, walk and jog the fifty yards to the row of three Shepherd wagons that abutted the fence beyond the lambing pens. Nobody had to say anything to him. Catherine had the look of young flower waiting to blossom. He reflected for a moment on how nice it was to be young and feel like that again. Would anything come of it was the real question.

❧

Catherine heard the hammering inside the wagon. She had seen this same thing for most of her life. The men, who lived in the wagons, wanted them to be able to resist the spring rains, the cold winds which rolled down the eastern slopes of the Cascades, the long hot summer weather with its thunderstorms, and the frosty weather of early fall. Each herder personalized his wagon so it became as comfortable as possible.

The wagons were simple affairs. The wheel base varied from eight feet to ten feet. The length of the floor varied, but it had to be practical. Fifteen feet long seemed to be the norm. Two sideboards, two and half feet high ran parallel to each other the length of the floor on either side of the floor. Another board formed the flat ledge that was the top.

The top of the ledge had to be wide enough for several storage drawers to fit underneath, strong enough to sit on, and accommodate a sleeper in a bedroll. A folding table stood near the front stood opposite the stove. The Coleman camp stove sat on the heat resistant brick on the other ledge. The opening for the stovepipe was directly above the stove. Man's ingenuity was at its best when figuring out how to get all the necessities into small, compact places.

The top was formed by long pliable wooden ribs which looped up and over the wagon bed. They were attached to the wagon bed by metal brackets. The waterproofed canvas top stretched over these loops. It could be rolled up from the bottom to let the summer breezes blow through or tied to the bottom to ward off storms.

Catherine had no trouble identifying Hank's wagon. It already sported one personalizing change. The wooden sideboards of the wagon were painted to match the clear February sky. The sky blue sparkled in the afternoon sun. She wondered what was happening inside. The trace of smoke escaping through the chimney pipe at the front of the wagon gave her the answer. The aroma said Hank was cooking. Catherine yelled, "Smells good. Is there enough for two?"

The small back door swung open and Hank's silhouette filled the doorway. When Catherine moved so the sun was at her back she saw the shape was dressed in his normal blue cotton shirt tucked into Levi's. He shoved one large lock of brown hair to one side. His face glistened with sweat. He held a hammer in his right hand. He grinned and motioned for her to come inside, "It's not a finished project, but you're welcome to come in, Princess, and see my summer home, and yes, there is enough food for two."

Princess, my daddy had always called me that.

"I'd love to see what you've done." She reached upward to Hank's outstretched arm. She knew what was coming and made no effort to escape. He pulled her up into a closeness that took her breath away. This greeting was far different than any other.

"Sorry about that, but this narrow door is too small for both of us at once. Come inside where we have some room." He pulled her inside where they could comfortably stand.

"You're doing it again, Hank."

"What."

"You pulled me up and in, but your arm is still around me. Don't you think it's time to let go?"

"Catherine, you have no idea how good this feels. You're pretty hard to hold with just one arm. Let me use the other." He wrapped his free arm around her and pulled her closer.

Her arms moved automatically around him and she lifted her face upward. Her mouth was dry, but she knew this was a moment she had wanted.

Hank's lips closed on hers. It was tender, soft and delightful. She kissed him back. Their moistened lips worked to capture their sudden need for each other. The kiss went far beyond anything Catherine had ever imagined. The suddenness of this moment startled her, and she wanted more. The kisses deepened. She pressed closer. That was not an option.

Finally she pushed away. She took a deep breath, which allowed her to sigh. "Wow. I certainly didn't expect a greeting like that."

"I didn't mean to do that, but I'm not sorry one bit, Catherine Sumertun."

"Good! Don't even try to apologize, Henry Hirsch! No woman ever wants a man to apologize for kissing her." She took a deep breath and pulled him down to her.

❧

This time Hank applied the brakes. "Whoa. Take it easy, Catherine. We've got to slow this train down. This could be a wreck if we let it." He pushed Catherine away to arms length and kept her there with both hands on her shoulders. Their eyes met. A little spasm shook his stomach. Who was he kidding? He already liked this woman more than he should.

The coaxing sprite tried to move closer.

He reacted with a slow grin. He couldn't resist this little she-devil. He let his arms drop from her shoulders to wrap around her waist and hug her. He felt the welcome pull of her arms. He knew exactly what this daring woman in his arms wanted. He steeled against the desire to push for more. He wasn't going to be that "damn Hank" who led the boss's daughter astray. On the other hand it might be worth it. With a sigh he pushed the reluctant woman away. "Let me show you the inside of my summer home."

⁓

She barely heard Hank's invitation to taste his cooking and see the rest of his wagon. She kept her hand in his. The fuzzy warmth gave way to attention at the work he had done. The most noticeable was the white paint on the inside sideboards and the ledge on each side. A small folding table was attached by hinges to the sideboard opposite the stove. The bedroll stretched out on the ledge toward the rear of the wagon. A small box, probably at least two feet square caught her attention.

"What is that?"

"That's my experiment. It is supposed to be an ice box. If I can somehow get ice on a regular basis, it will help me store food. Pretty good, huh?"

"Maybe I could get the job of supplying you with ice?"

He did the only safe thing. He ignored her. "Look at the end of the sideboard away from the icebox. Catherine rose, still holding his hand and inspected the small closet. An extra pair of Levis and several shirts hung from the hangers.

"Hank, it looks like a great summer for you. Are you looking forward to it?"

"Yes and no. Everything is furnished by the Sumertun Ranch, so it's a great chance to save some money and even study. That'll make it easier to get back to Washington State this fall. The down side is a long, lonely summer with 1,500 sheep that need attention, but furnish no company. That'll have to come from the sheep dogs and horses and the camp suppliers.

"Maybe I could come up on a regular basis as your supplier?"

Hank ignored that suggestion.

Her tour of the herder's Taj Mahal ended at the back door by the bedroll. Catherine had managed to stand squarely in front of Hank. She reached up and locked her arms around his neck. She turned her eager face up and parted her lips. She pulled his face directly to hers. The erupting passion felt like it had never stopped. She pulled Hank down to the bedroll on the ledge and flung her outside leg up and over Hank. He turned to face her. They pulled each other close and tight.

⁓

"Hank, get yourself down here. I need your help. Hank ... Hank ... Hank!"

Catherine knew that voice. She was being chaperoned whether she wanted it or not. She walked to the rear door and flung it open. She waved to Pete and yelled, "Don't worry Pete, he's on his way."

Catherine turned to Hank and causally mentioned, "By the way Hank, my mother is coming down to the lambing sheds at eleven o'clock tomorrow morning for the express purpose of meeting you. She has been hearing stories, so I invited her down to meet you. I think you're being inspected." Her droll laughed followed, "That's what I was doing today. I was inspecting you."

"Did I pass inspection?"

"I don't know, but we have all summer to find out."

8
Impressions

Pete heard the car making its way down the road to the sheds. It was not unusual for Sarah to come to the lambing sheds, but it was unusual for her to come down for the sole purpose of meeting Hank. Pete wondered what devious plan was being plotted, and by whom. Maybe the mother hen was just looking out for her chick, but he knew Sarah would not be subtle. He sauntered out of the lambing shed to meet the car.

Pete had heard many reports about Sarah's health from his wife, but he hadn't seen Sarah since she became ill. Pete was anxious as he opened the door and helped Sarah out. She barely stood up before his supporting arms engulfed her. "Sarah, Sarah, you're a wonderful sight! My wife said you were getting better."

Catherine noticed there were tears in his eyes.

The lambing season was all but over, but Sarah tagged along with Pete. Her eyes took in everything. Pete smiled as he watched Sarah's careful inspection of the unsuspecting Hank while he attended to a newborn lamb.

Catherine did the same, but for a different reason.

After the ewe and her new lamb were taken to an outside holding pen Pete introduced Hank to Sarah. Back inside the two gabbed happily over a characteristically strong cup of coffee. Catherine thought she may as well not been there.

When Sarah indicated it was time to go home Hank walked her to the car and politely held the door open. Catherine witnessed a miracle. Before she stepped inside the car her mother actually hugged Hank and thanked him for a great morning.

⤸

Catherine wanted an opinion from her mother on the drive up the grade, but not a word passed between the two. She let her mother out at the back yard gate, and drove the car into the garage. Back in the kitchen she found her mother waiting for the water to boil. "How does a nice cup of tea sound, Catherine?"

"Sounds good."

Sarah exclaimed, "Some things never change. They still make the lousiest coffee in the world down there. It borders on boiled poison!" Sarah knew her daughter was dying to hear her thoughts on Hank, but she enforced silence until the tea was poured and cookies served.

Catherine could wait only so long. She tapped her fingers impatiently on the table. Her urgent plea sounded across the table. "Well, Mother?"

"You're wrong if you think I'll base my approval on one meeting."

A shadow of doubt crept into Catherine's thoughts. Her mother said, "Did you know his father was a section hand?"

"No, but what difference does that make?

"Not much really. His tone told me he didn't think much of that job." Sarah mulled this over for several minutes before she spoke again. "This is not a 'like father like son,' scenario. There's quite a jump from a section gang foreman to a son who is studying to be a veterinarian. Something is driving him. That's impressive, especially if he pulls it off."

The shadow lifted when she noticed her mother's faint, teasing smile. "Catherine, I must say he's handsome and very impressive. Pete thinks the world of him, and he certainly charmed the socks off of me." She paused and sipped her tea before she casually tossed out her verdict. "You could do worse."

That verdict warmed Catherine's heart. She cupped her hot tea cup with both hands and blushed. She reached out and squeezed her mother's hand so hard her mother flinched. She didn't understand why her mother's approval should cause such a reaction, but it did.

In spit of the surging elation, she felt it was time to reassure her mother. She released the pressure on her mother's hand. "Don't worry, mother, I'm not going to run off to some motel with anybody I've only known such a short time." Catherine sighed, "But, he certainly lights up my day. I'll try to keep you informed."

When her mother left for her afternoon rest Catherine walked outside into the cool February air. Her raucous laugh could be heard clear down to the lambing sheds.

9
Transition

Lambing season was over. Two major jobs remained before the sheep left for Montana. The lambing shed had to be torn down and the three bands of sheep had to be gathered from the pastures along the Columbia River.

Catherine found Hank and his crew hard at work removing the canvas coverings from the lambing sheds. She cheerfully pitched in to help unfasten and pull the canvas from the wooden rafters. She helped fold the canvas and make it as flat as possible. The canvases were then compactly rolled up and safely put in a storage room that stood beside the wooden framework remains of the building. The skeletal building would stand forlorn against the sky until it was reassembled for the fall shearing.

After each roll of canvas was stored Hank made sure he located Catherine and gave her his "job well done" smile. His reward was her stomach-knotting smile. She didn't have to help with the canvases, but she acted like it was fun. She had been remarkable.

Hank reflected back yesterday's meeting with Sarah Turnoch. When Catherine and then Pete informed him she wanted to talk to him, his first thought had been, "Oh, oh, here it comes." He had easily fielded the snickers and the teasing from the other hands that came from romancing the boss's daughter. Rumors and half facts about how her mother ran the ranch with an iron hand were common. The visit from the "Queen of the Sumertun Ranch" had meant only one thing to Hank. She meant to protect her daughter from the likes of him. It wouldn't be the first time someone had objected to their daughter being involved with the son of a Gandy Dancer.

෧

His father had worked on the section for the Union Pacific Railroad. Hank thought of it as a labor scorned. Section hands were the grunts of the industry. They replaced the heavy rails, secured a good roadway by laying the ties that were the foundation for the rails, and last but not least pounded the heavy spikes into place that held the rails to the ties. They constantly aligned and maintained the gauge of the rails. Their reward for this was low pay. It was a job that wore men out. It was a job that Hank thought slandered the Gandy Dancer's family.

Hank had never been proud of his father's job. It had caused him social problems. He often heard jokes about the Pump Car which took the Gandy Dancers to work. Despite rain, snow or blistering heat two men alternately pushed down on the seesaw handle which turned the wheels of the Pump Car. It was work just to get to work.

Despite the hardships Henry Hirsch Sr. kept his family housed and fed. Hank knew and respected him for this, but he didn't respect his father job. He watched his physically exhausted father become bitter. The softness in his life disappeared after his mother died from pneumonia his sophomore year in high school.

Football at Pasco High School saved his life. He worked alongside his father on the section for two summers and his gangling six foot frame filled out to a muscular 190 pounds. His athletic ability had earned him a scholarship to the Washington State College at Pullman, Washington and showed him a way of life he didn't know existed. Injury stopped his football career during his junior year, but his scholarship stayed. His studies introduced him to his chosen field, Veterinarian Science.

Hank knew two things. He would never settle for a job he couldn't respect, and he would become a veterinarian. He had let romance interfere once, but it had only strengthened his resolve not to let it happen again.

⁊

Hank had watched Pete greet Sarah from a convenient hiding place in the lambing shed. They were obviously glad to see each other. The respect the two had for each other was there for all to see. Still a little frail from her long bout with the flu, Sarah carried the aura of someone who has the complete trust of those around her. This didn't help. Hank was already intimidated by the visit and what he thought would happen.

Sarah had pleasantly surprised him. The regal aura remained, but it didn't isolate her. Although she still looked frail her manner had been warm. She had actually seemed to enjoy talking to him. She had questioned him about his work and talked a great deal about the responsibility of taking the sheep to Montana. She had commended him for his desire to become a veterinarian. Her first big smile ended as she said, "I understand you and my daughter threw water in a worker's face to put out his cigarette. Is this true?"

"Yes, but she got there first. She was a tigress." His stammering response had been the ice breaker. The conversation turned easy until Sarah confessed, "She likes you a lot. When I asked her about you, she said I should meet you. That sounded sensible, so here I am."

When she had looked intently at him, he had thought, "Oh, oh, here it comes."

How could he have been so wrong?

She smiled. "I'm glad I came down. No one can tell young loves what to do, but I want the two of you to behave like you have some common sense. Can you do that?"

His answer had been almost a whisper. "I believe we can."

"Good." She had said, "That's all a mother can ask. Now come here and give me a big hug." As an afterthought she added, "By the way, Pete thinks you are okay. You can't get a better endorsement than that."

He had walked Sarah back to the car and her waiting daughter. Sarah had hugged him again before getting into the car. Both women waved from the open windows as Catherine drove away.

The ecstatic Hank ignored the questioning looks of the men; even Art Wheeler's sneer didn't bother him as he had sauntered back to the lambing sheds. He had wanted to jump into the air and kick his heels. His big challenge became how he would handle this almost, "too hot to handle" romance. The summer of separation would help, but he was not immune to the possibilities of romancing the boss's daughter. Big dividends were possible; dividends that might help him become a veterinarian.

He turned his attention back to taking down the last of the canvas coverings, but some thoughts of that meeting still invaded his thoughts. He had to balance desire with ambition. After her mother's visit Catherine had freely teased him, but let him know the wondrous touching had boundaries. He wanted more than she allowed. What would happen if she wanted more?

࿇

Catherine's voice jolted him from his memories of the meeting. "Hello. Hello in there! Hank, we still have some work to do."

He felt Catherine's soft caress on his shoulder. He shook his head to clear the cobwebs. "Sorry, I was just thinking about ... well, if you must know, about you. Okay?"

"That nice, but if we are going to finish putting away this shed tomorrow, it's time for you to get with it."

He accepted one quick brushing kiss on the cheek from the bedeviling creature. He blushed and returned to work and the knowing glances from his fellow workers.

Catherine's last job would be helping Hank, Rusty, Virgil and Art gather the sheep from the pastures along the Columbia River.

10
The Start—A Sudden Ending

The older, tall, silvery sagebrush protected the foraging flocks from the spring winds that whistled through the Columbia River Gorge. The sheep nibbled on the early spring grass which flourished on the large flood plain between the Columbia and the ridge of the Horse Heaven Hills. The ridge marked the beginning of the wheat farms. The frolicking lambs were cute, but definitely no longer cuddly. Catherine could almost see them grow, and this was vital. They had to be big enough and strong enough to begin the long, summer grazing trek which ended close to the Montana border. Catherine thought of the irony of the whole process. Most of them would be sold for mutton and lamb chops at the railhead, while the selected ewes, lambs and rams would return home for lambing and shearing.

Her morning ride was the start of that process. She opened the gates of the pole corral located tight against the abrupt rise of the ridge and began the day's adventure. Her stocky mare measured fourteen hands from the ground to shoulder point. Jiggles nickered softly and came when she was called. Catherine gently cooed into her ear and petted the sides of her neck and jaw. The mare found the raw carrot sticking out of her jacket pocket. Still talking softly Catherine slipped the halter over the mare's nose and fastened the long strap behind her ears before leading the mare into the large horse barn, which bespoke of days when large numbers of horses were required to pull the farm machinery.

Inside the deserted horse barn, she tossed the saddle blanket over the horse's back and smoothed it out. Next she threw the saddle on Jiggles' back and pulled the cinch tight under her belly. When she was satisfied the saddle was secure, she slipped the bit into her mouth, tossed the bridle straps over her ears and led her favorite horse out of the barn.

The gentle, easy riding horse was Catherine's first horse. While her mother and Alex watched, Pete taught her how to mount and dismount. He patiently held the reins for the first walks around the farm yard. When she rode solo around the farm yard Catherine complained, "This horse jiggles me too much."

She heard Alex snicker and yell, "It's not the horse Sis. It's you."

Alex's taunt struck home. By the end of the week she had a sore bottom and raw inner thighs, but she stuck to the horse like glue. She learned the secret of using her legs as shock absorbers. Her riding smoothed out, but the name, Jiggles, stuck.

Today she and Hank rode out into the fresh, March morning air to help gather sheep from the western meadows along the Columbia. She sat astride Jiggles while Hank rode his preferred, taller (sixteen and a half hands) Mr. Gray. When Hank asked her why the laughter she replied, "We must look like Mutt and Jeff when we ride side by side."

In a few days Hank's team pulling his Shepherd wagon, a trailing Mr. Gray and two joyously happy sheep dogs would leave the ranch. A few days later she would return to Western.

The knot in her stomach grew. She enjoyed Western, but she enjoyed Hank more.

The morning ride gave Hank more time to adjust to the two, energetic Border collies that now shared Hank's wagon-home. They would become like brothers during the summer. Only the different patterns of black, brownish-orange and white distinguished the two dogs. Their names really distinguished them. Malovich and Gilrakis would take some getting used to. Hank reined Mr. Gray close to Jiggles, reached over to put his hand on Catherine's as he joked, "Those two dogs know more about herding sheep than I'll ever know."

They approached the western end of the river range. The long ridge, which separated the farm land from the flood plain, angled south toward the river. The great Missoula Flood had washed away the soil here and uncovered a brown-black layer of ancient lava flows. The bare wall of lava met the river pasture at the river to form a natural barrier that defined the western end of the ranch's river range. The scenic vistas turned to lighter purples as the terrain stretched westward toward the Columbia Gorge, the Cascade Mountain and snow capped Mount hood. Catherine sat astride Jiggles and admired the scene.

The snow run-off from the high Canadian Rockies and the Rockies of northern Idaho and Montana had reached this section of the high running Columbia River at Pasco. March had come in like a lion. Snow in the mountains, and wind, rain and mixed storms had harassed the workers all spring. Spring work on the farm above the ridge lagged behind schedule.

Today was different. Every part of the ranch work looked rosier in the late March sun. The month was ending like the frolicking lambs they were going to move toward the large holding corrals closer to the ranch house.

The protected flood plain burgeoned with green grass and wild flowers. More flowers would follow until late May or early June. Gradually the grasses of the arid region would start to turn brown. The wild flowers' short life would end. Now the narrowing area between the ridge and the river seemed full of romping lambs, patient rams, and concerned ewes. The Columbia roared over a series of rapids to form the southern boundary of the Sumertun range. The sheep shied away from this loud water barrier like the plague.

Catherine centered her gaze on the rider who was a quarter-of- a-mile away to her left before taking the binoculars from her saddle bag. Her body stiffened in her saddle.

She handed the binoculars to Hank. "Is that who I think it is?"

Hank confirmed her suspicion and returned the glasses. She stared long and hard at one of the two riders heading for the southwestern corner of the range land. She asked, "What is he doing out here?" The angry, distrust in her voice was obvious.

"Relax Catherine; he's doing the same thing we are. He's helping Rusty gather the sheep and pushing them toward the corrals." He joked, trying to divert Catherine, from her anger. "Don't worry. Rusty is a veteran and will keep track of him." He dryly added, "We need all available help to gather the sheep from both ends of this long, narrow meadow." Whether that was enough information to derail Catherine's anger he didn't know, but it was the perfect time to show her the dogs. He glanced at the eager dogs. "Watch this, Catherine." He whistled to Malovich and Gilrakis and pointed to the small group of sheep standing near by. He commanded, "Cast, bring." The dogs became blurred streaks.

"Watch those two dogs work. This is what they live for." The dogs instinctively positioned themselves to start pushing the small groups toward Hank and Catherine. They trotted or ran around the sheep. They held positions as the situation demanded. They didn't allow a single animal to escape. Malovich and Gilrakis gathered a small group of sheep and moved them toward the two riders.

It had been a perfect demonstration. "I tell you Catherine, those two dogs are wonderful." He looked at Catherine and confided, "I'm just learning what commands to use."

He wanted to show off more of his new found knowledge. "Catherine, watch this." He put the slender pipe whistle to his lips and whistled two shrill blasts. The dogs stopped and looked toward Hank, ears up and all attention. He moved his arm in a come here motion and yelled, "Come back." Gilrakis looked at the moving sheep. Malovich stood still but watched with all senses alert.

Seconds passed. Catherine watched for the dog's reaction to Hank's commands. In one synchronized move they left the sheep and broke toward Hank and didn't stop until they sat at his feet. Catherine couldn't help it. She told them how wonderful they were. The two dogs wagged their tails at these justified compliments.

❧

Catherine continued to watch the two riders along the river while she and Hank rode among the sagebrush and small, open grassy areas closer to the ridge.

Malovich and Gilrakis continued to happily ferret out groups of ten, fifteen or more sheep and herd them toward the middle of the range. When this group approached three or four hundred they would push the sheep toward the large holding pens up river near the lambing sheds.

Each band of 1,450 to 1,500 sheep would be leaving for Montana around April 1st. Three Sumertun wagons and three bands would leave the ranch on closely staggered schedules and take parallel routes over state and federal rangelands all the way to Montana.

Hank's time on the Sumertun Ranch was limited, probably three to five days. Catherine sighed at the inevitability of the situation.

Loud yelling and gunfire captured Catherine's attention. She immediately dug the binoculars from her saddle bag to scan the river area. She found and focused on the wild shooting Art Wheeler. The yelling idiot held his rifle in one hand and wildly shot high into the air. In sheer panic the sheep scattered in every direction to get away from the shooting. Yelling and shooting, Art Wheeler pushed his horse among the small groups trying to drive them toward the rapids.

Catherine angrily shouted. "Who in the hell does he think he is, Hopalong Cassidy? This is not a cattle drive or a stampede."

Catherine knew sheep would act like sheep. They would follow any leader, even if it meant more danger. She knew the sheep were also scared to death of the roaring rapids, so they kept scattering. It would take all afternoon to get all of them back together again.

Hank on Mr. Gray galloped toward the melee.

∽

Catherine watched the whole episode through the binoculars. It was like watching a kaleidoscope in the slow motion. That crazy Art held the rifle high, laughing and shooting his rifle into the air. Sheep scattered everywhere. Rusty galloped into the circular scope of her binoculars. She watched him grab the shooter's arm and yell at him. Art resisted. Several more shots rang out.

She moved her binoculars to locate Hank and Mr. Gray. Mr. Gray suddenly reared up. Hank struggled to stay in the saddle, but the horse's abrupt move had surprised him. He fell backward, bounced off Mr. Gray's rump and hit the ground hard still holding the reins.

Catherine heard a shrill whinny. She saw Mr. Gray desperately dancing on his hind legs. Hank still clutched the reins. He suddenly dropped the reins and grabbed his leg. The horse bounced away a short distance, stopped, and shook his neck vigorously from side to side. Then he looked back at Hank and stood quietly.

She changed her focus to Rusty and Art. Rusty had wrested the rifle away from Art Wheeler. He yelled something and Rusty easily ducked the punch thrown at him. His quick retaliatory punches to Art's head were short and direct. Art clutched at the saddle horn in an effort to stay on his horse. It was a lost cause. He dropped down to the ground on his hands and knees. She saw Rusty yelling and pointing toward the lambing shed. "Rat Face" mounted his horse and rode away, shaking his fist at Rusty.

Rusty reined his horse to the left and rode toward the fallen Hank. Catherine estimated he had to cover 250-300 yards before he got to the fallen rider.

She had the shorter distance to cover. She and the dogs wasted no more time.

&

When Catherine arrived Hank lay on the ground, holding his leg; his face grimacing in pain. The two dogs stayed close by and whined. Like a true cowboy he pressed his lips together in an effort to remain stoically silent. She knelt down to examine the leg. She tried to push the pant leg up to see the spot Hank held. He moaned in pain at every movement.

Rusty galloped up, dismounted and quickly apologized. "I couldn't get to him in time to stop the shooting. That damn Art thought he was in a Wild West show. He was actually pushing the sheep toward the river. That shows you what he knows about sheep. How dumb can you get? Those sheep would avoid wild water like the plague." He grinned, "I took his toy from him." He knelt down beside Catherine, looked at the pant leg and the dark patch of blood. He reached into his pant pocket for his knife.

Rusty opened the longest blade of his pocket knife. "Hank, I'll be as gentle as possible. I'm going to cut the pant leg loose. I'll cut away from the side you're holding, but it will still hurt.

Brace yourself." He inserted the knife under the denim cuff and pulled the knife up along the seam. Three swipes with the sharp knife and pant leg flared open. Scraped skin and a developing ugly bruise were apparent. The blood was already drying.

Rusty had seen this type of injury before. "Looks like Mr. Gray stepped on you."

"Excellent diagnosis, Dr. Felcher. You rode from the river just to tell me that."

"Hurts like hell, huh?"

Hank nodded.

"Horseshoes usually cut, Hank, but the pant leg saved you from any deep cut." He probed gently with his fingers. Hank cringed at every point of finger pressure." Rusty put some pressure on the shin bone but nothing gave, and Hank didn't react with sharp cries of pain. He tenderly pushed the calf of the leg in a different direction. A sharp yelp followed.

Through gritted teeth Hank said, "That's the spot." He hesitated, "Is it broken?

"I think it is."

Rusty tenderly caressed the calf and murmured. "Maybe, it's only a crack or a bad bruise? We need to get you to a doctor and find out for sure."

Hank offered his own solution. "Look, I'm not trying to be tough or heroic, but the truth is that I can stand the pain. Why don't you two get me on Mr. Gray and I'll ride to the barns. Then Catherine can get me to Prentiss and Dr. Hobson."

Rusty and Catherine looked at each other, debating whether this was wise or possible. Hank became impatient. "Either put me on my horse and we will ride together to the barns, or one of you can ride to the house and come back with a car or pickup." He made his point. "Anything is better than staying here and doing nothing."

෨

Catherine looked at the ranch house. They were a mile away, maybe more. A small wisp of dust could be seen leaving the barnyard. Whatever they did would take time, more time for Hank to hurt. The dust turned toward them. Soon Catherine could make out a car coming toward them. The car bucked and bounced toward them on the rough road that ran through the river range.

"It's mother." Catherine wondered how in the devil she knew to come out. Sarah slowed down, left the trail road and came slowly over the grassland through the sagebrush until she stopped 10 feet from them. The car door flew open and she exploded from the car. "How is he?"

She made her own examination of Hank's leg. Any questions or explanations were put off until she rose from the ground and talked to Rusty. There was no doubt they had to get Hank to a doctor as soon as possible.

Fascinated Catherine watched her mother kneel, and reach to stroke Hank's cheek and reassure him everything would be okay. She stood, brushed the dirt from her jeans and directed Rusty and Catherine to lift him and get him to stand on his good leg. With his arms around their shoulders he hopped to the car. Once he lay stretched across the back seat Sarah fussed to make him as comfortable as possible.

Sarah turned to her daughter. "Catherine, get in the car and drive to the house before we go on to Prentiss." Sarah answered her daughter's unasked question, "I need to call Dr. Hobson and the hospital."

Catherine drove much slower and smoother than her mother's frantic drive out. Hank didn't need a another maniac behind the wheel.

༄

Rusty watched the car navigate back toward the house. It was a relief to know Hank was in good hands. He scratched his head in wonder at the whirlwind which just swept through. For years he knew Sarah directed everything that happened on the ranch. This just added to the legend.

He reached down and gently stroked Gilrakis and Malovich. "Don't worry, you'll get to work the sheep again; probably this afternoon." He scratched his head at this new dilemma. What happens if Hank can't make the trip to Montana?

Right now he had another problem to solve. He had to get Mr. Gray, Jiggles and the dogs back to the barns and get organized for the afternoon. He grunted. "It's also time to get rid of Art Wheeler."

The usually docile Mr. Gray was skittish. He backed away as Rusty approached. Rusty went back to his own horse and rode him toward the nervous Mr. Gray. The reassuring presence of another horse allowed him to get close enough to get the reins. While he held the reins Rusty dismounted and reassured the horse by scratching his ears, stroking his neck, and soft reassuring talk. He noticed blood on his hand. He ducked under Mr. Gray's neck to the other side and examined the neck closely. "I'll be damned, Mr. Gray. No wonder you reared up like you did. That crazy little bastard shot you."

He collected his canteen and bandana. Like riders the world over Rusty talked to his horses. Mr. Gray seemed glad to get the attention. He allowed Rusty to rinse the wound. After the first sense of water and cleansing on the wound, Mr. Gray turned his head and looked at Rusty as if to ask, "What are you doing to me?"

Rusty laughed. "It's okay Mr. Gray. I'm just washing the wound." He held his wet bandana close so Mr. Gray could smell it. That seemed to allay his fears. He continued to dab and wash the slight wound with his bandana. Rusty traced imaginary trajectory arcs with his hand to indicate where he thought the bullet that smashed into Mr. Gray's neck came from.

The bullet had to travel at least 250 yards to get to him. For a high powered rifle this wasn't long distance. He remembered

Art shooting wildly in the air. Maybe the high trajectory shot spent most of its energy before it hit Mr. Gray. If so, a little or no penetration was possible.

He cooed, "Easy, boy. It's okay, boy. I'm not going to hurt you, easy now. Let me push around this wound a little." He gently probed. There was no spent bullet lying under the skin. Maybe it only ricocheted.

He applied gentle pressure on the reins and coaxed Mr. Gray to take few steps. The horse hesitated. Rusty coaxed and reassured Mr. Gray everything would be okay. After a few test steps Mr. Gray seemed comfortable walking. A relieved Rusty took a rope from his saddle, removed the bridle and made a rope halter to lead the horse. He grabbed Jiggle's reins and swung into the saddle. Both horses led easy. Gilrakis and Malovich came quickly when called. He was no stranger to the two dogs. He was working at the ranch when he and Pete brought their plight to Sarah's attention. She hadn't hesitated to make a quick decision then. Funny he thought of that now.

ᴄᴏ

Catherine was still a gangling, slender girl in high school, and just beginning the late blossoming into a young woman. Carter still conferred with Sarah, but she had already earned her spurs as "The Queen of the Sumertun Ranch." Thanks to Carter the stories about that fated birthday party, the unweeded summer fallow story, and her declaration to run the ranch were already legendary. Rusty became part of the tale of compassion which made the rounds.

It had been late in October when the tattered, rubber tired Shepherd's wagon drawn by two tired, footsore, plodding horses turned off the Washington State Highway 14 along the Columbia and up Artesian Creek road to the Sumertun ranch. The driver arrived early for shearing, but the road-weary Edorta

(Ed) Arriota looked forward to a little quiet time. It had been a long, solitary ride from the summer sheep ranges of Montana.

Pete welcomed the veteran sheep shearer. For several years he had been a regular. This year the Basque sheep man seemed quiet and more resigned, like he'd been defeated by life. Pete had chalked it up to being exhausted and tired. Ed backed his wagon-home up against the ridge alongside the other wagons and prepared to stay a while.

Pete hadn't noticed the traveler for a couple of days, so he sent Rusty up to check on him, the dogs and the horses. When he approached the wagon he found two very anxious, thirsty, and hungry dogs at the front of the wagon. He talked soothingly to them a moment while he found some water for them. With his hand on Gilrakis's head, or was it Malovich's, he called out, "Ed, Ed, Edorta," loud enough to be heard.

No response. He didn't like that. The dogs followed him to the rear wagon door. Their whining made him even more nervous. He cracked the door and peered inside. The old man was stretched out on his bedroll. He called out again. "Ed, Ed Edorta." He waited. Malovich, or was it Gilrakis, nudged him gently with his nose. Rusty remembered thinking the dog was asking him, "What's wrong?"

It had to be done. He inhaled deeply, climbed the three portable steps and entered. He called again. No answer. He studied the stretched out figure. There was no rising and falling of the chest. The facial muscles were relaxed. He touched cold flesh. Rusty knew the answer before the next dreaded move. He tried to find a pulse.

It seemed the spent, tired Edorta Arriota had come home to rest. Rusty pulled up a blanket and covered his face. Sarah called the mortuary to take care of the body. The sheriff came to the ranch in the late afternoon to take care of the paperwork. He found nothing in the wagon to identify any close family. A couple of old letters had an address from the Basque region of Spain. He would have a letter sent to the address.

Rusty got his first glimpse of Sarah's decision making. She quickly told the sheriff she would pay for the burial, and a small headstone. She maintained, "No man should be buried at the county's expense. He should have a permanent resting place."

Pete nursed the two horses back to good health. They led contented lives in the grassy sagebrush plain along the Columbia River. Rusty and Pete figured the dogs, Malovich and Gilrakis, were three or four years old. A retired herder, Gorges Viscotti took them under his wing and trained them to do what they were meant to do; herd sheep.

❧

Rusty's thoughts stayed with the dogs. They were three year veterans of the trip to Montana. They would have been perfect for Hank Hirsch's maiden voyage. The two dogs came quickly when he called. He gently smoothed the ruffled hair on Malovich's neck. He smiled at the irony of it. "It looks like you two will have to break in a new herder." Gilrakis put his nose under Hank's hand and lifted it so he could be petted.

It was time to get back to the real world. Rusty picked up the lead rope for the two horses. He grabbed his saddle horn, stepped his left foot up into the stirrup, pulled up and swung his right leg up and over the saddle. He had a short time to enjoy this warm spring day and to think about the events of the day. His own rifle plus the one he wrested away from Art were jammed into his scabbard. The bulge under his leg constantly reminded him this episode wasn't over.

Art Wheeler just did dumb things. He tried to drive the sheep into the rapids. Why would he do that?" He puzzled on the problem a moment before he remembered the smoking incident. A fire in the straw pens would also kill a lot of sheep.

❧

Earlier Art Wheeler had ridden disconsolately along the river back toward the sheds. The shooting had been fun. Those stupid sheep ran away in every direction, except toward the river. There was no reason for Rusty to get so mad. The dogs would have soon gathered the scattered sheep. The incredulous look of amazement on Rusty's face had been worth it, but there was no reason to call him stupid, and even less reason to take his gun.

What rotten luck. The shooting accident could happen to anybody. What are the chances of a stray bullet falling from the sky hitting Mr. Gray, maybe a million to one? That family favorite didn't look so good when Mr. Gray threw him. He quickly thought about the Montana trip. If Hank was hurt he could step in and take his place. That thought brought a smile. He knew about the summer trek and Corwin had said he might get the job.

The daydream of a possible success instead of another failure was followed by some off key whistling. He'd talk to Pete about Montana before Rusty got to him. Then he would have some time to think of other ways to get even with that stuck up college girl. A brilliant idea would come along. Maybe it's not me that's a failure, maybe the plans were poor. He liked that thought. Meanwhile he'd stay out of trouble until Corwin got him the job to Montana.

11
On Hold

C atherine grabbed a pillow and blanket at the house while her mother made the necessary telephone calls. She filled a thermos with cold water before they scrambled out together. Her mother took the passenger seat. From there she could lean over the seat and do what she could to make Hank comfortable. Thirty miles over gravel roads seemed like an eternity. There was little talk. Catherine concentrated on getting to Prentiss as soon as possible. She pulled into the hospital's covered emergency entrance forty-five minutes later.

Two orderlies wheeled a gurney outside as soon as the car stopped. Dr. Hobson followed and supervised the two men gently lifting Hank from the car onto the gurney. Catherine lifted her hands to cover her face. It was a sight she didn't want to see. She was thankful for her mother's comforting arm around her waist.

Once inside Dr. Hobson lifted the blanket to observe the open pant leg and the exposed leg. "Horse stepped on him, huh?"

The two women mutely nodded. Catherine moved toward Hank and gingerly smoothed a stray wisp of hair into place before taking his hand and squeezing it. Sarah stood on the other side looking down at the injured leg. She shuddered at her second hard look.

In his best bedside manner Dr. Hobson informed them, "This isn't as rare as you two seem to think. This is horse country, remember? Those dang horseshoes protect the horse's hooves, but they're hell on legs." He checked the leg again. "You're lucky. There is no compound fracture poking through the skin. It has the look of a break in the fibula or maybe a stress fracture. Either way it's quite painful. I'll know more after the X-rays are taken."

The orderlies wheeled Hank into the bowels of the hospital.

Dr. Hobson smiled at Sarah and took her hand. "You look a little flustered after the hard drive into Prentiss, but you seem to have fully recovered from your bout with the flu." He paused a moment, "Can you tell me when Hank was hurt?"

Sarah quickly answered. "10:43 this morning."

Catherine stared at her mother. How could she know the exact time?

Even Dr. Hobson seemed surprised. "From an accident somewhere on the ranch to the hospital in an hour is very good time!" Like an anxious mother hen, he clucked, "The sooner the patients get here the better. Now, I'd better see what I can do. I'll see you two in the waiting room when I'm finished. Maybe you should get something to eat, instead of just waiting." They heard the click, click, click of hard leather heels against the polished floor.

❧

Sarah shook her head at the first sip of hospital hot tea. The hospital tea tasted like coffee. She never understood why anyone thought tea served in coffee cups, that still smelled of coffee, would have the clean taste of tea. She used the sweetness of a sugared doughnut to make the drink palatable.

It didn't surprise her that Hank and Catherine turned to each other when he was hurt. It confirmed what intuition had told her. Their eyes caught and held each other at every chance. This accident wasn't life threatening, but it made them aware of how fragile life was.

Catherine jolted her from these inner thoughts. "How in the devil did you manage to get to us so fast back at the ranch? We were making plans to ride back, and here you came barreling down that sheep path of a road like a bat out of hell. That saved a half-hour."

Her mother's answer was simple. "The Sumertun people looked ahead. You should know, Catherine. They built the house on the ridge. Your father taught me how to use the binoculars that hang in the pantry. You've seen them. I can see the farmland on the plateau or the lambing sheds and the flood plain below the ridge. Today I wanted to watch Hank handle Gilrakis and Malovich."

Sarah answered the obvious. "Yes, I heard the shots and saw Mr. Gray rear up and toss Hank. By the time I got my coat and looked again, Rusty was galloping toward him. You saw my wild drive on that trail of a road. I drove like crazy to get there."

Sarah answered her daughter's unasked question. "Burke--" she caught herself in the use of his name. He had had been dead fourteen years and sometimes the memories were still vivid. "Yes, Burke's responsible. He taught me to always know what was happening at the ranch. I just did what he had taught me." Her eyes twinkled. "That's how I knew the time."

She knew her daughter wanted more. She told her, "I saw everything, and I mean everything." Sarah wanted to make sure the identification was correct. "Was the man firing the wild rifle shots the same man you and Hank threw water on in the sheep pens?"

She hid a smile at Catherine's terse answer. "Yes, that's Rat Face, er, Art Wheeler."

"Good grief, Catherine, that's awful." Curiosity made her ask, "Why?"

"Because he has no chin. He looks like a rat. He's sneaky. Rat-Face fits him." Sarah heard bitter regret in her daughter's voice. "I should've fired him on the spot when he smoked in the straw pens. This wouldn't have happened if I had."

"I understand your regret, Catherine, but it wasn't your place to fire him." She added,

"But I would've supported you, so tell me, why didn't you fire him?"

"It was something he blurted out to Hank. Rat Fa--, excuse me, Art let Hank know he wasn't worried about getting fired. He seemed to think he was immune, even from Pete. The shooting this morning should get him fired, but we'll see."

℀

The tedious wait dragged on until clicking heels announced Dr. Hobson's approach. The two women rose as one to meet him. Catherine nudged her mother, "At least we don't have a life and death situation. I don't know how people stand waiting for that message."

Dr. Hobson reassured them. "Hank is going to be okay. It was a clean break, but it took some doing to get everything lined up. The last X-ray confirmed it's all together. Hank's leg is casted and he'll be back in his room soon."

"Getting him here as soon as you did helped a lot. We were able to set the bones and cast the leg today." He matter-of-factly told them, "Otherwise we may have had to wait for the swelling to go down before we could do anything."

They sighed collectively as Hank was wheeled past them on the way to the recovery room. Later the nurse would take him to room 208 on the second floor. Dr. Hobson gave the nurse final instructions before he spoke to Sarah and her daughter. "I know both of you would like to stay longer, but Hank still feels the affects of the sedation. He'll probably sleep through most of the day. You should be able to take him home in a couple of days."

Dr. Hobson's voice became serious. "I understand Hank is scheduled to take a band of sheep to Montana. I'm afraid you'll have to get someone else." He ignored their small gasps. "There's no way he can traipse around in rough terrain chasing sheep. It was a clean break, but the bone is weight bearing. There must be no pressure on the break while the bone knits. For now he'll need crutches and a cast to keep the bones in place. The leg will be as strong as ever after the bone knits. It's important there is no relapse while the break is mending. A second break would require surgery.

"I'll come to the ranch in a week to check his progress. Catherine had seen that same smile not long ago. "Maybe you can persuade your Mrs. Andreason to bake an apple pie."

Catherine reminded him that the apples ripened in the fall not the spring.

He groaned, "Such is life."

She smiled at his anguish and then showed mercy to this man to whom they owed so much. "Merigold probably has some more apples in her root cellar. Would that be okay?"

He smiled. "Tell her I'll make the drive in a week."

ॐ

The short days of winter had slowly stretched toward the longer days of spring. Sarah enjoyed the leisurely twilight drive home, so different from the earlier hectic drive to Prentiss.

Any drive to the unknown was always tiring. Both women were emotionally drained. Feeling the euphoria of knowing Hank would be all right, Sarah turned sentimental. In the twilight she scanned the fading yellow and orange sky above the plateau. To the west the light purple shadows of the foothills and the darker purples of snow capped Mount Hood gave the illusion of distance. The whole scene was incredible. She sighed, "This was Burke's favorite time of day. His work day in the dusty fields was over, except during harvest time." She suddenly burst out laughing.

"What's that about, mother?"

Her mellow mother was in sharing mood. "You were still little, when your father came storming into the house one day complaining about his daily coat of dust at the end of each day. He went to the tool room in the barn and punched holes in the bottom of a pail, and hung it on the wall in the barn."

The vivid memory brought a louder laugh. "Guess who got to pour warm water into the bucket so your father could shower. I was told to get a shower installed in the bathroom." She reminisced. "I got a remodeled bathroom from that little deal." A warm, light hearted laugh followed. "Your father loved his evening shower. I did too. Burke smelled much better when he came to bed."

Sarah cast a sideways glance at her daughter. "Don't look so shocked, Catherine. Those showers may be a reason Alex is here: not the only reason, but a reason."

∽

Catherine liked this new warmth which had developed during her mother's bout with the flu. This was a side of her mother she had seldom seen. Sickness and Hank seemed to be common meeting ground. Hank was more than a catalyst. Sarah openly cared for him. She now encouraged in words and action what she hoped would happen.

Catherine retreated into her cautious self. She knew she pushed Hank as hard as he pushed her. She really liked Hank, but sometimes the quickness scared her. There was no doubt in her mother's mind, but her mother was known for making decisions. She asked, "Where is Hank going to sleep when he gets out of the hospital? He'll need supervision and care for a few days."

The answer came characteristically quick and definite. "Why do you ask that? He'll be in the spare bedroom at home! You don't think I'd allow him to bounce around in that Shepherd wagon alone do you?" She thought about it some. "Maybe after a couple of weeks he can go back to his home in the wagon."

"Won't the wagon be on the way to Montana?"

"That's right. I forgot about that." Sarah stoutly declared, "I'll make sure he has a suitable place to stay, probably in the house until he can get around safely." She noticed her daughter's smile. "Got a better suggestion?"

Catherine said nothing, but watched her mother's face soften. She had seen this look often lately. "What are you thinking, mother?"

Her mother sighed deeply. "Memories, Catherine, just memories. Lately, I've been thinking a lot about Burke. We had a great love." She reached out to pat her daughter's hand. "I want you to have that same kind of happiness." She looked away, but not before Catherine saw a tear roll down her cheek. She looked unbelievably sad. "My world almost ended when he died."

A few miles of silence passed before Catherine heard her mother's sigh. "What's that about?"

"I was thinking of your birthday party and how the colossal sized weeds in the summer fallow jarred me back to reality." She dryly added, "If you don't remember, Carter will be glad to refresh your memory. That stopped the grieving part, but not the loneliness. I still miss him."

They rode on in silence, each to their own thoughts. Finally Catherine risked a question. "Mother, are you happy with Corwin?"

"There's nothing's wrong with Corwin." Sarah quickly apologized. "That came out a little too quick and snappish. Catherine, my life at the ranch is still full and very busy. What you heard was a woman reminiscing and singing the blues about a part of her life that is no more. That's all." Sarah quietly laughed. "Let's put it this way, Catherine, and then we'll talk about something else. Corwin doesn't shower before he comes to bed. "

12
Decision

Catherine drove into the farmyard before the sun dipped below the mountain horizon in the west. Alex enthusiastically bounded from the house to greet them. He kissed his mother on the cheek and told them, "I'm glad you two are home. I'm hungry."

Still in his own little world, he didn't notice their lack of enthusiasm. He opened the door for them to enter the kitchen. Alex happily hustled back outside when his mother asked him to get the blankets and pillows from back seat of the car. The blood on the folded blanket and the smattering of blood on the pillow caught his attention. Where had his mother and sister been, and where did the blood come from? Alex bounced back inside with the blanket and two pillows. He pointed to the blood stains. "What happened?"

Alex listened attentively to what his sister and mother told him of the day's events.

"I'm glad Hank will be okay. He is one of the good ones." He could see their nodding agreement. "You say Art Wheeler caused this. He's not one of the good ones. Everyone knows about Catherine's run-in with him." Alex heard a quick version of the day's events and laughed at the image of sheep leaping and running in every direction when Art's random shots shattered the mid-morning silence. He added an opinion. "It was stupid of him to try and move sheep by shooting and yelling.

It had seemed odd to Alex that Corwin wasn't home and his name was never mentioned. Where was he when all this happened? He wanted more information, but his mother got his full attention when she asked, "Have you eaten yet?"

∽

The little, wooden cuckoo emerged from the Black Forest clock at nine o'clock, sang its song, and then disappeared on its circular track back into the clock. Seven minutes later Sarah heard Corwin's pickup come into the barn yard. The pickup door slammed. Not a good sign. The outside screen door slammed shut. Another bad sign. When Corwin entered the kitchen Sarah instantly knew he'd had a bad day, but she had no idea why.

Corwin was normally fairly placid, easy going and manageable. Not now. Sulkiness contorted his face. Intense anger darted from his eyes. The smell of alcohol wafted ahead of him. Alcohol was really a bad sign.

When Sarah rose to greet him Corwin ignored her. She guessed he had stiffened his backbone with several drinks at Derk's, the little general store, small café and bar on the banks of the Columbia River. This wasn't the first time he had tottered home from Derk's. The ride over gravel roads had given him time to brood about whatever bothered him.

Across the table Catherine's eye's opened wide at the scene. Anger would soon replace embarrassment. Next to her Alex's face had turned pale. Corwin's behavior was a far cry from normal.

∽

74

Corwin pulled himself together to confront his wife. He stood straight and angrily declared, "This time Sarah, Pete went too far." He teetered unsteadily. His alcohol-induced, hard- nosed resolve almost vanished. Before it was too late he defiantly declared, "I fired Pete this afternoon."

A tight lipped smile appeared as Corwin feigned casual indifference. He had gotten her full attention. That would show them they couldn't ignore him. He walked to the stove to pour himself a cup of coffee. He smugly put the hot, steaming cup to his lips, cursed loudly and slammed the hot cup to the table. Hot coffee slopped out. When he regained his composure he loudly announced again. "You heard me. I fired Pete."

Catherine sat like a statue. She couldn't believe what she just heard. She wondered if Corwin had any idea of what he had done? Had he raised the bar to a point of no return? Why? The only real crisis today centered on Hank, and Corwin hadn't been involved with Hank nor even asked about him. What else had happened today? She thought back to the shooting and all the problems it caused. Was Art the cause of Corwin's anger? She remembered Art's casual reply when he had been caught smoking in the sheep pens? She had often wondered what caused this kind of confidence. There had to be a reason for Corwin's wild outburst. Did he throw this fit because of Art's shooting? She waited for the outcome.

Tenseness filled the kitchen. Catherine looked at Alex. He shrugged his shoulders ever so slightly and remained very quiet. Catherine knew he wanted to hear this out. She glanced at her mother and braced herself for the storm.

Sarah's wifely tolerance vanished, replaced by the deadly serious "Queen of the Sumertun Ranch." She sweetly asked, "Will you please repeat what you said?" She quickly added, "And please don't yell. That doesn't impress me." The icy tone should have warned Corwin.

It had taken him all afternoon to gather this much nerve. He obviously wasn't going to back down. He blurted out, "You heard me. I said I fired Pete."

"And why did you think he should be fired?"

"He forgot that he works for me! He fired a man I hired. He didn't even have the courtesy to talk to me."

"And is Art Wheeler that man?"

That question should have warned Corwin. It didn't. He replied, "Yes, but how did you know that?"

"He caused a lot of trouble around here today!"

"I don't know about any trouble, but I'm tired of Pete's superior attitude, and I don't intend to put up with it any longer. The lambing is over. I told him I would take charge of the Montana trek."

"What did Pete say to that?"

Corwin still hadn't noticed the frigid tone of Sarah's voice.

"He just laughed and told me the spring work on the wheat ranch needed my attention. He had the gall to tell me that I had plenty to do above the ridge."

"He's right, you know."

Corwin's voice trembled at the implication. "Is that what you think?"

Sarah knew it was time to placate her teetering husband, but she had no intention to plead with him. "Corwin, be practical. Pete knows more about sheep than any of us. He ran the operation before my Burke died and he grew up with the sheep part of the ranch." She gently, but very firmly admonished him. "No, Corwin, you stay away from that part of the ranch. There will be far less problems."

She hadn't noticed his face stiffen at her reference of "my, Burke."

Corwin smirked, "It's too late. I've already fired Pete and told him Art would stay. He's to be out of there by tomorrow. There's nothing you can do about it. Remember, I'm half of this ranch."

"Corwin, you've made a big mistake. There's only one person who can fire Pete."

Doubt lowered Corwin's reply to a whisper. "And who would that be."

"Me!" Sarah patiently explained, "Pete's been here longer than anybody. We go back too far and he's too valuable!" She matter-of-factly added, "He knows you can't fire him. Corwin, you have absolutely no authority down there. Leave it alone."

"We'll see about that! For God's sake, Sarah, I'm your husband." For the first time Sarah heard the whine in her husband's voice. "You have to stand with me." His eyes looked away, as he gathered his courage again. He stood erect, squared his shoulders and defiantly announced, "I'm half of this ranch and I'll have my say."

Catherine heard her mother's voice became factual, void of any emotion. The effect was chilling, like a mother disciplining a child. "We're not talking about that, Corwin. That's something altogether different." The stony silence forced Corwin to look up and listen. "Now tell me what started this idea that Pete should be fired?"

Corwin wilted. The false bravado was gone. He pleaded, "Damn it Sarah, I'll never get respect now. Pete should be fired for the way he treated me. He'll never listen to one word I say now." One spark of defiance remained. "You're right, Sarah, we'll talk about this in the morning when Alex and Catherine aren't around." He reminded her, "Until then, Pete stays fired." He spun around and left. The master bedroom door slammed, the bathroom door slammed, and finally the guest bedroom door slammed.

∽

Catherine mulled over the conversation she had with her mother on the way home. She smiled. There'll be no need for a bath tonight. She knew where that idea came from. Had her mother almost confessed something?

She had been fascinated by the entire exchange between her mother and Corwin. He had been transformed from the charged-up, determined aggressor back to the cringing, slump-shouldered man her mother hired the week after her eighth birthday party. Did her mother mean to do it? What would this rejection do to Corwin? One thing was certain; Corwin was not half of the Sumertun ranch. On paper the Sumertun Trust backed up Sarah.

∽

Ultimatums carried responsibility. Catherine had learned this harsh lesson early from her mother and Pete. Would Corwin have to learn this same lesson?

The childhood memory returned. The leisurely, summer evening horseback ride along the river was always one of her favorite things. After a delightful, summer ride the tired, happy Catherine put Jiggles into her stall and hurried into the kitchen to eat.

At 9:30 p.m. her mother had roughly rousted her from bed. "You didn't take care of Jiggles after your ride. You rode her and left her in the stall with no feed and no water. You can go back to sleep after you take care of your horse."

Catherine had haughtily told her, "It's my horse. You can't make me do that tonight. I'll do it in the morning."

Her mother did not take kindly to this, but all she had said was "fine." That was the first time she had noticed the icy, deadly chill in her mother's voice. Catherine had been too dumb then to realize what it could mean. Snug and warm in her bed she fell to sleep.

Catherine woke up early the next morning regretting her actions. She had neglected her very favorite horse. Before break-fast Catherine ran to the barn vowing to do better. Singing happily at this new found resolve, she had entered the horse stall area. She stopped to stare at the empty stall. Jiggles no longer stood there. She ran to the outside, but Jiggles wasn't in the corral either. She ran back through the barn, almost knocking Pete and her mother down as they came through the wide open door. Pete carried a rope and halter in his hand.

"What are you doing?"

"I'm hanging up Jiggles' halter."

"What have you done with her? I came out to feed and water her." She had quickly turned to her mother and apologized, "I really am sorry I didn't take care of her. I promise it will never happen again. Now, where is she?"

Sarah looked at Catherine and very matter-of-factly delivered her sentence. "We put her in the river range. There's plenty of grass and water there. She'll be there for a week." Catherine looked for forgiveness from her mother. None came.

Catherine had wailed and cried. Her temper kept rising although she knew why Jiggles was in the pasture. She emulated her mother's quiet tone, "Fine, she can just stay there." Catherine had looked at her mother as if to say 'I'll show you!' Then she stomped out of the barn before they saw her cry.

That had been the longest week of her young life. She was being hurt by her own stubbornness. What a hard lesson. It ended one evening on the river range when Jiggles came to her call and nuzzled her for a few carrots. Catherine had put her arms around her neck and scratched her ears and promised, "I will never neglect you again." The ultimatum to never ride Jiggles again was forgotten. The sunshine in her life became complete the next morning when her smiling mother asked her to share a ride down by the Columbia.

Both were glad the war was over. Catherine had learned ultimatums were no good unless you were prepared to be deprived of something you wanted. Winning an ultimatum was a hollow victory. Often you lost everything. Were Sarah and Corwin willing to test the ultimatums? Catherine's knew her mother was.

13
The Morning Ride

Gilrakis and Malovich trotted happily alongside Jiggles as Catherine left the barn and corrals to join Rusty and his dogs. They headed out to continue the job they were forced to leave yesterday. They talked about yesterday, the crazy rifle shots, and Mr. Gray. Rusty assured her that Mr. Gray had a minor flesh wound that would fully heal. "The wound was more nuisance than anything." He added, "Whoever is hired to take Hank's place on the Montana trip will be able to use him."

Catherine replied, "Hank is due to be released tomorrow. Mother and I will drive to Prentiss and bring him home. That means I won't be here to ride."

"That's okay. Alex can ride with us tomorrow." Rusty changed the subject. "I'm glad you and your mother got Hank to the hospital so quick. Hank's one of the good ones." He slyly cast his eyes sidewise to Catherine, "I don't have to tell you that do I?"

"No, you don't."

"Did Corwin say anything about the yesterday's fireworks?"

"No, he didn't say anything." Catherine didn't intend to share gossip about Corwin trying to fire Pete. "Corwin came home late. He'd been drinking down at Derk's." Her tone was icy. "Isn't that where he goes?"

"Not always, but that's the closest water hole. He doesn't get sloppy very often, but he pushed his luck when he tried to save Art. "

"What do you mean, when he tried to save Art?"

"You were using the binoculars, so you saw me send Art back to the sheds after I took his gun from him."

"Yes, I saw it with my binoculars, but I didn't know Corwin tried to save Art."

"You were on your way to Prentiss with Hank when I returned to the barn with the horses. Art was waiting outside. He demanded his gun." Rusty grinned, "I was still mad as hell at the little weasel. His stupidity could have killed either Mr. Gray or Hank. I deliberately pumped all the shells out of the gun and kept them. I hoped he would try to take them away from me, but he didn't. He was docile as a lamb when he quietly accepted the rifle.

"I told him, 'That was the dumbest thing I had ever seen.' I heaped another insult on him. 'If I was running on this outfit, you would have been fired on the spot'." Rusty exclaimed, "I asked him if he had told Pete what happened. The miserable little bastard hadn't said a word to Pete, and I bet he would sneaked away without a word if I hadn't taken him to Pete and reported what happened to Hank and Mr. Gray. He fired Art."

He pushed his cowboy hat back on his head. "Even then that insolent smirk remained. He seemed to think he couldn't be fired. That's when Pete decided to inspect Mr. Gray. We cleaned the wound and Pete put some salve on it. It was really a minor wound.

"The real fireworks started later when Corwin stormed in to see Pete about Art. Something had to happen."

Rusty got all of Catherine's interest when he confessed what he had done. "When Pete and Corwin disappeared into Pete's office, I hurried to get into a position to eavesdrop. You know I'm not a gossip, but I had to hear this firsthand. Corwin yelled so loud at Pete it was easy to hear every word."

"Is that what you meant when you said, 'Corwin tried to save Art'?"

He nodded "But don't ever tell Pete what I did. Okay?"

Catherine knew she would kill to hear this firsthand information. She leaned across her saddle and told Rusty, "I won't. Now, quit teasing me and tell me what you heard."

There were only the two of them riding on an open range, but Rusty spoke in a lowered confidential tone. "Corwin angrily accused Pete of going back on his word."

Catherine laughed. "Rusty, there is no one out here but you, me and the dogs. Quit talking as though the world's listening!"

Rusty straightened up and looked around and turned up his volume. "Sorry about that. Anyway, Corwin was steaming mad. He yelled at Pete, 'You told me that Art would not be fired. You lied to me.'"

Rusty watched Catherine closely for her reaction.

Her wide eyes said she wanted more.

"I didn't hear all of Corwin's next remark, but it was about cheating Art out of going to Montana. I did hear his loud boast, 'I'll take care of the sheep drive and let Art take Hank's place. You're not needed. What do you say to that?'"

"Catherine, I could've stayed with Mr. Gray and still heard Corwin when he yelled, 'You'll not lie to me again! Get your things out of here. You're fired, Peter Alzola.'"

She could imagine Pete's squared shoulders, the intense dark eyes and the same quiet, no-nonsense voice that Rusty heard. "There's only person who can fire me and it's not you."

"Corwin yelled, 'We'll see about that!' When he came storming out of the office I made sure I remained hidden."

Catherine absorbed all of this, and then compared it to what she heard last night. "Rusty, that's more or less what my mother said. She told Corwin that Pete would stay."

"What the devil does that mean for Corwin?"

Catherine didn't have the answer. She and Rusty rode quietly toward the river range to gather sheep. Both wondered where this would go, but for now there was work to be done. They would finish gathering the sheep and push them to the large holding pens that lay under the ridge. Catherine knew she needed to set the record straight, but that's was all. "That pretty much sums up what must have happened. My mother, Alex and I were in the kitchen when Corwin came home from Derk's. He had been drinking. He told us he had fired Pete."

Rusty leaned across the saddle, "And what did your mother say?"

"That she was the only one who can fire him, and she didn't intend to."

Catherine pulled Rusty's attention back to today's business. "That takes care of the firing. Yesterday was quite a day, but now it's time for us to finish what we started yesterday; gather sheep from the western river pasture." Catherine revisited an old dream.

જી

The germ of the idea had resurfaced after last night's tumultuous ending. It was part dream, part desire and part necessity. She needed to be out here today learning how to handle the dogs under the guise of helping Rusty. By 8:00 a.m. they rode companionably in the chilly March morning toward the western end of the river range. The excited dogs trotted alongside.

When it was time for Catherine to begin she struggled to pull a piece of paper from her jeans. She pointed to her scribbling. "I wrote down these commands for the dogs." She handed them to Rusty. "Are these correct?"

Rusty studiously deciphered the writing that covered commands and signals. "Yep, these are what I use to direct my dogs." He demonstrated each signal for her and asked, "Do you want to give them a try? That's the only way to learn. Don't forget that those dogs instinctively know sheep."

She spoke gently to Malovich and Gilrakis, gave one shrill blast on her whistle, and pointed to the visible pocket of fifteen to twenty sheep. "Find," she commanded.

Malovich and Gilrakis were off like rockets.

Rusty just grinned at her. "Looks like you will be okay. Let me give you a word of advice. Keep it simple. Don't use too many signals or commands. That confuses them. Good luck." He waved and left with his dogs for the river's edge to start his own collecting.

By 10:30 Malovich and Gilrakis had found and held several large groups of sheep. In a few days the Sumertun sheep would be leaving for Montana. Catherine wondered, what if?

The dogs never lost their exuberance for the game. After the initial "Find," which sent them zooming off, she rode to a small general recovery area. Here she used the command "Cast." She thought that was a funny command, but it worked. The dogs continually "cast" over the area and brought groups of grazing sheep into the larger group.

They had agreed to start bringing the sheep together at 11:00, so she picked up her binoculars and focused on Rusty. She laughed. He was looking at her. One waving arm confirmed they were checking on each other. She rode Jiggles toward the large group of sheep and again commanded "Cast." The dogs moved tirelessly around the sheep, never letting a single animal separate from the flock, while Catherine kept pushing them closer to the large holding pens.

She couldn't believe that one rider and two dogs could handle so many sheep. She used the binoculars again to check on Rusty. He and his dogs were busy bringing in more sheep. When the two riders and four dogs converged they had gathered between 1,500 to 1,700 ewes, lambs and rams.

They were still a good half mile from the woven wire fenced holding pen when the dirty, beige pick-up came clanging sedately toward them on the trail that passed for a road. Catherine looked at her watch. Both hands pointed to twelve. She couldn't believe it. Where had the time gone? It was lunchtime. The sheep still hadn't reached the pens.

When she complained she heard Rusty's laughingly explanation. "Sheep don't string out and move like cattle. It may seem hectic when singles keep bouncing out of the flock and the dogs cast them back in, but it's actually a slow moving body. All that shooting yesterday tells you just how little Art knew about sheep."

∾

Pete slowed to a stop, and yelled out the open window, "Time for lunch. Catherine, tell those dogs to 'hold.' We can get them get them moving again after lunch. Both Rusty and Catherine yelled and signaled "hold" to their dogs. The four dogs reacted as one to contain the morning's accumulation. Every so often one or two bold ewes would try to leave the group to find greener grass, but the dogs immediately pushed them back into the larger, loosely arranged flock.

Both riders dismounted, took their bridles off the horses so they could drink from the small, run-off stream, and then walked toward the pickup for lunch. Lunch was ham and cheese sandwiches, some potato chips and fresh, cool water in their canteens. After lunch Catherine found an open spot of grass, stretched out on her back with her hands cupped under her head and looked at the sky. On this idyllic day the fluffy white clouds drifted east pushed by the soft breeze rolling down the Cascades. Amid the euphoria of a full stomach and a languid warm day she dozed off.

Catherine abruptly woke to Malovich and Gilrakis licking her face, and Rusty's prodding voice. She pushed the dogs away and commanded, "Sit." She sat up to the grinning faces of two Border collies ready to go back to work. She good-naturedly petted each one and gently scratched their neck and head. She rose, stretched and brushed the dust and grass from her pants, and then scolded Rusty. "Thanks a lot for the gentle wake-up call."

"Anytime, Catherine." he grinned, "Anytime."

Pete stood a short distance away. He was pleased by the morning gathering of sheep and the easy camaraderie between Catherine and the two dogs. "You handle those two dogs pretty well. Dogs don't always take to new partners. They often confuse the dogs with different commands, but you kept it simple. They took to Hank like that too."

Catherine smiled, "I knew Hank liked them, but me?" She paused. Her clear-as-a-bell laughter rang out crisply. "I think they're just adorable and they're a heck of a lot smarter than I am. All I've done this morning is ride Jiggles, blow a whistle a few times, yell a few commands, and use my arms and hands to signal." Catherine reached out to Gilrakis, who had inched close and patted him appreciatively. A throaty chuckle soon escaped. Malovich had moved closer to demand his share of attention.

"See what I mean. Those dogs like you, and you like them. It's a good combination. Too bad you have to go back to school so soon." Before Catherine could think of an appropriate reply Pete had started walking back to the pickup. Lunch time was over.

She hadn't seen Pete wink at Rusty as he passed, but she saw the huge grin that suddenly plastered across his weather tanned face.

"Well, what in the devil are you darned so happy about?" She demanded, "What did Pete say to you? Did he tell you to take care of me? Are you here to baby sit me in case I couldn't handle the dogs?"

Rusty admonished her, "Don't be so suspicious, Catherine."

"Doggone it, Rusty. Why shouldn't I be? You just stand there grinning at me. It's time to get back to work." Each called to their dogs, whistled once, and yelled "Cast." Both of them derived the same pleasure from watching the dogs do what they loved.

By four that afternoon they had moved the gathered flock to the wide gates of the holding pens. Inside, the large gathering would be sorted down to a band of 1,500 ewes, lambs and selected rams ready to start the long summer trek. Her mother and Pete waited at the wide gates to receive and estimate the size of the flock.

14
Dilemma Solved

Sarah had walked from the house down the winter rutted road to watch the flock being pushed toward her and the large, wide open gate. She never tired of this spring ritual. Rusty and his two dogs patrolled the right side of the steadily moving flock. Catherine and her two dogs patrolled the left side. Virgil Lauda, another veteran Montana herder, his two dogs and Alex guarded the rear.

The dogs and riders pressured the flock hoping some rambunctious leader would step up to enter the gate. Once the leaders started the flock would eagerly follow. For this reason Rusty told Catherine to give particular attention to the front end of the moving sheep.

Sarah heard her daughter's confident commands to Gilrakis and Malovich. It pleased her to know she had adapted to this part of the gathering. She heard the command "Speak" when barking and more force was needed. If the dogs became overzealous she heard "Steady" to slow them down. On the other side of the flock she heard the same commands from Rusty. If a sheep strayed or bolted away, the dogs quickly forced it back into the flock. Sarah smothered the laugh that wanted to escape at Alex's cracking voice commands, but everyone operated on the same page.

The dogs enforced their will upon the sheep. They moved tirelessly along the rear and flanks of the group. Sarah waited patiently as the first sheep approached the wide open gate. It hesitated, leery to enter any opening smaller than the wide open range. It watched for any threatening movement. It smelled the ground and nervously checked out Sarah and Pete on either side of the gate. Gilrakis barked. The wary sheep inched ahead. Suddenly the first ewe leaped forward over some imaginary line. The following sheep couldn't wait to do the same and follow her into the large enclosure. Sarah heard the occasional command to "Walk Up." There was confidence in Catherine's voice. Gratified she watched the dogs obey and quietly nudge the slow moving sheep along. It was one thing to know the commands. It was another for the dogs to execute.

Sarah forgot everything as soon as the first sheep walked inside. Estimating the size of the flock began. When the last sheep had entered she would compare numbers with Pete who stood on the other side of the gate. Today's closest guess was between 1,570 and 1,600 sheep. Tomorrow's count from the eastern river range should be higher. In three days the holding pens should be bursting at the seams with sheep.

Sarah and Pete had to make a big decision before the sheep left for Montana. She tagged along with her daughter to the barn. Catherine rewarded Jiggles for a hard day's work. Jiggles munched on several carrots, and nickered with pleasure at the careful grooming and the usual amount of scratching, patting and cooing. Catherine made sure Jiggles was well taken care of after the ride. She had learned this lesson long ago.

At the house Sarah went to the refrigerator, pulled out two cold sodas and handed one to Catherine. "Catherine you did a very good job with the dogs today."

Her daughter looked up in surprise.

"Surely you haven't forgotten these." Sarah pointed to the binoculars that sat on the kitchen's window ledge. "That's right. The kitchen window is my view of the world." She reported the days count, "You did very well with the dogs today. You're calm with them. They understand and obey you. That's not always the case." She dryly added, "You'll notice they followed you to the barn and they're waiting for you now at the back door."

Catherine took a long drink of Coca Cola. She casually pinched her nose to stop the bubbles from tickling her nose before thoughtfully rubbing her chin. "What are you trying to say, mother?" She remembered Pete's little innuendos at lunch. "What have you and Pete been talking about?"

Sarah shrugged her shoulders nonchalantly. "We needed to see how you and the dogs worked together." She eyed her daughter and then innocently asked. "Did you enjoy today's experience?"

Catherine took another long, cold drink and thought for a few seconds.

Sarah waited patiently to hear it from her daughter.

"Surprisingly so! I studied and practiced Hank's list of commands. That helped me more than anything." She directed the obvious to Sarah. "It's the dogs that deserve the credit. They're wonderful. They do all the work. To answer your question: Yes, Mother I thoroughly enjoyed the day."

"Catherine, I've been thinking about Hank. He'll be coming home tomorrow, and we agreed he should stay in the guest room for a while. You know Corwin is no longer staying at the house. If he decides to remain stubborn, well, my dear, would you consider sleeping in Hank's wagon after he comes back from the hospital?" She added extra emphasis. "That will let the dogs sleep in a home they are used to."

༄

Catherine kept her amusement hidden while she finished her cold Coca Cola. She set the empty bottle on the table and faced her mother. Maybe her wish had a chance to come true. Why didn't her finagling mother just say what she wanted to hear?

She quietly chuckled, "Let me analyze what I've heard today and see if I understand clearly what has been implied. Pete sends me out with Malovich and Gilrakis. Everyone helps me learn to use the commands. Rusty tells me I really get along well with the dogs. Pete brings lunch and tells me I'm doing extremely well with the dogs.

"You focus the binoculars on me all morning. The first thing you tell me when we get the sheep into the holding pen is how well I'm doing. Now you suggest I spend my nights in Hank's wagon, so the dogs have a place to sleep." Catherine waited for her mother to absorb this before she asked, "Is everyone trying to tell me something?" A small, intensified "Hmmmm" escaped. "Maybe, something about the Montana adventure?"

She waited for an answer. Catherine tantalized her mother with a silence that seemed to go on forever before she said, "My dear Mother, maybe you just need a little nudge to say what you want. Perhaps I can give you some help." She folded her arms over her chest. She enjoyed this cat-and-mouse game. The expression on her mother's face slowly changed. Was it enlightenment? She remained quiet. Did her mother understood?

"Don't we always need the income from the sheep to make the annual payment to the Federal Agri Bank? You know I love this ranch. Even as a little girl I wished someday I could go on the trek. It's always been a dream." She bluntly said, "I would like to take Hank's place. What do you say to that?" She thoroughly enjoyed asking, "Isn't anything better than considering Art Wheeler?" There! Her desire was out in the open.

Sarah snapped, "Art Wheeler was never considered. Hank could probably do limited herding in a couple of weeks, and there will be plenty of help until the sheep get through Prentiss." She watched her daughter absorb that information. "But that's too risky. And the ranch always needs a successful drive. The first week of April is spring break so we considered sending Alex out for two weeks. That would give us time to find someone, but he's too young. Besides he's not interested."

"How do you know that?

"I asked him."

"You asked him before you even considered me?" Her voice became intense. She stared at her mother's. "Don't tell me you thought this was a man only job."

"Don't be silly. Catherine." She hissed, "No, it wasn't that. I wondered if going back to Western wasn't more important."

"But isn't going back to Western my decision?"

Sarah sighed, "Maybe, but I still want what's best for you."

"Why put me through all this dog stuff if you didn't think I was good enough?"

"You were the logical choice and you are good enough." She apologized, "I just had to see. After you, my first job is to protect the ranch. I hope you're strong enough to make tough decisions. Pete thinks you are." She peered at her daughter. "Can do it?"

She quickly answered her mother. "Yes, I can and I want to!" Catherine had never had sensed she belonged on the Sumertun Ranch like she did at this moment. She couldn't wait to tell Hank who his substitute would be. The summer trek to Montana loomed ahead. Was this her destiny?

"Good. That's settled. There's one last thing Catherine. The ranch comes first. If you can't handle this, I won't hesitate a minute to put someone in your place."

15
Heading Out

Goose pimples rose on Catherine's arms and neck. Every nuance around her intensified. Her dream started. The first band of 1,500 four-legged fleecy clouds drifted out the big gate of the western holding pen. Malovich, Gilrakis and Rusty's two dogs darted back and forth as they prowled the flanks. The dogs moved excitedly to the "walk up" or "speak up" commands. They continually barked as they pushed the first band of sheep up the graded road toward the wide fenced lane they would follow until they cleared the ranch.

For the second year Alex used his spring break to ride. He couldn't help the urge that broke into a smile. "Rusty, do you mind if I stop at the house a minute?"

"What for?" Rusty demanded. "We've just got started."

Alex turned away to keep his smile hidden. "The sheep should be moving faster. I thought a few rifle shots in the air might help." Alex peeked cautiously at Rusty to see how he took his little joke.

His tone was severe. "You know what happened to the last guy that did that." Then he reached over and playfully cuffed Alex on the shoulder and smiled. "Forget being funny and let's move these sheep along."

Most of the ewes had been on this trip before. They knew the way. The docked tails of the frisky lambs constantly waved as they stayed near their mothers. Even the bum lambs stayed close. The lambs' shortened tails wouldn't get caught in the sagebrush and low bristly burrs of the rangeland, nor would the sheared coats of remaining wool. They were in their summer dress. Catherine waited until the last sheep started up the grade.

She had heard stories about this journey since she was a small girl. Would she have stories of her own to add? Would coyotes and bears raise havoc with the flock? She knew she wouldn't get drunk and take the wrong trail like one sheep-herder had. She had many thoughts, some questions, but the joy could not be squelched. It was her turn to be a part of Sumertun history. She thought of her father and her first bum lamb. Her father thought his daughter taking care of the lambs was an omen. Maybe he had been right.

She gulped in the morning air to clear her mind. This was everything she thought it should be. Western College for Women was a pleasant preparation for whatever came her way, but this was where she wanted to be. This was life, and she was right in the middle. Never had she felt so much a part of anything as she did now. She laughed as the last reluctant sheep joined the flock on the road up to the ridge and beyond.

She and her mother sat in the driver's seat of the Shepherd's wagon until the last animal was on the road. Then she untied the reins from the wooden brake lever, slapped them against Thunder and Lightning's rumps and yelled, "Giddy-up." Her home on wheels creaked and groaned as it rolled into action. Jiggles trailed behind the wagon. The most exciting foray of her young life began.

She felt the reassuring hug from her mother, and noticed the glitter in her eyes. Tears? Excitement? Maybe she remembered earlier times.

"Mother, did you always feel this great when you started on the trek?"

"I did. It's a marvelous feeling. I always expected to hear the blaring of trumpets and the entry of gladiators when we started." She shrugged her shoulders. "If that makes me sound sentimental, so be it."

Catherine let her imagination capture the Roman gladiator scene. She agreed. "Yeah, the beginning does feel like that. I know it won't last long. The trail will change everything to some tedious routine, but it can't blunt the pleasure of today, can it?"

"No, it can't!"

Catherine posed another question. "I know you often went with my father, before he quit going on the drive, but did you ever stay with the sheep for the entire summer?"

"Never, but I loved the time on the trail with Burke."

Catherine noticed that far-away look again.

Sarah said, "This may or may not be some big adventure, but the open range can be big and peaceful. You'll see." Sarah steepled her hands to the point of her chin, and remembered. "It can get lonely, but think of it as an adventure; an adventure you should record in a log book. My part of the journey was short, just like yours will be, so I'm no expert. I stayed with them twice until the sheep crossed the Columbia River on the old Vernita ferry. That was the longest time." Her question popped up again. "Why don't you keep a log?"

Catherine considered this suggestion. She divided her imagination between the horses and the sheep. She heard her mother's voice. "In the future you can visit fresh, precise memories whenever you want, and not just some fuzzy pictures that time has dimmed when you try to remember. Photos and a journal together would be ideal."

"That's not a bad idea, Mother." She liked the idea, but she laughed, "You'll have to buy it for me. I won't have much time for shopping this summer."

⁓

The imagined entertaining trumpet fanfare and the gladiator's glorious entrance into the Roman coliseum faded the moment she spotted Hank standing on the porch. He leaned on his crutches and waved. She returned his wave.

The thought that she was headed north while he stayed here jarred her. The sinking feeling in her stomach hurt. Pathos replaced joy. The trek no longer seemed as glamorous as it did a few moments ago. She turned to her smiling mother. "Mother?"

"Go ahead, Catherine. I've driven teams before. Remember?" Her heart melted at the sight. Her disciplined, strong willed daughter was doing exactly what she wanted to do, yet she wilted at the sight of Hank.

For a split second she remembered her past. It had been very nice; very nice.

Catherine kissed her mother on the cheek, stepped on the ladder steps on the driver's side, leaped to the ground and sprinted the 20 yards to the house. She managed to put on the brakes before she knocked Hank flat. In one motion they quickly embraced and pressed their eager bodies together as close as possible. Hank bent down to kiss her eager mouth and she ardently returned the kiss.

Sarah knew her daughter would devour him if possible. They were only 20 yards away, but Sarah swore she could feel the heat.

They faced an age old dilemma. They ached to be together, but were being forced to part. Sarah watched the lingering kisses grow short. Her daughter's hand touched Hank's out- stretched fingers as long as possible before she broke away. She took four hesitant steps   before she suddenly turned and hustled back to frantically kiss Hank one last time.

There were tears in her eyes when she climbed back up the steps to the driver's seat. Neither Sarah nor Catherine spoke for several minutes. Both seemed absorbed in the moving flock, but they were thinking of the men who shaped their lives.

Up ahead of the wagon Alex, Rusty, Virgil and the dogs kept the sheep moving. This pushing would cease the moment they hit the open range north of the Yakima River. For the next six or seven days she would have ranch help to move the band twenty-two miles to Prentiss and the seven blocks of havoc through the town and across the river.

For years Catherine had seen photos of sheep and cattle driven through the streets of Prentiss. Every year the Tri-County Review featured at least one picture of the Sumertun sheep or some ranch's cattle marching nervously through the small town, or crossing the Yakima River on their way to the open range. Maybe she would be in the photograph this year? Taking three bands of sheep through town was not an everyday occurrence.

16
First Hand Education

Catherine swiped the back of her hand across her eyes. She looked past her mother and over the milling sheep. "Mother, will you please drive the wagon for a while. I need to be alone for a few minutes."

No explanation was needed.

Once again Catherine stepped on the first step and leapt to the ground. She retrieved her saddle and bridle from the wagon. She slipped the bit into Jiggles' mouth and adjusted the bridle straps around her ears. She continually caressed Jiggles' neck, scratched her ears and cooed softly to the mare. She threw the saddle blanket on her back, smoothed it out, tossed the saddle over the blanket and pulled the cinch tight under her belly. There was one last caressing. Whatever was said brought a slight whiny and a gentle nodding from the horse.

Sarah watched her daughter gallop by. She kept pushing Jiggles until she was well ahead of the flock. She carefully opened the wide gate at the end of the ranch making sure there was no stray wire to catch the sheep or a horse as they passed through.

The sheep would pass from the Sumertun ranch, onto the large strip of rangeland between several ranches and follow this to the county road that led down into Prentiss.

Catherine treated herself to a pity party for several minutes. There was no reason for her to feel any despair. This was where she wanted to be. She dabbed her eyes one more time with her moist handkerchief and stiffened her shoulders. It took several minutes for her swirling emotions to calm down. She rode back to join the human race. The soft breeze in her face was the final healing element.

Alex waved his arms as she approached the flock. She understood and rode toward him. Her anxious brother snapped, "What in the devil are you doing? You'll kill yourself riding like that over rough ground." When no answer came his casual observation came. "We've at least another hour before we get to that gate, so take it easy."

"Did you get me over here just to tell me that?"

"Something made you ride like crazy." He studied her face carefully before she turned away. "You've been crying. Care to tell me about it?" He waited. There was no answer. "Okay, let me guess. Hank was on the porch. You went to see him. That means you're crying about Hank. What I saw didn't seem like a reason to cry."

She stoutly defended herself, "No, it wasn't. It's just that I suddenly realized I'll be out there and he'll be here. That's what my summer will be."

Alex sat in the saddle like Solomon. "Sis, you aren't really dumb enough to think that you'll be alone all summer, are you?"

Catherine looked at her brother. Slowly some understanding of the possibilities brought a smile. Her eyes brightened. "Little brother, you see things that others don't."

He couldn't avoid his sister's light kiss on the cheek. After thoroughly embarrassing Alex she asked, "That isn't why you waved for me to come over, so what did you want?"

"I want to go to the wagon, see mother and get a cool drink of water. I'll be right back." He pressured the rein against Mr. Gray's neck and left at an easy lope for the wagon.

Catherine took her brother's place with the flock. Soon she was absorbed in the movement of sheep, horses and dogs. It gave her little time to think about Hank.

Alex didn't come back on Mr. Gray. Her mother did. She asked, "Are you okay?"

Catherine nodded, and then told her about Alex.

Sarah only smiled. "He thinks deeper than people give him credit for. You have to dig to get an opinion, but in many ways he is an open book. He came to the wagon for water, but what he really wanted was something to eat. He's always hungry. If you want anything left for the trail, I suggest you get back to the wagon."

Catherine started for the wagon, but stayed long enough to hear her mother say, "Tell your brother Pete will be here with lunch soon. We'll eat as soon as the three bands are outside the ranch. Until then it's my turn to enjoy this moment."

෴

The exercise through the gate didn't vary. Pete sat beside Catherine on the driver's seat of the shepherd's wagon and watched. The dogs gathered Catherine's band and the horsemen gently pushed them toward the wide open gate. Malovich and Gilrakis barked and continually prowled the outside of the flock. Gradually a small lead group came to the gate. The leaders stopped and inspected the open gate. Only the hard pushing from the dogs caused any motion. Catherine wanted to laugh at this animal comedy.

The leader looked like it was being crunched up against a wall. She finally leaped over the line and scampered into the open range. The ice was broken. For a while every lamb and ewe jumped over the line at approximately the same spot. Soon the constant noise from the riders and the barking dogs drove all three bands through the gate.

After the horses, the Shepherdess wagon and Catherine were through the gate, Pete left his wagon seat to wait in his pickup, while Rusty and his band were followed by Virgil and his band through the gate. Then the gate would be closed and made secure. The sheep were free to wander in the open range between the ranches.

∽

From the protection of a large lava rock outcropping Art Wheeler watched the three bands of sheep leave the ranch. Catherine and her mother were pointing, laughing and talking about something. It was obvious they didn't know he existed.

He mumbled, "My bad luck started when that snooty college girl saw smoke."

Corwin wasn't any happier. "You knew better than to smoke around the straw, but a fire would have killed a lot of sheep. Maybe Pete would have been blamed and I would still be there. That would be you riding out there instead of Catherine."

Art said, "The shooting was a lot of fun, but even worse luck. How could I know sheep wouldn't stampede but only scatter when panicked? What were the chances that a stray bullet would hit Mr. Gray? That damn Hank also threw water in my face for smoking, and his broken leg caused me to lose my job. No one could save me from Pete, not even you. How could anyone know "The Queen of the Sumertun Ranch" would go against her own husband?"

Art searched Corwin's forlorn face hunkered down against the rocks. "Why didn't you go back, Corwin?"

"Go back to what? She let me know there was no future there. She told me to stay with the wheat. I had absolutely no real say in anything. I was just a glorified hired hand."

"You're not even that now." Art reminded him. "We should be with the sheep not that damn Catherine. It looks like they don't have much use for us anymore.

Dejected, Corwin took one last look. "Yeah," he mumbled, "Looks that way." He wondered if he should have gone back. He shrugged his shoulders. Too late, now! Hatred for anything Sumertun grew.

೦౦

The sheep were free to graze at their own pace. Pete, Sarah and Alex left with the promise to see everyone tomorrow. This luxury would stop as soon as they crossed the Yakima River. Today had been a sneak preview of the future. It had taken all morning to get the flock out of the holding pasture, up the grade, and off the ranch. Now Catherine had her first solo time of with her sheep.

She reread the typed paper, "Lamb Facts," Pete had left with her. It had been written by a shepherd who had a lot time to read the Bible. The writer's stated source had been Psalm 23, John 10 and Ezekiel 34. According to the author; "Sheep are creatures of habit. If they are left to themselves, they will graze the same ground over and over until it becomes barren. They will walk the same trails until the land becomes wasteland. That is why sheep need a shepherd. They need to be managed."

The idea amused Catherine. She had known sheep were dumb animals for a long time, and this authority was really old. She chuckled. If I wasn't being hassled, had plenty of food and water, I'd be content too.

Rusty unsaddled the horses and led them to Alder Creek, a small, spring-fed stream, which started five miles north in the foothills of the Rattlesnake ridge. The thirsty horses drank their fill of cool water. Rusty filled a one gallon, canvas water bag for each rider. The riders would enjoy a cool drink tomorrow. Next he staked out all the horses close to the camp wagon where they had plenty of fresh spring grass. Then he reminded Catherine, "One of the most important chores, tired or not, is to take care of the horses every night." He gave her the two fingered Boy Scout salute and left for his own shepherd wagon.

Catherine was left alone with the horses, the sheep and her two dogs. She sat on the driver's seat of the wagon and watched the evening fade away. With a sigh and a lot of unanswered questions she went inside and unrolled her bedroll on one of the wooden ledges that ran the length of the wagon and crawled in. It would be a cool night, but the determined Malovich and Gilrakis ensured her warmth.

In the morning she walked toward the small stream. The ice cold water on her face jolted her awake. The second handful felt good. She used soap after the third to wash her face and the fourth to rinse. She left the stream wide awake and alert.

Back at the wagon she used the small pump to aerate the kerosene for the Coleman camp stove. This jumped into flame at the touch of a match. Soon she wrapped her hands around her first cup of hot tea. From the driver's seat she and the two dogs, one on either side of her, scanned the area. It was impossible to talk to them and not pet them. The sheep seemed to have spent a quiet night. She chuckled at her thought. They were probably relieved not to be pushed and barked at.

Her empty stomach looked forward to breakfast. She found the big bag of dog food stored in one of the outside boxes attached to the side of the wagon and poured out the morning rations for the hungry dogs. Then she fixed the standard bacon and eggs for herself.

Afterwards she stretched and reached toward the early morning sun. A good day beckoned. Maybe a little breeze would come up the Columbia in the afternoon, but all in all, a good day to be a shepherd.

"A shepherd," she exclaimed. Wait a minute. I'm not a shepherd. That means a man. I'm a woman. She mused, "Would that make me a shepherdine? Perhaps, a shepherdette? Maybe a shepherdess?" She pursed her lips and tossed off the different names. Shepherdess had the nicest ring. Yes, a shepherdess is what she would be.

She found a pencil and added the letters "ess" to the word "shepherd" every time it appeared in her lamb fact paper. Satisfied, she tacked it up at eye level on one of the wagon's rib frames.

Another item caught her eye. "The welfare of sheep depends solely upon the care they get from their Shepherdess. Therefore, the better the shepherdess, the better the health of the sheep." These weren't the flocks of biblical times, but the thought remained the same. The sheep needed tending. Every year they helped secure the future of the Sumertun Ranch with wool and the sale of lambs. The importance of her summer began to sink in.

She began a ritual she would observe every morning. She stood on the driver's seat of her newly named Shepherdess wagon and scanned the area to locate her flock. Then she saddled Jiggles and rode among them. The morning passed swiftly.

She became aware of Pete's pickup bouncing toward the wagon. Lunch time was here. Where had the morning gone? She went out the back door and down the steps to greet the crew the same as always; one step down and a leap to the ground.

During lunch they set the afternoon schedule. Her mother would stay with the wagon. With the help of the dogs, Alex, and Catherine would ride with the flock. Every hour they would rotate. The difference became subtle. Instead of driving the sheep they allowed them to roam about in search of food. If needed a singular command sent one or both the dogs flying to bring the errant ewe, lamb or ram back into the fold.

Alex and Catherine guided the sheep toward better looking grass. They kept them away from dense patches of sagebrush, burrs and nettles. Catherine remembered the paper said a good shepherdess inspired confidence in the flock. She and Alex rode among them and talked to them. It was surprising. They seemed to like the soothing affect of a voice.

All but one determined black lamb. It continually left the flock to seek greener pastures, and the dogs kept bringing him back. Catherine left Jiggles the third time the dogs forced the lamb back into the flock. Both dogs sat there and growled until Catherine caught Blackie, his newly bestowed name, and held him. She sternly talked to him. He accepted the forced cuddling, but roamed off as soon as he was left alone.

So much for scolding.

Otherwise it was a tranquil afternoon. The sheep grazed with drifting guidance. She happily greeted her mother when she rode out, who in turn told Alex, "It's my time with Catherine and the sheep, so go tend the wagon until supper." She good-naturedly chided her son, "I know you'll be hungry by then."

From the other side of the flock Sarah watched her daughter cajole and keep track of her charges. When they met, Sarah joked, "Now you know how a mother feels."

Catherine peered at her mother and laughed. "So that is what it feels like. I can see where you could get very involved with them. That's what a shepherdess does, isn't it?"

Sarah's eyes twinkled at the term. "So that's what you are. When did that title come about?"

The story amused her and she agreed that Shepherdess was a very descriptive name, one that would apply to her daughter.

Catherine asked, "As a Shepherdess aren't my duties the same as before?"

Sarah laughed. "They've never changed."

The pleasant camaraderie between mother and daughter continued to grow. It was akin to friendship, only better. They quietly led the slow moving flock toward Prentiss. Amused, Catherine noticed a few of the ewes and their lambs began to identify with her. Mother to a large band of sheep had never been her view of a shepherd's; a shepherdess' job. Her summer's education loomed ahead.

Her thoughts drifted to the future. What would happen when Hank was ready to come back to the job that was his in the first place? Would she be bumped? She felt some reluctance to accept this possibility.

Sarah had some doubts when she and Pete thrust the job upon her daughter. As a quick substitute for Hank, Catherine had been a welcome surprise. Sarah had critically observed her daughter's performance since then. Catherine had settled into the job like an old pro. Her self-given title, "Shepherdess" was indicative of how she viewed the job.

Sarah stepped forward. "After lunch you'll be alone as the Shepherdess until tomorrow morning when we come back."

She noticed Pete's arched eyebrow at this announcement. Sarah quickly summed it up. "In case you haven't noticed Pete, Catherine's a woman." Her steely gaze at Pete and her son told them to listen. "She's decided she is not a woman shepherd; she is a shepherdess. As a shepherdess this flock is her total responsibility." Sarah loudly announced, "Starting today, that is what you are."

She announced to everyone, "Now it's time to eat."

ᗯ

After lunch Catherine watched all of them leave. She secretly wished Hank had come with Pete this time, but she forced herself to remember her first responsibility had to be the sheep. The desert grass was green and growing. The sheep would have good feed. For now, they were safe in the natural alleyway between the ranches. After they left the safety of this area, Catherine's long wish would turn to reality.

She tied Jiggles to the wagon and climbed into the driver's seat. There she untied the reins and yelled at Thunder and Lightning, "Giddy-up, it's time to move on." They worked their way through the scattered sheep to a position a mile or so in front of the grazing flock and stopped. All her life she had heard that sheep were followers. It became apparent. Some of them followed the wagon at a discreet distance, but others followed her on her morning ride. She unhitched the team of horses and picketed them in a good grassy area and rode Jiggles back to the flock.

She spent the afternoon riding or walking among the flock leading, not pushing, them toward Prentiss. She was amused. She spent the afternoon getting acquainted with as many sheep as possible. It was easy to identify the 6-inch red "S" painted on the right front shoulder of each Sumertun sheep. Other things became apparent. The ewes and their lambs stuck together and the rams stayed to themselves. The occasional head butting among the rams would turn serious later in the summer when the ewes came into season. She cultivated a few leaders by speaking to them and getting them to follow. That might come in handy going through the streets of Prentiss.

Catherine also experimented with the dogs. The summer would be impossible without them. They were smart, hyperactive and just flat adorable. She practiced the commands, "come-bye," circle to the left of the stock, "away," circle to the right of the stock, and "look back," return for a missing animal. "Look back" was particularly important for sheep like the stubborn Blackie. Catherine enjoyed practicing and the time quickly passed. She thought it ironic that the afternoon was probably more profitable for her than for the dogs. Good grass and Alder Creek remained as the flock nonchalantly moved past the shepherdess wagon.

She attacked the sandwiches, salad and the cold cola from the ice chest in the evening. When the sun settled below the still visible Mount Hood in the west, she turned in. She stretched out, put her hands under neck and looked at the canvas wall. It had been a good afternoon. The whines beside the bedroll reminded her that her company for the night wanted to sleep. They also had a hard day.

༄

Catherine started her day by washing her face in cold water again. This time the water came from the two-gallon canvas water bag that hung from the wagon frame. This would often be the case during the summer. She would carry water between streams, springs or domestic water along the way. She was lucky. This was not a worry for her. The herders of the past had mapped water sources on the meandering route to Montana. The sheep had it over her. Between water holes they could get needed water while they munched on the dewy grass. Only extremely dry conditions caused problems. Morning and night her first chore was to take care of the horses and dogs.

With her first cup of morning tea in hand she stood on the driver's seat with her binoculars and scanned the area. From the ground the dogs looked up at her in anticipation. Their tails thumped the ground. They wanted to do something. She again scanned the flock, and said, "Cast." The two took off like rockets to cover both sides of the large area.

Soon movement became apparent. The wanderers were brought back to the scattered grazing group. The sheep merged into larger, slow moving groups. Amazed, Catherine stood on the bench seat with her mouth agape. Those two dogs would make her summer. Her loud yell, "That'll do" or a long shrill single blast from her pipe carried well in the cool morning air. She could see their ears stand up. The dogs stopped and trotted back to her. They accepted her compliments of "good dogs" and "great work" and her caressing hands while the nearby flock contently grazed.

⁓

At noon Catherine went to the wagon for a cold drink of water. She lifted the water bag to her lips when she heard Pete's pickup approach and stop.

A familiar voice called, "Hey, Catherine. Are you there?"

She rushed to put the water bag on its hook, slopping some of it on the small table. She pushed open the back door, found the top step, leaped to the ground and suddenly stopped. The object of her affection stood five feet away. He leaned on his crutches, his right calf in a cast.

He looked so good she wanted to crush him, but she just stood there. He was the best looking man she had ever seen. He took her breath away. She was aware of no one else, but all she could manage was a small voiced, "Hi, Hank."

He too, became afflicted with a case of shyness. "Hello, Catherine."

Pete, Alex and her mother eagerly waited for the robust greeting they expected. The tension of expectancy hung in the air, but nothing happened. These two people, who intensely wanted each other, did nothing. Alex couldn't stand it any longer. "Will you two just kiss each other and get it over with. I'm hungry."

Catherine watched the shyness on Hank's face melt into a bedeviling smile, then an open, teeth-flashing grin. He ran the fingers of his right hand through his hair. Catherine thought to stay in character, he should have said, "Ah, shucks." He didn't. Pete poked Sarah playfully in the ribs to keep from laughing. Alex innocently asked, "Well."

The shyness vanished. Catherine walked gingerly into his opened arms. The kiss was the gentlest, warmest and most welcome kiss Catherine had ever known. She whispered, "God, it's good to see and feel you. I never missed anyone so much in my life." She pulled him tight.

"I missed you too." Then he held her tight.

Alex informed them it was time for lunch.

After lunch Pete left with the reluctant Hank. Alex, Catherine and her mother again rotated their time between shepherding and driving the wagon. The second "cast" command of the afternoon kept the browsing sheep moving north toward Prentiss.

෴

Gilrakis and Malovich trotted alongside the two women but not before they barked ferociously a couple of times at the flock. Catherine laughed and asked her mother, "Do you suppose they're telling the sheep to stay out of trouble until they get back?"

"Who knows? What I see is two dogs and one shepherdess who like each other. You'll have a good summer; one that won't be nearly as lonely as you think."

Catherine turned in her saddle at that little zinger. "What do you mean, mother?"

"I'm taking Hank into Prentiss tomorrow for a check-up. I bet Dr. Hobson will clear him for limited duty." She noticed the surprise on her daughter's face and then the worry. "You do realize it will be 11 days tomorrow, don't you?"

Catherine mumbled, "That doesn't seem possible."

"Think about it. It's been 10 days since he broke his leg." Her mother held up her hand and marked off the days on her fingers. "The day he broke his leg and got it set, two days in the hospital, four days with us at home, and you've been out here three days. He's young and healthy and is healing fast. I bet Dr. Hobson will give him the okay for limited work. That means he can probably drive the pickup by the time you need supplies again."

Sarah cast her mischievous smile. "That's something I can give you to both of you."

She watched Catherine's dawn of comprehension smile, followed by some doubt "Hank doesn't know?"

"It doesn't matter if Hank knows now. Sometime in the future his leg will heal and he'll deliver supplies to you plus the other two wagons. That should make you happy, huh, little one? Happiness is a great thing. If this helps, then I'm a happy mother."

"It does help." Catherine noted a fleeting, wistful look. "Mother, you're not telling me everything." She applied pressure on her mother. "Now, why did you do it?"

Sarah pulled up on her reins to slow Mr. Gray. She turned in her saddle and told Catherine in a sure, precise tone, "I want you to know happiness. Don't settle for anything less." A thoughtful expression, like she had made a decision, spread across her mother's face. "I settled for less when I married Corwin." She shook her head. "Big mistake."

Her dark blue eyes remained calm, while Catherine's face registered astonishment.

Sarah matter-of-factly said, "Corwin hasn't been around since that night in the kitchen. I have no idea where he is, and I want more out of life than that." She emphatically added, "Whether it works out for you two or not, you've opened my eyes."

Catherine's eyes opened a little further at her next casual announcement, "I plan on filing for divorce soon." She reached over and patted her daughter's hand. "Don't worry, my little one, I've been through worse, much worse." She kicked her horse in the flank, left Catherine standing there, and galloped the last 50 yards back to the wagon.

She knew her mother must be hurting. She had already called her little one twice.

ೲ

When everyone left in Pete's pickup Catherine didn't mind. It gave her a little time to think. She was elated that Hank would see her several times during the summer, but did that mean Hank would relieve her when he had fully recovered? Her new ambition came out loud and clear. She wanted to be Shepherdess all summer.

17
The Road to Prentiss

In mid-morning Catherine left the sheep to their endless graz-ing and rode Jiggles to the edge of the plateau. The Yakima River bisected the impressive valley below. The river made the difference between the valley and the plateau. Irrigated farms along the river were famous for apples, potatoes, alfalfa, hops, high yields of grain and sugar beets. On the plateau grain and alfalfa depended on the sparse rainfall to survive and grow profitable yields. In the valley the farms were generally small, 40 to 240 acres. The ranches were large on the plateau. The Sumertun ranch was 3,000 acres while grain and sheep were the ranch's income.

Her gaze wandered west to the towering snow-capped Cas-cade Mountains, the birth place of the river. Catherine savored the spectacular view. The valley, the river, and the mountains on a glorious April day; how much better could it get?

Would the Sumertun sheep begin moving toward Prentiss this afternoon or tomorrow morning? Could they get the sheep down the five mile grade this afternoon and safely in the city corrals before nightfall? Maybe Pete and her mother preferred to let the sheep forage on the plateau today, and push them down the grade in the morning. She asked the dogs what they thought, and they answered with enthusiastic barks. She laughingly told them, "You don't know any more about it than I do."

Catherine had her answer when Pete drove the ranch's truck pulling the large horse trailer close to Rusty's wagon. She watched him guide Pete to a suitable, flat unloading place. Rusty and Virgil Lauda pulled down the solid tailgate, which also served as an off-ramp. The two men walked up the ramp into the trailer, untied their haltered horses and led them to the outside world.

Sarah's horn announced her arrival. Catherine didn't have to count any further. She knew her mother and Alex were there, but she sucked in her breath when she spotted the cowboy hat. He opened the door, pushed his crutches out and carefully slid off the seat to the ground.

Catherine needed no coaxing. She skipped happily to Hank's waiting right arm. She said, "It's time to eat, Alex. You'd better get going."

Six riders, six dogs and three wagons were poised to escort the sheep down the steep five and half percent grade to the waiting Prentiss corrals.

Catherine waved her hand forward like Tom Mix in a western movie. She reined Jiggles right from the rangeland onto the gravel road. Since her band left the Sumertun Ranch Catherine had worked to become familiar with the sheep. She had purposely cultivated the few ewes that seemed to be natural leaders. At first Catherine had looked around the self-consciously to make sure no one saw her talking to the sheep. She had worked to establish the shepherdess-sheep bond the paper said was necessary. Would she pass this test?

She chided herself for being as dumb as the sheep. Twenty yards down the road. She looked back and laughed. "Look Mother, we have two followers." Dolly and Ulla walked toward her. A few more lambs followed their mothers. Elated Catherine knew an important test had just been passed.

Soon a steady line of sheep followed her down the grade to Prentiss. The sharp rise of the slope above the road formed a natural barrier. The slope fell away fast on the lower side of the road where the six dogs patrolled. Any strays were quickly pushed back up to the road by the perpetual-motion dogs. Traffic was the one thing that could cause a trouble.

The myriad of county roads that served the ranches of the plateau all funneled into this gravel road down to Prentiss. The sheriff's office didn't have the manpower to cover all the feeder roads. Any drivers and their cars would have to be ushered through the flock. Catherine hoped there wouldn't be too many. The deputy stationed at the bottom of the grade stopped the sparse, upward bound traffic and redirected it to the state highway further east or asked them to go into town and wait.

After Dr. Hobson declared him fit for limited duty, Hank quickly accepted the chance to drive the wagon he still thought of his own to bring up the rear. The cars or pickups stopped at Hank's waving hand and listened to his explanation of how to go through the sheep. Many drivers were ranchers with stock of their own. They knew the importance of the cattle and sheep drives, and were cooperative and patiently followed Pete or one of the other herders through the sheep. In this organized chaos the sheep and their escorts moved steadily toward the bottom of the grade.

Above the rim to the south the long, dust trail billowing up behind the car headed west spelled trouble. Sarah first spied it as she rode up the grade to see how Hank was doing. She noticed the dust clouds approaching the top of the grade. No one came west from the state highway unless they had made a mistake. Someone was traveling much faster on the gravel road than they should. She hoped the car kept going west. The car would eventually wind up in the little village of Lincoln, if it didn't wreck first.

Pete had just completed guiding Sam Judd, a local rancher, down the hill through the slow moving sheep. There was plenty of time for the two to chat. Pete learned that Sam's wife was feeling much better, so he was coming to town to get a load of Purina Chicken Chow. He was glad to learn the road would be clear when he came back from Prentiss. The taciturn Pete smiled at Sam's ability to keep talking about nothing. He rode up the grade to be ready when the next car or truck needed an escort through the sheep.

Pete pulled the canvas water bag from its customary place, hanging from the bed of the Shepherd's wagon. When he noticed Sarah riding toward him he waited to offer her the first taste of cool water. Sarah wasted no time in formalities. She savored every gulp before she returned the water bag.

"Thanks Pete."

He reached for the bag and his own drink when he saw the reflection in Sarah's widening eyes. He turned in time to see the shiny black car turn right onto the top of the canyon road and speed downhill. "Damn fool," exclaimed Pete. "That's no local."

The large black car followed the road down and brought its dust cloud with it. The cloud left the car at the first sharp right-hand turn to sink into the canyon below. Across the canyon Pete and Sarah could make out the outline of the driver hunched over the steering wheel. The big touring car followed the road south back into the hill before it doubled back on the hairpin curve under the ridge. The dust cloud began building again. Pete rode uphill past the wagon and waited. The driver seemed intent on making a mad dash down the grade. It roared downhill toward Pete, and then disappeared behind one of the slopes.

Coming around the slight, right-hand curve the car suddenly reappeared. Pete plainly saw the driver's astonished face as he slammed on the brakes. The driver fought to keep control. Pete tensed, ready to spur his horse in any direction. The car skidded to a stop fifteen yards from the Pete and his horse, and thirty yards from the helpless wagon Hank drove. Sarah stood frozen. The dust cloud engulfed them as it sped over the black car, Pete and finally the wagon and Sarah.

Oblivious to any danger he might have caused the driver bounced angrily from the car shaking the wrinkles from his dark blue, three piece-suit. He appeared to be in his late forties. The jacket draped over the strong shoulders and tapered to his waist. He rearranged his tie and marched toward Pete sitting atop his horse. "What the hell's the matter with you? This is a highway, not a stock trail. I could have been killed if I hadn't seen all those sheep in time."

On horseback Pete towered over the driver. "Mister, you could have killed me! That's a lot worse than running over the sheep." He pointedly asked, "Or don't you think so?"

No reply.

Pete pointed out an obvious fact. "Besides you could see us and the sheep from the curve across the canyon. These roads are not speedways, so why were you so reckless?"

The driver remained combative. "I took a wrong turn off the state highway on what I thought was a short cut." He raised his arm to read his wrist watch. "I'm running late as it is, and now these damn sheep--." He threw his hands in the air, "I guess I'll just have to push through them." He returned to his car and opened the door. He looked over the open door up at Pete sitting in the saddle. "Now if you will get out of the way I'll drive through. It will give me great deal of pleasure to scatter those sheep." There was no mistaking his anger.

Pete stood in the left stirrup, swung his other leg over the saddle to the ground, and in three quick strides confronted the man. Only the open door separated them. Pete's voice was controlled fury. "My name is Pete Alzola and I'm responsible for getting this band down the hill to the city's corrals." He stuck his hand out for the handshake that didn't immediately come. He waited, but didn't move.

Reluctantly the man shook hands and introduced himself. "I'm Glenn Simons." He drew his hand back and glared over the open door. "That doesn't change anything. I have to get through -- now!"

Neither noticed Sarah's quiet approach until she spoke. "Pardon me, Mr. Simons, but I couldn't help but hear your name and your intentions. My name is Sarah. Pete and I have been making this run down this grade for many years." She flashed her beaming smile. "We apologize for the inconvenience. If you'll be a little patient we'll get you through the sheep and down the grade as soon as possible."

She noticed the car for the first time. "Is this the new Packard Touring Car?"

Glenn Simons stepped back and smiled at the petite woman with dark blonde hair, who stood before him. "Yes it is. I've had it all of two months."

"Is it as good as the advertisements say?"

His dubious expression said, "Lady, do you really know anything about cars?" His tolerant voice asked, "You mean the slogan, 'Ask the man who owns one?'"

Sarah nodded.

He answered her. "Yes, you should ask, and yes, it is a very good car, probably the best on the market. That's why I bought it."

Sarah slowly walked around the car to inspect it. "I apologize for being forward. May I call you Glenn?"

He cautiously answered, "Yes." He quickly countered, "That doesn't mean you people are off the hook for blocking the road. It's a damn inconvenience. They shouldn't be allowed on the road. I have a very important business meeting and I'm getting later by the minute." He fixed a stern stare at Sarah. "I intend to talk to the law when I get to town."

Sarah turned to Pete and winked, and then she gave the belligerent Glenn Simons another smile. "Then we had better get busy, Pete. This man has important business in town."

Pete smiled and said, "Get in your new car, Glenn, and we'll get you there as soon as possible." He silently laughed at his thoughts and the comparison. "I'm not smooth like Sarah. She can charm the birds out of the trees. That poor guy doesn't have a chance; and he thinks he impresses her with his tough guy act." He put his left foot in the stirrup, grabbed the saddle horn and pulled up. He adjusted his seat in the saddle and looked down at the fuming driver. "Sarah, get in the car. You can help Mr. Simons and ride in that new Packard at the same time."

Sarah blithely opened the passenger door and slid in before there was a chance to protest. She ran her hand over the shiny dashboard and the posh seat upholstery. "Glenn, it's as nice on the inside as it is on the outside. It must have cost you a pretty penny."

Sarah could see him puff up.

"Not pennies, Sarah; dollars!"

Sarah acted suitably impressed. Glenn Simons didn't notice she had quietly assumed command. Surprisingly he listened to her say. "Just drop in behind Pete's horse and watch the dogs and the other riders. They will clear the way. Just be thankful it's sheep and not cattle."

An amused smile appeared. "Why is that?"

"Cow manure splatters on everything, even new cars. The only thing you have to worry with sheep is one may suddenly jump in front of you. They're nervous little creatures, so you have to drive carefully."

She cheerfully admonished him, "Don't blast your horn every few seconds. That only makes them scatter. Then it will take you longer to get down the hill. Don't fret and fume, you'll live longer and get to the meeting in a much better mood." She caught his flashing brown eyes and held them with her open, guileless ones. "Shall we go?"

Glenn Simons eased the big Packard sedan in behind Pete and resisted the urge to constantly honk the horn. He lived by the clock and felt those he dealt with should do the same. He wanted to be mad as hell, but he wasn't. Time didn't seem to matter to this Sarah person.

He sneaked a sideways peek at her. She obviously had been riding, but she looked fresh as a daisy. Her red, gray, and white plaid shirt had not lost any of its crispness. Not a hair was out of place. She doesn't seem to have a care in the world. Otherwise she would have reacted differently when he half-threatened her and that Pete. He thought she probably works on a ranch or is married to someone who lets her enjoy life. That was why she looks so young, although she must be about my age. He thought it would be nice not to have any responsibility.

Through the open window he heard Pete call out, "Gilrakis, walk up -- speak."

"What does that mean?"

"Walk up, means just that. He wants Gilrakis to move closer to the sheep and bark to make them move faster."

"Gilrakis? Is that the dog's name?"

"Yeah, that's the dog's name. His partner is Malovich. Quite the names, aren't they?" Her gentle laugh reminded him of chimes.

He drove slowly into the wedge shaped opening created as the sheep split. With no thought he reacted to the lamb that darted in front of the car. He jammed on his brakes and honked his horn. Several more sheep broke away. Pete turned in the saddle and glared at him and yelled, "Don't honk that damn horn. It makes matters worse."

To his great surprise Glenn apologized to Sarah. "I couldn't help it. That blasted lamb darted in front of me. I couldn't help it. Darn it! That's what I mean when I said they shouldn't be allowed to clog the roads."

The woman sitting beside him remained serene, "What business are you in, Glenn?"

"Construction. I own a construction company. Why?"

"Are you in complete control of everything?" Her calm voice penetrated his anger. "Don't accidents and work interruptions happen?"

"Darn it Sarah, I try to be in control, but yes, things do happen." He felt guilty for his outburst. He couldn't seem to get mad at this woman. "I see what you mean." A self-effacing smile appeared. He wanted to say "Damn it Sarah," but it came out "darn it Sarah."

"Why the smile, Glenn?"

"It was just a thought, Sarah. I have to sit back and do the best I can, huh?" Curiosity got the best of him. "You said you and Pete have done this for several years."

She nodded.

"Surely someone occasionally runs into a lamb or a sheep, maybe a calf or a cow. What happens when the animal is killed?"

She simply replied. "They have to pay for it."

He immediately protested. "That's not fair. The animals are blocking public roads. I would refuse to pay." He knew this lady didn't have any power, but he needed to know. "What would you do?"

"I wouldn't need to do anything other than file a claim." Her tolerant smile reminded him of his high school English teacher's reaction, when an answer should have been obvious. "Large areas of the west are considered open range. Didn't know that, did you?"

She waited for an answer.

To his chagrin he had to tell her he didn't.

"There are no fences on the open range. All livestock is protected. Whoever kills an animal pays for the animal. No court decision required. That may not seem fair, but that's the law. However you didn't kill the animal, but you were mad enough to, right?"

He was ashamed to admit it, but she was right.

In a non-sermonizing voice, she told him, 'You need to relax a little, Glenn. You're too uptight about everything. Life's like that frightened lamb that darted in front of your car or like any accident in your construction business. You can't control everything. You need to relax, enjoy this unusual sheep-on-the-trail thing, and be ready for the meeting. By the way you never told me what you do in construction, or what your meeting is about."

He sneaked a peek at the woman beside him. He thought of her as a blithe spirit. He didn't believe she cared what he did. Still, he realized he was a little more relaxed. Glenn Simons focused his attention ahead to the split in the moving flock and drove carefully forward.

He wanted to impress her. "I build grain elevators, those big ones you see around Pendleton and the Palouse country in eastern Washington. My meeting is with the Tri-City Grain Growers. They want to build a grain elevator in Prentiss." A quick flush of irritation crossed his face. "That is, if they're still there."

He drove grimly behind Pete as he split the flock. As they approached the deputy at the bottom of the hill he glanced at Sarah again. She still wore that urbane look of contentment. This is just a lark to her. He thought she didn't have any real responsibilities, so there was no need for her to worry.

"This has been a pleasant break, Glenn. Thanks for the ride down the hill. I can tell people I rode down the hill with a man who owned a Packard and liked it." She pointed to the deputy.

"You turn right when you get past him and you'll be at your meeting in five minutes. The sheep are continuing on to the city's corrals. It's a short distance for the sheep, but it will take us another half hour to get them there."

She pointed up ahead to the figure on horseback. "That's my daughter leading the sheep to the corrals where they'll spend the night." She sighed at the inevitability of the summer. "After we cross the Yakima River tomorrow they have a summer's journey ahead, but my part of the drive is ended."

"Where will your daughter take the sheep after they cross the Yakima."

"To the railhead in Sandpoint, Idaho or some little town in western Montana you've probably never heard of." She laughed. This time the melodic laughter sounded like harmonically blended bells. "Can you understand why a couple of miles on a steep grade is a very minor journey?"

"Yes, I can see why." Glenn Simons heard the wonderment in his own voice. He hated to see his short drive down the grade end. It had to be the company. He heard that gracious voice. "This is where our time together ends." She touched his sleeve. "Glenn Simons, you've made this part of the adventure better. Good luck at your meeting. Remember to relax and enjoy those around you. They'll listen and consider what you propose. I bet you're good at what you do. Just tell them that Sarah said to listen."

Before he could reply, she was out of the car and trotting toward the deputy. He ran his hand over the sleeve she had stroked. It was unbelievable. He was ready to fight at the top of the hill, now he hated to leave for the meeting. He slowly turned right off the county road and onto a paved street that would lead him into Prentiss and the meeting. He found her in his side mirror. That unpretentious woman rode double with Pete back up the grade where she would lead more cars through the sheep.

18
The Banquet

The small town of Prentiss, population 3,854, served as a railroad center for the cattle, sheep and wheat ranches of the area, plus a growing fruit packing industry for the irrigated farms of the valley. Agriculture was the lifeblood of the vigorous, growing town. The city had erected the corrals to serve the many cattle and sheep drives that passed through the town going north to open rangeland. They also served those who used the railroad to ship their livestock to market. The rodeo grounds were adjacent to the corrals. The corrals portrayed both the past and the future. They were an important part of the Prentiss community.

Monty Sherwood had opened his small Sherwood Inn to serve those who needed a room while they loaded their livestock or farm commodities on the train. Sherwood Inn prospered during the boom era of the 1920s and Monty replaced it with a new, larger Sherwood Hotel a few months before Black Friday, the October, 1927 stock market crash day. The tradition of good service and clean, pleasant accommodations helped Monty and the hotel survive the Depression. The hotel had served the Sumertun family since 1928 when they started using the open range across central Washington to Montana.

Every year before he died Burke Sumertun had reserved several rooms for himself, and Sarah, Pete and the men who brought the sheep this far. After Burke died a few years passed before Sarah started the custom again. At this moment Catherine enjoyed this tradition with a luxurious hot, soapy, bubble bath. She sank down in the tub so only her head showed. She surrendered her body to total relaxation. "Ah-h-h" expressed the joyful feeling of hot water against her tired body. Catherine stretched her arms upward. It felt wonderful. She wondered how long it would it be before she would have this luxury again.

Catherine thought about the last few days. She regarded them as a dress rehearsal. She had only begun to understand what being a shepherdess meant. After going through the streets of Prentiss and over the bridge of the Yakima River she would get to the real thing. No more practice, no more daily help from the ranch, and no more food service from home. There would only be herself, Rusty and Virgil, each with their band of sheep and their dogs. That would be daunting, but my, oh my, did she ever look forward to it.

She sank languidly below the surface completely engulfed by hot water before she came up sputtering and happy. She had become a vital part of the Sumertun Ranch. How great was that? Would this be her destiny that began with the first bum lamb or would she be relieved by Hank and go back to Western?

⁓

Dining at the Sherwood was Sarah's special treat. Everyone enjoyed being an honored guest for one night. Sarah had thought it a waste of money when Burke did it, but after she decided to live again, she looked at things differently. She laughed and told Catherine, "That darn Burke had always delighted in doing this, and now I know why."

Sarah and Catherine waited for the men in the hotel's small conference room, which doubled as a private dining area. Both had discarded the dirty, dusty riding boots, the jeans, and cotton blouses under flannel lined Levi jackets of the trail for casual evening dress, nothing fancy, just good quality dresses, with custom gold accessories, silk hose and one inch heels. Sarah counted the place settings, which lay on spotless white linen tablecloths. The fresh roses flanked by white baby's breath caught her eye. She bent close and smelled. The Sherwood Inn had done everything just right.

∾

Glenn Simons sat in the lounge nursing his bourbon on the rocks when the two women passed through and disappeared behind the curtain into the private dining area. He observed their animated conversation as they sashayed casually through the regular dining room, unaware of anyone else. They obviously enjoyed each other's company. They were a far cry from the two serious women he had seen this afternoon. He looked again. Maybe they weren't so different. Their facial expressions were still open, still friendly, and still fearless. He kept his attention riveted on Sarah. What made her so different? He slowly sipped his bourbon, remembering how she had changed his attitude in one short ride, and then how she saved his afternoon meeting.

∾

Pete, Rusty, and Virgil and the late arriving Alex fidgeted and looked nervously around as only outdoor men dressed up for dinner can. They pushed their way through the hanging drapery and wandered around the table until they found their designated place cards. Sarah hid her amusement as she watched her daughter move around the table. When Catherine sought her eyes for an explanation she assured her, "Don't worry, Hank's not left out. He'll be here as soon as the deputy brings him."

"Deputy?"

"That's right. Every year I hire a deputy to patrol the corrals at night. He has an added duty this year. He is Hank's chauffeur. Is that okay?" Her blazing smile simply reinforced what she already knew. Catherine wanted to spend every available minute with Hank.

Catherine heard the telltale squeak and scuffling of crutches and watched the tip of a crutch push the light drapes to one side. Hank stepped inside and waited. She hurried to him and did what everyone expected her to do. There was no fuss, just a firmly planted kiss that was returned. Even Alex seemed pleased. Dinner was about to begin.

Sarah stood at the head of the table with her champagne glass lifted. Her toast was an imitation of what Burke had said long ago. "Here's to all of you. You make all this possible. You've worked through some tough times to make the Sumertun Ranch prosper, and get only a fine dinner once a year." She took the first sip, felt the released bubbles tickle her nose and joked, "I'd say that's a fair deal." She grew solemn. "Thank all of you for everything!"

The sound of clinking glasses followed. It wasn't Pete who stood up. It was Rusty. In his laconic, dry voice he spoke, "Yep, I'd say that's a fair deal. You're the only rancher I know who does this. You make us feel like we're important. You've discovered the secret. It's not the money. We all like the good pay, but we love being appreciated."

Sarah barely heard Rusty's toast, "Here's to Queen Sarah" and the applause that followed. She had noticed the shadow fall against the curtains. Someone stood outside listening. She kept stealing quick glances at the curtain as she responded to Rusty's toast with another drink of the bubbly.

She found Catherine's questioning eyes. "What is it Mother?"

"I don't know."

Sarah left as unobtrusively as possible when the food arrived. She parted the curtain to peek outside, but saw no one. She felt certain that someone had stopped and listened. It was probably a waiter or someone on the way to the restroom. The explanation didn't satisfy her, but for the moment, it was all she had.

Back inside everyone enjoyed the meal and more champagne. Sarah turned her attention to the prime rib, cooked to perfection, a dazzling large baked potato and delicious spring asparagus. The irony of sheep in the corral, but beef on the table was not lost on her.

The party for the well-fed, happy ranch hands officially ended with one final toast to Catherine wishing her luck on the summer adventure. The tired ranch hands gradually faded away. All of them thanked Sarah and bypassed the lounge on the way to their rooms. Tomorrow promised to be a long, busy day. Hank walked Catherine to her room. Their good-night kiss threatened to become much more before they finally pushed apart. With a sigh, Catherine went into her own room.

She felt too tense and keyed up to turn in. Hank did that to her. So did the fact that tomorrow she would be leading a band of sheep through the main streets of Prentiss. She absent-mindedly looked out the window to the deserted street below. Tomorrow, on this same corner the sheep would turn north toward the river. She thought about the sheep and her dogs.

She remembered every word on the Lamb Facts paper that hung in her wagon home. *When a shepherdess senses fear in the flock she moves quietly among them and quiets them.* Another section jumped out from her memory. *As soon as the sheep become aware that the shepherdess is with them, the fear is replaced by trust.*

Tomorrow the sheep would be pushed from the corrals down Western Avenue and turn north at the corner and past the hotel. The storekeepers would be out front to protect their store. Deputies and volunteers would line the intersections. Catherine had seen pictures in the National Geographic magazine of small flocks of goats passing through villages in the Swiss Alps on their way to alpine pastures. This parade would be sheep not goats. It was not an everyday occurrence and there was a big difference in the size of the flocks. Sleeplessness plagued her because of one question. *If she didn't tend to her flock, who would?*

Wide awake she changed back to her work clothes and left her room. She knocked on her mother's door and impatiently waited. She knocked again. No answer. Maybe Pete wanted to talk to her after the dinner. Maybe she stopped at the lounge to talk.

The bartender hadn't seen Sarah leave, but thought he had seen someone waiting outside the dining room. Maybe someone was waiting to talk to her? Catherine was relieved when she heard voices coming from the private dining room. She called out.

∽

A pensive mood had descended on Sarah after everyone left the dining area. She sat alone at the head of the table. Duke Ellington's recording of "Solitude" wafted in and out of her consciousness from the lounge jukebox. Her mood was broken only when she sipped the champagne and thought about the future. Corwin caused some regret, but she thought of her divorce as procedure, not sorrow. She had fooled herself into an accommodating marriage. The end had been coming for some time. She had not seen nor heard from Corwin since the kitchen scene. In a very short four years she would be fifty. Hank and Catherine had shown her surviving wasn't enough. Now, she wanted more. She wanted to live again.

The fact that Corwin had never tried to explain anything nor ever made any effort to keep connected was a painful eye-opener. The mystery of why he put himself so far out on a limb for Art remained unanswered. Her musings were interrupted when the last person she expected to see stood before her and asked, "Mind if I join you, Sarah?"

19
After the Banquet

S arah focused her eyes on the blurred figure. "No, no, come in, Glenn." She emptied the last of the bubbly into his glass. They touched glasses and sipped champagne. Sarah peered at the rugged face in front of her. He presented a full, thick head of short, wavy, dark hair and bushy eyebrows to match. The brown eyes, which were so angry this afternoon, seemed to be laughing. His deeply tanned complexion was probably the result of outdoor work. He loomed even larger than this afternoon.

"This is a surprise. I thought by now you would be on your back way to Vancouver."

"I should have been, because I was very late for an impor-tant meeting." He pulled out a chair from the table, turned it toward him, straddled it, and sat down facing Sarah. "But a funny thing happened. There will be another meeting tomor-row morning."

"How on earth did you manage that?" Her giggle was slurred. "I thought you said the people you deal with are on time ... just like you."

"Touché."

Sarah thought he looked just like a little boy caught with his hand in the cookie jar. "What happened?" She burped. Her hand moved quickly to cover her mouth.

"When I finally arrived at the law offices of Patrick C. Greenworth, only three members of the commission were still there. I suspect they were waiting to tell me that I wasn't wanted in not so gentle terms. One older man, Sig Rasmussen, just sat there and listened to the other two. Finally, it was his turn. Without a doubt I was through before I had a chance to explain anything. Almost word for word that old wheat rancher reiterated my own philosophy about the responsibility of being on time."

Glenn Simons was too interested in his explanation to notice Sarah's tiny smile.

He pushed the chair closer to her and leaned his face even closer. "There was nothing left for me to say. The irony of me losing an opportunity because I was late was too much. I laughed. Not just a little, muffled teehee, but a real tension-releasing belly laugh"

"And what did Sig Rasmussen do. It sounds like you insulted him."

"You're right. It wasn't meant to be, but it was very insulting." He leaned even closer to Sarah. His eyes searched her face.

Glenn's position in the chair left her no where to turn. Besides he looked good. He smelled like a man. Even the slight whiskey breath was enticing. His masculinity charged the atmosphere. *Be careful girl. The champagne is getting to you.*

"For some reason your last words popped into my mind. I told him, 'By the way, Sarah said that you should listen to me.' You wouldn't believe the difference in that man. He was somewhat incredulous when I told him why you rode down the hill with me." Glenn sipped his champagne and almost whispered his observation. "You certainly have one great believer in your worth as a human being."

Glenn leaned even closer. Sarah didn't object. "Sig, he insisted I call him Sig, arranged everything. Thanks to you, there will be another meeting tomorrow at eleven tomorrow morning. I'll be on time!" He leaned back in triumph. "What do you suppose caused that?"

Sarah smiled and yawned. "Another chance is wonderful, Glenn. Sig is a very dear friend and one smart, but tough son-of-a-gun. He will do anything for you until you let him down. I know being late didn't set well." She stretched her arms, blinked a few times and apologized. "Glenn, I'm not used to drinking champagne. I'm suddenly very sleepy. Will you please excuse me?"

"Of course, Sarah, but you have to answer one question."

The demand amused Sarah, but she kept slipping away. She slurred, "If I can."

His eyes stared relentlessly into hers. "Who in the devil are you?"

༄

"Mother, are you still here?"

"In here, Catherine."

Glenn heard the quickening of boot taps on wood. Catherine burst into the dining room. She had changed back to her work jeans, boots, and a bright orange and blue western shirt. For protection against the chilly night she carried her flannel lined denim jacket. She cast a curious glance looked at Glenn, then again at her sleepy mother. Her perplexed voice asked, "Mother?"

Glenn answered. "Your mother has had too much champagne tonight. I'll help you get her to her room." They stood Sarah up. Glenn picked her up as easily as he would a rag doll and carried her fireman-style up to her room and laid her on the bed.

Catherine wanted to know what happened.

Glenn told her, "Don't ask. You know as much as I do. Catherine, your mother is one rare woman. When she wakes up in the morning tell her, 'Thanks for everything'."

After he left Catherine was too busy getting her mother into bed to decipher what that meant. She softly closed the door and left her mother gently snoring.

20
A Busy Night

The night air had a cool bite to it, but the short walk to the city corrals was pleasantly invigorating. In the morning she would ask her mother what had she done that warranted a thank you from Glenn? Why were they there alone in the dining room? He seemed unusually concerned. Why? Catherine felt the foolishness that comes from worrying about something you had no control over.

The fears might be baseless, but her heart had told her to find out. Two wagging tails bounded out from under the wagon to greet her. Gilrakis and Malovich were priceless. The three of them walked quietly through the first corral. Catherine assured the sheep that everything was as it should be. In the second corral, she felt a slight push against her leg. 'What the"— She looked down to see the demanding Dolly. Catherine scratched her head and talked to her. The ewe followed Catherine until she opened the gate and stepped toward the third corral.

Catherine swore the three corrals were quieter when she headed back to the wagon to finish the night. She had followed her heart and a drowsy, warm, fuzzy feeling of self-satisfaction followed when she nestled into her bedroll. A lot of that warmth came from the two dogs which snuggled up tight against her. She lazily reached down to pet them.

❦

Low whines and growls roused her. Catherine quietly slipped on her pants, grabbed the loose sweatshirt from the ledge, and slipped into her boots. It was too dark to check her watch. Her mother had said there would be a deputy here until midnight, but it had to be later . She reached down to pat the dogs. "I'm glad you're here."

Catherine spotted the flashlight beam flitting around the farthest corral and some uneasy sheep ready to scatter. She yelled, "Who are you and what are you doing here around the sheep?" Several skittish sheep moved quickly aside.

The strong flashlight beam swung toward her and stopped. It was quiet for several moments. Finally a clear, strong voice rang out. "Hello, I'm Deputy Daniel Jerrigan. I'm just checking to see if everything is okay. You must be Catherine Sumertun."

"Yes."

"We didn't know there would be anyone here after Deputy Barnes went off duty. The city wants us to check the corrals during the night." She heard a chuckle. "Three years ago some cattle got out and raised Holy Ned with some front yards. Waking up with a steer in your yard tends to make people angry."

"How could something like that happen? Cattle and certainly sheep can't open a gate."

"Someone probably got careless and didn't secure the gate. Cattle are bigger and they rub against the wooden fences. They probably worked the latch loose. You'll notice the gates have new wooden sliding bars with large notches that are held in place by a wooden dowel. You have to remove the dowel, and lift the top bar so it will slide. Without that you can't open the gates. Believe me, the gate is secure. That's what I was checking when you came out of the wagon. You gave me a little start, you know. I didn't expect to see anyone here." He tipped his hat and apologized for waking her.

Catherine watched his taillights disappear toward Prentiss. All seemed quiet. She spoke to the dogs. "Come on you two ... false alarm." Back in the wagon, she found her own flashlight and checked the time. It was 2:00 am. She crawled back into bedroll and felt the reassuring comfort of the dogs curled up beside her and began drifting off.

∽

Half asleep, Catherine mumbled, "Not again." The dogs moved toward the door. The sound of uneasy bleating came from corrals. It must be the deputy checking the gates again. She drifted toward sleep. A different sound persisted. The deputy didn't have that much trouble before. She rolled out of bed and yawned. Barefoot she padded to the back door and peered out. There was no one there.

Sitting back on the open bed she heard the noise again. Suddenly she was wide awake. She hastily pulled on her pants, threw on her sweat shirt, jammed her sockless feet into her boots, grabbed her own flashlight, and hit the ground running. Gilrakis and Malovich bounded out and quickly sprinted past her. Their menacing growls grew stronger.

Catherine heard cries of "Damn dogs. Get away from me, Gilrakis, no. Damn dogs." Despite the dim moonlight obscured by a distant cloud she made out the form of a man running. Whoever was running stopped and picked up some kind of a stick. She heard a menacing growl and looked toward the sound. A sharper yelp of pain came next, then some more cussing, more growling and the sound of tearing cloth. When the growls stopped she cautiously trotted toward the noise to investigate. Her two tail-wagging sentinels met her halfway. It was a job well done, and they seem satisfied. They gladly accepted her few words of "good job" and a few strokes of affection.

A pickup started in the distance and sped away.

Catherine petted and hugged her two dogs. Not only could they keep sheep moving, but they would protect them from varmints, human varmints.

She examined Gilrakis and Malovich. Neither limped nor behaved as if it had a severe injury. Gilrakis flinched when she ran her hand over his shoulder, probably a bruise would develop. Whoever had done this had called him by name. Before she could tell them again how wonderful they were, a car approached on Western Road.

Catherine and her dogs were almost to her wagon when they were caught in the deputy's spotlight. She put her arm up to protect her eyes. The dogs stiffened and growled. They quieted down as Catherine stroked them and said, "Relax, you two. He's on our side."

She heard the familiar voice of Deputy Jerrigan. "What do you mean on our side?"

Catherine told him of the prowler who fled. "The dogs evidently bit him a couple of times, but I don't know where or how bad. I think whoever it was will have torn pants or a torn jacket, and maybe a sore leg. You just missed him" She pointed in the direction where the sound had fled. "It sounded like he left going west on the highway."

The two walked to the far corral. The flashlight beam centered on the gate caused a chuckle to rise. "It looks like you interrupted someone who wanted to open the gate. His flashlight spotlighted the dowel. Notice the wooden dowel has been pulled part way out. The dowel is usually wedged pretty tight into the drilled hole He was probably fumbling around in the dark trying to figure out the dowel's importance. Unless it was completely pulled out, the bar wouldn't move."

Catherine watched the deputy grab the dowel, pull it out of its hole and move the wooden bar. He bounced it hard a few times and looked at her. "Does that sound like what you heard?"

She smiled at the recognition. "Yes it does."

"You said you heard someone tinkering with the gate. How did you know it wasn't me? I was here earlier."

"At first I thought you were on your regular patrol. I looked out and saw nothing. Back inside the wagon the thought struck me. You used your flashlight. Whoever was there this time didn't use a flashlight. Why? That's when the dogs and I came running out of the wagon and the dogs chased him away." She puckered her lips in thought. "It's too bad the dogs couldn't have treed him."

They both laughed.

Catherine said, "Whoever it was called Gilrakis by name."

"Got any ideas?"

"Yes, but it's just an idea, no proof." She gave the Deputy Art Wheeler's name.

21
Fireworks

Sarah had looked forward to this day. The sheep would be moved from civilization onto the open range for the summer. It was also another day of discovery for her daughter; the beginning of a long summer with huge responsibility. Sarah didn't feel any excitement. Her head throbbed and her mouth felt like someone had left stale coffee in it. The pounding on the door sounded like artillery. She pulled a pillow over her head and moaned, "Go away."

The pounding persisted. Sarah rolled over and moaned when the rising sunlight stabbed her eyes. Sleep became an impossible commodity. "All right! All right! Keep your shirt on. I'm coming." As an afterthought she asked, "Who is it?"

"It's Pete, Sarah. Mind if I come in?"

Sarah pulled the blankets up around her neck and croaked, "No, come on in Pete."

The door opened and Pete tentatively entered. He took one look at Sarah, suppressed a grin and asked, "Holy Mother of Mary, what did you do after we left last night?"

"Nothing!" She snapped, "And you didn't come here to ask me that. What is it?"

"Everyone's at breakfast but you and Catherine, so I came looking."

That got Sarah's attention. She looked questioningly at Pete. "Is Hank in his room?"

Pete clucked at her like an old mother hen. "Don't even think like that, Sarah. If I know Catherine, I bet she already checked the sheep and the dogs this morning." He diplomatically added. "Maybe you just need a little time to get ready for the day. I'll have black coffee and breakfast tray sent up." Tongue in cheek he dryly asked, "We can expect you in the lobby by eight, can't we?" He fled before Sarah gave him a very inappropriate answer.

After an invigorating, cobweb-clearing shower, Sarah further braced herself with vigorous toweling. Next she forced herself to look at the breakfast tray. It held little appeal, but she sipped the coffee and toyed with breakfast. It took most of her will power to rise and dress. Her uniform of the day was her usual faded blue jeans, a plaid western shirt, and shined boots.

She sighed when she looked in the mirror. There was a surprising malaise in those blue eyes. She tersely told the image, "Get with it, Sarah. You're a lucky woman." She left the hotel room wondering if Glenn Simons would have a successful meeting today. At precisely 7:55 Sarah entered the hotel dining room.

When she encountered the slightly amused faces she knew what had to be done. She cheerfully told them, "Good morning, everyone. I'm sorry to be late for breakfast, but Pete has already taken care of that for me." She confessed to her friends. "Last night was a wonderful night. Unfortunately, I forgot that champagne has a way of sneaking up on you." She playfully quipped, "My head is paying the price for my forgetfulness." She acknowledged their friendly smiles and low laughs, but went on. "Today is our usual, unusual start to this annual trek. We take the sheep from the corrals, through the main streets of Prentiss and the bridge over the Yakima River to the open range." She shook her head to clear the usual, unusual sound and smiled, "Whew, the cobwebs aren't completely gone. I'm glad I'm not riding all day."

She sat down, sipped her coffee and listened while Pete went over the day's plans.

❦

Deputy Jerrigan had picked up Hank at the hotel at 6:30 a.m. The deputy delivered the first surprise on the way to the corrals. "Someone messed with the gate on the lower corral last night. Catherine said it was someone who called Gilrakis by name. No sheep got out, but someone tried. Do you have any idea who would do that?"

Hank thought this was a sneak's way of causing trouble. One person fit that mold. Hank told the deputy, "Maybe." He gave the same name to the deputy as Catherine had.

His second surprise came when the deputy delivered him to the corrals. Catherine stood outside the wagon with the dogs. He chuckled. It was obvious she had slept in her crumpled clothes. Her hair was uncombed, but she still looked good. He didn't hesitate. He slowly went in on his crutches, took her in his arms and soundly kissed her. His eyes sparkled at her delightful and eager acceptance. How she did it, he didn't know, but his spirits always soared at moments like this.

She carefully stepped away and looked at the crutches. "You're getting pretty good on those things. A girl doesn't stand a chance of getting away; that is, if she wants to."

Deputy Jerrigan smiled. He didn't see enough happiness in his job.

Hank's arm rested about her shoulders and asked, "Will you two please explain what happened here last night?" He listened attentively while they told him their part in thwarting the early morning attempt to open the corral gate. There wasn't a logical explanation except someone wanted the sheep out and scattered about.

Hank thanked Deputy Jerrigan for the ride, and casually turned to Catherine. "Breakfast is waiting us at the hotel." He teased Catherine, "You can ride back to the hotel in the comfort of the deputy's car or with me and the Shepherd's wagon. There's still enough time to get cleaned up and ready for the day." He tilted her chin upward and kissed the willing Catherine. He playfully teased. "From the looks of those clothes, I'd say you need it."

❧

She sat beside him on the driver's bench with one arm hooked inside of his. Behind the veteran Lightening Striker and Thunder's easy clip-clop, clip-clop his thoughts wandered to the cast on his leg. This was his drive before Mr. Gray unceremoniously dumped him. The stories of past journeys, the romance of the summer and the time to study for his veterinarian courses made him eager to be where Catherine was. It worried him some when Pete had told him Catherine was becoming a good shepherdess. All was forgotten when he pulled back on the reins and stopped the wagon behind Overton's Mercantile. He tied the horses securely behind the store before he and Catherine left for breakfast. His second job was to assist Pete with any last-minute organization.

After breakfast his third job was to make sure the ordered supplies from Overton's and Keene's Hardware Store were loaded in Catherine's wagon. Then he would stay at the stores and help channel the sheep away from both stores.

His last job was to drive the loaded wagon out of town and over the bridge behind the sheep. When the wagon, horses, every sheep, and every dog were at the edge of the open range, it was time to leave Catherine as if she were a medieval knight ready to start on her noble quest. He looked down at the cast on his broken leg and sighed. The quest was his originally. He looked forward to returning to his role as shepherd.

୧୬

At 8:30 a.m. Catherine yelled, "Open the gate, Pete." The corral gate slowly opened wide. The sheep eyed it curiously. Some inched closer to investigate. Gilrakis and Malovich barked and channeled the sheep toward the gate. Rusty, Virgil and their dogs patrolled the back of the corral, pushing the sheep until they crowded forward. A fine dust cloud rose above the milling animals. Finally Daisy, Dolly, Ulla and their lambs responded to Catherine's familiar voice as she walked among them. They stepped to the invisible line, smelled it, hesitated and made a little hop across. Then the corral emptied and the sheep followed her up Western Road. When the second corral gate opened Rusty and his dogs led the way. When the last corral emptied in a similar fashion for Virgil all three bands were on their way down Western Road.

୧୬

Nothing had worked last night. By the time Art figured out how the dowel kept the wooden bar from moving in the gate, it was too late. He had failed again. He seemed destined to fail in his attempts to make Catherine look inept and a failure. All he wanted was simple revenge for the bucket of water in his face. His new plan couldn't fail. Catherine would look like the failure when her sheep panicked.

He leaned against the fender of his old, black pickup and watched from the eastern end of Western Avenue. As soon as he spotted Catherine and the sheep coming toward the city's lone stoplight he started the multi-dented pickup and drove to his parking place at the old livery stable. He pulled the two large gunny sacks from the pickup bed, hoisted them over his shoulder and limped toward his hidden perch at the edge of town. The sheep would turn left off Western at the stop light and head north on Main Street. He would be waiting. His hollow giggle held no mirth.

He planned to panic the sheep. Catherine would be unable to control them. They would scatter; maybe some sheep would be lost in the Yakima River. Finally he could get some revenge. She would feel shame. Art laughed softly at the prospect.

⁓

The stores, hotels and cafes of Prentiss welcomed the annual sheep and cattle drives. They filled their streets several times a year. Cattle and sheep ranchers spent money while waiting to put their livestock on the train or driving them through town north to the open rangeland. Experience had taught the town how to handle the drives. The town stood ready to keep the sheep funneled in the streets. The streets were devoid of parked cars. Each business guarded their store front. The street intersections were cordoned off by portable wooden fences, deputies and volunteers. The sheep followed the only direction left open.

Approximately 4,500 sheep moved easily on Western Avenue. Catherine and Sarah turned left at Main and looked behind them. Sure enough the leaders were right there. The dogs were merciless as they barked at any sheep that offered to stray onto the downtown's new cement sidewalks or the older wooden ones. The corner stoplight meant they were halfway through Prentiss.

The Sherwood Hotel stood on this corner. Every available window of the three story building was filled with viewers and well wishers. Sarah had seen this phenomenon before. She had witnessed cattle drives and she had been a part of the sheep drives through downtown Prentiss, but she had never led them. The parade of animals was a festive event to witness. She smiled at the spectacle. A little bit of the Old West lingered in everybody.

At the present time, Sarah was also concerned with the sheep making the turn, but she had been forewarned. On her way to the dining room this morning Glenn Simons met her in the hallway. She suspected he had waited to make sure this meeting took place. His tone was caring and concerned, but somehow solicitous. "Good morning, Queen Sarah. How do you feel this morning?"

She had snapped, "I feel fine. Evidently, I'm not as dumb as you seem to think."

His dark brown eyes expressed his surprise. His face went from smug to concerned, "What on earth does that mean?"

"It means you were the one who came to the curtain divider last night to listen. Why would you want to listen to a bunch of sheepherders having dinner?"

"Yes, it was me, but it wasn't them that interested me. It was you I wanted to thank you for getting me a second chance, and why you are known as 'Queen Sarah'?"

"That's not important." She had tersely replied, "My daughter tells me you helped get me up to my room last night. I apologize for that. That should have never happened. I'm thoroughly embarrassed that it did. For helping me, I thank you." In self-defense, she tossed out, "Don't be late for your meeting this morning. Sig won't be so forgiving the second time." With a turn of her regal buzzing head, she had dismissed him, and started walking toward the dining room, the breakfast meeting and her staff.

Glenn Simons didn't back down. "I won't be, but first I'll see you in the big parade."

෴

Sarah and Catherine led the flock through the left hand turn from Western onto Main Street. Sarah looked behind her. The sheep were strung out behind and moving at a decent pace. Her low, musical laugh signaled satisfaction with the whole morning.

Catherine seemed to be taking to her assignment like a duck to water.

Almost absent-mindedly Sarah violated her own determined resolution made in the hotel hallway. She looked up. Sure enough, Glenn was waving at her like an enthused high school kid. Worse yet, she waved back and a spontaneous smile slipped from her stern facade.

Sarah heard his shout. "You look great on horseback. How's it going?"

"It's going great. Thank you!" She waved one more time and he returned it.

She quickly turned away.

Catherine impishly teased, "What's the matter, mother? A man waves to you and you turn red. It must be the excitement of the drive through town. Then you wave and smile back and pretend it didn't happen. Hasn't anyone ever waved and yelled at you before?" She observed, "It looks to me like a whole bunch of giddiness going around. Anything you want to tell me?"

This was a complete role reversal to Catherine. She enjoyed it immensely when her mother said, "Shut up, Catherine."

⁓

Overton's Mercantile stood on the right side in the middle of the block next to the Keene Hardware Store. Hank waited at the front of the store to help protect the store and to watch the Sumertun women and their sheep come around the corner. Both Sarah and Catherine spotted Hank, who waved enthusiastically. Catherine waved back and turned to her mother. "See, mother, everyone waves during these parades." Hank waved again. With the sheep funneled north toward the open range he disappeared inside to pick up his supplies.

The old abandoned livery stable marked the northern edge of town. From there Catherine could see the bridge over the Yakima River. Main Street faded into a county road, which served the few irrigated farms north of the river. Once past the old livery stable the collage of riders and barking dogs would coax, soothe, and push the three bands of sheep over the bridge and onto the open range. Rehearsal time for the Shepherdess would be over.

When the truck and trailer carried the riders and their horses back to the ranch she would be completely alone. Being alone probably wouldn't sink in until much later. A deep, remorseful sigh escaped; so deep it caused her mother to ask. "What is it, Catherine?"

"Nothing, Mother. I was just thinking about tonight and being truly alone. It's a little scary, isn't it?"

"Yes it is." She reached out and wrapped an affectionate arm around her daughter. "It's scary, but you can do it, Catherine. I have no doubt of that."

"Thanks for your vote of confidence, mother. I was suffering a few moments of doubt and maybe a little self-pity."

Two weeks in the saddle and the outdoors had already bronzed her skin. Her mother observed the difference, "You already look more like a Nordic goddess than a school girl who was pulled from college in the dead of winter to take care of me." She nodded toward the moving flock and the bridge that loomed ahead.

Catherine yelled at Gilrakis, "Come-bye. Let's move 'em." Gilrakis moved to the left side of the flock. Malovich responded to the command, "Away" and moved to the right side with Sarah. The sheep were moving slowly toward the bridge. Catherine breathed a sigh of pleasant anticipation. Another half-hour and they would be over the bridge with no obstacles between them and the open range.

છ૰

From the cupola atop the livery stable Art watched the last sheep pass by. He had unpacked the large burlap sacks, which contained his goodies. He chortled at what lay ahead. His toys were all lined up and ready to do their job. He could hardly wait.

The truck pulling the large horse trailer inched past his lofty perch inside the copula. He looked down on everything. Now was the time. He gloated. Those stupid sheep would scatter in every direction. He knew water and wool coats don't mix, but he had hoped a few would run into the river and drown. He would teach the Sumertun's not to treat him as a   nobody.

∽

The fire arched down from the sky. It was a brilliant, intense burning ball of yellow. It headed right for the sheep, bounced off the road and exploded in a loud frightening blast. A second ball of orange followed and then blazing flying rockets filled the air. The panicked sheep bolted in every direction. Catherine easily controlled Jiggles, but she sat mesmerized by the sudden onslaught of rockets and noise.

Malovich and Gilrakis didn't need commands. Instinct told them safety lay in keeping the sheep together. The dogs immediately started to "Cast" the terrified ewes, lambs and rams. One rocket exploded close by the placid Jiggles. She spotted her mother still working the right side of the flock. Catherine screamed, "Where are the rockets coming from?"

No answer. Catherine kicked Jiggles in the flank and headed toward the river. She didn't need to start the drive with drowned sheep and lambs. Pete's yell stopped her. "Don't worry about the river Catherine. Those sheep are more scared of moving water than anything." She suddenly remembered her Sheep List. *The shepherdess is the only cure for panic in the sheepfold. When the shepherdess senses fear she quietly moves among them reassuring them of her presence.*

How could she do that? She was close to panic herself. A few more rockets shot toward the flock. Catherine laughed at her own stupidity. They weren't rockets. She had seen firework displays before. The delayed fuse for the explosive powder was ignited by lighted Roman Candles. She reined Jiggles into the panicked sheep and rode among them, constantly talking. A funny thing happened. A true sense of calm possessed her.

One more fact from her memorized "sheep list" jumped forward. *Sheep are frightened of swiftly moving streams. They cannot swim and are easily carried downstream. Their wool absorbs water and they become heavy. Sheep and rapid water do not mix.* Catherine doubled her efforts to calm the sheep. The dogs had done their part. They had "casted" the sheep into one large group. They were still uneasy and frightened, but a sense of normalcy was returning. She was secretly amused and pleased at the calming affect of her voice.

Pete and her mother rode quietly toward Catherine. Pete's loud voice announced, "The sheep are settling down, Catherine. They aren't quite as wild as banshees anymore. Keep up the good work." He had seen Catherine coaxing and soothing the flock. It was a sight he had often fretted about. Now he knew. She would tend to her flock, no matter what.

He complimented her. "Everyone has been busy as flies around buttermilk, but I notice you did what good shepherds, excuse me, what good shepherdesses do." Mother and daughter smiled at this correction. That was his reward. "You calmed your charges. Good work." That was Catherine's reward.

Compliments from Pete were rare. Her ego swelled beyond its normal size.

Her mother heaped one more compliment on her. "I guess you could say, you passed your first critical test with flying colors."

"Oh, mother," but she smiled at her pun.

She saw her astonished mother's eyes widen. Containing the sheep during the array of brilliant, flashing colors and the devastating noisy explosions had left no time for anything else. Catherine gasped when she swung around in her saddle and looked in the direction of her mother's gaze. They looked at rapidly expanding flames licking at the old, dry, wooden walls through ever enlarging holes. In another few minutes the fire would completely engulf the old livery stable. The few people who stayed with the drive after leaving Prentiss retreated as far as possible from the blistering heat.

Catherine leveled her gaze at her mother. With a raised eyebrow she answered. "I think you're right. Those Roman Candles must have been shot from the old livery stable. It looks like one of them started its own fireworks."

She and her mother turned as one toward town to listen. Catherine confirmed her mother's opinion. "You're right again, Mother. The fire engine is already on its way."

Despite all the excitement Catherine's main job never changed. The sheep had to get back on the county road and over the bridge. She yelled with confidence and authority at the men and dogs, "Let's get these sheep over the bridge."

Sarah and Pete exchanged glances. Their temporary choice for the trek looked good.

෧

The twenty-fourth Roman candle missed the open window, hit the wall and fell into the remnants of straw and dried manure, and aged, dried wood. Art Wheeler stood hypnotized. This couldn't be happening. The Roman candle ignited the explosive he had attached to each candle. It thrust the burning candle mixture at him. Panic grabbed his soul. The explosive flash-burn seared his flesh. Instinctively he jumped away. He clamped his lips tight to mute his scream. He half dropped, half scrambled down the ladder and sidled like a spider to an open door.

The fireworks worked to his advantage. He furtively crawled out of the barn amidst all the confusion and dropped into the nearby irrigation ditch. Thankfully it was not carrying water, but he cursed the remaining mud.

The cursing stopped when he realized the damp mud relieved some of the pain. He grabbed a short, gnarled branch from the ditch bank and used it to help him crawl through the mud and a few shallow puddles of water until the ditch ended at the town's irrigation head gates. He was two blocks away from the fire before he peeked out from the protection of the grassy ditch bank.

He clamped his teeth together and ignored the pain. Hard luck continued to plague and frustrate him. Last night it was the dogs and today it was the fireworks. Didn't anything ever go as planned? He knew he had been very lucky to escape the raging fire.

The few spectators who were gabbing and gawking at the unexpected fireworks retreated from the heat when the barn became engulfed in flames. No one noticed the wretched, mud-covered figure that crawled from the ditch. With the aid of his improvised cane he limped painfully into the alley. His pickup was still two blocks away.

⁀

Hank and two clerks had watched Catherine on Jiggles lead the trailing sheep around the corner and past the front of Overton's Mercantile. It was easy to see the pride Catherine must be feeling. She wasn't the "Queen of the Sumertun Ranch" but she was rapidly becoming very important. A gray cloud of doubt entered his thoughts. The plan had been for him to replace Catherine on the summer trek. What if mother left daughter in charge? That thought disturbed him.

The two clerks were bent on keeping any uneasy sheep like Blackie from straying into the store. Hank's stomach felt pinched when Catherine flashed a beaming smile at him. The moment of doubt was washed away. He solemnly watched the bunched up sheep follow their shepherdess around the turn onto north Main Street toward the river bridge. He sighed and crutched his way back into the store to supervise the chore of getting the supplies into the wagon. He looked forward to his first supply trip.

Overton's had supplied the Sumertun needs for many years. In three weeks he would load up here again, and then deliver new supplies to all three bands of sheep foraging on the open, isolated rangeland. He laughed. Who was he kidding? Catherine was foremost in his musings. Maybe the broken leg was a blessing. He would see her more than if he was tending the sheep. Hank shook his head at the ironies of life. His loading chore was almost finished when he heard the explosions and the outcries.

Hank looked north toward the bridge and scanned the sky for the source of the whooshy sound he heard. Above the sparse tree line a randomly spaced series of bright red, green, orange and yellow fireballs arced through the air toward the bridge area. He heard the explosions that followed. Those fireballs and explosions would cause sheep to scatter everywhere. Worse yet, Catherine would be right in the middle of whatever happened. How would she respond?

The nervous nickering of Lightning and Thunder drew his attention. Their ears picked up every nuance of the fireworks. Hank put his arms around their necks and talked to each horse. He scratched their ears and stroked their heads. They relaxed. Hank wondered who got the most benefit from this, them or him.

The light colored, yellow-orange flames steadily grew larger. Clouds of smoke billowed high above the trees. Hank knew it had to be the old livery stable. That old barn would burn like kindling and grow hotter and hotter. He heard the city's fire truck speed by on Main Street. This confirmed the location. It also dramatically increased his nervousness. Catherine might be in real danger and there was nothing he could do. The ache and the size of the knots in his stomach hurt.

He yelled as loud as possible to anyone inside the store. He waited impatiently for someone to come out. Emery, who helped him fill the supply order, looked out the door.

"I'm going to the fire. Catherine's down there somewhere." He started to move. He disgustingly looked at the crutches and snarled at the startled clerk, "Hell, I can't even run." He leaned against the back of the wagon and looked helplessly north toward the fire.

If he had ears like his horses they would be standing straight up and alert. A smallish limping man with a make-shift cane slipped into the alley a block and a half away. Furtively the rumpled figure came toward him. He ducked into every doorway and peeked out before flitting into the next hiding niche. He hesitated several minutes where the alley emptied onto First Avenue. He waited in the shadows and fidgeted like a scared rabbit that didn't want to be exposed in an open, sunlit area where a predator might prevail. Hank knew the exact moment the familiar figure decided to scud painfully across the street.

Sympathy flew out the window. He couldn't believe his eyes when the scared rabbit crossed the street and limped up the alley toward him. Mud covered most of his clothing. His pant leg was torn. The image of a dog tear on his pants came to Hank's mind. He came from the direction of the old livery stable. What did that mean? Hank ducked back behind the Shepherd's wagon and hissed at Emery, "Call the police. I think the man who started the fire is coming toward us." Emery stood motionless. Hank mouthed the words, "Do it now!" The startled man quickly ducked inside.

Hank stole another quick peek from behind the wagon. The fugitive was nowhere to be seen. Panic pressed heavy against Hank's chest.

He looked again and sighed. The mud covered figure had stepped out of the recessed doorway of the Stillman's Clothing Store. His muddy shirt sported a large burn spot on the right upper chest. His pants were torn and muddy. Hank quickly appreciated this irony. A new wardrobe from Stillman's would certainly help. Anguish crossed every feature of his face. He could almost feel sympathy for the weasel, almost.

He waited. The man was in a hurry. Hank would bet his last dollar he knew why Art Wheeler was fleeing, and from what.

The foot scrapings and the dull clop of the gnarled end of the branch became louder. Hank waited and waited until Art Wheeler was even with his wagon. Then he stepped abruptly out from behind the wagon. He stood face to face with the harried man. He had the satisfaction of hearing a sharp intake of breath. A surprised, anxious question of disbelief followed. "Hank, what are you doing here?"

Hank wanted to pound a fist into that face. He reluctantly accepted that this was not the time to fight. This was a time for using smarts. He took a deep breath, relaxed and asked, "My God, Art, what happened? You look awful." His voice was reassuring. "Why don't you sit down on the wagon tongue and I'll get something for that leg. It's been bleeding. It looks like you tore it open running. Why would you run that hard, Art?"

"That's none of your damn business. Leave me alone and just get out of my way."

"What kind of a friend would I be if I didn't want to help?" Hank solicitously added, "Wow, I just noticed that burn on your chest. You do need some help."

Art stepped away and pleaded. "Hank, just leave me alone."

"I can't do that Art." He pointed toward the fire. "That old livery stable is on fire. Know anything about that?"

"Why in the hell would I know anything about that?"

"Did you cause that fire, Art? Did you want to scare the sheep when you set off those fireworks?" Hank voice grew tense and angrier. "You know Catherine's out there, don't you?" He watched Art's frightened face grow paler. "You know I can't let you leave until we know what happened, so use your head and sit down."

Art's shaky voice belied his bold curse, "Go to hell, Hank. Yes, I and everybody else know you're playing around with the bosses' daughter. Why wouldn't you? That's a rather nice hunk of woman you have for yourself. Huh?"

A glint appeared along with a slight, crooked smile. "What does Alyssa think of this? Does she know? I could keep quiet if you let me go."

"Alyssa is no longer involved, so don't try blackmailing me. I shouldn't have ever shown you her picture, but that has nothing to do with you and the fire. Now, tell me about the old livery stable fire and the Roman Candles before the police get here."

"I'm leaving and you can't stop me. I can outrun a man on crutches."

"You probably can, but you had better make it good."

Art's cheek jerked. His mouth twitched. Just like his crossing the street to get into this alley, Hank sensed the exact moment Art made his decision.

He took three painful running steps. Hank waited.

Art didn't believe the relief he felt. Hank was going to let him go. *What a dumb clod.*

Art was even with him and grinning lasciviously. I'll lay low when I get away, but those sheep will be in the open range four months. That gives me plenty of time.

On Art's fourth step Hank jammed his crutch between Art's legs. He saw the hard fall and Art lying crumpled on the ground. He heard the satisfying yelp of pain, and witnessed the despair in Art's eyes. He pinned the desolate figure to the alley's surface with his crutch and told him, "Now stay there until the police come. If you don't I'll enjoy clubbing you with my crutch." Hank's eyes turned into narrow slits.

Art Wheeler cringed at the hard, quick anger shining from those eyes.

Hank vehemently asked, "Got it?"

Art nodded and sank back to the ground. He quickly rolled over and tried to rise, but Hank rammed the end of the crutch into his shoulders and commanded him to stay there.

Art surrendered and his captor relaxed a little.

Hank's weight rested on one crutch, while the other kept Art pinned. Art rolled to one side and swung the gnarled end of the cane at the same time. It struck the bottom of the crutch and knocked it out from under Hank. He went down. Before the stunned Hank could grab him, Art hit Hank on the shin of his good leg.

Hank yowled at the instant pain!

"You can't catch me." His voice dripped sarcasm. "You won't be a hero again." Hank watched helplessly as Art limbed away and disappeared from the alley. He heard a motor start, the crunch of tires on the pavement and the blatant horn honk. Art Wheeler had escaped again.

22
Open Range

From the back steps of her Shepherdess wagon Catherine watched the pickup and the truck with the large horse trailer leave. The taillights grew smaller and smaller, until they disappeared in the twilight. The riders should be home by nightfall. Catherine went inside to check the kettle sitting on the Coleman Camp stove. It was boiling and ready to brew her a cup of tea. Later she sat on the wooden ledge in the wagon and punched her bedroll to make it fluffy.

She looked northeast to the distant Wahluke Slope. The open range lay there in front of her. The rising foothills seemed close. Their color changed from the silver and green of the nearby open range to a blue-green color that faded into a light purple of a far distance. It would be a month before the slow moving sheep would munch their way to the top of the slope and turn into the Crab Creek Coulee. She fondly stroked Malovich's head. She wrote in her logbook. "I feel contentment with the silence of the open range."

Catherine awoke the next morning to the same engulfing quiet. She had to listen hard to hear the quiet bleating of grazing sheep, the raspy squawking of a few magpies and the melodic call of the meadow lark. She rolled out of bed, stood and stretched. A vague memory of the dogs leaving her side earlier came to her. She filled the tea kettle from a half-full water bag that hung inside and lit the camp stove. She poured some of the cold water into a metal wash basin, cupped her hands to scoop some water out and splashed it on her face several times. After she vigorously dried with a soft towel she was awake and ready to face the day.

She spied the single typed sheet of lamb facts and shepherdess philosophy and smiled. She had hung it where it would command her attention. Her biology classes and the word, "osmosis" ran through her mind. *The welfare of the sheep depends solely upon the care they get from the shepherdess.* She was gradually absorbing that list by osmosis.

With a cup of hot tea in hand she moved to her first solo morning assessment of the flock's whereabouts. She reached down into the box marked, Keene Hardware Store, and picked up the binoculars that would be a near-constant companion for the next five months. The box reminded her of the next job. The contents of every box had to be sorted out and stored. The necessity of this was driven home again when she stumbled and almost fell trying to step over the third box. Darn it! Hank loaded the wagon, but he didn't put anything away.

She laughed, but forgave him. After all he had identified Art Wheeler for the police.

Yesterday! Was it only yesterday that the sheep had left the corrals in Prentiss?

Enough had happened to last Catherine for a long time. Getting the sheep from the corrals and through town had seemed like the biggest problem, but it turned out to be the least of her worries. Never had fireworks and a burning barn been a problem to the annual Montana drive, but of course, Art Wheeler hadn't been around until this year. That man carried a bagful of unanswered questions.

She smiled at the thought. Hank probably got a great deal of pleasure in capturing Art, and then suffered a great deal of anguish when he escaped. How ironic! Art's stray bullet that hit Mr. Gray had put Hank on the crutches and now, Hank had identified him as the man who probably fired the rockets and caused the fire. That fit Catherine's definition of poetic justice. It was a real shame the little rat got away.

Catherine stepped to the front of the wagon and climbed on top of the bench seat to get a good view of the range around her. She scanned the flock with her binoculars. The sheep were scattered over a large area. Was the grouping too large, or was there no need to worry? This problem would have to be answered every single day on the trail. Pete knew sheep. She would heed his observation, "Herd the sheep with a loose hand. Nervous sheep are hard to handle." With this thought she went inside to find breakfast somewhere among the boxes.

At 11:00 she returned to the wagon to take on the tedious task of arranging and storing her supplies. She had quickly tired of stepping over and around the boxes on the floor. She surveyed the cluttered floor of the wagon again and confirmed what she already knew. Everything in the wagon must have its own place. Clutter meant trouble. She looked in her notebook for any notations from previous treks that would give her a place to start.

The portable camp stove and her bedroll took up most of the one ledge. The one common usable space on both sides was under the ledge. Four 2'x18"x 2' pull out drawers sat side by side under each ledge. She pulled them out and checked her list of food supplies and gave serious thought to what would go where. The list wouldn't please the epicures of the world.

The staples, flour, sugar and salt, had been put into smaller, usable heavy-duty paper bags for storage in the bins. Catherine wondered how many times Overton's had done this for the Sumertun ranch. She smiled. There were a lot of people looking out for her. It was her first time out, but it wasn't their first time. She cheerfully pushed the first drawer under the ledge. Sorting wasn't the tedious drudge she thought it would be. It became a celebration of knowing she wasn't alone. It didn't take long to sort the dry goods into drawers.

She placed the tea in one empty coffee canister. Some thoughtful soul had screwed three large coffee cans to the wooden ledge to hold kitchen utensils. Nothing would jiggle loose when the wagon moved.

The task she had dreaded became a time of discovery. The potatoes, beans, carrots, onions, rice and oatmeal took two drawers. The consumables, canned, condensed milk, carefully wrapped cured ham, a slab of bacon and the precious cloth-wrapped eggs, laid on top of these rated a drawer. She resisted the urge to open a bag of dried apricots, peaches and raisins her mother had included and the tempting beef jerky Pete sent.

She had discovered these treasures when she pulled out one of the large drawers. They also contained a new Kodak Brownie camera and several rolls of film. The simple message read, "Enjoy. We're thinking of you." It was signed, "Your Mother and Pete." These were presents she would use.

At noon Catherine scanned the wagon's interior. Everything except the box from Keene Hardware had been emptied, sorted out and stored. Only the small drawer in front of the wagon had been ignored. She knew it contained miscellaneous stuff like pot holders, string, and probably much more. She would tend to it later. Would summer bring, more mess or more organization? She didn't know, but right now that was not very important.

Her four clean shirts and two pair of jeans hung from one of the arched wooden ribs, which supported the canvas covering of the wagon. Her personal lingerie was stuffed into the shallower drawers under her bed roll. There was still some room in the bigger storage drawers for fresh vegetables in season. By then she would probably kill for fresh produce.

After a ham sandwich washed down with some cool water she stretched and embarked on a ritual she repeated when she was undecided. She stood on top the driver's seat and scanned the area with her binoculars. All seemed quiet. Catherine had never thought about it before. It seemed when the sheep were content they didn't move. Nowhere did she see any unusual meandering. Some sheep were grazing. Some were lying down. It was an idyllic scene from a master painting, only on a much larger scale.

She got the message. On the cloudless, cool April afternoon the tensions of being the shepherdess from the Sumertun ranch, through Prentiss, through the rockets and the burning livery stable and over the bridge took their toll. Catherine laid on her bedroll, relaxed and took a short nap.

She awoke to cold pressure against her bare arm. Still groggy she pushed herself up on her elbows. She shook her head to clear the cobwebs, but the cold against her arm persisted. An eager bark followed. Malovich pushed his head under her hand demanding attention. Catherine sighed. "What is it Malovich?" She absent mindedly stroked the white, brownish- orange spotted head while she yawned. One look at the clock setting by the camp stove roused her from her drowsiness. She couldn't believe she slept two hours.

Catherine used some of her precious water to wash before she climbed to her command post on the driver's seat. She looked down at the adoring Malovich. "Did you wake me up to tell me something is wrong or because you felt neglected?" This evoked a low whine as Malovich cocked his head to one side. She reached down and cradled his head with both hands. "Are you trying to understand?" One paw reached up and rested on her hand.

Catherine straightened up and scanned the area. There was nothing unusual out there. She laughed at the attentive sheep dog. "Looks like you just wanted some company. Come on, let's take a little tour." Gilrakis eagerly joined them. They spent the next two hours riding and walking among the band of sheep. She talked to them, observed them and stopped to scratch the heads of few ewes that had come to recognize and trust her.

Her first full day alone as the shepherdess came to an end as she enjoyed the smells from the cast iron Dutch oven. Before her afternoon patrol she had combined water, carrots, onions, potatoes and the only fresh meat Overton's had sent into a delicious stew. Not every day would be as pleasant as this one, but the trek was off to a good start.

23
North to the Vernita Ferry

The next day started with a different scanning of the vista. She looked back at the flock and not from the middle. That darn sheet of paper about sheep was the reason. Over her early morning strong breakfast tea she had read, *"Sheep are creatures of habit. If they are left to themselves they will graze the same ground over and over again, walking over the same trails until the land becomes wasteland and their paths erode into gullies. Ground overgrazed by sheep often becomes polluted with parasites and disease. That is why sheep so desperately need a shepherd. They must be managed.*

Catherine also knew some history about the west. Sheep could overgraze and destroy the grass. Their front incisor teeth enabled them to cut the grass below the tender light colored growth region of the stem. This killed the plant. Heavy foraging ruined the range.

Cattle could not nibble down as far. The plants survived their grazing. The range land remained intact after heavy usage.

In every western state sheep and cattle wars had been fought over this very issue.

Pete had emphatically told her to not let the sheep stay in one place too long. His exact words were, "Use your judgement about the time, but in general keep the sheep moving. A pleasant campsite is a temptation to stay too long. The three bands of Sumertun sheep will be moving north in three distinct lanes. There will be little overlapping of feeding areas, but movement will keep the range protected."

Catherine's charges were in the eastern-most lane. The sheep would have to average 2 to 3 miles a day to get to Montana by September. The spring grass was plentiful, vigorous and growing. Progress here would be slower.

Catherine had followed Pete's instructions and moved her wagon ahead of the flock. She carefully followed some of the older wagon trails and kept the Yakima River, which meant fresh water, in view. She shied away from rocky, rough terrain of the lower Rattlesnake Hills until she found a small, suitable grassy lea. A small feeder stream flowed from the foothills through the grassy meadow toward the river. The small line of poplar trees and two willow trees huddled along the stream made it the perfect campsite.

She could ride back to the flock, then stay in the middle and finally let the sheep pass her by as they moved parallel to the river. She would head north when the Columbia turned south at Horn Rapids. When Catherine checked her map she noticed a sparsely used county road connected Prentiss with State Highway 240.

Catherine did her early morning chores. The horses drank their fill at the little stream before they were staked out in good grass. She fed the dogs before she cooked her own breakfast of bacon and two eggs. After breakfast Catherine saddled Jiggles and rode back to the sheep to spend the morning. Two happy dogs trotted alongside Jiggles. At the first "Cast" command of the day, they were off and running. Soon the loosely organized band moved and grazed contently. Blackie was an exception to the rule.

Catherine spied the rebel lamb at the far western reaches of the flock. She shook her head. That little sucker is always out there alone. She pointed and sent Malovich after Blackie with the command "Find." Gilrakis wasn't about to be left out of this chase. It was always fascinating to watch the two dogs work. Her fascination stopped abruptly. Through her binoculars she glimpsed the tawny coat loping through the sagebrush. "Coyote!"

Automatically she reached down. She touched the empty scabbard. She felt the quick fear of failure; failure that was rooted in a petty distaste for guns. She didn't want a loss from a coyote stalking Blackie after only four days on the trail. She was thankful the two dogs running toward Blackie had stopped the coyote. Her responsibility for the sheep was driven home. She would not leave camp again without the rifle in its scabbard. She gritted her teeth. She didn't want to give Pete and her mother a reason to feel they had made a mistake.

෴

Back at the wagon she eyed the box that sat on the floor of the wagon. It contained the order from Keene Hardware Store. She noticed the compass that lay on top. Catherine had general knowledge of the lay of the land on this early part of the drive. The compass was not needed now, but it might be needed later. She examined the small, round instrument, which would have a new home in her saddle bag.

Catherine sighed and looked into the box again knowing what she would find. There was a real need to be disciplined and practical. A common enemy lurked outside. The four boxes of 30-30 ammunition lay on the bottom of the box. That meant some shooting practice. She reluctantly lifted the rifle from its rack near the back door, checked the lever action a couple of times and peered through the sights at an imaginary target. She pushed six shells into the magazine. She checked to make sure the chamber was empty. There was no exhilaration. History told her predators would kill a few sheep along the way. This morning's experience just confirmed the need to protect the sheep. Shooting didn't excite her. She put the rifle back on the rack like she was hanging up muddy clothes.

The telescope fishing rod was another matter. Its three sections could be extended out to six feet. Fishing might be the best way to get fresh meat. Unlike the gun lying benignly on its rack, the fishing rod offered a little fun and excitement. She wound the fishing line onto the reel and slid the reel into its slot on the rod's handle. Anticipation crowded away the smoldering rifle feelings. She needed to attach the hook to the line, add a sinker or two for weight, and dig some worms and she was ready for action. She picked up the small box that lie in the corner and found some spinners. Heck, she might not have to dig worms. She placed the pole on the rifle rack with a little more satisfaction.

Her lunch of reheated stew lived up to expectations, and the hot tea afterward revived her ambition. The dogs finished off the last of the stew mixed with their regular dry dog food. After lunch she and Jiggles were headed south toward the resting band of sheep. She removed the binoculars from her saddle bag and swept the area. She loved what she saw. Blackie stood on the outer edge of the flock, but the dogs thwarted every attempt to stray. They seemed to take great delight in tormenting the errant lamb each time it started to leave the flock.

It was a sight she appreciated. "Good dogs. Keep it up."

She spent the early afternoon riding and walking among her flock, always assuring them that everything was fine and dandy.

Late in the afternoon she sat in the saddle and swept the area. That damn coyote was back snooping around the edges. She pulled the 30-30 from its scabbard, pumped a shell into the chamber and soothed Jiggles with quiet talk. Catherine squinted through the sights, found the shoulders of the coyotes and squeezed the trigger. A puff of dust jumped from the sandy soil two or three feet left of the unsuspecting coyote. It jumped in the air, turned and looked in Catherine's direction. Catherine swore the coyote grinned at her as it nonchalantly loped into the sagebrush cover.

Two thoughts occurred. She needed some target practice and she needed to sight in her rifle. It was ironic. This morning she had second thoughts about using the rifle. Now she had none. She grimly thought, "No coyote is going to get one of my sheep. Not if I can help it!"

She looked forward to a second chance.

24
Surprise

Catherine awakened to the soft sound of bleating sheep. It took a moment to register why they sounded so close. Yesterday she and the dogs had left them behind at the edge of the meadow to graze. The sheep just followed the grass and had casually invaded the long grassy lea with its fresh water. She remembered the sheep paper that hung on the wall.

If they are not led to proper pastures, sheep will obviously eat and drink things that are disastrous to them. Therefore the shepherdess goes before them and prepares a table or mesa for their grazing. The shepherdess must be sure there is an adequate supply of good water.

Did this mean she was a good shepherdess? For the time being there was the inner contentment of a job done well. She laughed at this observation. That could change in a heartbeat, but so far, so good.

The band's northeastern progress had been slow and leisurely. She could stay here two or three more days. The grass was that good. The small stream from the foothills provided fresh water. She thought that it might be big enough to have fish. It ran the year around, so why not? This morning's sweep would be right in front of her. She stretched, rolled out of her bedroll and started another day.

Her morning sojourn had become routine. More of the sheep were addressed by name, and some of them followed her short distances. Some expected to be scratched; others bleated but shied away; some came only so close. A few lambs satisfied their curiosity and come close enough to smell her. Each animal was different. She began to understand why the herders became close to their charges.

Catherine checked her watch; 3:00 p.m. She peeked out of her wagon to quickly check her flock. Dust from the county road caught her attention. The pickup probably used the gravel road as a short cut to State Highway 240. The pickup slowed, left the county road and started picking its way through grass and sagebrush toward the camp. Soon a waving arm appeared and the horn sounded. It was her mother. Catherine wondered why the devil she was here? This was followed by what's wrong?

The passenger stayed hidden in the shadowy side of the pickup. Catherine's heart flip-flopped. Maybe she brought Hank with her. She stepped away from the wagon to greet her visitors. The pickup stopped. Her mother waited until the dust drifted past the pickup before she opened the door and stepped out. The usually sedate, poised Sarah galloped toward her. Catherine's jaw dropped. Her mother never ran or galloped. What on earth could cause this? She braced herself for the collision.

Her mother arm's engulfed her with a monstrous embrace. They stumbled two steps together. Their arms flailed about for balance. They grabbed each other to keep from falling, but neither could keep the other from bouncing onto the soft meadow grass.

Sarah rolled over on her elbows to face her daughter. Her full-throated laugh followed. "Good afternoon, Catherine dear. Quite a surprise, huh?"

Catherine didn't think "surprise" really covered the sight of her disciplined mother running to hug anyone. She cautiously asked, "Mother, what are you doing here?" As an aftermath she added, "And yes, this is quite a surprise. Is everything okay?"

"Everything is fine now." Sarah wiped a tear away. "The fact is your mother just got lonely and nosy. I had to see how you were doing." They stood, brushed the grass off their jeans and shirts before Sarah asked, "How is it going? Are you okay?" She checked the grazing sheep. "From the looks of it, I'd say the answer is yes on both counts"

Catherine didn't intend to wait any longer. "I saw someone in the passenger seat. Did you bring Hank with you?"

She watched her mother motion to the pickup. The passenger door opened and Glenn Simons stepped out to greet Catherine. "Sorry to disappoint you Catherine, but it's only me. I wrangled a ride from your mother to come and see for myself why Sarah was so proud. Now I understand. You look wonderful. The sheep seem to be doing well." He flashed a smile. "That was some ballet you and your mother just did. Is that the customary way you greet each other?" His eyes couldn't hide his mirth.

Catherine knew blarney when she heard it. Still it sounded nice. She laughingly replied, "No, this is not the customary way we greet each other, but you have to admit it got your attention."

The vivid recollection of Glenn Simons carrying her mother upstairs to her room after too much champagne traipsed through her memory. A shadow of doubt crossed her mind. A force like Glenn did not casually drop in on anyone. This was absolutely the wrong time for her mother to do anything romantic. This shouldn't be happening.

Catherine did her best to recover from her disappointment. "Welcome to the humble Sumertun sheep camp, Glenn. It's good to see you again." She flashed her best welcoming smile. With good humor she told Glenn, "You're not what I really wanted, but it's still good to see you. What brings you back to this country?"

Glenn Simons liked Catherine's honesty and forthrightness. She wanted Sarah's passenger to be Hank, was honest enough to say so, and yet considerate enough to say she was glad to see him. He answered her question. "Business."

"Business?"

"Yes, business, just business. I came to Prentiss to sign the contract with the Tri-Cities Grain Growers to build them a new grain elevator. Thanks to Sarah, I had a second chance and they accepted my bid. Construction will start next week. They want it finished before this year's harvest. That's pushing it. They understand so they're offering me a bonus if I finish it in time. I stopped yesterday at the ranch to see Sarah and to thank her for all the help." He smiled and added, "And to see if she recovered from her champagne headache."

His chuckle came from deep in his chest and rolled out as a pleasant rumble. "Catherine, your mother wasn't champagne sick this time. She was daughter sick! I wanted to thank her and to visit. She wanted to see you, so we killed two birds with one stone. It's as simple as that. She picked me up at the hotel this morning." He apologized, "I'm sorry I wasn't Hank, but we did bring some steaks to grill and some ice cold Coca-Cola. Will that help?"

His next move was foreign to him. Did it come from a wish to please? Glenn stepped forward and extended his arms. When Catherine returned with a little hesitant hug of her own, it brought smiles to his sun-weathered face. He looked over Catherine's shoulder and saw Sarah smile and wink at him. What more could he ask for? His day was complete.

He knew Catherine's invitation to ride Jiggles and inspect the meadow and the sheep was a pretext for talking privately to her mother, but he accepted the offer with a smile. Catherine went with him to Jiggles. She inserted the bit into her mouth, checked the cinch to make sure the saddle was tight enough and handed the reins to him with a smile. "Enjoy your ride."

He lifted his left foot into the stirrup, grabbed the saddle horn and swung easily into the saddle. He noted Jiggles' surprised look at the unaccustomed weight. Glenn reached down and patted the horse on her neck "Quite a lot more than the 125 pounds you're used to carrying, huh Jiggles?" The dogs looked at Catherine, then at Jiggles and then at new rider heading for the sheep and obediently followed the horseman.

~

Once Catherine was inside the Shepherdess wagon with her mother she demanded, "Mother! What on earth are you doing?"

Sarah's eyes popped wide open in amazement. "Catherine, I don't like your tone!" She struggled to keep her resentment from showing. "If you're referring to Glenn, then I really don't like your insinuation. I think you owe me an apology." She crossed her arms and looked directly at her daughter and waited.

Slowly a tentative smile graced her face. Catherine opened her hands into a palms-up gesture. Her voice softened. "You're right, mother. That came off badly. I apologize." She coyly asked. "Okay, what are you doing here and why is Glenn with you?

"I told you. Glenn told you. The reason is simple. I've really missed you. I wanted to see for myself how you were faring. It's not my fault if you can't accept that." Sarah softly asked, "Is that really so bad?" Her hope came out as a question. "I thought you would be glad to see me."

Catherine sighed and relented. "No, it's not bad at all. My thoughts just came out all wrong." Both stepped forward. The embrace between the two was comfortable and pleasing.

Sarah told her daughter, "I'm glad that's settled."

Catherine hesitated before prying. "I'm dying to know if there's anything is going on between you and Glenn. He seems pretty interested."

"No, my suspicious daughter, nothing is going on. He stopped to say thanks. I told him that I missed you and he suggested we come today. Alex wanted to come, but he's still has school." She summed it up for Catherine. "Glenn is not one to sit idly by and do nothing. I imagine that's part of the reason for his success." A smile appeared. "Even when he was a real tough guy on the hill complaining about sheep being in his way, you could see little chinks in his armor. Now I'm sure that toughness is just a put on. He really is nice. He makes you feel like you're important."

Catherine watched her mother's mood turn sober. "You had no way of knowing, and you need to know. I stayed overnight in Prentiss after we left you alone with the sheep." She noticed her daughter's quizzical expression. "It had nothing to do with Glenn. The next morning I talked to Morton Waterford."

"Your attorney?"

"Yes, and you can guess why."

Catherine nodded.

"It's now official. I filed for a divorce. In the State of Washington this is serious business. It will take a year before the decree is final."

She knew Catherine was eager to ask questions. Sarah held up her hand. "Please let me finish and then it will be time to get serious with those steaks and call Glenn." She glanced down at her hands twisting around each other and laughed. "I'm pretty nervous about it. Anyway, Morton told me he would file the necessary papers, try to find Corwin, and get things started. I'll see him today when I drop Glenn off at the hotel." She sat up a little straighter and set her jaw a little tighter. "It's started. You should know there is no way I'm going to cause a mess for Glenn or myself by being an idiot. When I tell you nothing is going on, I mean just that." Sarah saucily added, "I must say though, that Glenn Simons could probably get all my juices flowing." Emphatically she made her point. "That's exactly the reason nothing is going on. Satisfied?"

She enjoyed the startled look on her daughter's face. "Come Catherine, let's get ..." Three rifle shots rang out in rapid succession and the three echoes reverberated through the nearby Rattlesnake foothills. "Good heavens. Why would Glenn be shooting?"

Catherine felt no need for alarm. She casually answered. "Maybe some jackrabbits, but it's probably a coyote. There's been one nosing round here the last two days. I hope Glenn got him. I missed him yesterday."

The meal preparations were interrupted by the familiar sound of sheep moving and bleating.

Catherine noted, "It sounds like Jiggles is returning."

Sarah moved eagerly to the front of the wagon to locate the returning horse and rider. She gasped and pushed her hands up to her face. She turned back to Catherine and lost her balance. Her face turned ashen. For the second time in one day Catherine grabbed her to keep her from falling.

"What is it Mother?

"It's Jiggles." She hung onto Catherine.

Catherine quickly made her mother sit, put her head down and breathe deeply.

Sarah slowly regained her composure. "How silly of me to act like that when I saw Jiggles. There has to be a reason"

"Reason for what, mother?"

Sarah took another deep breath. "Jiggles came back to camp without Glenn. I wonder what happened?" Catherine heard panic in her mother's question.

Catherine took two quick steps to the front of the wagon and looked out. Jiggles stood next to the staked out Thunder and Lightning like nothing had happened. Did the three shots cause Jiggles to unload Glenn? That would be easy if Glenn wasn't a good horseman. Was he injured if that was the case? She sighed. She looked back at her mother. Who would have thought her mother would have reacted like she did. The image of calm, steely composure in a time of need had disappeared. Glenn certainly stirred unaccustomed emotions in her mother. An unanswered question surfaced. Could Corwin have caused a reaction like that? That was an absurd idea. She knew he couldn't and didn't.

The practical Catherine thought for a moment. If Glenn was hurt, she would have two problems not one. She knew what to do and sooner she started the better. "Mother, I'm riding out on Jiggles to find Glenn!"

Her mother stood up, poured cold water into the metal wash basin and doused her face. Then she declared, "I'm going with you."

Catherine had seen that face before. There was no arguing. "Okay, you take Jiggles and I'll ride bareback on Thunder. Let's go."

Catherine hopped to the ground. She turned to help her mother. Both her hands clasped her face again. Her eyes were wide open. She mumbled incoherently. Catherine turned to look in the direction her mother pointed.

Glenn walked nonchalantly toward them carrying the rifle over his shoulder. He waved and yelled. Catherine felt the whish of cloth brush past her. Her mother had jumped from the top step and ran by. The astonished Catherine watched her mother cover the short distance to Glenn and throw her arms around the surprised man.

They approached camp arm in arm and chattering like magpies. Catherine thoughtfully watched. Her mother may mean it when she says nothing is going to happen and so might Glenn, but hot embers can burst into open flame at any time. These two definitely were not cold ashes.

"What happened, Glenn? We heard the shots. The next thing we knew Jiggles came back to camp without you." She dryly observed, "You can see my mother wasn't worried."

Sarah had the good grace to blush and drop her arm from around Glenn.

It was time for an explanation and Glenn obliged. "There wasn't any need for either of you to worry although I can see why you did. You heard the shots, right?"

The two women nodded.

"You assumed that I shot while in the saddle, right?"

They both nodded again.

Catherine interrupted, "Yesterday I shot at a coyote from the saddle. I sweet talked to Jiggles before I shot, because I didn't want her to bolt when I shot. She didn't seem gun shy. I know this wasn't the first time someone shot over her from the saddle." She coyly looked at Glenn and grinned. "Maybe you're not as good a rider as me."

"Probably not, but that wasn't what happened."

Catherine and Sarah anxiously waited. Finally her mother broke the silence. "Well?"

"The truth of the matter is I dismounted and pulled the rifle out of the scabbard and walked a few steps away from Jiggles to locate the coyote along the edge of the meadow. I fired three quick shots and missed all three. Guess what?" He chuckled as he recalled the scene. "Jiggles was half way to the camp when I turned around. There was no dumping the tenderfoot from the saddle. There was no injury. Your horse ran back to camp leaving me to walk." He broke out laughing. "By the way Catherine, you need to sight in that rifle. Every shot was left of the target. I'll be glad to do it for you."

"Go ahead. Maybe then I can hit something."

25
The Vernita Ferry

Catherine smiled as she reread the part of the paragraph that suited the present situation. *Sheep are creatures of habit. If left to themselves, they will graze the same ground over and over again. That is why sheep so desperately need a shepherdess. They must be managed.* She had followed the herder's log book and guided her charges to good grass and water. This campsite and meadow certainly fit this description. Her reward was a pleasant campsite and a slow moving flock that found plenty to eat. She hated to leave. It was probably her imagination, but she sensed the sheep were also reluctant to move.

On this cool April morning she had other some things to think about. Her mother had come out to see her because she was lonely. This seemed like normal behavior for anyone who had just filed for divorce. She believed her mother when she said nothing had happened with Glenn. Her mother could protest, but right now she was vulnerable. The two of them together looked like an affair about to happen; like kindling ready to burst into flame. She shrugged her shoulders. Why worry about events where you had no control.

Catherine shook off her thoughts, took her command post on the driver's seat and scanned the area. Malovich and Gilrakis sat on the ground eagerly awaiting the now familiar morning command. Watching them always pleased her.

She gave them a laughing "Cast." They eagerly bounded out to the small outlying groups and began pushing them toward the center. After saddling Jiggles she rode among the sheep and helped. By mid-morning the band had turned north and left the Horn Rapids area. They would placidly graze their way 26 miles north to the Columbia River, and then turn left and follow the river upstream. April was almost over when they approached the Vernita-Arrowsmith Ferry landing.

Wooden triangular pole towers stood deserted like forlorn sentinels of the past on either side of the river. Catherine had seen photographs when the ferry used them. The three long stout timbers were bolted together at the top. Then cable had been tightly wound around the poles to reinforce them where they crossed each other. At ground level the poles were secured in concrete. The cable was the heart of the old ferry system. It stretched across the river from these towers. A steel eyelet attached the ferry to the cable guided the ferry back and forth across the Columbia River.

The Vernita ferry that now sat in the Columbia River no longer used a cable. It was a simple, 60 foot long by 30 feet wide, open-decked barge. The major difference was the large Haines engine in the stern. The steering system was housed in a pilothouse on the right side of the barge. Catherine's band (1,463 sheep) and the other two bands would ride across the Columbia, 350 sheep at a time. The sheep were contained by permanent wooden panels along the sides of the ferry and by temporary partitions across the deck. The partitions kept the sheep evenly distributed on the deck for the crossings.

Catherine, Virgil and Rusty needed help to get their sheep safely across the river, and to tend to the sheep on the Arrowsmith side while the next 350 sheep were ferried across the river. This meant Pete, Alex, Hank and Sarah would be present for the crossing. Goose pimples rose on Catherine's crossed arms. She gave herself a little hug. Thoughts of that darn Hank did this to her.

The herders and their wagons made camp a quarter-mile from the Vernita landing and waited for the extra help. Catherine had a momentary dread of Glenn coming with her mother, but that quickly passed. She wrote in her journal to help pass the time. Last year the three bands were in the vicinity four days before they crossed. She wondered why they waited so long. She checked her supplies. Hank should resupply all three wagons before they crossed. She let the delicious thoughts of delivery linger.

Catherine used her binoculars to watch the ferry while they all waited. The ferry didn't sit idle. It was one of several essential ferry connections between eastern Washington and the rest of the state. The ferry carried 16 autos or pickups or 8 big trucks across the Columbia. The crossing took just 15-20 minutes.

The second day she left the grazing flock and rode to the landing. One conversation with the operator, Bill Longingden, told her why they were waiting. The three bands were scheduled to cross the next two days. If the car traffic was heavy it might take longer.

A quick three o'clock binocular scan from the wagon's driver seat confirmed their positions. Rusty and Virgil were ready to cross when the word was given. Rusty had the same idea. He also used his binoculars to scan the area. He waved to Catherine. She waved back. There was something else. Her stomach tightened. She followed his pointing finger to the canopied pickup approaching Virgil's flock.

She rode Jiggles out for a quick inspection. She talked to all her favorites and the time still dragged by. What was taking him so long? It tantalized her. Then the black scallywag of a lamb got her attention.

It strayed from her grazing group towards Virgil's flock. She whistled to get her dog's attention, and then commanded, "Bring" and pointed toward Blackie. It took a good 20 minutes to start the stubborn lamb back toward the main bunch.

Finally she heard the familiar tinny beep-beep sound as she wiped the perspiration from her brow and the sweatband of her hat. The pickup rounded the same grassy knoll that had attracted Blackie. The horn, the bouncing pickup and the dogs sent the straying lamb scampering past her. Now she could give her attention to the pickup and its driver.

Hank was out of the pickup almost before it stopped. "Having a little trouble, Catherine?"

No man ever looked so good. She swung out of the saddle, left the reins hanging loosely on the ground, and ran toward his waiting open arms. She stopped short. Her hand pointed to his leg. "No crutches?"

"No crutches. The doc released me two days ago. He said to be careful until I quit limping and that's already happening. Your job is safe until then." He warned her, "That doesn't mean I want you to run into me like a locomotive." He motioned, "Gently, please." In three seductive steps Catherine stepped inside the arms reaching for her. "Better?"

"Much." There was no more talking, just a quiet consuming emergence of two people, who wanted to touch and hold each other. Their kisses progressed from tender to demanding, from startling to possessive. Soft touching became caresses. Their bodies fought to get closer.

Hank looked down and noticed the dogs. Malovich and Gilrakis were sitting nearby grinning with their heads tilting to one side. "Do those darn dogs have to know everything that goes on?" Two tails wagged in unison. Hank sighed, "I guess they do."

That's when Catherine remembered. "I bet that darn Rusty is watching everything."

She caught Hank's questioning look, so she explained the morning exchange through their binoculars.

"Sounds like Rusty." He quipped, and waved in the general direction of Rusty's camp, He peered upriver to the northwest at the darkening clouds which were rolling down the mountains slopes and following the river toward them. Hank suggested, "Maybe we had better get these supplies unloaded before the rains come."

She agreed, but left him with one lingering, promising kiss. Her heart still pounded when she got in the saddle. On the short ride to her wagon Catherine wondered what would happen after the supplies were unloaded and put away. If three weeks alone in April left her this lusty, what would she feel like in May? She was absentmindedly humming, "April Showers" when the first sprinkle of rain fell.

Despite some controlled between-loads nuzzling, they finished unloading and sorting the supplies. The sprinkle continued. Both Hank and Catherine reached for light jackets to keep warm. The water vapor laden clouds above the Columbia were pushed up by the heavier cooler air rolling down the mountain slope. The clouds darkened as they were squeezed by the cooler air. The rains became heavier.

Catherine thought about tomorrow. She asked, "How will the weather affect the ferry crossings tomorrow?"

He shrugged off her worries. "It really has to get stormy and wet before the ferry stops running. Wind causes more trouble than rain." He looked out through the open hole hidden under the canvas overlap at the front of the Shepherdess wagon. "Right now I'd say the rain will get worse before it blows through tonight." They sat down on the ledge beside the Coleman Camp stove and enjoyed a cup of hot coffee and the warm comfort of the Shepherdess wagon. The rain beat against the canvas sides and fell harmlessly to the ground.

Catherine leaned back into Hank and nestled into his left shoulder like it was protection from the spring squall. "Phew, that feels good." Hank's arms rested around her waist. They both enjoyed the comfort and warmth.

He casually leaned down and kissed Catherine's neck. She reached up to pull his face down to hers. Their response was explosive. Open mouth met open mouth. Tongue met tongue. She turned up to get closer and his hand slid into her shirt and bare skin. Catherine moaned. She pressed against him wanting more.

Her vivid imagination captured an ember waiting to burst into flame. She had compared her mother and Glenn to this. What was she? She was following the same script. In the midst of a raging conflict between desire and reason Catherine pulled away and stood up. Her knees threatened to buckle. She reached up and held on to one of the wooden ribs that supported the canvas top.

Catherine stood before Hank, her shirt partially open. She exhaled deeply and delivered the awful truth. "We can't do this. We have said as much before, but here we are and we can't keep our hands off each other." She sucked in large gulps of air to gain some control. She gasped, "I want more, but it can't be that way." She hastily tucked in her shirt to get outside... rain or no rain.

Hank protested, "Hey, it's not my fault. You just said you wanted more. You left me in no man's land. Now you stand all purity-like saying it can't be that way."

Catherine yearned to be held. Torrid heat surrounded her. The cool rain called.

 She popped the back door open to step outside. Two wet sheep dogs hurled themselves into the warm, dry wagon. Catherine yelled, "Gilrakis, Malovich, get out of here. You're wet." She reached for a towel to dry them, but it was too late. The two dogs shook every inch of their rain soaked hair. Hank and Catherine threw their hands up in front of their faces. Water came out in flurries. There was no way they could defend themselves from the drenching. Not satisfied with the shower they had already provided, the dogs gave one last shudder that proceeded from head to tail. Satisfied, they lay down on the floor to absorb the heat and stay dry.

Catherine sternly told them, "There is no way you two are getting off that easy." Catherine found another towel and tossed it to Hank. They dried their hands, face and clothing. Then they turned on Malovich and Gilrakis and vigorously dried them.

Her voice turned warm and affectionate. "Now you can stay inside and get warm." Catherine observed the grin on Hank's face. She felt the same laughter welling up. The dogs provided the needed comic relief. Catherine joked, "I guess we'll have to be pretty careful as long as those two are around."

She walked to Hank, embraced him and apologized. "I'm sorry I came onto you like an Amazon claiming her mate. You do that to me. I'll be more of a lady in the future. That doesn't mean I won't have these wild emotions. It means they'll be held in check." Catherine put her arms around Hank. She felt his arms around her. A very warm pervasive aura surrounded them, but she wouldn't be lulled into the physical desire game again.

If she allowed it once then there was no turning back. So far Catherine had been able to resist. Could she survive such strong emotional moments in the future?

∽

Hank merely nodded. He had just escaped a mauling by a mountain lion, a sweet, passionate mauling, but still a mauling. Catherine had said in no uncertain terms that she wanted him. The dogs had done a very spontaneous, effective job of stopping what seemed to be happening. Catherine's switch from passionate to resistance had been sudden.

Then he remembered she had said no before the dogs jumped into the wagon. That memory jolted him. In fact she had opened the door to go out into the rain. That's when the dogs jumped into the wagon. Was he happy about escaping? He had just followed her lead. How could she say no when they both wanted the same thing? Today's resistance could be reversed in one second, one kiss or one teasing caress. Hank smiled. There was plenty of time.

Hank thought about his predicament. It looked like a summer of "do we or don't we?" He knew he wanted Catherine and that she wanted him. The tilt of her jaw and the determined jut of her chin didn't give him much encouragement ... strong woman.

His thoughts wandered to his leg. The limp would be completely gone when he returned again with supplies. Three lonely weeks on the Wahluke Slope might make Catherine more willing, especially when he replaced her at Othello.

❧

The gentle, sod soaking rain continued. It would die as soon as the clouds passed. As the evening faded away two sets of headlights left the highway and came toward the campsite.

That had to be Pete, Alex and her mother. Tomorrow would be a very busy day. Getting three bands of sheep mixed in with cars and trucks for a ferry ride across the Columbia would take time and a lot of patience. Catherine went to bed thinking of tomorrow. The sheep crossing was one problem. How to slow down the Hank juggernaut was the other.

26
The Crossing

Catherine rolled out of her bedroll at first light. Outside the light drizzle continued. Thanks to her mother, the aroma of hearty coffee, the smell of sizzling bacon, and the sight of frying eggs temporarily pushed aside thoughts of the day's waiting adventure. When they finished the last piece of bacon and downed the last drop of coffee the business of the day became pushing the sheep toward the Vernita Ferry. Catherine looked forward to her first Columbia crossing with her sheep. Rusty's and then Virgil's sheep would follow.

In an unusual way that darn Blackie was being stubborn again. He insisted on being in the lead group. Catherine laughed at this new Blackie, but knew it spelled trouble. Once on the other side Blackie would be free to roam while the other sheep were being ferried across. That could be disaster. Finally Pete and Alex cornered the exuberant lamb and put him in the canopy that covered Pete's pickup bed.

The light, cool morning rain continued to fall. The riders had draped their colorful, cape-like ponchos around their shoulders.

Their broad-brimmed riding hats diverted the rain out to their shoulders. They would remain dry as possible. Catherine looked out of place in her denim jacket, but the rain was light. Her mother reassured her, "If you wish, Catherine, I'll leave you my poncho when we go home."

"Not necessary Mother. I have one in the wagon for heavy rains."

Hank cautiously led Thunder and Lightning pulling the shepherdess wagon to the front of the ferry. First on, first off was the rule for wagons and cars. Alex led Mr. Gray aboard and left him by the wagon. Jiggles whinnied at being left behind, but Catherine had to have a horse when she returned for the second load. Once the wagon and horses were on board, and cars parked, the sheep were pushed and cajoled past the wooden panels that funneled them toward the ferry. Pete released Blackie to go back to the remaining sheep.

There was no cacophony of endless yelling like a cattle drive. It was a quieter litany of men yelling and whistling and dogs barking. They cut the first sheep from the flock and pushed them toward the ferry. The line they had to cross this time was not imaginary. The heavy steel loading ramp presented a real scare to the sheep. Each footstep made its own, new, metallic sound. This took a little time. The dogs barked and men on foot urged them onto the ramp. Virgil and Rusty actually lifted some sheep on board. At last the first load was ready to transport.

From the pilot house Bill Longingly signaled to the deckhand to close the gates. Catherine made her way toward her wagon. She felt a slight push. She looked down at Dolly and Ulla. Her two leaders wanted a little assurance. She talked softly to them and scratched their heads before she climbed up to the driver's seat to sit with Hank. She was ready to witness another first when she heard a very determined bleat.

She craned her neck around to see what caused the disturbance. One half of the rear gate had been swung to the middle and secured. The deck hand started to shut the other half, when the little black streak squeaked past him. Blackie was not to be denied. He had somehow managed to scamper onto the first crossing.

Hank laughed. "Determined little cuss, isn't he?"

Amused, Catherine agreed. "No wonder the dogs had so much trouble with him."

In the pilothouse Bill Longingly kicked in the clutch to shift the gears. The cogs meshed, the propeller wash surfaced behind the ferry, and the ferry started its short trip across the rain punctured surface of the Columbia River to the Arrowsmith landing.

The little black sheep spread all four legs on the deck and braced himself while he watched the passing river through the outside railings. He never moved.

The unloading at Arrowsmith was much easier than the Vernita loading. Hank drove the wagon off, followed by three cars and three pickups. He tied the team to the nearby hitching post. Alex led Mr. Gray to shore and waited for the sheep. Malovich and Gilrakis barked at the sheep, which didn't hesitate to leave the ferry. It was Alex's duty to move this first bunch away from the landing and tend the sheep until other loads, 350 sheep at a time, arrived.

After the sheep left the ferry eight cars and two pickups were quickly loaded for the return trip. Catherine took this opportunity to garner a quick good-by kiss before heading back to the ferry. The deckhand waited for her before he closed the gate.

The black streak brushed past Catherine again. She grabbed the railing to keep from falling. Blackie was back on the ferry. From the front he spread his legs for balance. He looked at Catherine as if to say, "Come on. Let's get going." She looked at the deckhand, who looked at his captain, who looked at Catherine. They all burst out laughing.

It took thirteen trips to transport the sheep across the river. From there, Virgil, Rusty and Catherine aided by Pete, Sarah and Alex continued their efforts to put the sheep into three distinct forage lanes. By evening they had partially accomplished this. Catherine's first off flock grazed in the eastern lane; Rusty would be in the middle and Virgil in the western lane. They wouldn't merge again until they crossed the Columbia on the Grand Coulee Dam.

That evening Sarah and Pete hosted a large cook-out before the herders left the next morning. Hamburgers, potatoes and baked beans from the little general store at Arrowsmith made the preparation easy. Over the outdoor fire pit the sliced potatoes were frying in the large camp skillet. The grill, darkened by years of use over a hot camp fire beckoned to the large hamburger patties. Each hungry herder cooked their own. A cold soda or beer would slake their thirst. The crossing was over. The grazing sheep could be heard bleating softly in the distance. Tomorrow they would head up the Wahluke Slope.

Hank sat on the wagon tongue to enjoy the meal with Catherine. Catherine leaned against him and laughed. He looked down at her. "What's so funny?"

"Blackie! Think about it. That lamb has done his best to stray away from his flock. Now he made every effort to stay with them. He made every single crossing. Bill Longingly told my mother and Pete he had never seen anything like it. When the last of the sheep in our band left the ferry, he left with them. How unusual is that?"

"Yeah, it's odd, very odd."He gently caressed her shoulder as he spoke. "Do you think he'll keep straying while the band grazes up the Wahluke Slope?"

"That's a question that only he can answer, but my guess is yes." His pleasant touch warmed her. She turned her face upward to be kissed.

"Easy Catherine, remember we don't want to get all stirred up."

Slightly taken aback, she coolly replied, "Don't worry, Hank, I'm not going to attack you." She confessed, "I just felt the comforting touch on my shoulder, and I liked it. I wanted a little more." She asked, "Are you going to kiss me or not? After all, a girl doesn't like to offer and get turned down."

He bent down and kissed her lightly on the lips.

Catherine felt the reluctance in his lips and saw it in his eyes. "I didn't want this to be a duty kiss, Hank." The ache in her heart increased. "Is that what it was?"

"Don't be silly, Catherine." he protested. "Have you already forgotten the last time we touched? We climbed all over each other until you got a guilty conscience. You let me know 'this was not the way to go.' You acted like you were the only one who could see or cared about the dangers. You set the rules. Now, you're upset because I try to live by them.

He conceded, "It wasn't a moving kiss for either of us, but it was a comfortable safe kiss. Isn't that what you wanted or were you just teasing? Think about it while I take our plates in the trash pit." He asked, "How much touching are you willing to accept? I want more than that last kiss. Remember we won't see each other again until Othello."

Did this mean Hank wanted more now? Catherine felt her resistance rising. "I thought we had agreed on how far to go. At least I have."

Catherine watched Hank disappear toward the rear of the wagon. She sighed at the resentment she felt. She tried to see the rosy side of the kiss. Was he trying to keep their desire under control? If so, that was okay. She certainly understood that. Their last passionate encounter had scared her. It could have led to so much more, clearly too much more, but his last question, "How much touching are you willing to accept?" upset her. What the devil did that mean? Did that mean he wanted sex to keep this romance flourishing? He might as well have hit her. She had made her position clear. They couldn't go on playing with fire. Maybe Hank didn't think so.

She had a few minutes to think before Hank returned. She still struggled to interpret his meaning, but she always came back to the same thought. Hank wanted a lot more than a few hot kisses. So did she, but it wasn't going to happen. The delicious thoughts of his hands on her still lingered. It seems that wasn't enough. She waited for Hank's return.

Catherine's rising anger cooled with each cold drop of moisture that reached her upturned face. There would be no more light-hearted kidding tonight, if it was light- hearted kidding. Everyone sought shelter from the steady, chilling rain. Catherine simply opened the overlapping canvas behind the driver's seat and entered her wagon. She hoped a hot cup of tea would combat the rain, cool her anger and relax her soul.

Fate had intervened in Catherine's life several times. She regarded this increasing April rain as such. It had stopped either one from issuing any ultimatums. The heavy downpour had forced the celebrating group to cover their heads and scamper for the protection of their sleeping quarters. Pete drove Rusty and Virgil to their wagons. The two canopied pickups had the necessary bedrolls for Alex and Hank. The crossing celebration was over.

ᕦᕤ

Catherine sat with her hands wrapped around her tea cup when her mother entered the wagon and walked to the back door to let the dogs in. They had stayed under the wagon, but they weren't going to miss a chance to get inside. Gilrakis and Malovich sat there and gloated because they had escaped the rain. Catherine had to laugh at the satisfied looks on their faces.

"Well, I must say, it's nice to see you laugh. Except for the entry of the dogs, you've not been the most cheerful person I've seen today." Catherine peered at her without moving her hands from the cup of hot tea, so she tried another tack. "I noticed Hank left with Pete when he took Rusty and Virgil back to their camps." Still no answer came.

Sarah felt forced to use the direct approach. "The rain was the reason Pete drove the others to their camps, but why Hank? Did you two have a fight? Care to tell me about it?"

Catherine poured refills, but didn't reply. Sarah quietly sipped the magic potion that is tea and waited while Catherine set the hot kettle back on the camp stove. She waited and watched Catherine gently stroke Gilrakis' head.

"Mother, it was horrible. I had no idea anything was bothering him. We were talking about Blackie's unusual behavior today when he casually stroked my shoulder. It was very natural and pleasant. I automatically leaned into him and turned my face up. I wanted nothing more than a casual kiss; nothing earth moving, just a quick, easy kiss. He didn't want to kiss me. I could see it in his eyes and felt it with my lips. It was like kissing a dead fish."

"That's no reason to be mad and stay mad. Is there something else?"

"There's more." Her daughter replied, "The part that upset me. He implied that I needed to accept more in our romance."

"That doesn't sound like Hank." She bit her lip and absent-mindedly reached down to pat Malovich. She needed a moment to think. "He said that?"

"More or less."

"Tell me exactly what he said. Maybe you misunderstood."

"Mother, I know you think Hank can do no wrong, but he implied more than a few kisses were expected. He accused me of teasing and then changing my mind." That's when the rain hit and he dashed away with our plates.

"Are you saying sex was expected."

Catherine nodded.

"Do you remember what he said, or were you too mad to remember?"

The words were deeply etched in her memory. "How much touching are you willing to accept? I'm just like you. I want more.'" She added, "I wasn't angry then, but after he left I got to thinking about what he said. Then I got mad."

Sarah thought about this statement. "That doesn't sound like an ultimatum to me." She fixed her gaze on her daughter until she fidgeted. "You're more aggressive than Hank. You two were alone when he delivered your supplies. How glad were you to see him?"

"Mother!"

"Oh, don't worry, Catherine. I'm not accusing you of anything." Sarah hid behind her smile while she formulated her next observation. "Do you remember how upset you were when I showed up with Glenn?"

Sarah noticed Catherine's tiny smile.

"You warned me to be careful and not to make a fool of myself. Now I'm asking you the same question. What were you doing that let Hank think there would be more?"

Catherine bit her lip before she replied, "Mother, I'm afraid you're right. I hadn't been alone with Hank since the sheep crossed the Yakima River onto the open range." Her entire face bespoke embarrassment.

Sarah smiled and waited for the confession.

Catherine reluctantly admitted, "When he delivered my supplies I jumped on Hank like a dog on a bone. I left little doubt of my intentions. We had the time, place and emotion. He felt wonderful." The aura remained very quiet. A pixie like smile appeared. "You're the cause of all this, you know."

Sarah snapped, "Be sensible Catherine. I wasn't even there."

"In a sense you were. Remember how indignant I was with you and Glenn? You just said it. I realized that was exactly where I was with Hank. I wondered how you would feel if you walked in at that very moment."

Sarah smiled at the irony of Catherine's statement.

"Oh my, oh my, Mother. That might be why Hank said I had set the rules."

Sarah wanted more details, but Catherine didn't need prompting. "I was so glad to see him. I was his last stop on his supply route, and I knew why. After the last bit of supplies were stored in their proper place we turned to each other. It was exciting. We couldn't get enough of each other. I pulled him down on top of me on the very ledge where my bedroll is. Mother, I made no effort to stop him, until I thought of you and Glenn. That's when I stood up and told him it couldn't go that way. I started to go outside into the rain to cool down. That's when the dogs bounced inside. Believe me, they stopped everything."

"The dogs?"

'I see you haven't heard about the dogs. I thought Hank would have that story in every camp by now."

Sarah laughed heartily at the story of Gilrakis and Malovich flinging water on everything and everybody. She wryly said, "I can see how that stopped any romantic notions. It was probably a good thing."

Catherine nodded.

"But you had made up your mind before the dogs came in, right?"

"Right!"

"The fact you had the good sense to make your decision before the dogs made it for you makes me quite happy." She put her arm around her daughter's shoulder. "I know now you can and will make the right decision. What you did takes a lot of guts. I'm sure Hank will see this for himself." Sarah paused for a moment. "You and Hank haven't really talked about this, have you?"

"How could we, Mother? Eating together this evening was the first time we've been alone, if you can call a camp full of people alone."

"You know, little one, sometimes its better not be too open and too demanding. Everyone likes to think they have a share in an important decision. You're aggressive and also very trusting. Maybe you need to step back and think about what Hank really wants. Maybe you have to learn what I had to."

She noted Catherine's surprised look. "I wasn't always what you see now. Everybody has to grow and learn." She paused to collect her thoughts so she could tell her story. "You were there, so you already knew about my drive alongside the weed-covered summer fallow after your eighth birthday and the tempestuous meeting with your grandfather the next day.

You didn't see the aggravating year that followed. In my desire to reclaim the Sumertun ranch I bossed everyone, including Pete and Carter.

Catherine leaned a little closer at this revelation.

"Oh yes, my dear Catherine, I rode herd on everyone ... hard. Several men quit rather than put up with a woman who constantly harped at them. They either did it my way or they were gone. They didn't call me 'The Queen of the Sumertun Ranch' then." A smile crossed her face. "I don't know what they said, but I'm sure it wasn't that good.

"After a very stormy session with Pete at the lambing shed, Carter came to me. Once again he sat me down in the parlor and patiently explained that I was driving everyone away with my blunt, aggressive behavior. I remember it well. He told me, 'Sarah, you can't drive every tractor every day, you can't harvest the wheat by yourself, and you can't shear the sheep or run the lambing shed by yourself.'

"I remember protesting, 'That unfair.'

"His answer was simple. 'You will have to do all these things if you don't start trusting the men to do their job. You've made a magnificent effort to right the ranch you neglected. The men understand. They feel the same urges you do, and they appreciate jobs in this time of want. They want the ranch to prosper.

It means a better future for everyone. You forget everyone relies on you, and even more important; you rely on them. Everyone has a role to play, or everyone fails.'"

Catherine was intrigued. "Did Grandfather Carter make you change your ways?"

"Not me. I was too stubborn. He couldn't make me do anything, but I didn't want the ranch to fail because of my neglect. Carter was a patient and loving rock to cling to. It took a while before I noticed he nudged me along with little suggestions. Later he would ask questions about the suggestions. He made sense. I could see improvement. Our discussions became more philosophic. It was a slow process, but eventually I became what you know. I learned you're nothing by yourself."

Catherine held in the laugh that wanted to escape. "Are you're saying I'm a little stubborn, pushy and aggressive?" The laugh escaped, "I wonder where that came from?" They shared a laugh. Mother and daughter touched hands and draped an arm around each other's shoulders. The simple, shared moment touched both. Amused, Catherine asked, "And I can get what I want by sharing?"

"That's it, kiddo. You don't lose a thing and what you can gain is immeasurable."

Sarah wasn't quite finished. "Being stubborn, pushy and aggressive is not necessarily a bad thing. What you must do is learn to manage these traits. Taking what comes your way is easy and alluring, but it's not managing your life. Western College and being 'Shepherdess' has given you knowledge and time to grow so you can manage your life. Managing simply means you aren't drifting; that you have some purpose in life. Time, learning to share and discipline are tools."

She continued her thoughts. "Your sharing starts by talking this out with Hank. Find out where you're going." She quipped, "Personally I don't think you have a problem, but if you and Hank don't work out, so be it. I'll love you either way."

Sarah reached up and turned off the Coleman gas lantern. The half-moon furnished an eerie, faint light inside the wagon as it struggled to find openings through the diminishing clouds. She prepared for the assault that would come when the eager dogs jumped up to their bedrolls and curled tight against them for the night. She whispered. "Good night, Catherine. Don't worry, it will all work out."

Gilrakis left the floor to snuggle in close to Catherine. She fondly petted the dog. "Affectionate dogs aren't they? Good night, Mother, and thanks for caring and sharing. I love you." She had a lot to think about. Malovich took the opportunity to jump up beside Sarah.

⁓

Catherine couldn't sleep. Her brain kept going over and over the whole Hank episode. She rose to make herself one final cup of tea. Maybe that would help.

"Catherine, why are you up?" Sarah looked at her wrist watch. "It's 1:00 o'clock."

"I'm sorry, Mother, but I haven't slept a wink. I'm going to make myself a last cup of hot tea to go with one of the doughnuts you bought from the Arrowsmith Store." Her mother turned back into the bedroll and pulled the top over her head. She chided, "Don't worry mother, I'll be very quiet."

When the tea kettle began boiling she reached absent mind-edly into the miscellaneous drawer under the stove for a large pot holder. She pushed her log book aside, then her camera and finally a half-full box of 30-30 shells. She cursed herself for using the drawer as a catchall. She reached in past all the collected items to seize a large pot holder and pulled it up. A glossy, 4"x6" photograph fell to the floor. She picked it up and studied the large photograph of a young woman dressed in formal dress. Her light colored gown plunged deep enough to feature a firm roundness. She stood almost as tall as her escort.

Catherine gasped. Hank Hirsch, dressed in a dark suit, a white shirt and a tie stared back at her from the photograph. This picture was taken at Washington State College. This had to be a woman from college; a woman who indicated Hank was much more than a casual friend. Across the bottom a message was scrawled. "To Hank with all my love, Alyssa."

Catherine sank quietly to the floor. She turned off the camp stove and stepped outside with her tea to let the damp cold air soothe her anger. She had too many questions that only Hank could answer.

27
No Mans Land

Catherine watched the ferry pull away from the Arrowsmith landing with the horse's reins draped loosely over the railing for the crossing. This arrangement took up more space, but her mother still refused to cross with the horses tied up. She reasoned, "They would have no chance of survival in case of an emergency." No one disputed her authority.

Bill Longingly didn't care whether the horses were tied or untied as long as he was paid for the space. He knew they would soon be riding home in their trailers.

Catherine stepped back as the landing gate closed. She made sure no Blackie streaked through the gate before it closed, but the little fella made no effort to break away from his own band. The surface wash from the ferry's propeller pushed the craft away and the Sumertun ranch group waved good-by, except the solitary Hank.

His lean, angular frame slumped against the end rail until the ferry was halfway across the Columbia. His good-bye wave was as feeble as his kiss last night. Catherine would remember that pouting face for a long time. She had no idea what the wave meant. Her emotional tie to Hank was stronger than anything she had ever experienced, but she had made her point. Had she been wrong? Her jaw jutted out like bulldog. She didn't think so.

∽

The sheep were in no mood to be pushed after the ferry crossing. The dogs made their normal morning cast and Catherine allowed the sheep to stay with the good grass, still wet from the rain. She guided Thunder and Lightning and her wagon toward a campsite she had located from the dog-eared pages of Ricardo Urritia's logbook.

Looking west back to the mountains, she understood why the sheep were ferried across the Columbia River to continue their way. There was no place to graze in the rockier, steeper terrain west of the river.

The gentler eastern Wahluke slope was the result of the giant alluvial fan formed when the colossal Missoula floods spilled out over the south rim of the Crab Creek Coulee. Good soil, winter moisture and spring rains allowed large sagebrushes, clumps of bunch grasses and plenty of vibrant, wild grass to grow. Already she enjoyed an early scattering of desert daisies and purple lupine.

She unhitched the horses and staked them out at the new campsite. Then she rode Jiggles back through the flock, assuring them that green pastures and water awaited them. Her flock moved sedately up the lower Wahluke slope toward the distant crest of the Saddle Mountains. Always the rising slope and falling crest presented contrast. On the other side of the crest the Crab Creek Coulee waited. The busy Catherine almost forgot about Hank.

∽

Hank's brief morning visit had given her plenty to think about. He had visibly tensed after she asked, "I thought you would be at the ferry by now. How come you're here?" She had wondered if he was just nervous or gaining courage before delivering his reason for being at her back door. Hank had said, "We won't see each other until Othello. That should give you enough time to decide how you want to continue. Will it be friendship or more teasing?"

"If you think caring warmth and desire is teasing, then there will be no more. I must have seemed like easy pickings to you, Hank Hirsch." She stared up at the face she once thought of as tender and giving. "Actually I enjoyed every minute, but I don't tease, thank you! I'm honest with my emotions."

"What the devil does that mean?"

Catherine walked to the miscellaneous drawer and opened it. The telltale photo stared up at her. She almost tore it in half as she jerked it from the open drawer. "Who is Alyssa?"

Hank was clearly surprised by the photo. His laughing reaction startled her. "I see you found the picture. I wondered where it was. I kept it to remind me."

"Of what? Just how easy women are?"

He sighed, "Just the opposite, Catherine." He stepped forward to touch and embrace the resisting Catherine. Hank stepped back to cast his eye at the stubborn Catherine. "You like things straight forward, blunt and honest. Right?

Catherine glared at him.

"Will you listen?"

She slowly nodded.

"You act like you should be the only woman I've ever known. You surely can't be that naïve, but my past dates shouldn't matter if I treat you right. Sure, I pushed you a little. I guess that's human nature. We both enjoyed the flirtations, but you proved you're not 'easy pickings' and I respect that. I came here this morning to apologize, but you waved the photograph around and acted like a wounded bear. Do you want to know about the photo?"

"Yes."

"The woman in the photograph is Alyssa Tanner. You can see she's beautiful. We were classmates at Washington State, and yes, we were very close, but we broke up after that picture was taken. I kept the picture to remind me of how close I came to getting married. If I had done what she demanded, I would never become a veterinarian. He father is a partner in a big mining company around Coeur d'Alene, Idaho. I had a very good job waiting, a willing wife and secure future if I did what they wanted. They didn't even consider that I wanted to be a veterinarian. They wanted more than I was willing to give.

"I haven't lied, and I've been honest with you. The picture reminds me what must be done for me to become a veterinarian. My father thought work was more important than education. I appreciate that he worked all through the depression and took care of his family, but ours was a hard relationship, especially after my mother died. He never gave me one penny toward my education." He flatly declared, He'll be working on the section until he dies.

"I worked a couple of summers beside him on the railroad as a section hand, and hoarded every penny I earned to get through undergraduate school. After working at the ranch and finishing this summer with the sheep I'll be able to enter the School of Veterinarian Science at Washington State. My undergraduate grades have been very good, and I have a partial scholarship."

Catherine finally asked, "Does that mean you didn't ever think of marriage?"

"You have caused me to think, but my position is the same. I must keep focused on the prize." He hesitated like he was thinking of what to say. He smiled. "I guess the question is still, 'Will we see each other in Othello as good friends or as a good romance'?"

"At this time I'd say a good friendship is hell of a lot better than a romance." Her terse reply continued, "You have a lot to learn about me. When you come to Othello, we'll just have to see how it goes. Make no mistake, Hank, you'll not be forgotten but things have changed."

In clipped tones he said, "I'm looking forward to relieving you at Othello."

Catherine understood the rebuke. How long she stood there unresponsive, she didn't know, but it had to be long enough for Hank to have some doubts. "Well, Catherine I've had my say. I'll see you in Othello." He reined Mr. Gray to turn and gallop to the ferry, but paused for one last blast. "It's too bad you didn't want to play. We were awfully close to some great lovin'."

If Catherine could have found a rock she would have thrown it at him.

More than ever she was glad she had said no. The promise of lusty romance had been wonderful, but now that she understood Hank's priorities the romantic future looked bleak. It was time to give her attention to a new campsite, her sheep and her dogs.

28
The Wahluke Slope

The three bands continued the long climb east up the gentle Wahluke slope toward the upper Columbia Plateau formed by the ancient, tumultuous lava flows, glaciers which changed the flow of the Columbia, and the unimaginable sized Missoula floods which formed the great coulees of the present landscape.

Rusty and Virgil had done this before. Catherine hadn't, but she recognized the tedious, lonely stretch of the trek was about to begin. She looked forward to it. During these solitary moments she slowly realized she did not want to be relieved at Othello.

How things had changed. It had been forty days since she had jumped from the wagon to run into the ranch house for one last, tearful farewell from Hank. Now she steeled herself to wait until Othello to find out where they stood. Right now, Catherine thought they didn't stand anywhere.

She checked her crude map to locate a path up the large triangular slope. The sheep would travel along the long southern leg of the triangle. She found a landmark listed in the dog-eared notebook, checked her compass and headed northeast toward the end of the foothills. The soil, the small creek and the rain were responsible for the grass and campsite that made Catherine's job easier. When she cleared the eastern foothills of the Saddle Mountains she would reverse her direction and graze west in the large Lower Crab Creek Coulee where the Columbia River once flowed.

Last night's rainfall was an added blessing that spurred plant growth. Already she enjoyed a new scattering of yellow desert daisies. The flowers would lose their vitality soon after they bloomed. By late June everything would fade under the summer heat. Only the silver-green sagebrush and sturdy bunch grass would grace the hot, dry land in July.

This was the land the Washington Post decried in its opposition to the Grand Coulee Dam as fit only for insects, rattlesnakes and coyotes. Springtime on the Wahluke Slope refuted this. Catherine knew her progress over the grass-covered slopes would be slow. The rain revitalized grass and water from the small creek were too good to pass up. What other discoveries would be revealed? That night she noted her thoughts in her log book.

The normally clear stream ran serenely down the gentle slope toward the Columbia. The sparkly surface was muddied some by recent rain. Her first campsite on the slope was where the creek flattened out and slowed through the meadow. Catherine could leisurely move the sheep east along the small stream and up the slope for another ten to twelve days before she dropped over the last foothill into the Crab Creek Coulee. She looked upward at the thin cloudy, gray sky. Did that unusual sky mean more rain?

Catherine finished her evening sweep of the flock. The sheep browsed contentedly along either side of the creek and the two dogs seemed satisfied. The excitement of the ferry crossing and starting up the long slope caught up to her. She slept peacefully in the cozy warmth of her bed and the added warmth of the cuddling dogs.

She awoke in the early morning to the sound of rain beating steadily against the canvas covering of the wagon. It was four o'clock when she looked at her watch. The dogs seemed unconcerned, so why should she worry? She drifted back to sleep in the early morning darkness with her hand resting on the sleeping Malovich.

The morning drizzle greeted her as she stuck her head outside. There was no wind to blow the storm through. Trees were few and scattered. The sheep stood stoically in small groups on either side of the creek. They looked like little white clumps of cotton against the lush, green meadow. All morning she listened to the steady beat of the falling rain.

Not used to being cooped up in her shepherdess wagon, she sighed, looked out at the unchanging sky and poured herself some more tea. By now the day should be warming up. That would stop the rain. The little thermometer hanging by the back door didn't give her any encouragement. Gilrakis watched her pace the floor and sip her tea.

Catherine read the "Sheep Facts" paper for the fifth time. *Sheep are frightened by swiftly moving streams. They are easily carried away by the current. Also their coats of wool become waterlogged. Sheep and rapid water do not mix. And sheep know it! Whenever they have to cross water that has any depth to it, there is only one safe place for the sheep and that is next to the shepherdess.*

She gave little credence to this "dangerous waters" information, but a little nibble of fear surfaced. How much rain did it take to make the small creek overrun its banks? There was plenty of good grass on either side of the creek, so there was no worry. The wet grass took care of their thirst. She shouldn't have let this bother her, but doggone it, it did.

She sighed and set her mug of hot tea on the table, put on her broad brimmed hat, pulled on her denim jacket, and hustled outside to the passing stream. Small traces of muddy water were mixing in, but it didn't look menacing. She felt foolish, but thought it was better safe than sorry. She stuck a stick into the mud at the edge of the creek and left.

The sun peeked through the scattered clouds by one o'clock. The rain had slowed to a few hit or miss droplets. The dogs wanted outside, so Catherine saddled Jiggles and her entourage followed as she rode out to move the sheep back into manageable groups. Jiggles carried her through the shallow ford in the creek. The dogs splashed happily alongside. At the familiar command, "Cast" they whizzed off to the outlying areas to bring the sheep together.

A third of the sheep grazed complacently south of the stream. They seemed content and happy to see their shepherdess as she rode among them and talked to them. A few of them followed her. They didn't leave until their shepherdess gave them some individual attention. After her morning sojourn she thought it best to leave the sheep alone. It was time to test her fishing prowess before the stream got too muddy.

The stream meandered in slow curves through the slope. Some of these curves had severe banks that had been cut in the soft soil during previous high waters. Fish might lurk there or in the riffles that entered the slower part of the pool. She slid her telescopic rod out to its full length, and tossed the shiny spinner into the slower pools of water, sans worms.

The rain from the upper reaches of the slope had started to swell the stream. Two inches of water showed above the earlier water level. This amount of water would cause no inconvenience. Catherine didn't feel a need to move, as she turned her attention to fishing. The isolated creek yielded six, seven to eight inch trout in thirty minutes. That was two fish for each ravenous dog and her. It was an enjoyable afternoon.

When the temperature dropped in the late afternoon the rain reappeared. The horses stood with their rumps toward the falling rain. The few trees around the campsite gave them little protection, but they had faced this before. The dogs stayed under the wagon, but soon were whining to get inside. Rolling claps of thunder followed the Columbia River down from the mountains. Lightning ripped from the clouds to the ground striking the higher parts of the Wahluke slope. When Catherine looked out through the canvas loophole in the front she witnessed a late spring thunderstorm at its best.

She tried her best to describe what she saw in her journal and decided her writing skills needed a lot of improvement. She laughed. This job gave her plenty of time to think and write. This must have been the case for one of the earlier herders. Ricardo Urritia possessed definite drawing skills. His drawings dominated the little notebook she kept in her saddle bag or in the drawer under her bedroll. His laborious block printing had taken some time to decipher, but his drawings had showed her the way to her present campsite.

Stories of the trail would be interesting; if she could make them come alive. She had already used most of her Kodak film. They could be replenished at Othello. Photos to illustrate and writing to describe her passage seemed like a good way to pass some time.

Catherine slept fitfully during the heavy rain and the thunder. Thankful for the security of the dogs she snuggled deep into the warmth of the bedroll. Around three o'clock in the morning she awakened suddenly. The silence almost deafened her. No rain fell and no thunder tore the sky asunder. The increased noisy gurgling of the stream caught her attention. In the morning she would have to be out bright and early among the sheep. For now she sank back into a deep slumber.

She stuck her nose outside at 6:00 a.m. to greet the clearing sky with an enthusiastic stretch. The day was a far cry from yesterday's dark clouds and angry storms. She scanned the muddy creek hustling down its channel. The stick no longer stood. The stream had risen a foot. Was it possible to get the shepherdess wagon to the other side? Should she? The sheep had good grazing so they were in no danger. She could always ford the creek on Jiggles. She decided to wait before making any sudden moves.

After a rare morning coffee she rode among the sheep. The heavy rain had not affected them. She had laughed at her Sheep Facts which read, *"Sheep and water don't mix. The weight of water from heavy rains and a wool coat, mixed with mud and sticks could force a sheep to go down and be unable to get up."*

That list of sheep fallacies came from biblical times. Her sheep did not have mud, sticks and burrs in their coats. Furthermore they had not grown their full coat of wool. Nevertheless Catherine rode Jiggles across the torrent to the north side to check the sheep. The dogs seemed to view the forced crossing as challenging fun. After they shook themselves dry they sprinted off to gather the flock and move them along the stream toward the distant eastern end of the slope. Then they splashed eagerly through the stream again, shook dry and moved the sheep on the south side.

The water receded on the second day. Catherine forded the creek with the wagon to the north side of the meadow and set up camp three miles further up the slope. Since most of the sheep were already on the north side the sheep could stay separated until she moved the wagon again. The exception was Blackie.

Unlike the ferry crossing Blackie wanted to be on his own again. Catherine diligently scanned the large flock each morning with the binoculars, especially the small clumps of white that needed to be brought in closer by the dogs. Blackie remained at the outermost edges of either group. Catherine swore when she found him grazing on the edge of the southern side.

The most dangerous predator the sheep faced stalked her favorite stray. The coyote's tawny coat sparkled in the morning sun. The characteristic unapologetic grin was evident. "You S.O.B." Catherine snarled. She slipped the 30-30 rifle from its scabbard, pumped a shell into the chamber and sighted in on the critter.

Before she could shoot she watched in horror as the coyote suddenly lunged to grab Blackie by the throat. Blackie didn't run, didn't try to get away. He stood terrorized and frozen to the spot.

She exhaled and aimed at the rear flank of the coyote. Catherine prayed. "Please Lord let me hit the coyote and not Blackie." Absolutely motionless, she gently squeezed the trigger. The sharp blast reverberated up the slope. The coyote immediately dropped Blackie and flopped away to escape the unknown attacker. One hind leg was useless as it struggled to move the short distance into the protective sagebrush on the outer edge of the meadow. Paralyzed by fear Blackie stood like a statue. Catherine drew down on the coyote's shoulders and squeezed off two more shots. Again she was conscious of the echoes rolling along the slope. The coyote flipped over once and raised its head one time trying to locate the danger that just struck him down. The grin was gone.

Blackie still didn't move. How much damage had the coyote done?

There were tears in her eyes as she prodded the surprised Jiggles across the creek. Her two bodyguards ran abreast of Jiggles until they came upon the bleeding carcass. They sniffed and growled while Catherine dismounted and carefully approached the coyote. She pumped a live shell into the chamber, just in case. The coyote's lifeless eyes were glazed over. She silently thanked Glenn for sighting in her rifle. Using the barrel of her rifle she cautiously turned the coyote over. A bloody hole appeared on the left shoulder.

Catherine didn't know whether to be happy or sad. She didn't like killing anything, but saving Blackie was paramount.

But did she save him? The lamb stood frozen to the same spot.

Quote number three came back to her. *Because they are helpless, timid and feeble, sheep easily fall prey to other animals. When they do they will often freeze instead of running for safety or crying out. Without the shepherdess, they are totally defenseless.* Catherine muttered, "How true, how true."

She knelt beside the terrified lamb. There was blood on the shoulder and throat, but no life threatening gash, no spurting stream of blood. Either the bullet saved the lamb from the coyote's deadly slashes or his growing thick wool didn't allow the coyote to get a good choke hold with its teeth. Either way was good.

Blackie's pitiful bleat stirred Catherine into action. She slipped off her Levi jacket and wrapped it around the trembling lamb. She spoke softly as she gathered Blackie in her arms and scrambled into the saddle. She laid the stricken lamb across the saddle in front of her and stroked him all the way to her wagon.

Over the Coleman camp stove she boiled water to wash the wound. Upon closer examination it didn't appear to be a deep slash, but it would be sore. Her medicine kit included some powdered sulfa, the same new anti-biotic her mother had taken in pill form. She sprinkled the powder liberally over the small wounds. She heated some canned milk, diluted it with water, and force fed the complacent lamb she held. She fondly told him. "You're a very lucky little fella. Maybe now, you'll stay closer to the flock." Little did she know how true this idle prophecy would be.

೧

"Hello, hello, anybody in there?" Catherine welcomed the voice. She yelled, "In here, Rusty."

He had ridden into the camp, dismounted and wrapped the reins around a wagon wheel. "I heard the shots, and couldn't help but worry. What happened? First, are you okay, Catherine?"

She explained all that had happened. Rusty took one long look at Blackie. "You aren't the only one with coyote trouble.

Virgil shot one back closer to the Columbia." He grinned. "Make sure the game warden knows about every coyote you kill. In case you didn't know, the government pays a bounty for coyotes." Rusty reached for the hot coffee pot, filled his cup and drawled out his verdict."You might be rich before the summer is over."

29
Tsmee-toos

The rains were a curse and a boon. The sheep huddled together in little bunches and didn't move. Catherine struggled to stay dry, but she didn't want to stay inside. The rain was inconvenient, but it kept the grass vital, green and growing. That was a major boon.

Finally the warm sun burst through the few, remaining wispy clouds. Standing atop the driver's seat she marveled at the wonder of what two days of warm rain could do. Her laughter was lost in the emptiness of the slope. A new profusion of yellow desert sunflowers had burst open as far as she could see. The Mariposa lilies, which had waited for the magic rain and sunshine, burst open in the secluded, wet spots along the creek.

According to Ricardo Urritia's little notebook, Catherine was falling behind schedule. She thought a few extra days spent here wouldn't hurt. Free feed for the sheep was one purpose of the drive. As a shepherdess that was what she was doing. She hoped Pete and her mother wouldn't get too upset about the loss of time.

Blackie became an amusing nuisance. There was no more straying. He followed her everywhere. He stayed in the camp area, slept under the wagon, and demanded extra attention with numerous head butts whenever Catherine was afoot. She substituted her name in the nursery rhyme; "Everywhere that Catherine went the lamb was sure to go." The lamb definitely gave her a character for her nightly writings.

❧

After circling the last foothill of the Saddle Mountains, Catherine made her first campsite in the very large Crab Creek coulee. The French-Canadian trappers gave the word "coulee" to the areas carved out by glaciers and further defined by flood.

While her flock grazed on the south side of Crab Creek Rusty and Virgil and their dogs drove their bands north of Crab Creek. All three bands would lazily graze in their lanes while they drifted west toward the Columbia River. The creek originated as Upper Crab Creek 163 miles to the northeast and flowed as the longest continuous creek in the state. That fact wasn't important to Catherine. A constant water supply while the three Sumertun bands grazed westerly was important.

The wide coulee, which once contained the Columbia River, did not contain the lush grassland of the Wahluke Slope. The silt and sand which made the Wahluke Slope productive had been washed out of the Crab Creek Coulee and deposited south on the slope during the Missoula floods. The remaining gravelly soil and the arid weather of the coulee was fit for the deep rooted sagebrush, greasewood, bunchgrass and the spiny hopsage, which provided a bare minimum of browse for the sheep.

The large stands of native, protein laden bunch grass could sustain the flocks, but the spring rains provided water for the grass which would be the main source of food. When the heat of late May and June arrived the livid green grass would soon fade to brown. Their pace in Crab Creek Coulee wouldn't be as leisurely as the Waluke Slope and Ricardo Urritia's journal told Catherine her assumption was correct.

&

After her afternoon inspection of her troops Blackie eagerly left the shade of the wagon and ran toward her. She had to laugh at the comical black lamb. She swung out of the saddle to the ground and greeted her new pet. If Blackie could've jumped into the wagon like Gilrakis and Malovich he would. As it was, he stayed under the wagon. Woe-be-gone bleats followed until the dogs snarled at him.

Catherine chose a campsite on the southside of Crab Creek under one of the few groves of poplar trees. Her flock would remain on the south side. The other two bands would work westward on the wider northern side. There was plenty of grazing room for the three bands as they wandered west before climbing the Royal Slope north to the Columbia Plateau rising 200 feet above the Columbia River at the Grand Coulee Dam.

The prospect of taking the sheep over the dam, the largest concrete structure in the world, was getting closer to an awesome reality. Would she get the chance? Would Hank take her place at Othello? She sighed. The answer would come tomorrow. Deep in thought she unconsciously reached down to pet Gilrakis. He raised his head to her touch. The tail thumping on the floor was a welcome sound. Those two dogs were two more reasons she wanted to stay.

&

One gravel road connected the three cattle ranches inside the coulee with the outside world. The road ran the length of the coulee and connected Othello in the east with the Columbia River in the west. Sitting on the bench at the Shepherdess wagon Catherine couldn't help noticing the lone dust trail that approached. She recognized it as a paneled delivery van before it turned off the road and followed one of the obscure trails toward the poplar grove and Catherine's wagon. She focused the binoculars on the approaching truck. A smile appeared when she read "Odets Mercantile" in large red and black block letters on the side paneling. Someone other than Hank was delivering her supplies. What did that mean?

Catherine walked out to meet the driver. The young man stepped out of the delivery van, shyly smiled and held out his hand. "Hi. I'm Tim Odets. I take it you're Catherine Sumertun?"

Catherine nodded. The young man was about her age. Tall, maybe six feet with good shoulders that tapered down to small-ish hips. His ginger, not red, hair and impish hazel eyes gave the impression of constant good humor. His narrow face featured high cheekbones. His faded Levis, an Odets shirt and dusty work shoes completed her quick, once over. She answered, "Yes, I'm Catherine. I take it you have supplies for the three bands."

"Nope, just you. I've already delivered supplies to Rusty and Virgil." He moved toward the back of the delivery van and unloaded her supplies. She issued directions where to set the boxes. Next she showed him Hank's home- made ice chest and watched him drop the block of ice into the storage unit. For a few days she would have cooled fresh produce and ice for a cold drink.

He finished unloading her supplies before he announced. "Catherine, I have two surprises ... no charge." Another grin followed that announcement. He handed her the first surprise, a bottle of ice cold Coca-Cola. "Can't beat that, can you?"

They sat down on the back steps of the wagon and enjoyed a satisfying break. His second surprise was the last two issues of the Spokane Review. In large, bold print the May seventeenth headline read, "THE UNITED KINGDOM STANDS ALONE AGAINST HITLER."

Catherine quickly read the complete story and looked up. "Out here with the sheep you forget what's going on in the rest of the world. This looks pretty grim, doesn't it?"

Tim finished his drink with one last big gulp. He burped and then agreed. "My dad thinks it will only get worse. That means America will be involved." He paused as if thinking aloud. "I hope not. If there is a war, kids my age will be in the forefront." Tim switched the subject. A mischievous smile lit up his face. "Did you happen to notice me the past few days?"

"How could I? Today is the first time I've ever seen you."

"No, it isn't. You just didn't know it."

Perplexed, Catherine told him, "Okay, stop it. Where would I have seen you?"

"Did you notice a little yellow airplane flying over you the past few days?" Tim obviously enjoyed this little game.

Her eyebrows arched. "Was that you?"

"Yep, I kept track of you and the other two bands of sheep as you came up the slope. That way your supplies were ready when you arrived. Pretty good, huh?"

Catherine nodded before she asked, "Tim, I have a favor to ask. Would you take me into Othello so I can use a telephone? There's an important call I want to make."

"Not a problem. You can use the same phone Rusty did. I'll be glad to take you in and bring you back on one condition."

Catherine's tensed at any unexpected proposition here in the middle of nowhere. She suspiciously asked, "What's the condition?"

‿

The Hank problem was put aside when Catherine complied with Tim's condition. Her first airplane ride was the condition he had set for taking her into Othello. After her call home Tim drove her to the county airport and the little, yellow Piper Cub tied down on in front of a hangar. Tim helped her get into the back seat. Tim took the pilots seat in front. Soon they were airborne flying east over the scablands of central Washington. As they approached the scablands he pushed the joy stick, the steering wheel of the Piper Cub, to the right and banked into a gentle right turn. Tim gave her a great view of the motley looking lava field called the scablands. She held onto the seat for dear life on the first turn. By the second turn her fear disappeared. Catherine also understood why the sheep were going west through the Crab Creek Coulee before they headed north over the French-man Hills. Nothing could pass through those lava scablands.

The broken lava field looked like scabs that appeared on your arm if you scraped it. The scabs would dry and lift up. The rough scab over the skin looked just like the land below. From her geology class at Western she knew this area was formed by lava flows and then torn asunder by floods which washed the soil away from the lava. She had also heard about these wonders from all the herders. Ricardo Urritia drew several sketches of these scablands in his logbook. He caught them just like they were.

⁓

It had been a good day. She went to bed thinking about the excitement of her first airplane ride. Tim was an entertaining, intelligent pilot. He could pass for a classmate. Was he right about the war in Europe expanding? According to the editorial page, he was. If so, he would join the Army Air Corps. By look-ing ahead he could do what he loved and still fight.

She turned her thoughts to Hank. He was looking ahead by going to Vet school. What would a veterinarian's place in the war be? She smiled at the grim irony of her situation. If her telephone call to her mother had the desired result, Hank might be too angry to be a problem.

Was she being too selfish or was this looking ahead? She remembered some of her mother's counsel on managing your life. Weren't she, Hank and Tim doing the same thing? Didn't managing mean working to get what you want? Did her desire to continue the trek make her selfish? She looked to it as getting what she ultimately wanted; to be an active part of the Sumertun ranch.

Tim, Hank, the plane ride, her request to her mother and the myriad of questions evolved into a restless sleep.

⁓

"Okay you two, 'Cast.'" Gilrakis and Malovich never changed. They were off and running toward the outer flanks of the flock. Their barks and unflagging energy started her flock moving farther west into the wide coulee. In the clear, cool morning air she could hear Rusty and Virgil doing the same thing. The bleating cries of three bands of sheep were a constant in the coulee. Catherine stood on her driver's bench, used her binoculars to sweep the area on the north side of the creek. She swept the area and spotted Rusty and Virgil riding among their charges. She would be doing the same thing as soon as she saddled Jiggles.

The spring grass and the flowers were the main courses for the sheep; bunch grass and the early silvery sagebrush growth were the alternatives. Crab Creek furnished the water. It should be idyllic, but unanswered questions remained.

The next day she again watched the yellow Piper Cub approach. What in the devil was Tim doing here today? He flew the plane west past her and the sheep. She watched the little yellow plane become a distant dot. When she turned to follow the dog's gaze she saw the yellow dot become a high, fixed wing Piper Cub coming toward her. The plane mesmerized Gilrakis and Malovich. They barked, and kept it up. She heard the throttle being cut back as a prelude to landing. The gliding aircraft slowed and descended toward the gravel road.

She remembered Tim had called them flaps. Catherine located them on the back edge of the wings. They slowed the plane for landing. Her hand shot to her mouth. That fool was landing on the only road in the area. She watched the plane almost hover over the gravel road and then the plane's nose flared upward. The plane settled lightly on the gravel road. Tim revved the engine enough to taxi toward her. He stopped in wide spot and cut the engine.

She rode Jiggles toward the plane. Tim pushed his dark glasses up to his forehead and stepped out from the plane. He received no welcoming smile.

"You fool, that's no smooth runway. You could get killed."

He shook his and laughed "Why do you think that? I take off and land on the runway at the Othello airport on coarser gravel. The danger here is a car on the road, or in your case some sheep on the road. That's why I went so far west. I wanted to check the traffic. The sheep weren't close to the road, so it was safe. Satisfied?"

Catherine didn't know what else to say. "Yes, I'm satisfied." She teased, "Now, why did you come out this way; to see me or just to practice landing in strange places?"

He took her outstretched hand and kissed it. Catherine was amused at the ease she accepted this prankster's kiss.

Tim bowed from the waist and gallantly replied, "Why, to see the fairest blossom in the coulee. Why else would I come?"

"Okay, you've seen the desert flower. Now why are you here?"

"I took advantage of your mother's request. Flying was the quickest way to get her message to you."

"You flew out here just to deliver a message?"

"That and to see if you wanted to go up again. I hoped you might like to fly over the Frenchman Hills and locate your routes." He gave her a little half grin. "Besides, you can see the Tsmee-toos from the air."

"Never mind the Tseemo-t...er, or whatever you said. What did my mother say?"

"She will be here tomorrow and she plans on staying overnight, maybe longer."

Catherine remembered Tim had said Rusty had also used the phone yesterday. Was his call tied to this visit?

She barely heard Tim's urgent request. "Now, what do you say to another plane ride?"

"I can't! My sheep are grazing in the coulee."

"You left them yesterday and today's flight will be shorter. You can tie your horse back at your wagon and the dogs will stay close." He squeezed her hand. "A half-hour at the most. What do you say?"

What could she say no to such an innocent plea?

They flew west past several Tsmee-Toos to Wahatis Peak. It became her landmark to turn north over the Frenchman Hills. She located several sheep trails. The Tsmee-toos of the coulee were no longer a mystery. She wondered how many stories each of them could tell her.

Her short tour ended when Tim set the plane down softly of the gravel road again. Her second flight had been just as entertaining as yesterdays. She stepped out and away from the plane holding her hair in place against the swirling propeller backwash. She doubted he ever heard her "Thank You."

Her sheep were grazing peacefully. Her dogs and Blackie stayed with the wagon. Sheep Facts kept telling the shepherd was all important, but she wasn't, at least for a half hour.

Two questions loomed large. Why did Rusty want to use the phone and what did her mother decide? Were the two related? Perhaps Tim's showing her the way through the Frenchman's Hills might be an indication.

꙳

That evening she turned to her journal and wrote, "Long ago the coulee was the connecting short cut for the Indians coming south to fish in the rapids of the Columbia. Tsmee-too was the name the Indian tribes gave to the mesa and buttes that dotted the Crab Creek Coulee. They used the basalt walls of the Tsmee-toos for protection from attack. They used ladders to get to the top of the Tsmee-too and pulled the ladders up after them. The stark outlines of large, two to five story rocks were believed to be magic. In reality the Missoula floods had ripped huge chunks of the lava walls away from the northern rim and rolled them out into the flat bottom of the coulee. Other buttes were formed by the rampaging waters washing away every bit of earth from around the existing basalt formation. One butte was said to be several acres on top. Another was balanced like an inverted cone that managed two stories of height. The Tsmee-toos were located on the north side of Crab Creek, close to the huge lava cliffs that were tossed about like pebbles by the floods.

"From the air I counted at least twenty five of these ripped-off chunks of lava called Tsmee-too, and probably missed that many more. I imagined the glaciers coming south from Canada, damming the Columbia River and raising the level of river high enough for the river to flow south in a new bed. The river was large and it follows logic that it would carve valleys flowing through this new area of central Washington. Tim took a few extra minutes to follow this flow from the air. For the first time I could follow the old Columbia River bed through the Crab Creek Coulee.

"I can't imagine the size of the wall of water that roared west from the Missoula Glacier Lake floods. The coulee was inundated with a 400 foot wall of water. The rampaging water formed the final extent of all the coulees. When we get over the Frenchman Hills the sheep and I will see the greatest coulee of them all, the Grand Coulee. I still can't imagine what it must have been like."

She still looked forward to taking the sheep across the Columbia River atop the Grand Coulee Dam. Catherine reread her entry. It took her thirty minutes to edit and rewrite. To make this a story might be a lot harder than she thought.

Tomorrow her mother would be here. What direction would her life take then?

30
A New Skill

From the start being the shepherdess had exceeded her every expectation. The responsibility of the large band of sheep had been new and scary, but the challenge had been fulfilling. When she came home to care for her ailing mother she had no idea fate would give her this chance. Now she didn't want to give it up. Tears would follow the decision, whether it was giddy ecstasy or bitter disappointment.

After her morning ride among her flock relief came again from the air. Tim ran his customary landing pattern and settled softly onto the road. Catherine didn't hesitate to accept his late morning invitation to fly.

"You have to wait for a while." He went back the plane before the puzzled Catherine could ask any questions. He returned with a package of breakfast sausages. "Your mother wanted me to deliver these. She also said she would deliver Rusty and Virgil for a cook-out tomorrow. With a twinkle in his eye he explained, "I plan on delivering steaks tomorrow. That way the meat will still be fresh and ready for grilling." Before Catherine could protest or ask why she wanted five steaks he revealed his plan. "I know now you have plenty of time for a flight." His eyes sparkled. "There is something special to do"

They flew over the other two sheep camps with Tim in the front seat where he could see the instrument panel and Catherine in the student's seat. Tim wangled the wings at each camp and Catherine waved. She chuckled when the always happy Rusty waved back. Again she wondered why he used the phone. She was drawn back to reality as they flew west over Crab Creek. Tim again pointed out the Tsmee-toos that marked the ideal routes Rusty and Virgil should use to leave the coulee.

Catherine absorbed all this, but as they turned north she asked, "What is the surprise you said you had for me?"

Tim teased her. "I didn't say surprise. I said 'something special'."

Catherine challenged him. "Okay, what is it?"

"See that stick that is between your legs?"

"Yes."

"Gently hold it and follow where it takes you."

Catherine remained skeptical but obeyed. Tim pushed the stick to the left and the plane banked to the left. Astonished, she felt her hands move left as the plane banked to the left. When the plane leveled off her hands followed the stick back to the middle. She felt elation and some comprehension at what Tim was doing.

For a half-hour Tim coaxed her through level flight, going up or down and banking using the rudder pedal in co-ordination with the joy stick. During all of this he was always gentle and low key. She actually flew the plane on a straight and level ride and made one gentle right hand turn flying back toward camp.

She listened and allowed her hands to follow the "stick" while Tim brought the plane back to camp and flared the little Piper Cub to drop onto the road. He left the motor idling, while his student hopped out. His voice rose above the noise of the engine.

"That's it, Catherine, your first flying lesson. You did very well." A mischievous tone of voice followed. "Care to do it again?"

"Yes, if you can. That was wonderful!"

Tim's grin split his face. "You have few more days before you head over Frenchman Hills. We can do more." He waved to her and yelled "See you tomorrow."

Catherine spent the rest of the afternoon among her charges. Almost by instinct she turned eastward to see the dust trail on the gravel road from Othello. She quietly turned Jiggles toward the sheep wagon. Would it be shepherdess or shepherd at day's end?

Catherine arrived at the camp first and waited for her mother. Sarah seemed to be in control this time. There was no grappling with each other to keep from falling; only a gentle hug and a welcoming smile. Catherine spoke first. "It's good to see you. How was the trip?"

"It was an easy day, and I enjoyed the drive, even if it's dusty. This part of Washington could certainly improve their roads. It's good to see you again, little one." She thought about tomorrow's steak fry. "Did Odets deliver the steaks and sausage I ordered?"

"Yes, he flew the sausages out. Odets wanted the steaks perfect so they'll deliver them tomorrow."

Her mother nodded.

Catherine reached down to casually scratch Blackie's head, before he butted her for attention. "No, Blackie, not now! Now go back to the wagon." She affectionately patted the lamb, and looked at Gilrakis. He understood. With a few barks he deftly moved the bleating lamb back under the wagon.

"What was that all about?" Sarah listened appreciatively as her daughter told how Blackie became her shadow. She finished, "Blackie is a nuisance sometimes, but he doesn't stray any more." She remembered the stray shots at a coyote at Horn Rapids. "Give Glenn my thanks for sighting in that rifle. He saved Blackie's life." She coyly added, "He does still stop by, doesn't he?"

"Funny you should ask. He stopped at the ranch three days ago, but only as a friend. That's it." She eyed her suspicious daughter. "Don't worry, nothing is happening, but that's not important. What's important is the sheep are in good hands." She laughed and scanned the coulee around her. "I've never been through this area with the sheep. It looks interesting, so maybe I'll drive home along Crab Creek and cross the river at Vernita.

"What a great idea. You'll get to see how big the coulee really is."

Both women shunned diplomacy as a way to solve problems. The time for small talk passed. Both of them knew it. Who would broach the subject first? Catherine walked with feigned nonchalance to the ice chest, took out two Cokes and handed one to her mother.

"Well?"

"Well what?" Sarah took a long drink of her cold Coke, before she broke the spell. "You don't have to worry, Catherine. You're doing a great job. That's what I came up to tell you. The first thing I saw when I arrived was that lovable lamb you saved. That just confirmed what I had decided. That was one more example you care. I'm very proud of you, Catherine. You're growing each time I see you."

A small tear fell before Catherine dabbed it away with a tissue. She embraced her mother and held her tight. "Thank you. I really, really wanted to keep on going. What a great adventure this has been." She straightened, stepped away and asked the question that had been on her mind for the past few days. "How did Hank take the news? What did he say when you told him?"

"He was disappointed, but he didn't say anything. I left an option of relieving Rusty and Virgil from time to time. Later in the summer he's more important at the ranch." With a wry smile she admitted, "I bribed him with a raise that should help when he goes to school this fall. I believe he understands the situation. Plus, Alex is old enough to work and knows the ranch so I have flexibility."

Sarah knew this was not the concern her daughter felt. "Don't worry little one, he will not stop liking you" Some of her underlying steel emerged. "If he can't accept this, he's not the one for you."

Catherine wistfully replied, "Managing your life isn't always easy, is it?"

"It certainly isn't. Life is making your options work for you. That takes discipline. You wanted this and you've made it work. Can you keep it up?" Sarah looked plaintively at the vastness of the surrounding coulee and waited.

She heard her reward. "Yes, Mother, I can and I want to." "I do have another question, Mother. What did Rusty say when he phoned you?"

"I asked him what he thought about you continuing on as the "Shepherdess?"

"And?"

"Remember your eighth birthday and the anger that followed?"

Catherine nodded.

"It was then I realized the ranch was my responsibility. I couldn't use Burke's death as an excuse any longer. Do you remember that time?"

Catherine's smile became a loud laugh. "How could I forget? Grandpa Carter was very glad to see you back again. That was the start of 'The Queen of the Sumertun Ranch'."

Sarah lifted the cold Coca-Cola bottle to her lips and drained the last three swallows.

"Catherine, you have to know I made this decision based on what I thought was good for the ranch. Being my daughter didn't hurt, but getting the sheep to the railhead is too important to just give it to you." She admitted, "Yes, I talked to Rusty. I also talked to Pete, but most of all I observed. I made the decision based on what I thought was best for the ranch." Her eyes locked onto Catherine's. "If I hadn't thought you were best for the job, Hank would be here today."

Catherine felt like her knees would buckle. She couldn't think of an endorsement better than that.

31
A New Development

Catherine viewed the world through rose colored glasses. Her morning bareback ride on Thunder was rougher than usual, but that was a small inconvenience. She looked across the flock and smiled as her mother on Jiggles enjoyed the morning inspection. Her enthusiasm for life was never far from the surface. She coped with the good and the bad in the same manner. She just bowed her neck, made her decision and took them in stride. Catherine wondered if she could ever achieve that same confident poise.

That her mother wanted her to continue on the trek had filled her soul with elation. There may have been some sentimentality, but when she said the selection was good for the ranch, well, nothing could have been better. Catherine belonged and that was that. Now she had to live up to that billing

~

The yellow Piper Cub came in from the west. This was becoming a normal, but welcome sight. Amused, Catherine observed her mother watch the plane approach.

Wide-eyed surprise spread across her mother's face. "That damn fool is going to land on the road!" The engine was cut to glide speed. The plane flared up and gently set down on the road. Sarah gasped, "I was right. Why is he landing here?" She waited for a reply from her daughter. None came. She turned to Catherine and saw the light smile of beginning laughter. "You know something you're not telling me." She gave her daughter a playful poke in the ribs. "Tell me. Why is that plane landing here?"

"You'll see soon enough Mother."

Tim Odets taxied the plane to the wide clearing of the road and cut the engine. He stepped out of the yellow plane, reached in and pulled out a flat box. He waved to Catherine, grinned and ambled with the package toward the two women.

Catherine waved back.

Sarah poked her daughter again and probed, "Who is that, and why is he flying here?"

"Oh, that's Tim Odets, you know, from Odets Mercantile. He's delivering your steaks for the evening cook-out. He wanted them kept chilled. Even in an icebox, meat has a tendency to spoil quickly in any heat. He delivered the sausages yesterday." She laced her arm confidentially with her mother's, "They keep better. Now, let me introduce you to Tim."

Sarah whispered so only her daughter could hear, "That's a handsome young man." Her eyes rolled upward in mock exasperation. "Are you telling me everything? Is the mouse playing while the cat's away? Tell me, is anything going on?"

"Of course not! How can you possibly think that?"

"That's what you thought when you saw Glenn with me."

As one they laughed, and watched Tim approach.

⁓

Tim set the box of steaks down, slyly grinned before taking advantage of the situation. He put his arms around Catherine and hugged her. She elbowed him in the ribs before she made the introduction. "Tim, this is my mother, Sarah Turnoch." After the introduction Tim put the steaks in the ice box. He returned and commented, "Sarah, it must be a big party tonight. Five steaks and I've counted four people who will be here. I know Virgil, Rusty and Catherine are the herders...and Sarah makes four. Am I right?"

Tim continued his musings. "That leaves one for someone else." He casually checked the two smiling women. "Am I right Catherine?"

Sarah smiled. Catherine nodded.

"Why would you include me?"

"Ooh, you know darn well why I did."

She found her mother watching the charade. "It was to be surprise, but Tim has forced me to tell. He's offered to take you up in his plane to show you the Tsmee-too."

"The Tsmee-too," She exclaimed. "What is that?"

"That's also what I asked him. He'll tell you while he shows you the same view of the coulee he did me."

৵

Forty-five minutes later Tim sat the little Piper Cub down on the road like a feather.

He taxied to the clearing and cut the engine. Smiling, Catherine trotted to the plane to help her mother out. "Well, how did you like your surprise?" She laughingly asked, "Did you learn about the Tsmee-too?"

A wry smile appeared. "Yes, Catherine I learned Tsmee-toos were once lava buttes that had been torn loose and shaped by the flood waters, and that Indians spirits are connected to them. Tim is good guide. Seeing the coulee from the air certainly gives you a different view. It's interesting how clearly you can see the routes all three bands will take when they leave the Crab Creek Coulee, but most of the time I stared at what nature had carved out. The sheep have traveled this route for years, but the sheer size of this coulee is surprising."

They thanked Tim for the plane ride and stepped back as the motor started again. Catherine heard her mother say, "Don't forget the steaks are thrown on at 6:30." The Piper Cub taxied onto the road and soon disappeared on its way to Othello.

"So Mother, you invited Tim to a steak barbecue tonight? You didn't even know him until today. "

"Yes. Not only that, but I told him to meet us at the Coulee City airport for a view of the dam and the surrounding area. That should be fascinating." She paused, but no reaction came. "By the way, Tim told me that you have been flying the airplane some. True?"

"Yes. That was a big surprise, but it's fun and not as hard as I thought it would be."

"Are you thinking of learning."

"Yes, but Tim isn't certified to instruct. I can learn from him, but I can't take-off and land. I do what he can correct while we are in the air. He's a nut with a purpose." She noticed her mother's questioning look.

"Tim brought out a couple of papers when he delivered the supplies. I saw the big headline and read the story about the war in Europe. He is learning to fly so he can enlist in the Army Air Corps. He thinks America will be drawn into the war against Germany. I'm ashamed to admit that I don't really understand what is going on. Do you think we'll be drawn into the war? It seems so far away."

"I can understand that. You're a long way from everyday events. It's easy to stay in your own little world of sheep. That's your full-time job. I hear about Europe every day on the radio and read about it in the paper." She grew very serious. "I think about Alex. He'll be 18 in a couple of years, and that scares me to death."

"That also means Hank and even Tim, doesn't it?"

A far away look crossed Sarah's face as she added, "And maybe you."

Catherine quickly turned her attention to her afternoon flight and evening cook-out. Those were much cheerier prospects.

32
Reconnaissance Flight

The steady drone of the engine reassured Catherine. She tapped her instructor on the shoulder. "It's a different world up here Tim. I can see why you like to fly. How long have you been flying?"

"Two years. My father wouldn't pay for my lessons until I graduated from high school. After I got my license I took him up. Now he's worse that I am. In this arid country the population is spread out, so he looks forward to delivering merchandise to the outlying ranches. He thinks it's a wonderful excuse to fly."

Tim pointed to a small ranch in the coulee. The peeled, pole corrals reflected the bright sunlight. The old frame ranch house sparkled in its fresh coat of white paint. An open shed served as a garage for a pickup. A barn was under construction. A small herd of cattle browsed on the slope that led down to Crab Creek.

He spoke loudly over the drone of the engine. "According to my calculations your three bands of sheep should reach here in two or three days. Two of them will be north of the creek. Right?'

Catherine nodded. She wondered where this was going.

He banked the plane right over the corrals again. She could clearly see everything.

"Notice anything unusual?"

She looked again. "Not really." Then she took another look. A single worker was building a fence from the corrals down the slope toward Crab Creek. Catherine loudly exclaimed, "He's building a fence! It's right where the sheep will go. He can't do this! This is open range."

Tim circled high above the ranch. The small herd seemed content. Like the sheep they would gravitate to good grass and water. That meant cattle and sheep would collide.

Tim told her. "I noticed it earlier with your mother, but didn't say anything. It seemed wise to show you and see if I was right. It looks like the fencer is through for the day, but the fence is further along than it was when your mother flew over. If the rancher's intent is to stop your sheep from grazing through here, he'll probably get that fence completed before your sheep get there. Knowing gives you some time to do something."

He told her to take the controls, make a big right hand turn and follow Crab Creek west. "I've got something else to show you."

Flying took all of Catherine's attention, until she heard Tim say, "Drop down to 1,000 feet and tell me what you see."

She got a good look at the largest Tsmee-too in the coulee. The huge, oval shaped butte had been left standing after the Missoula floods subsided. Most of the butte was defined by sheer lava walls, but the west end had been torn apart by the swirling vortex of angry eddies that formed when the rampaging waters from the Missoula flood from each side met. This left a ramp of sand, gravel and rock to the grassy top.

Tim explained, "The Indians used this as a fort. They could quickly get to the top and have only a small area to defend. If you look close enough you'll notice old fence posts. There used to be a gate there. In 1905 the U.S. Cavalry rounded up the wild horses of the coulee. They would gather small groups and drive them to the top and shut the gate while they rounded up others. There is about ten acres of bunch grass on top, a rare artesian spring, and the sides are vertical. It was perfect. Nothing was going to escape. That's how Pen Butte got its name." Catherine flew around the lava-walled Tsmee-too three times before heading home.

Crab Creek Coulee was an unexpected, pleasant surprise, but maybe one with problems.

⤳

She had one immediate problem to solve and she needed to think. The solitary sentinel on horseback watched her from the north side of the creek. From Tim's description the man had to be Ernst Ostlermann.

According to Tim, he had worked construction on the Grand Coulee Dam. He had toiled with a purpose, saved his money and purchased the small deserted ranch lying on the top bench of the Crab Creek Coulee. From the air they had seen him building the fence.

Now he sat astride a scruffy looking, deep-brown, barrel-chested horse guarding the area between his deeded land and the creek. Catherine waved as she rode west past him on the way to the known crossing. He didn't wave back.

She eased Jiggles down the trail through the high earthen walls and forded the creek, and then rode up the less arduous trail to the north side. Catherine rode east past some grazing cattle toward the house and the partially completed fence. She drew a deep breath as she approached the menacing, stern faced Ostlermann sitting in the saddle. It didn't help when he pumped a shell into his rifle. Her stomach flip-flopped at this implied threat. She mumbled a quick prayer for a peaceful solution.

⤳

The man glared at the approaching woman, who would want only one thing, the passage for her sheep on the north side of the creek. The story of sheep destroying the range was as old as the hills. They wouldn't do that to this range. His 320 acre farm and small herd of thirty-five white-face cattle represented five years of hard labor on the Grand Coulee Dam.

Ernst Ostlermann had been desperate and out of work when he rode the rails from Pittsburgh west to Washington hoping for one of the construction jobs the Grand Coulee promised. He had been lucky. He had poured concrete in freezing temperatures, hammered nails in 100 degree weather and in the rain. He had lived in the lonely Spartan atmosphere of a barracks, but he never missed a day of work, and he saved his money.

Ranching here in the arid past had been a dire occupation. Ernst was looking to the future. His saved money allowed him to bargin for the deserted farm. Cash was a powerful incentive. At last he had something of his own, and he was determined to make sure his cherished dream survived until the promised irrigation from the Grand Coulee Dam reached his land.

In the past bands sheep had caused no problems when they had come through the coulee, but this year was different. He had cattle to feed. No wisp of a girl, who probably had no authority, was going to talk him out it. The rancher sat still as stone and waited.

⁓

The man was impressive. Even in the saddle Catherine guessed he was over six foot and probably over 200 pounds of hard muscle. His broad-rimmed hat covered his dark eyes and unshaven face. Nothing suggested a willingness to listen and cooperate. Catherine steeled herself. "Good morning, sir. Are you Mr. Ernst Ostlermann?"

There was no movement. "I am."

"Mr. Ostlermann, my name is Catherine Sumertun, and I have two bands of sheep coming this way on the north side of the creek. They need to keep on moving on the northside. As you probably already know, there is not a good crossing up stream for three miles. That's two days of pushing the sheep just to get them back to the crossing and back to here. They need to keep going, but your fence is in the way. The quicker we get through here the sooner we'll be out of your hair."

She saw his broad shoulders straighten. Was this stubbornness?

She heard his gruff voice. "I know what you want." He pointed to his herd. "I have thirty-five young steers and heifers that need grass." He pointed the rifle toward the farm house, the dry land wheat field and the unfinished barn. "This area is next to my place and those cattle will stay in the coulee when it's fenced. You'll just have to go around." Ernst laid the rifle across the saddle and leered at Catherine. "I'll shoot any sheep that gets past this fence."

Catherine gathered her wits. She could feel the nervousness. Did it show? This was not going to be easy. Could she be a strong shepherdess? She cringed at the thought of having to use her mother. Her resolve strengthened. "I appreciate your wanting to feed your cattle. I'm sure you appreciate that my three bands also have to be fed. The two bands on the north side of the creek will be here in two days, maybe sooner. We do not plan to stay here and overgraze the area."

She directed her question to him. "That's what you're worried about, isn't it?"

For the first time she noticed some hesitation.

Catherine decided to keep on the offensive. "Sumertun sheep have been coming through here for years. Have you seen any destruction of the range?"

"No, but I intend to make sure there isn't any." His fierce stare was frightening.

Catherine pondered this threat. There had to be a way out of any direct confrontation. She followed his glare to the east. Her heart skipped a beat. Two wisps of dust followed the approaching horsemen. That had to be Rusty and Virgil.

She exhaled. This is great. Two hostile sheepherders weren't what she needed!

She made her decision. "Look, Mr. Ostlermann, there has to be a way out of this problem."

"There is. Take your sheep back up stream and cross to the south side of Crab Creek and go past here on the south side."

She remembered her mother's talking to tight lipped, demanding Glenn Simons on the grade down to Prentiss. In a far more aggressive manner than she felt Catherine leaned closer. She willed herself to speak quietly. "You do understand this is open range and you're not allowed to fence it, don't you?"

He sat quietly in the saddle, but said nothing.

Was nothing some sort of hesitation? Maybe some understanding of what I said?

With the same quiet intense voice she informed him, "You're breaking the law by threatening me with a gun, and you'll be doing it again if you shoot any of my sheep." She saw a tiny break in Ostlermann's steely determination. She decided to push on, "That means you'll have to pay for each killed animal or any damage you have caused. Going to court is not an escape. Too many lawsuits have set precedence in this matter".

She pressed on in a confident manner she didn't feel. "Mr. Ostlermann, if you're like us money is scarce, and you don't want to waste it."

Ernst automatically nodded.

Good, he understood money might be involved.

⌖

Any further talking stopped when her two herders arrived. Rusty and Virgil swung aggressively swung from their saddles and approached. They did not seem happy to be there. Rusty looked at Ernst and back to Catherine. "Any trouble here, Boss Lady?"

"Boss Lady?" Ernst could hardly believe his ears. How could this young thing be the "Boss Lady" of two men and three bands of sheep? She couldn't be more than 21, if that. He did some quick arithmetic. Three bands meant she owned or was in charge of 4, 500 sheep. That meant money, and money meant power. He reluctantly took a serious, objective look at this young woman, who was not scared by the grim persona he had forced upon her. He faltered. She did seem to be dealing from some kind of strength. Ernst leaned forward in his saddle.

That body language encouraged Catherine to remain focused on the problem. "If the sheep come through here as the law says they're allowed to, what is your biggest problem?"

She patiently waited while Ostlermann thought it over. He replied, "Driving my cattle back to the corrals and having to feed and supply water for them while your sheep graze slowly west. That's another reason I can't let you go through. I would have to bring the herd to the creek for water once a day." His sarcastic voice rang out. "I can't hire two cowboys to move my herd like you do—and I don't have the manpower or money to spend a whole day separating your sheep and my cattle. Law or no law you stay on your side of the creek—that's it."

Catherine very sweetly informed him, "Within a day I'll have the Sheriff out here to make sure the law of the open range is followed. Then I'll have an attorney serve papers for financial damages." She looked the rancher right in the eye and sternly warned him. "Don't think for a minute I won't do it." She patiently waited and watched Ostlermann for any sign.

The normally quiet Virgil surprised everyone. "Mr. Ostlermann, the Boss Lady means it." He beamed a dry, humorless grin at the uneasy rancher. "If you think she's tough you ought to see her mother. 'Like mother, like daughter.'"

For the first time Ernst's grim smile disappeared and he appeared thoughtful.

෴

The idea literally came to her from out of the blue. "If we can keep the sheep and cattle separated, so that it doesn't cost you any money for hired help, will you open your fence and let the two bands pass?"

He rubbed his chin thoughtfully.

Great! He actually seemed to be considering this. Catherine outlined her plan. She recapped her offer. "No cost to you, your herd is protected and no more fencing will be needed, and there will be no need for the sheriff." She appealed to him, "Okay"

"And if I don't?"

"Like I said, the sheriff will be here as soon as possible to enforce the law."

Catherine waited until Ernst quietly nodded.

He listened to her plan with amazement.

∽

It took the better part of day for her, Ernst, Rusty, and Virgil to drive the thirty-five steers and heifers up the slope to the top of the "The Pen" Tsmee-too. Ten acres of good grass on top and water from the artesian spring took care of every problem. At the top Ernst braced the old gateposts and strung a rope across the ramp. He was absolutely stunned that he had relented so easily and how happy he was that he did.

Catherine wore the happy smile of one who had solved a difficult problem as she rode back to her charges.

Ostlermann casually asked Rusty on the short ride back to the ranch house. "Would she have really called the sheriff, if I hadn't let her sheep pass?"

With a straight face he answered. "She would have. It's like Virgil said. 'If you think she's tough, you should see her mother. Between the two, you wouldn't have a chance.'" He leaned over and confidently confided to the troubled cowman. "This summer with the sheep is her first real responsibility. She gave herself the title of 'The Shepherdess'. I believe she deserves the title 'Boss Lady' even more. What do you think, Virgil?"

Virgil nodded

Subdued, Ernst Ostlermann went to the ranch house with a lot to think about.

Three days later the last of the sheep passed "the Pen."

Ostlermann's small herd was driven down the ramp from their Tsmee-too and eastward toward their open rangeland.

The next evening Ernst was their guest at the grilled steak cook-out. Tim flew in with the steaks, cold beer and the sheriff came from Othello. In a much friendlier atmosphere the sheriff explained the open range laws to Ernst.

Ernst was stubborn, not stupid. He gracefully agreed with Rusty's observation. He stood no chance with the captivating Catherine. He lifted his cold beer and promised, "Here's to next year. I promise not to be any trouble. I'm looking forward to seeing all of you again." He set one condition. "Next year I furnish the steaks."

33
Wahatis Peak-Dry Falls

C atherine guessed the height of the Tsmee-too to be about 100 feet. The top had been eroded into a cone-shaped hat sitting on a layer of lava, which was the brim. It marked the turning point north for the three bands of sheep. Catherine pushed her band two miles past the Wahatis Peak before turning north. Rusty turned north at the Wahatis Peak and Virgil two miles east of the odd looking Tsmee-too.

Life settled into routine once past the Wahatis Peak. They passed over Frenchman Hills and grazed up the long, gentle slope toward the higher, flatter Columbia Plateau. The morning routine seldom varied. It started with the dogs eagerly casting scattered sheep into a loosely organized band moving northeast toward Ephrata. In the morning and evening she was especially aware of coyotes hunting any sheep that strayed. She shot at any coyote that wandered within the rifle range. They had an uncanny knack of knowing how far was safe.

Every two or three days she rode east to visit Rusty and Virgil and co-ordinate their progress.

The small creeks of Frenchman Hills ran full, so water was no problem. Mornings were cool, but the days were turning warmer. The vigorous grass stayed green. Prolific Desert Daisies sported white and yellow blooms on short stems wherever any moisture accumulated. The purple Lupine blooms were fading away. The ever present sagebrush would soon sprout its silvery pods of seeds. Catherine reveled in the routine and the occasional fish fry with Rusty and Virgil.

❦

The sheep moved contentedly northeast toward Ephrata. The mild days of late May held. Thunder and Lightning pulled her wagon ahead of the grazing flock toward a small rise and a campsite that overlooked the area. She urged her team past a wind- break of eight skeletal poplar trees into a deserted farm yard. Several elm trees grew on the other side of the ramshackle farmhouse. The trees were probably planted by a homesteader, who long ago had called it quits. A small, cluttered ditch once carried water from the spring to livestock, the farmhouse, and even a garden. What water got through the eroded ditch banks and the weed gauntlet now danced merrily downhill until it joined a meandering creek that ran around the base of the last foothill to join Crab Creek.

The country road from Ephrata wound its way close to the area before disappearing as a thin line east into desert land. This land would be irrigated when the Grand Coulee Project was finished. She selected a campsite on the outskirts of the former farmyard. The shade and the water would serve her well, while she waited for her flock to graze past her. The campsite was like all the X marks she had found in Ricardo's notebook: perfect.

Someone had loved roses. Several beautiful rose bushes had once adorned the homestead. They survived summer heat and winter cold until they were deserted. Then the vivid colors of cultivated roses had turned into muted yellow and orange wild roses.

The entwined, thorny, smaller faced wild roses were still beautiful. They probably survived because the old ditch seeped enough spring water to them, some poplars and three elms. Bees called a hollow in the branch of one elm home. Catherine watched the energetic colony work in the flowers. Catherine laughed. "Everyone needs a little honey."

Someone had labored mightily to bring a little beauty to this arid plateau home a zillion miles from nowhere. Catherine tried to imagine the battle some pioneer woman fought to keep some beauty in her life. If she saw how her rose bushes had mutated into wild patches of thorns and smaller blooms would she still be happy? Probably. After all she had tried and she left something beautiful behind. Catherine marveled at the human spirit and its effort to make life better in the most unlikely of places.

Catherine couldn't resist a few roses for a bouquet. She reached through the thorns to cut a few. Their home would be an old tin can full of water inside her wagon. She laughed at the irony of beautiful roses in a tin can. Nobody said life out here would be filled with refinement. Satisfied with her new camp, she rode Jiggles back toward the flock.

∾

Back in camp after her afternoon inspection Catherine staked out her horses amidst good grass and water. She filled her water bags from the spring before preparing a sandwich of cheese and fried bacon. She poked around for something else to complete her lunch. Her storage box contained one skinny carrot and a few dried apricots her mother had left. She gnawed on these and enjoyed the northwest view.

∾

The small, bustling town of Ephrata sat on the edge of a rosy future. It nestled in among the last of the tapering foothills of the Wenatchee and Badger Mountains. The foothills provided the Indian tribes with hunting, fishing and shelter. The mountains offered lumber for the current population. Thanks to the construction of the Grand Coulee Dam the real future lay in irrigating the arid, but fertile land Catherine crossed.

The entire Columbia Plateau sloped slightly from northeast to southwest all the way to the Columbia River Gorge. This peculiar fact made gravity flow irrigation possible for large areas. Billy Clapp, a local attorney, had pushed long and hard for the proposed dam site on the Columbia River at the head of the Grand Coulee. When the papers were signed and construction started in 1933 Billy Clapp became a celebrity. Soon the town and the region would benefit by his tireless efforts. Irrigation was the future. The Reclamation Act of 1902 was alive and well.

34
Sarah

Sarah rolled over in bed, away from the penetrating morning sunlight. She pulled the blankets up close to her and snuggled deep into the comforting warmth. Her eyes focused on the gold framed picture she had put back on the wall. She saw a lanky, handsome man standing beside his happy bride. She sighed, "Darn it, Burke, why did you have to die? You made life so good." She sat up and hugged her pillow. She studied the portrait and the young-eager-for-life bride, who stood proudly beside her new husband.

She pulled a smaller framed wedding picture from her dresser drawer. She studied the wedding photograph with a critical eye. Corwin was handsome enough. He was very thin when he was hired, but by the time they married he had filled out thanks to steady work and food. Sarah had seen to it he dressed a lot better. His nondescript brown hair, medium height and a fairly rugged looking jaw caused no problem. What had she missed?

She checked both photos again. Burke looked straight into the camera. Corwin was looking off to the side. Of course! Those damn eyes had fooled her. There was no strength there. She remembered the wishy-washy look when he came looking for a job. That was it. He was a fair looking man, but no confidence came through the eyes. Why did she think she could change him? Did it get that lonely here in the middle of nowhere? It must have.

She flopped back on the bed and stared at the ceiling. "Damn it!" Her life lacked any oomph, any pizzaz. She absent-mindedly patted the other side of the bed. There was no one there and hadn't been since Corwin left. Actually he wasn't a loss, but he did leave a vacuum. She sighed deeply at her situation. Life could not exist in a vacuum.

She thought of Catherine and the loneliness of the trek. The irony of it hung in the air; like mother, like daughter. She smiled at her thoughts. There was a lot to be said for her having the strength to resist temptation and wait for the right moment. Sarah was grateful that her daughter possessed the strength to do it. Whether this strength would bring happiness was the unanswered question.

Her telephone ring, one long and one short on the party line of six, interrupted. She rose from the bed to answer the telephone. Everyone knew whose ring it was. How many would quietly lift the receiver to listen? She lifted the receiver from its hook. "Hello."

"Hello, Mrs. Turnoch. This is Tim Odets. I delivered your supplies at Othello."

She raised her voice. "Oh yes, Tim, of course, I remember." She hesitated a moment. Why did long distance telephone calls always scare her? "Is everything all right?"

"There is no need to worry, Mrs. Turnoch, everything's fine. Your daughter wanted me to inform you when she camped close to Ephrata." There was a short pause. "Catherine wanted to make sure you called the Warburton IGA store about the supplies."

"I've done that, Tim. Will I see you at Ephrata?"

"If you want to."

"I do, and thanks for calling."

"Good. I'll see you in two days." He didn't hang up, but reluctantly spoke, "Sarah."

"What is it, Tim?"

"You'll need directions to find Catherine. I drew a map and left it at Warburton's. It will be good to see you again. Maybe you'll want to fly again."

Sarah smiled. That young man was taking care of her. That means Catherine will be happy. *And to think I worried about her.*

She hummed a familiar tune as she put the receiver back on its hook. She couldn't help but smile. Tim understood party lines. The call said a lot, but it didn't give much to the gossips who listened. Tim would fly to Ephrata from Othello in two days and she knew a plane ride would follow. Nothing had been said about Catherine flying. That would be too personal, but Tim had been with her yesterday. Fresh supplies meant fresh meat and a cook-out. That would please Rusty and Virgil.

It had been a great telephone call.

She playfully tossed her blankets into place, rolled her pillows into the head of the bed and pulled the multi-colored bedspread over them. From there she headed for the shower. Streams of hot water and foamy, soap suds restored Sarah's spirits even more. The doldrums faded away as she shampooed her short, summer-cut hair. She briskly dried her body with the beach–sized towel. The show tune escaped again from her lips. A different Sarah emerged from the bathroom. Tomorrow she would drive to Ephrata see her daughter and maybe get another lesson from Tim.

༄

The drone of an approaching plane interrupted Catherine's afternoon. It was a sound she knew. She looked to the east and scanned the sky. Sure enough, the familiar Piper Cub appeared. The plane approached and then circled lower and lower until

Catherine could make out the waving arm. She waved back, and then watched Tim fly toward Ephrata.

That answered one question. Hank wouldn't deliver the supplies, but how would Tim get there? An hour later the trailing dust answered her question. The pickup left the road and followed the faint wagon trail through the sagebrush to the campsite. Smiling, Tim popped out and warmly greeted her. "I told you I would find you."

Catherine knew his greeting would be enthusiastic, maybe too enthusiastic. She was in no position to confuse him. Nice and friendly with no embarrassment was the way to go. She did not move toward him as she cheerfully greeted him, "Hi Tim. Imagine seeing you again."

Tim reached into the front seat and pulled out an ice chest. "It's been a while since you left the Crab Creek Coulee. By now, you probably would like an ice cold pop." He opened the ice chest, pulled out a bottle and handed it to her.

Catherine accepted the bottle covered with sparkling cold beads of ice and water. She rubbed it against her forehead and cheek. The chill refreshed her almost as much as the first long sip followed by the usual satisfied burp. She touched her bottle to his, heard the characteristic clink and toasted him. "You not only fly like an angel, Tim, you are one."

Tim laughed and reached out to Catherine. He put one arm around her shoulder and squeezed. "And you look like an angel."

Catherine thought the relationship was just where it should be.

༄

Their afternoon flight was awesome. Once Tim had the plane in the air Catherine took to flying again like she had never left. She followed his direction and banked the yellow plane north and flew over the east side of the Lower Grand Coulee.

A succession of five lakes lay on her left; each formed by the undercutting action of the great floods. They sent their shimmering reflection skyward. The lakes were surrounded by good grass and protective timber. On her right side lay the flatter land of the plateau. Sheer lava cliffs and a few breaks formed the definition between the lower coulee and the flatter eastern plateau.

As they approached the storied Dry Falls. Catherine heard Tim above the engine noise. "Circle back over Dry Falls and then look east to the plateau on the way back. You should be able to see the trails of the past and the route you want your sheep to go."

Catherine studied the arid plateau. It was true. She could see the various trails and the singular dirt road that led east to several isolated ranches and disappeared as a tiny thread in the east. Tim broke into her silent observations. "Take the plane up to 5,000 feet. It's easy. Just gently pull back on the stick and give it more power."

Catherine felt the exhilaration of power as she climbed. She concentrated on flying until the altimeter read 5,000 feet and she leveled off. Pleased with herself she eased the throttle back to normal. She turned back to Tim and asked, "Now what?"

He calmly answered, "This is about the safest plane there is to fly. It literally can almost fly itself, but you must be able to handle emergencies when they arise. Always be aware of the ground below and notice any place you could land in case of emergency. Always be thinking ahead, just in case. Now do what I tell you and don't be afraid."

A small shiver ran up Catherine's back. What was he planning to do?

He told her, "Ease off the throttle so your air speed decreases. When it reaches the area marked on the dial gently pull back on the stick so you don't lose altitude too fast.

"Are you nuts?"

"Just do it." He confidently chuckled, "If it makes you feel any better look out and find a likely looking place to land."

Catherine did and pointed it out to him.

"You're doing fine. Now, cut the engine to glide speed, just like you do when you practice landing. Pull back on the stick. Don't worry! I'm still here to help you."

Catherine hesitated.

"Do it Catherine!"

Catherine reached out and eased the throttle back. Then she pulled back on the stick until the Piper's nose slowly rose. Then the plane shuddered and the nose dipped below level flight. A tremor of fear set in. Her stomach almost revolted. She had experienced the same feeling at the first plunge down from the top of a roller-coaster.

Tim told her she had experienced her first stall. He urged her, "Now push in the throttle, hold the stick level Catherine and keep it there until you get to glide speed." Her hands followed his on the stick, until she felt the plane holding steady on its glide path. The churning in her stomach eased.

Tim's voice was calm and reassuring. "Now keep a steady pressure on the stick, Catherine."

Her hands sensed the proper pressure. The plane's nose maintained the proper glide path, even rose a little. The air speed decreased as the plane descended at a controlled rate. A huge sigh escaped. She grinned. She yelled over her shoulder at Tim. "I did it, didn't I?"

"You certainly did. You were great. This is what you have to do when landing the air plane." He was satisfied. "Now increase the power and get up back to 5,000 feet."

As they approached the airport he reminded her, "Now, cut the air speed by pulling out the throttle."

The plane continued its slow descent until she heard Tim. "Let me have it now, Catherine." She listened to his reassuring voice, followed his every move with her hand on the stick and her eye on instruments. She even understood the feel when he pulled back on the stick to flare the plane up and cut the engine before touching down. She relaxed as he taxied the plane back toward the hangars. Already she looked forward to his next trip to Ephrata.

*

The rain and mild weather of April and May had meant green grass and the beginning of wild flowers in central Washington. Catherine still saw the few scattered wildflowers, but knew their time was limited by the increasing heat and lack of rain.

On the semi-arid land north of her campsite the ever-present sagebrush, the vigorous, protein rich bunch grass thrived and some green prairie grasses lingered. These would sustain the three bands until they entered the Grand Coulee. The feed in the coulee would be sufficient to maintain the sheep. Catherine, Rusty and Virgil hoped to be over the Grand Coulee Dam and into the cooler forest grassland north of the Columbia River by late July or early August.

*

Catherine had been at camp a half-hour when she spied two pick-ups kicking up a dust cloud on the dry dirt road. They barely stayed in front of the dust cloud. The dust engulfed the pickups when they slowed to turn off the road. It was left behind when they turned right and came toward the camp. Sarah stepped out of the pickup, just as the second one came up and stopped.

"Mother! What are you doing here?"

Without a word Sarah reached into the ranch pickup, and lifted a box from the back. With a dead-pan face she nonchalantly said, "What does it look like? I'm delivering your supplies from Warburton's. Your cupboard should be getting bare by now." She waltzed past her daughter and set the box down inside the wagon.

Catherine watched in stunned amazement. She looked at the second pickup where Tim stood hiding the IGA label on the door. He grinned and hunched his shoulders as if to say, "I don't know."

When returning to the pickup for more supplies Sarah's stoic expression remained. It all ceased the minute she was even with Catherine. Sarah reached out and threw her arms around her daughter. Her laughter filled the air. "You big boob, why else would I come? I came up here to see you. I was feeling blue yesterday morning when Tim called with your message about the supplies from Warburton's IGA. That was all the push I needed."

Sarah and Catherine continued talking, until Tim fetched each of them an ice cold Cola he brought with the supplies. This signaled he was ready to sit down and be included. He held up his bottle up to toast, "Here's to seeing you two again." He cheerfully asked, "Now, when do you want to fly? I'm ready and available this evening and all day tomorrow."

∿

At twilight the plane appeared, circled once and headed toward the airport. Thirty-five minutes later Catherine heard the pickup approach the campsite. She had guessed right. The evening meal would be on time for the elated fliers. When the pickup stopped, her excited mother stepped out. Evidently the flight over the lower Grand Coulee and Dry Falls had the same affect on her mother much as it had her.

"Catherine, that's a marvelous flight."

Tim stood behind and grinned. A pleased mother was a marvelous thing.

Sarah babbled on, "I've heard about Dry Falls as long as the sheep have come this way." She took a deep breath. "I've even seen it twice with Burke, but never from the air." The effervescence kept bubbling up. "Flying over it lets your imagination soar. Today I could almost see the wall of water leaping out over the three and a half miles of rim rock. If I could find a painting where the artist showed the flood waters leaping out and over the precipices I'd buy it."

The excitement lingered. A wound up Sarah was something Catherine didn't see every day. Tim sat back to enjoy Sarah's enthusiastic praise. "Tomorrow Tim is going to take us over the Upper Grand Coulee all the way to the dam." She eagerly held out her plate to get the roasted potato Catherine had pulled from under the embers. She used a knife to peel away the tin foil and soak it with butter filled before spearing a large hamburger patty from the grill with her fork. This was followed by a large portion of pork and beans spooned from the opened can. She glanced at her plate and then poured herself a glass of iced sun tea. Sarah said, "Out in the middle of the nowhere this is as good as it gets. Better dig in, Tim."

Pleasant, relaxed conversation followed while the disinterested sun slid down behind the mountains in the west. After Tim drove back to the Ephrata airport hanger and the small room in the back of the hanger reserved for pilots, the mother and daughter sat outside in the engulfing darkness and stared into the fading embers. The aura invited quiet talk. Sarah asked, "Well, Catherine, what's going on? It feels like Tim is almost courting me."

Catherine laughed good-naturedly. "Mother you're trying to make it something it isn't. He loves to fly. You and I are just good excuses." She hastily added, "There's nothing going on, but he is attentive and pleasant." She pried a little. "Why so interested in Tim? Are trying to protect Hank?"

"No, but I can't help wondering about you out here and alone. Do you miss Hank?"

"Yeah." The admission had come slowly. Catherine hesitated before discussing her feelings; feelings which seemed to be slipping away. "We seemed so close to being something really special. Now we're on hold. I hate that and trying to decide if we were wrong or right. Maybe we should have gone ahead and done it. At least I would know."

Her improbable laugh startled her mother. "I bet it would have been great." She continued probing. "How about it, mother, is sex that great?"

Redness spread across Sarah's cheeks. "Catherine, what kind of a question is that?"

She giggled at her mother's embarrassment. "If I don't do it, how else can I learn what making love is like?" Impishly she asked, "Maybe I should work my wiles on Tim?" She let her innocent gaze fall on her mother and waited.

"Oh, all right, Catherine." An uneasy composure returned as she gathered her thoughts. This was a subject they had barely touched on. Finally she confessed. "It can actually be pretty wonderful. You can conquer the world. You're empowered to love some one as only you can. With Burke life was as good as it gets. He loved me and I loved him." She mulled over the usage of the word. "Love is the key word. Without love it's not so great. Oh, it can be comfortable, maybe even destructive. Comfortable was Corwin. That's about it. Catherine. I've only known two men in the biblical sense. I married young, so I wasn't doing anything wrong. That is probably the curse of sex. If you aren't in love and married it can be a damaging act. One you have to hide from society. That hurts your pride. When you love someone you shouldn't have to hide it. You need be proud of your love and able to shout it to the world."

She studied Catherine's face a moment and reached out to touch her daughter's hand. "You had the strength to say no to your emotions and to Hank. That made me very proud. Sex will be something special for you when the right moment comes."

She sighed. "To answer your question, no, I'm not trying to protect Hank. You know I like him a great deal, but what happens between you and Hank is your call, not mine. Things have been a little cooler and more distant since the decision that you would continue on as shepherdess. He has moved back into the bunk house. I see him every day but it's not the same. It's more boss to worker now." She mulled over her answer. "It's strange because we talk about the wheat part of the ranch, but very seldom talk about you or the sheep. I don't know what that means, and for that I'm sorry."

She paused, gathered her thoughts and changed the subject. "I know it was the right thing to let you continue with the sheep. The way you handled the Ernst situation was simply magnificent. Rusty and Virgil were very impressed you know. I can see why Rusty hung the title 'Boss Lady' on you."

She was amused by her daughter's surprised reaction to that observation. "I know I'm just a nosy, proud mother, but you don't realize how much you've grown. Every time I see you it gets better. I'm impressed."

Catherine smiled, "Mother, I never think of you as nosy. Let's just say you're aggressively interested. Tell me. What do you think of Tim?"

"Tim is a very nice young man. He hasn't been battle tested yet and he's safe."

Catherine digested this opinion. "Mother, are you happier with a safe Tim or a dangerous Hank?" She waited for an answer that didn't come. She was thoroughly amused. "It makes no difference you know. There isn't any time for romance out here. Besides Hank told me that nothing will interfere with his becoming a veterinarian." Her mischievous grin appeared. "Now it's my turn, Mother. Is Glenn still coming to Prentiss to build his grain elevator?"

She chuckled, "Yes, smarty, he is still coming to Prentiss to build the grain elevator. That's a big project and it keeps him very busy. Yes, I've had dinner with him a couple of times. Am I safe? Yes. Is he safe?" She quipped, "Only because it has to be that way."

Sarah noticed her daughter's surprise. She was glad to get Catherine's attention. Sarah grew solemn. "I do have news that might interest you. We've located Corwin."

"Really. Where in the devil is he?"

"He's in Marksville, a small sawmill town in central Oregon, 100 miles south from the ranch. He has been served divorce papers. Now we wait and see if he wants to contest the divorce or if he fades quietly into the past."

"How do you feel about the divorce?"

Sarah rested her face in her cupped hands. She gazed off into the quiet night. Finally she whispered, "I hate to admit it, Catherine, but I probably did Corwin a disservice. Loneliness makes people make weird decisions. I tried to make Corwin into another Burke and that doesn't work for either party. I'll be glad when it's over."

The patient Malovich and Gilrakis trailed the two women into the wagon, hopped up onto the sleeping bags and waited. Nobody slept until they were comfortable.

❧

At the Western Bar and Grill in Marksville, Oregon Virgie Wheeler had opened the envelope of the registered letter. The return address read T. J. Morton, Attorney at Law, Prentiss, Washington. She pulled the papers from the envelope to scan them.

"Well, well, well, Corwin. Sarah is divorcing you." Virgie read the papers for Corwin. "It looks like you're out in the cold again." She remembered the past and cackled, "Looks like I'm not the only one who divorced you. Corwin, you're such a loser! Corwin managed a wry smile while his stomach churned. *First it was Art and now it's me. Will anything stop those women?*

35
Stingers

Everyone enjoyed the evening steak fry at Catherine's newest campsite. It was a welcome break from the sheep. Most of the talk centered on the wonders of the Dry Falls, the Grand Coulee and the dam. They were still talking when Rusty decided to leave the group to stroll past the wind break of poplars toward the abandoned cabin.

He tipped the cold bottle to his lips and enjoyed a long drink of Seattle's Select beer. He thought Tim was all right to include beer in his delivery to the camps. It might be a while before he savored another one.

He pushed a loose board aside with his toe and surveyed the shambles that once was a cabin. His eyes wandered to the wild roses that grew beneath the branches of the elms. He poked his finger into the soil. It was damp. His eyes followed the dampness up the slight slope to the source of the seepage. At one time this must have been a pretty good looking homestead. Rusty knew of several such relics on the way to the dam. The trouble was always the same; little or no water. Nothing flourished without it. Grand Coulee Dam was the hope of the future. Rusty pictured the settlers starting with such high hopes and some like this one fought valiantly against the odds. Each defeat eroded the will to survive and diminished the spirit. Finally the settlers left. It had been a sad, but oft repeated story.

A rusty, one furrow plow, which horses probably pulled to form the original ditch, stood alone as a piquant reminder of such early hopes. In the abandoned fields north of the farm house the scattered surviving remnants of fields of grain and grass turned wild would help feed the sheep on the way north. The area was a great campsite for Catherine, but it left Rusty feeling philosophic.

He stared at the thorny brambles and the surviving roses. They had been distinct vibrant colors before they turned wild. Rusty's romantic side told him to cut a few roses and take them back to his wagon. The color and scent would last a while. He carefully reached into the thorny brambles. Rusty cut one stem with his pocket knife and then reached out for another yellowish-orange blossom. His foot slipped on the damp soil. An unnoticed, far-reaching runner from the main bush caught his sliding foot. He automatically reached out for support.

✑

Catherine, Sara and Tim turned as one from around the fire when the howls of pain reached them. "Good grief, what is that all about?" Catherine asked.

Virgil had been sitting in the driver's seat of the wagon while watching Rusty inspect the roses. From there he saw everything. "That's Rusty. He fell into the rose bush. That bramble is protecting its roses." He stepped down from his perch and casually walked toward the campfire. "Come on, let's get him out of there. Those thorns are long and sharp. He reached out and pulled the two women to their feet.

Rusty falling into the roses would be a good yarn for a long time. They had no idea of the consequences.

❧

Once past the row of poplars they saw Rusty struggling to stand. Every time he tried to get a hold of support he angrily pulled back from a thorn stab. He tottered a few seconds and reached up to grab the overhanging elm branch. He steadied himself.

"Look out!" exclaimed Tim. They all followed the shaking limb to where it joined a hollow branch. They all saw the same thing.

Wild mountain bees came buzzing from the hollow branch. The roses were their coveted prize. Catherine remembered seeing the busy bees in the morning and thought nothing of it. Now they were not busy. They were angry. Their home had been disturbed by the vibrations Rusty started when he clutched at the overhanging limb. Before anyone covered the twenty yards to Rusty his cries of frustration turned to pain. The little black and yellow bees darted from their home on a search and destroy mission. They angrily targeted Rusty.

Tim got to Rusty first. Catherine was right behind. He gratefully reached for both their hands. They pulled him free of the entangling bushes, but not the bees. They stung every rescuer. They followed the retreating party to the wagon and tried to get inside the wagon before Sarah could pull the back door shut.

Sarah and Catherine each grabbed a newspaper to swat the invaders. A few of the small black and yellow bees were swatted away. They didn't look very menacing lying on the floor. Sarah quickly swept them out of the wagon. Peace was restored, but no one was eager to step outside. They waited until ominous buzzing around the wagon quieted.

They turned their attention to the victims. Sarah was thankful for the evening chill of the high sagebrush desert. Her light jacket and her late arrival at the rose bushes kept her bee stings to three. Catherine and Virgil had a few more. The bees largely ignored Tim.

Rusty presented a far different picture. Lying in the roses had left him exposed. He had been defenseless against their attack as he struggled to get out of the brambles. Sarah counted thirty-five stings on his arms and across his neck and shoulders. Rusty had lost his hat during his struggles and his head sported a few red blotches. Long scratches from the thorns streaked up his arms and blood dotted the edges. The thorns had penetrated his light shirt and even his heavier denim pants.

Outside of the pain and the inevitable swelling there didn't seem to be any danger. Catherine and Sarah used bicarbonate of soda mixed with warm, soapy, water to wash everyone's stings. Only the redness around each sting remained. All seemed well as could be expected when Tim took the two men back to their camps. Before he left Rusty grabbed two bottles of Seattle Select beer, declaring, "I've damn well earned these."

The evening get-together had been the usual success until the sudden onslaught of bees. When the taillights of Tim's pickup faded out of sight, Catherine turned to her mother and asked, "Have you ever run into anything like this before?"

"No."

Her sudden laughter seemed out of place to her daughter. "What's so funny?"

"You!" She kept laughing. "You have no idea how you looked when that bee got in your hair. That dance should get you on Broadway."

"Oh, sure. You can laugh, but I was stung not once, but twice before you smashed the bees with the newspaper." She bowed her head toward her mother. "It still itches. What does it look like?"

Sarah ran her fingers through her daughter's hair and parted the hair at both stings.

"It looks a little red, probably swollen a little. It will start going down through the night. Everybody reacts a little differently to bee stings."

Little did she know how right she was or what it would lead to.

36
Soap Lake

Sarah waited impatiently in the doctor's office reflecting on the events that led to this visit. She had driven to Rusty's camp this morning to say good-bye. Virgil was there to greet her.

Never given to a lot of words, the soft spoken Virgil told her, "I'm glad you're here ma'am. Rusty needs help." She had walked up the three steps at the rear of the wagon, opened the door and entered. Sarah gasped at the appalling sight.

Rusty sat on the edge of the bed, naked to the waist, holding his head. She barely heard his greeting, "Good morning, Sarah."

She expected his bee stings to itch and probably a headache. The vivid image of bee stings which were large and swelling from an infected core was something else. This demanded a doctor's attention. One angry swelling had spread to the size of a half-dollar. The yellow infection which surrounded the sting now looked angry and dangerous. The other stings graduated downward in size until only a white core was seen. One infected boil grew on the inside of Rusty's elbow. He groaned at any movement.

Sarah had wasted no time. She waited while Virgil got Rusty ready to travel. She stopped at Catherine's camp and told her about Rusty and then drove her ailing shepherd to Ephrata and the doctor.

❧

Sarah waited in the doctor's office. For an hour she heard a few yelps, moans and the mumbled voices of doctor and his nurse. Finally Dr. Newcombe came her way.

She anxiously asked, "How is he, Doctor?"

"Mrs. Turnoch, this is not something we see every day. The reason it took so long is simple. We had to lance each sting and drain away the infection, and then remove the forming core before we could dress the wound." He smiled. "Each was like getting rid of a big boil. I asked you before, but now you've had some time to think. Is he allergic to bee stings?"

"Not to my knowledge. Did you ask him?"

"I did. I also asked him if he had this reaction before. This is a first for him."

"What should do we do? There are three bands of sheep to keep going, and he's pretty much alone with his flock. Will that be a problem?"

"I don't think so. Give him a couple of days to rest and check with me again."

"Don't worry Doctor. We've been together a long time. He'll get the rest he needs."

"Good. This isn't an allergic reaction. Anaphylaxis is a very serious reaction to bee stings. Any bee allergy is usually quick to appear, is quite violent and very dangerous. The fact that Rusty's reaction is more than twelve hours old says it's not anaphylaxis.

"One sting is normally not a problem. There is some swelling and a lot of itching, but it soon passes. Rusty's problem is simply too many bee stings. He had a lot of toxin pumped into him. That poison has to come out somewhere, and the fact that it's coming out as painful boils is better than having his body upset internally." He handed a prescription to her. "This salve should be applied directly to the open wound. Keep the wound dressed each time you apply the ointment. You can get it filled at the local drug store."

Dr. Newcombe gave Sarah time to read the prescription. She nodded her agreement, and looked up to see the pale faced Rusty come down the hall leaning on a petite, brunette nurse. He gave Sarah a weak wave and an even weaker smile as he plopped down heavily on the nearest chair. The nurse with the sympathetic eyes stayed close. Rusty's face was almost as pale as her white uniform.

Sarah directed her attention to paying the receptionist for the visit, while the smiling Rusty pitifully kept his arm around the nurse on the way out to the pickup.

Sarah wondered why Dr. Newcombe lingered. "Is there something else?"

He replied, "Have you ever heard of Soap Lake?"

෧

Sarah stopped to tell her daughter about Rusty before she delivered him back to Virgil's camp. This allowed her to tend his sheep in the afternoon.

That evening the tired Sarah relaxed and enjoyed an evening cup of hot tea. She brought her daughter up-to-date on the day's events, and then handed her the Soap Lake pamphlet. "It seems Dr. Newcombe has a lot of faith in the healing powers of the lake.

Catherine glanced at the pamphlet. "The location is perfect. Rusty can soak in water and mud for a couple of days at Soap Lake, maybe more, while the sheep keep moving. without interruption. What do you think?"

Sarah smiled at this unerring call to duty. She pointed to the well illustrated "Soap Lake" pamphlet. Catherine smiled and read it aloud.

"The name of the town, Soap Lake, came from the local Indians, who called the waters, 'Smokiam' which means 'healing waters'. Some say it came from the soapy feeling of the waters and the foam which often appears at the shoreline. The tribes were known for the annual horse races they held each year on the north shore of the lake. They used the lake to heal themselves and their horses.

"In 1933 the Veterans Administration selected Soap Lake as a special project to treat Buerger's Disease, which affects the circulation in the arteries and veins of the hands and feet. Smoking and the use of smokeless tobacco are the main causes of this disease. The very high mineral content of the lake is especially beneficial to the victims of Buerger's disease.

"Of the five lakes existing along the Coulee Corridor, Soap Lake has the highest mineral content. The first layer is mineral water. It contains 18 different minerals and its second bottom level is a mud-like substance which contains stronger mineral composition with concentrations of unusual substances and microscopic life forms. The two layers do not mix. The scientific community refers to lakes with this rare condition as meromictic. There are eleven such lakes in the United States and Soap Lake has the most concentrated mineral content.

"We invite you to spend some time with us, to soak in the waters and cover yourself with mud. People come from all over America and the world to do just that. Stop at one of our marvelous, modern hotels that cater to the bather's every wish. Enjoy the healing, mineral waters or the miracle mud of Soap Lake. Enjoy our hospitality and leave refreshed."

"Thank you. The Soap Lake City Council and Chamber of Commerce."

Catherine looked at three pages of photographs. She put the pamphlet down, ""Beautiful little lake isn't it? It looks good to me, Mother. Have you talked to Rusty?"

"He's a typical man. He hurts, but says he's okay. He'll suffer, but will be out with his sheep tomorrow. According to him he doesn't need any more medicine. We both know he'll moan and be miserable and itchy for a few days, but he won't admit the water or mud might do him some good." Sarah sighed in frustration. "Oh, well, we'll just have to live with it."

Catherine smiled. She's seen that determined look before. Her mother's firm jaw meant stubbornness, pure stubbornness. She would get Rusty to Soap Lake tomorrow.

༆

Sarah stepped into the long rectangular therapy room of the historic Siloam Hotel and waited. She critically examined the image in the mirror. Why had she told Rusty she was interested in soaking in the mineral waters? She chuckled at the obvious answer. It made it easier to get Rusty to the lake. He didn't want to come by himself, but he did come with her.

She looked back at the reflection in the mirror and decided it wasn't too bad. The hotel's guest shop offered the latest thing in bathing suits. She fell in love with the bright scarlet suit. It was certainly better than some of the older, frumpy looking models. The skirtless, one piece bathing suit was the latest thing. The Latex took care of figure control. The shiny rayon and cotton were woven tightly together for style and strength. Sarah didn't want frumpy. She was ready to live.

There were fifteen cubicles in the room. Each cubicle contained a white enameled tub inlaid into the white and brown tiled floor. Today the cubicles were only half occupied but a constant chatter echoed throughout the large hall. In the morning Rusty would soak in the mineral laced warm water inside the hotel, and in the afternoons, he would wallow outside in the private mud baths, while Sarah went back to help Catherine and Virgil tend the flocks.

❧

Sarah inspected the large functional room while she waited for Rusty. The room was painted a neutral, bone colored enamel. Enlarged photographs of the lake, some horse racing scenes from the north side, the Indian Chief Moses, and bathers using the waters and mud dotted the walls. Several comfortably curved, wooden chairs were scattered around the room to provide the guests a place to sit, rest and discuss their time in the lake's waters. One large spigot fed warmed mineral water into each tub. A valve at the base of the tub drained the tub into a shallow U-shaped trough, which returned the water to the lake.

Rusty and a woman attendant entered the room and greeted Sarah. Rusty stepped out of the heavy, white terry cloth robe furnished by the hotel. It was the first time Sarah had seen the opened wounds. "Rusty, all I can see on your arms and neck are big red bumps with empty, dark red spots in the middle. That must have hurt like the devil, or worse."

"Sarah, you should've seen that one. He pointed to his inside elbow. When it was lanced the pressure must have shot the infectious stuff two feet in the air. You probably heard me yell clear out in the waiting room. After that one, the rest of the boils seemed minor."

The petite brunette attendant had the same affect on him as the nurse from the doctor's office. He put his arm around her, whimpered like he suffered some hidden pain and leaned on her for help. Sarah couldn't help but smile at the male animal in action. She took Rusty's robe and gently guided him into the tub and explained, "The warmed lake water doesn't do more for you than the cooler water and mud at the lake. It's just more comfortable. Let me know if you need anything."

The attendant accepted Sarah's robe. The scarlet bathing suit drew Rusty's whistle. "Sarah, you like a million dollars in that red suit. The magic water can't do any better."

She blushed at the compliment.

They left the curtain between their two tubs open. They chatted whenever the need arose, or accepted the pleasant quiet as they soaked in the warm water. Later Sarah would check her scratches from the rose bush to see if the waters actually helped heal the skin.

They left the Siloam Hotel tubs at noon. Sarah told him, "Catherine will be back at four. That allows us time to check on the sheep and gives you time for lunch and some more time to flirt with that young lady." With a mischievous smile and a slight giggle she added, "Make sure you don't slip in the mud and pull her down with you."

&

At four o'clock Catherine drove into Soap Lake to pick up Rusty. She followed her mother's instructions and parked close the hotel's private lake area. When she found him he looked like one of the pigs at the ranch. Only his face showed above the mud.

She sat and waited for him on one of hotel's wooden benches while he showered away the mineral saturated mud. Before he could leave an attendant would rub salve on each sting and apply bandages. When he finished Rusty walked out of the dressing room toward her with a warm terry cloth towel wrapped around his neck.

It took one look at Rusty's face for Catherine to know something was wrong. "What's the matter, Rusty? You look like you've seen a ghost. Is it the mud?"

There was no smile. "No, I actually feel better. I think the mud acts as a poultice. My skin feels like little tingles moving around. My arms are definitely getting better. That's not a problem." He pulled the towel tight around his neck. "In a hundred years you'll never guess, who is using the public mud baths. I didn't recognize him in that mud, but after he left the shower, there was no doubt. I thought we were done with him, but his sneer told me different." He leveled his gaze at Catherine, "It's just a feeling, and it's not a good feeling."

She felt the hair rise on the back of her neck. Only one man fit Rusty's warning.

"That's right, Boss Lady. Art Wheeler's here in the flesh and that's not good."

37
Comrades in Arms

Rusty's words wrecked Catherine's day. Art Wheeler didn't possess one redeeming feature. She exploded, "What in the hell is that little weasel doing here?" The anxiety in her voice surfaced. "Did he talk to you?"

"Of course he did. He went out of his way to make sure I did. His first snide observation was, 'Rusty, you look awful. You really need to soak here in the famous mud!' He made a point of counting the many stings." The irritating memory of his meeting with Art still lingered. "When I told him what happened in the rose garden, he just laughed his degrading snicker."

Catherine knew exactly what Rusty meant. She'd heard it first after she had thrown water in his face.

"He told me the burns from the barn fire have caused a lot of pain. They've been slow to heal. He heard about Soap Lake. Evidently someone paid for him to stay a few days and soak in the mud. His last words were, 'I'll see you later.'"

Catherine protested, "I hope we don't see him. The fire and his burns were his own fault." She remembered the panic she felt when the fireworks blazed through the sky toward her sheep. "That creep should still be in jail."

"That may be true, but it ain't so! The insolent little bastard"... Rusty blushed and immediately apologized for his slip, "He's out of jail and more devious than ever. He made sure I knew an attorney had paid his fines. Medical treatment was a reason for his release.

"He even whined about having to use the free public facilities. His exact words were, 'It must be nice working for the Sumertun ranch. They have money. At least Sarah takes care of you. I bet that snooty daughter wouldn't do it. She's got me fired, but don't worry. Her time will come.'"

Red streaks of anger crept up Rusty's neck. "That's when I jabbed my knuckle into his chest and told him in no uncertain terms, 'She's not the reason you got fired. You shot Mr. Gray. Hank broke his leg because of you. Remember? You're the reason you were fired! Your burns are your own damn fault!'"

Catherine patted Rusty's hand. "Thank you."

He ducked his chin and murmured, "I was glad to do it." Then he remembered the petite attendant by his side. He introduced the small, trim, late thirtyish woman as Florence Fredrickson. He added, "Call her Flo. She may be small, but she is gentle and strong."

Flo smiled as she shook Catherine's hand. "I feel like I know you. Rusty is always telling me about you." Her lyrical laugh sounded like bells. "I'm happy to meet you." The unflinching handshake made Catherine smile.

"As soon as Flo gets me bandaged again I'll be ready to go home." Catherine watched them head for the small first aid station, close to the dressing rooms and showers. Rusty leaned on her. She put her arm around him.

Catherine smiled. Her mother was right. Flo is petite, capable, strong, and willing.

❦

Back at camp they relaxed with cold drinks. Rusty sipped his cold beer and patiently answered their questions.

Catherine listened to his comments, leaned toward her mother and said, "Whether it's the doctor's treatment, sulfa or the mud I don't know, but Rusty says he feels better." She innocently added, "Mother, you were right about the petite Flo and Rusty's willingness to lean on her."

Rusty almost choked on his beer.

Catherine paused. It wasn't good news she had to pass on. "Rusty has another surprise for you. It seems Rat F... Art Wheeler was a fellow mud bather." She passed on what Rusty had said about seeing him and she looked to him to add to it, but the warm day of soaking in the miracle waters and mud of Soap Lake had caught up to him. He closed his eyes for a moment while Sarah thought about his disturbing news.

❧

Sarah knew Art Wheeler wallowing in the mud at Soap Lake wasn't good. A few moments of aftershock followed before she calmed down to think. He presented a dilemma. Rusty's bizarre accident with the roses and bees couldn't be planned or known, so Art's appearance might be pure chance. Sarah grimly reasoned that anything connected to Catherine and the sheep wasn't chance. Their route was easily followed. If Art was here for any reason connected to the sheep it was planned, but planned by whom and for what reason?

Her worried gaze fell upon her young daughter. Catherine had filled in admirably for the injured Hank. She didn't need this. "Rusty!" He opened his eyes at Sarah's intense call. "Rusty, are you sure he blamed Catherine for getting him fired?"

"He sure did, but I wouldn't worry much about what Art says. His kind talks a lot."

Sarah passed it off for now. "Yes, I know. He probably said that to show off, but the fact remains he is here and has tried to cause trouble in the past." She thought it was time to find out more about Mr. Wheeler.

The sound of Tim's Piper Cub coming from Othello interrupted her thoughts, but offered Sarah one solution.

Catherine waved at the waggling wings. She eyed the rapidly tiring Rusty, who didn't rise from his seat. He looked half-asleep. She touched him on the shoulder. "Rusty, are you okay with going back to your camp?" He nodded, stood and took the last sip of beer.

"Mother, I'll get Rusty back to camp so he can rest." Sarah nodded. Catherine had to make sure. "Do we take him back to the lake for treatment tomorrow?"

"Yes. You and Virgil can cover for him. He needs to take it easy one more day, maybe two. I'll take him back for treatment day after tomorrow. After that the sheep should be well past Soap Lake, and hopefully he'll be able to return to work. If not we may have to get someone up here a few days."

"Who?"

"Probably Alex or Hank." Amused, Sarah noticed her daughter's quick reaction. She had no doubt which one Catherine wanted to come. But it was Tim she looked forward to seeing at camp this evening. That airplane was going to come in handy.

⁓

Catherine enjoyed the short morning drive from the airport back to camp. It had been a very busy morning. Her mother had left early with Tim to fly home. After Catherine returned she rode Jiggles out for a quick morning inspection. She sucked in the fresh, exhilarating plateau air. June was the rarest of months. Cool mornings and warmth, not heat, and a few scattered showers still dominated the weather. She picked up Rusty at 10:30 a.m. That left plenty of time to get him to his 11:00 o'clock treatment at the Siloam Hotel.

After she picked him up, she asked, "Do you think we'll see Art today?"

"Not this morning. I'm using the hotel tubs. That would cost him money." Rusty thought back to yesterday's meeting. "He made a point of telling me how lucky I was to work for the Sumertun Ranch, and not you."

Rusty turned quiet and serious. "He blames you for getting him fired and that alone worries me. There are also two scruffy looking men hanging around with him. Fact is, everything about that guy irritates me. To answer the rest of your question, he'll make sure I see him this afternoon. It will be like bees looking for flowers."

"Oh, that's rather good, considering why you're here."

"Glad you appreciate a good pun. You could laugh you know."

She flashed her best smile before asking her second important question of the day. "How do you feel? Stick your arm over here. Let's see how it looks."

Rusty warned her to watch the road, but extended his arm. "The swelling's way down and most of the itching is gone. I feel much better. Today should do the trick."

She drove into Soap Lake on State Highway 28, turned west at the main intersection and followed the road north around the mineral rich lake to the Siloam Hotel and the waiting Flo. Catherine quipped, "Looks like a good day to me." She caught Rusty's slightly red face. "Yes, yes, a heavy leaning day."

He quickly slid out of the pickup. "See you at four."

⁓

Catherine arrived back at camp to eager greetings from Malovich and Gilrakis. Quiet time among the sheep was welcome. In twenty minutes she sat astride Jiggles for the late morning ride. So far it had been a very busy day.

Just before take-off this morning Sarah had hugged her and told the already edgy Catherine, "We'll probably return sometime tomorrow." She laughed, "You'll know when we return by the waggle of Tim's wing." She hastily added, "Try to bump into that weasel and find out what you can. I can't believe he's here just for the mud treatment." She sweetly admonished her daughter, "And Catherine, try to control your temper. Information might be more important than slugging him."

"I'll try mother, but it may be difficult." She had no idea of hard that would be.

Her late afternoon trip into Soap Lake wasn't as pleasant a drive as yesterday. An uncharacteristic tenseness prevailed. Why? It had to be Art Wheeler. Her mother wanted information. Catherine didn't even want to see him, let alone try to be nice and get some information. Any question to Art would be twisted around or answered by a lie. Could she take advantage of this willingness to lie and cheat? Catherine grimaced in frustration.

Not one good way to start a conversation with Art had surfaced when she pulled into the private parking space reserved for the Siloam Hotel's mud bathers. The oxymoron, mud bathers, brought her first relaxed smile of the afternoon. She stepped out of the pickup and surveyed the bodies lying submerged in the hotels mineral laced mud. No way could she recognize any of the men and women wallowing in the mud.

She located Flo leaving the dressing room area with a large beach towel. She spotted Catherine and waved. Catherine made the obvious observation. "I take it's time for Rusty to leave the mud."

"Yes." She laughed. "Have you picked him out of the group yet?"

"No. How can you tell?"

"He's the one waving. That's the only way."

The two of them walked to the warm outdoor shower and waited while Rusty rinsed away the miracle mud. Catherine inquired about Rusty's progress. Flo told her, "The mud is doing its job. The swelling is almost gone and the color is close to normal. He's right, you know. The warm soak in the morning penetrates and soothes. Like Epsom salts, only better. The afternoon mud acts as a poultice and draws out any impurity."

"Damn it, not again!" Catherine saw alarm spread across Flo's face.

She turned to see a smallish, mud-covered man being pushed along by two attendants. They didn't seem happy with the muddy man, whose old, tattered cut-off Levi's dripped mud. His mousey, light brown hair was hard to distinguish from the mud. The same arrogant smile and accusing pale blue eyes he had flashed at her in the sheep pens remained. He pushed back at the attendants, who firmly held both his arms. Grim faced, they marched him toward the public shower.

Flo asked the closest attendant, "Do you want me to call the police? This is the third time he has sneaked into the hotel's mud area to bother Rusty."

Art Wheeler flashed Catherine a weak, thin lipped sneer and then informed Flo, "Don't worry. I won't be troubling you any more today." He doffed an imaginary hat to Catherine. "Good to see you, Kate. I take it Rusty has already told you he saw me." He cast a disparaging leer at the attendants, "You guys can dump me at the public shower. You'll not be needed anymore."

They took no chances. Fifty yards away on the north-east tip of the lake she watched the two attendants roughly shove Art under the showers and hold him there.

"Do you know that guy?" Flo's icy tone insinuated, "Why would you?"

In the few minutes before Rusty would reappear Catherine gave Flo some history on Art Wheeler. That seemed to appease her. The atmosphere became warmer as Rusty stepped out from the dressing rooms. It soon became apparent they both had ideas of their own; Ideas that would leave her alone in a situation she didn't look forward to.

Rusty suddenly turned shy. "Flo and I plan on having dinner together tonight." His quiet statement seemed a request. "I'm feeling much better, so I'll be on the job in the morning."

Catherine hid her amusement. Rusty didn't have to ask her permission. She replied, "That's great Rusty. You're lucky. Enjoy the evening."

He gave Flo his conquering hero grin. Flo's demure smile accepted him in that role.

Flo added, "Don't worry about getting him home, Catherine. That's my job tonight."

They leaned on each and started up the slope toward the hotel and her car.

Rusty turned to look back one last time. "Are you sure you don't want me to stick around a few minutes?" He nodded toward the public shower. "You know, just in case?"

She warmed at the assurance Rusty offered. "No thanks. You two enjoy the evening." She wistfully watched them lean into each other as they walked up the hill. It would be nice.

∽

Catherine sauntered down to a bench by the lake, sat down and relaxed. It was a lovely warm afternoon in June; one which let her stretch out and sense the coming heat of summer. She did some quick arithmetic. They had to cover fifty miles before they crossed the Grand Coulee Dam with the sheep. The sheep would quickly graze across the arid plateau to Dry Falls. The feed would get better and the progress slower in the wide, Upper Grand Coulee.

She would celebrate her twenty first birthday in the majestic Grand Coulee surrounded on both sides by 900 foot lava cliffs. Long, long ago lava flows covered the area, before glaciers and then mighty floods formed this magnificent corridor. Thinking of these monumental happenings she felt rather small and insignificant. She picked up a small stone and flipped it into the lake and watched the rings get wider. The farther they went the weaker the ripple effect became. She forlornly thought; kind of like Hank and me.

It had been nice to see Rusty and Flo leaning into each other as they had left. A trace of loneliness changed her smile to a sigh. She hugged herself remembering the warmth and tenderness she and Hank had once shared; when they had really wanted each other; when they couldn't keep their hands off each other. Another sigh escaped.

The strident voice penetrated her warm thoughts. Then a louder "Hey Kate" jerked her further away from the pleasantness of the evening. She turned in the direction of the voice. Art Wheeler!

Instantly Catherine became aware of the stark difference between her warm thoughts of Hank and the reality of the disgusting twerp limping toward her. How could her mother expect her to be nice to a troublemaker?

She bit her lip. Her response was curt. "My name is Catherine, not Kate!"

"Still the spoiled college girl, I see. Kate's too common for you, huh? Must be nice to get everything you want. I wish it could happen to me."

Catherine angrily replied, "Maybe if you hadn't smoked in a danger area, or shot Mr. Gray out from under Hank, shot Roman candles at the sheep, or even worked harder, you might not be here using Soap Lake to treat your self-inflicted burns."

She abruptly stopped. Maybe this wasn't the way. What had Grandfather Carter said.? Oh, yes. "You can catch more flies with honey than with vinegar."

She laughed. She had almost called him Rat Face. Then Catherine forced herself to speak in a more subdued tone. "In a way Art, I owe you for the job of taking the sheep to Montana."

He sneered, "I doubt that! I never did anything for you. Why should I? Don't bother to deny you always wanted Pete to fire me? Everyone knew I didn't mean to shoot Mr. Gray or hurt Hank, but nobody wanted to listen. Corwin defended me and had to leave." Art noticed Catherine's wide-eyed look. He boasted, "Yes, I knew he was forced to leave. Surprised you didn't I?"

How could he know that? Pete had hired him as a favor to Corwin, who repaid the favor by trying to fire Pete when Art shot Mr. Gray. Only one person had been told to stay away from Pete and the sheep. Abruptly she asked, "How well do you know Corwin? Why was he protecting you?"

She saw his surprise.

He shrugged his shoulders indifferently as he searched for an answer.

"Somehow he's related, isn't he?"

"No." Art was a poor liar. He knew it and so did she. He looked away from her unrelenting stare.

Good, he was being defensive. Catherine changed the subject. "I noticed you were limping more than I remembered. What happened?" She hated acting sympathetic, but maybe that was the way to reach Art.

Like an angry cat his defiant voice spat out, "Nothing more has happened. You caused it when you sent your dogs after me in Prentiss."

"So it was you," she exclaimed. "Hank and I thought it was you, but we never knew."

There was no retreat from his unguarded moment of admission. Anger and guilt slid into embarrassment.

Catherine quietly gave him a way out. "It doesn't make any difference. No harm was done. All the sheep were safe." She waited for him to regain some bravado before she went on. "Just so you'll know, I didn't sic the dogs on you. Someone was bothering their sheep and they went out to protect them." She softly said, "It was poetic justice to hear their snarls, the ripping of your pants and your noisy cries of pain." She gasped as the truth suddenly came. "Gilrakis or Malovich didn't hurt your leg, did they? They might have nipped you and drew some blood, but that limp wasn't caused by the dogs. What really happened?"

"Okay, so you figured that out. You are right; the dogs didn't really hurt me. They nipped me some and tore my clothes, but I was okay when they left. I fell in a ditch as I ran away and sprained my knee really bad. When that cop came looking I thought it was over, but he turned away before he got to me. My knee hurt like hell. It seemed like hours before I limped to my pickup and left."

"I understand why you were mad at me for throwing water in your face, but why are you still mad at me?"

"Why wouldn't I be mad? Everything went downhill after that. You're the fresh college girl who gets everything she wants because her mother owns the ranch. I was told about these summer treks, and given hope that I could do it."

"You expect me to believe Pete encouraged you?"

"No, it wasn't Pete. It was someone who knew the Sumertun Ranch needed a good sheep drive to survive."

Incredulous at that statement Catherine asked, "Whoever told you that?"

"It doesn't matter. I wanted to be one of the shepherds who took the sheep to Montana, but you got my job. My troubles started the first day you came to the lambing sheds." He bitterly complained. "It's too bad it wasn't you that fell into the roses."

Catherine probed, "Who told you that you could lead a band of sheep?"

"Someone who thought I could do it, but it doesn't matter now."

"Yes it does. Is it because that person is no longer at the ranch?"

Art Wheeler ducked his head. "I told you it doesn't matter. First you and then Hank made me feel small." Palatable, angry belligerence filled the air.

Catherine was appalled by this man dealing her such a bunch of crap. She curbed her temper as best she could, but her voice was demanding. "Have you listened to yourself and all the garbage you're dishing out? I already know you burned your leg and chest getting away from a fire you set at the livery stable. What happened? Did a Roman candle get away from you? What did you hope to accomplish with those fireworks? We kept the sheep under control. Didn't the wild shooting at the ranch teach you that sheep don't stampede?" She waited for another confession. None came. "Hank said you were limping badly when you came into the alley toward him."

"Oh yeah! That didn't stop him from tripping me in the alley when I tried to escape. Then he held me down with his crutch, but I got even. I knocked his crutch out from under him and then hit him hard on his good leg. He was forced to watch me escape." Art Wheeler gloated, "Too bad your precious Hank looked bad."

He had just confirmed what she suspected, but he showed no regret, only defiance. He undid the one button which held his shirt together. The skin on his stomach and his legs below his cut-offs showed burn scars. "I don't have all the attention that Rusty gets, thanks to your mother, but the burns feels a lot better after three days here in the mud. I plan to stay a few more days." He sneered, "Don't worry. You haven't seen the last of me."

Catherine had heard "Rat Face" go from anger, to sarcasm and now to a threat. The threat caused the most concern. She forced her voice calm and coaxing. "Why so angry at me? You've caused all the scars you're carrying. I threw water in your face for smoking in the holding pens, but that's it. You weren't fired then and you should have been. Corwin tried to fire Pete after he fired you for shooting Mr. Gray and Hank broke his leg. Why?" Catherine bored in for the truth. "Now tell me. What is Corwin to you?"

The insolence flashed. Grim silence followed. If looks could kill, Catherine knew she would be dead. She enjoyed a smug satisfaction watching him trying to figure what to say and where to go. He looked helplessly at his nemesis.

As sweet as maple syrup on pancakes she told him, "All the loafing at every possible chance told Pete you weren't responsible. After Hank broke his leg and with the starting date for Montana staring them in the face the ranch had to hire someone quickly. You left my mother and Pete with only one possibility." Catherine beamed, "Me."

She pleasantly informed him, "I was glad to help. It's always been my dream. When Pete and my mother decided Hank wouldn't replace at Othello, and Rusty called me "Boss Lady" I knew I had earned my spurs."

Catherine stood as erect as possible. She pulled her shoulders back. On the slope she stood a good four inches taller as she looked down on the little wart. "Art, you're much too free with accusations. I'm sorry you don't feel good, but as far as I can tell, you brought all your troubles to yourself."

She started down to the lake walkway that led to her car.

Art Wheeler stepped in front of her. "You can't talk like that to me. Nobody can."

"Oh, for God's sake, Art. Don't cause any more trouble for yourself. You're out of jail and free. I'll never understand that fireworks effort, but you need to get yourself under control." She tried again to leave.

He didn't move.

Catherine would be forced to step around.

His sneer widened.

She shot an angry glare at him. "What the hell is the matter with you? Let me by."

He didn't budge.

She saw hatred in his eyes, and defiance in his face and stance.

He hissed the ultimate challenge. "Kate, there's no one here to protect you now."

Catherine's temper climbed like a thermometer on a hot day. The low timbre of her voice, the steely determination in her eyes, and stubborn forward thrust of her jaw should have warned him, but it didn't. She coldly told him, "I don't need them to deal with you." Her intention was just to push him aside and go on, but her emotions, already rubbed raw by this jackass, kicked in. She spun him around and shoved the smaller man stumbling ten feet up the slight slope toward the hotel. She glared at him and yelled, "I tried to be nice but that doesn't work with you. Now leave me alone!"

She ignored his raging curses as she angrily strode away.

She heard Rusty shout, "Look out, 'Boss Lady.'"

❧

She looked back. She saw the yelling maniac; saw the upraised fist. She retreated three quick steps toward the lake. That was no good. Catherine turned to face her tormentor. She would not throw her hands up in surrender. It was time to make her stand against this inept coward who snuck around and blamed her to cover his own hide. This man had become a constant thorn in her side. She planted her feet and waited.

Rat Face wanted a free rein to hit her as often and as hard as he could when he rushed down the hill at Catherine's back. At Rusty's warning she turned. She noticed spit spraying from his mouth. She gulped and instinctively ducked low. Wheeler's first blow flew harmlessly above her head. She grabbed his waist with both hands. In one motion she lifted the ranting, wild swinging man.

His wild swings missed her face.

❧

Rusty had felt an unaccustomed nervousness when he and Flo left Catherine at the edge of the lake. Any meeting with Art

Wheeler was not a meeting he wanted to happen. He told Flo to drive around the hotel on the road that rimmed the grassy approach above the hotel's mud baths. He could observe, but not be seen. Rusty quietly moved down the slope. The moment Art called her "Kate" Rusty knew there would be sparks.

Rusty kept walking slowly down the hill to be ready if needed. He saw Catherine attempt to pass by Art several times before she shoved him up the slope. His reward was to witness action which would make a great yarn for years to come. He would never forget the sequence.

When he saw Art arise from the grass and charge Catherine. He yelled "Look out, Boss Lady!" He saw her duck beneath the wild swinging blows.

৵

Catherine felt the angry rush of adrenalin. Like a shot putter she explosively shouted the moment she lifted Art above her head. She staggered under the weight of the fist swinging coward, but somehow she maintained her balance long enough to reach the edge of the lake. In one continuous motion she crouched, gulped in a deep breath and launched her burden with both hands. She pushed up with every bit of energy from her legs. Her explosive scream echoed along the lake. Power swept upward through her shoulders and into the flexing arms. An incredible feeling of triumph followed as she threw her onerous burden into the lake. She fought to retain her balance and not fall in the lake. She won. Catherine looked out at the lake

She saw and heard the rewarding splash. The ringlets of water at Art's entry point were spreading.

Art landed face down in the shallow water. His landing was further cushioned by the lake's soft mud. Every time he pushed down with his arms to get out, he sank in a little deeper. Cathcrine watched the struggling man try to get out of the mud. He was trapped in the mud and water.

She felt some alarm as she started toward the lake. He saved her the trouble of rescuing him. Desperately he pushed out of the mud, and then struggled to get his face above the surface. Catherine heard his hungry gulps for air. When he was able to stand she blasted him. "Stay there, Rat Face. I don't want to ever see you again!"

Catherine turned into Rusty, who wrapped his supporting arms around her. He shouted loud enough for all of Soap Lake to hear. "That was the greatest thing I ever saw."

Flo arrived in her car from above the lake at the same time the sheriff's car pulled in. She joined Rusty and Catherine to watch him reach out to the scrambling Art Wheeler and toss him a towel. With a hint of a smile the sheriff commanded, "Wash the mud off in the lake before you get out. You're a mess."

The wet, mud covered man dutifully complied. The sheriff waited until Art had toweled himself dry. Then he told the incredulous victim, "The hotel called. They've been getting complaints about you, young man. You've been using their facilities, making a pest of yourself, and not paying. Unless want to go to jail on a misdemeanor charge, I suggest you pay them the $12.00 you owe them for using their mud baths. "

"I don't have $12.00."

"Then come with me to the station. You can be our guest. I'm sure we can accommodate you for a few days." They relaxed and watched Art Wheeler being hauled away.

Every muscle went limp, but there was no relaxing. Catherine had seen the silently mouthed threat, "I'll kill you for this." She had seen the hatred in his eyes as he left the lake in the custody of the sheriff. A little tremor of fear had swept through her body. There would be no possible appeasement if they met again.

38
The Grand Coulee

Catherine held her breath. The view from the eastern side of the ancient Dry Falls was even more impressive than it had been from the air. It would take her sheep three, maybe four days, of normal grazing to move past the three and a half mile precipice carved out the lava rock by the historic floods.

She was even more impressed when she rode Jiggles closer to the edge of the lava cliffs. She dismounted thirty yards from the edge and cautiously walked closer before kneeling down to her hands and knees to crawl the last five yards. Then she lay flat clinging tightly to the rocky surface to peek over the edge of the high lava cliffs. Vertigo threatened to engulf her. She gasped for breath, inhaled deeply and drank in the sight.

Catherine tried to imagine the facts about the Lower and Upper Grand Coulee and turn them into something alive and vibrant. She couldn't. The stark image of a 400 foot wall of flood water traveling at 65 miles an hour and leaping into space over these 300 foot rock walls was incomprehensible. She very carefully crawled far enough from the edge far so she didn't feel fear. Then she stood and walked to Jiggles.

Catherine took her binoculars from her saddlebag and contemplated the magnificent view south. The lower Grand Coulee and its five lakes had been carved out of the coulee by the repeated undercuts of flood waters. In a very short time the flood had worked its way north to create to Dry Falls. Who knows what Dry Falls would be today if the glaciers hadn't receded or Missoula Floods hadn't stopped.

❧

Since she had dunked Art Wheeler in Soap Lake her nerves were on high alert. She had constantly found herself on the lookout for anything out of the normal. Every little unexplained noise caused her imagination to run amok. Malovich and Gilrakis sensed the nervousness and stayed close. Several time Jiggles turned to look at the nervous bundle sitting in the saddle. Petting the three of them had given her more comfort than she had given them.

Catherine absorbed some of the natural serenity of the plateau. The ever moving flock demanded some attention. This also had a soothing effect, but the shroud really lifted with the morning appearance of the yellow airplane. Catherine yelled and waved at the waggled wings. She watched it bank left and head for Ephrata.

She reined Jiggles around and rode through the brush and uneven terrain to the dirt road. On solid footing she yelled "Yippee-I-Oh-Ki-Yea at the top of her voice, and kicked the startled Jiggles in the flanks. The short, high spirited run to camp elated her soul. Happy and laughing she dismounted and took care of Jiggles.

❧

She had endured a great deal of anxiety since the incident at Soap Lake. It was forgotten as she raced to greet the airport's pickup. As soon as Tim stopped her mother stepped out of the pickup Catherine and threw her arms around her mother. "Oh, it's so good to see you again. What took you so long?"

"Whoa, whoa, slow down, little one! I've only been gone three days, and I did some things that will be of interest to you." She got right to her point of concern. "How's Rusty?"

After Catherine's detailed report which included a brief flash about Flo satisfied her, Catherine knew a second question would have to be answered.

"Did you learn anything from Art Wheeler?"

Catherine's face fell. Why did her mother have to ruin this reunion with questions about that man? Her voice became lower and resigned. "Yeah, I learned something. That man is not to be trusted and he is up to no good. That last time I saw him, the sheriff was taking him to jail. That's a good place for him."

"Don't tell me you got into an argument with him?"

Catherine's nodded.

Sarah sadly shook her head. "I asked you not to do that, didn't I?"

"Slow down Mother. Everything is going to be okay." Catherine laughed at the irony. She had been chomping at the bit for two days and now she told her mother to slow down.

She patiently explained, "Art was taken to jail because he had been pestering Rusty at the hotel facilities. Watching the sheriff fish him out of the lake was a satisfying sight."

"Catherine, you're not telling me everything." Sarah's voice became wary. "How did he get in the lake?"

"I threw him in."

Her mother dryly answered, "That figures."

⁂

Tim watched and listened to this meeting evolve from exuberant happy greetings into a series of teasing questions and half answers. He had no idea where it would end. He stood absolutely amazed when the two women stepped farther apart to stare at each other. What had looked like a squabble turned into relief and smiles because two people understood each other. He smiled when they smiled and laughed when they laughed. Then he invited himself to the love fest. "Okay, you two, how about letting me in on all this hugging?"

The surprised women quickly recovered and converged on Tim. With tussled hair and lipstick smudges on his cheek, he fit into the middle of the giggling arm-in-arm threesome as they walked to the camp wagon for refreshments. There were still enough small chunks of ice in the homemade chest to keep four bottles of Coke and two bottles of beer cool. Each of them sat down with a cola to set up a schedule for the rest of the day. Tim volunteered to take Catherine up first while Sarah visited Rusty to see how he was healing. Tim and Catherine would pick up supplies at Warburton's IGA store and deliver them after the flight. The usual cookout would follow at day's end.

Catherine enjoyed this schedule. She loved to fly, and later after the cookout she really enjoyed hearing Rusty tell her mother what happened that evening. He was a born storyteller. Her mother was entertained with a very lively version; one Rusty had rehearsed.

~

Catherine liked having the cook-out at her wagon. She enjoyed having people around. Her uplifted spirits had started with the appearance of Tim's plane and continued unabated throughout the day with the flying lesson. Tim was good company. Flo was the great surprise. Catherine warily watched Rusty introduce Flo to her mother as his guest. She relaxed a little when she spotted Flo and her mother talking and laughing. Rusty had the look of the cat that swallowed the canary. How much had her mother been told?

Rusty sidled close to Catherine. "I know Flo is a surprise, but I did ask Sarah while you were flying. She said it was fine. That was before she started asking me a lot of questions." Rusty fidgeted uneasily, "You know I had to tell Sarah everything I could about your fight with Art Wheeler, don't you?"

"Yes, I know that." Her eyes twinkled. "Did you tell her the truth or did you tell her your version."

He sounded offended, "Oooh, that wounds me, deeply wounds me. You know I told her the truth." He grinned at the remembrance of what he saw. "I only wish you had thrown him a little higher and he had sunk a little deeper in the mud. He deserved everything he got. I was proud of you."

"Thanks Rusty. How did she take your version?"

"Your mother is a tough lady. She can shoulder a lot of hurt, but you're something special to her. I really couldn't read your mother, but she's upset." He leaned close to Catherine. "I didn't tell her Art mouthed some pretty bad words." He nodded his head toward Sarah. "It looks like she's coming over to say something."

Sarah came right to the point. "Catherine, why is his story different from yours?"

"He saw it from a different angle, that's all. Just say his has more detail and is probably very entertaining. Let's not allow someone like Art to spoil a good evening. He's in jail and that's where he should be." Virgil interrupted further talk when he announced, "Come and get your steaks while they're hot and not burnt." The diners found scattered seats. Flo sat close to Rusty. Tim seemed more attentive than usual to Catherine. Her mother seemed to be a little distant.

Catherine wondered what was she thinking?

ভ

Only the warm starry night remained. Both Catherine and her mother had settled into   their bedrolls, and the two dogs had managed to snuggle up close. Catherine knew her mother. Something unsaid bothered her. She probed, "Okay mother, what's bothering you? Neither of us will get any sleep until you tell me."

She heard her mother's short laugh. "You do know me too well, little one."

"Well."

"You were flying with Tim when I finished talking to Rusty. It's like you said. His story covered a lot more ground than yours did. That was okay, but I wanted more information, so-o-o I drove into Soap Lake to see the sheriff and talk to Art."

"And how is the little twerp doing in jail? Did he want you to bail him out?"

"He didn't have to." She had matter-of-factly answered, "Someone beat me to it."

Catherine exploded, "What!"

"That's correct, Catherine. A local attorney, H. B. Dunn, appeared today and paid his bail and any expenses that were incurred. Art Wheeler walked out of jail a free man just as Tim and I arrived. Naturally, Mr. Dunn is not at liberty to say who his client was." Sarcasm dripped from her voice. "Mr. Wheeler had no such restriction. He let the sheriff know he wanted to enjoy the miracle mud of Soap Lake for a few more days."

Catherine snuggled deep into her bedroll like it could give her some protection from more bad news. She conceded, "Oh well, as long as he doesn't bother us, I guess its okay." She remembered Art's threat. Should she keep quiet? Did he have the courage or the smarts to carry out his threat? The more important question was who kept supporting Art Wheeler. Someone had to be responsible. Support meant planning and that made Art more dangerous than she thought. Catherine was positive he couldn't operate alone.

She sat up and looked across the wagon at her mother. "Mother, there is something you should know." She tried to make Art

Wheeler's threat sound as trivial as possible, but she voiced her concern. "Maybe it's time to find out more about him."

She wasn't prepared for her mother's laughter.

Catherine was a little piqued by this attitude. "Why is that so funny?"

Sarah's laughter subsided to a twitter, "Because I had come to the same conclusion. I told my attorney to check into his background." She dryly added, "I really don't like threats against my daughter."

೧

Catherine took one more appreciative look at the lower coulee from atop Jiggles and Dry Falls. Soon the sheep would be grazing inside the Upper Grand Coulee. She would be celebrating her twenty-first birthday on July 15th between the high cliffs that defined the coulee. Despite a few eroded openings in the lava cliffs it was impossible for the sheep to leave the coulee until they entered Electric City on the northern end and followed the paved road down to and over the Grand Coulee Dam.

Her thoughts drifted back to Art Wheeler. She knew him as a bumbler who botched almost every assignment he attempted, so why did his threat bother her? She knew why. It was because of the venom she sensed behind his threat. For the past eight days she had frequently used her binoculars to search the surrounding landscape for any trace of him and the two men Rusty had seen at the lake. The Soap Lake sheriff told her the two men, Anthony and Sam Tom, were both members of the local Siloam tribe and didn't seem dangerous. She wondered about the three men Tim had seen north of the camps. Maybe it was them. Nothing really fit. Art's threat at Soap Lake was too personal. If someone was behind Art's efforts Catherine sensed with every fiber of her being that Rat Face would be the messenger and the Grand Coulee would be the site.

39
A Knight

The distance from Soap Lake to the entrance of the Grand Coulee had been an easy 26 miles. The plateau terrain east of the Little Grand Coulee was a slight, ever upward slope. The topsoil was thin. The feed, though sparse was adequate. Hungry sheep meant a constant search for food and a constant search meant movement. Catherine and the two dogs kept the pace as the sheep meandered northeast from Soap Lake. Two days away from Dry Falls she checked on Virgil in the morning and then stopped at Rusty's camp for lunch. She had coyly teased. "Are you getting any more special attention from Flo?"

He drawled. "Well, you know, the Hotel Siloam does have a certain responsibility to see that its clients are satisfied. Sarah wouldn't want to waste money. Flo is making sure that my recovery is complete. That's why I camp where it's easy for her to find me." He chuckled at his defense.

"You're a sly dog, Rusty. I bet you've left a trail of broken hearts every summer between the ranch and Montana."

"That certainly sounds good. I wish I could live up to that expectation. I'm 32 and still single or have you noticed? There must not have been too many broken hearts."

"That just means no one caught you, yet."

Rusty's joshing turned serious. "I don't mean to pry, but what about you and Tim? He seems like a nice young man."

"He is very nice. I like him a lot." Catherine searched for words to answer Rusty. "He pays a lot of attention to my mother and me. It's always pleasant. I love flying, I enjoy our time together but that's about it." She sighed, "He's not Hank. I guess that says it all."

"Yeah, I guess it does, but don't worry, you'll figure it out." He ducked inside his camp wagon and returned with two ham and cheese sandwiches and some dried fruit. He opened two bottles of cold Coca-Cola. "Flo keeps me supplied," he shyly explained,

They were finishing their lunch when Rusty ventured his opinion. "Catherine, I know it's not my place to be giving you advice, but I've known you as a teen-ager and now as a young woman. I don't believe you understand just how much you changed. This drive has made you a lot stronger. It was no birthright thing that caused your mother to keep you on as the Shepherdess, and it is no currying for favor that either of us called you Boss Lady. It just slipped out the first time, but you've earned that respect. Virgil and I have talked about it. You work hard and make good decisions."

He cleared his throat and went on, "Now we know this Art Wheeler thing is causing you some trouble. Virgil and I wanted you to know that we're on the lookout and we'll be there to cover your back if you ever need it."

He teased, "It's not the same as Flo you understand, but we love you and we'll do all we can to protect you." Rusty suddenly became uneasy. "Enough said, Okay?"

"Rusty, you're wonderful!" Then she really made the tender-hearted hero turn red. She wrapped her arm around him and squeezed, thanked him and kissed him on the cheek. "I imagine Flo has done better than that."

"She certainly has!" Rusty's quick retreat to the wagon with the dishes was her reward.

A happy, recovering Rusty pleased Catherine, and if Flo made that happen; so be it. She could write several pages in her journal about the wonderful feeling Rusty had given her.

He left lingering images of a knight in shining armor.

Soap Lake faded into the distance. Catherine thoroughly enjoyed the peace and quiet of the Columbia Plateau as the three bands headed toward the Grand Coulee.

&

Coulee City, located on the south end of the Grand Coulee, was the railroad's entry to the Grand Coulee Dam. It became the distribution center for all supplies, including Portland cement. Every morning the loaded supply train left Coulee City on specially constructed tracks for its thirty mile journey through the Grand Coulee to the northern end of the coulee.

Construction of America's largest dam demanded an inexhaustible amount of sand and gravel. Concrete was created when these were mixed with water and Portland cement. Catherine thought it ironic, but very considerate of Mother Nature to let her monster floods of the past form the necessary large gravel and sand deposits all around the area. These were transported by endless miles of conveyor belts to the main mixing plant at the dam site.

She had to wait until the early morning traffic from Coulee City to Grand Coulee Dam cleared before the sheep were allowed to cross Washington State highway 155 and the railroad tracks. When approval came, Catherine and the barking dogs pushed the flock over the highway.

Once the sheep started across the road it was déjà vu again. Blackie bolted past the leaders and then stopped on the other side of the highway to wait for Catherine to finish pushing the sheep across. She couldn't help laughing. After the last sheep had safely crossed the highway she dismounted to hug and pat her black rebel on the head to remind him of what a good sheep he was. After one final hug she swung back into the saddle and began urging the sheep toward the railroad tracks and the west side of the coulee.

By evening the three bands of Sumertun sheep were browsing contently in their lanes inside the high lava walls that defined the coulee. The sheep would be in the coulee until they reached Electric City. Catherine was getting closer to having her dream photograph taken.

The 1938 photograph of sheep crossing the dam was firmly implanted in her mind. She wanted a similar photograph taken as the 4,500 Sumertun sheep crossed the dam. Catherine thought this the epitome of the summer drive. She grinned and chewed her lip at the thought. She had approached her mother about the possibility of a photo for a birthday present, but there had been no promise.

∽

It wasn't dreams of sheep crossing on the dam that made Catherine suddenly sit up in the early dawn hours. She trembled as she wiped cold sweat from her forehead. Malovich whined and stayed close as though he understood and shared her ediginess. The bad vibes and fitful sleep stayed with her until she arose in the morning. She remembered every dreadful detail of the dream.

She stepped outside to inspect the high black cliffs speckled with orange and yellow impurities. They stared stoically back at her. Did they cause her nightmare? She certainly hoped not. According to her loose schedule the sheep would be in this corridor two more weeks. Catherine didn't want to wake up every morning tired, scared and sweaty because of some darn dream she didn't understand.

She searched her mind for a name from her "Beginning Psychology" class at Western.

The term, claustrophobia followed. She paused to think about her dream. If this were true she should feel hemmed in. On the warm July morning she didn't feel this. The lava cliffs of the Grand Coulee were miles apart. This gap would become even wider before the western side disappeared at the northern end of the coulee. That shouldn't cause claustrophobia.

That night Catherine suffered another intense nightmare. Again she awoke in a cold sweat. Her head left a damp imprint on her pillow. This time she had a name; premonition. It was so real she could see where and when. It also meant she didn't get back to sleep.

40
Reinforcements

Catherine sat astride Jiggles and watched the pickup veer off the highway. It bounced its way toward her through the sagebrush, bunchgrass and the dying desert grasses like a drunk coming home.. She reined Jiggles to the left and headed for camp. She heard her mother honk as she passed the other two camps on her way to Catherine's wagon in the western third of the coulee.

She allowed her time to stretch before she enthusiastically embraced her. "Mother, you're right on time!" She noticed her mother's surprised look. "I didn't know whether you'd be here today or tomorrow, but I know your habits. 11:30 is on schedule."

Sarah chuckled. "That new highway is a pleasant wonder. It took me four and a half hours to drive from the ranch to your camp. That's been gravel or an ill-kept state road for as long as we've been bringing sheep this way. If the reason for the wider asphalt highway is the Grand Coulee Dam, then it's worth it."

Catherine pointed toward the western wall of lava, "Mother if you miss driving on dirt roads, there's always the old gravel road on the west side of the coulee."

"I'll stay on the new pavement, thank you." Sarah found the back steps of the wagon and plopped down. "I don't care how you cut it though; it's still a long drive from the ranch. She looked around at the sheer walls while she waited for the cold sodas from the ice box.

When Catherine returned with the cold colas they touched their bottles in a ritualistic toast, "Here's to you." Sarah took a long exhilarating drink and continued looking at the lava sentinels which the glaciers gouged out long ago. She wistfully observed, "It's hard to realize what this is destined to become. You don't think about it much until change is in the works."

Catherine followed her mother's gaze, studied the cliffs. She didn't think of them as any type of future, and then the premonition flashed by. Her face paled. She held her breath.

Her mother's instinctively tuned in. "What is it, little one? You're deathly pale."

"What did you mean when you said, 'what this is destined to become'?"

"I only meant that this area between the cliffs will become Bank's Lake when the Grand Coulee project is finished. That thirty mile lake is destined to irrigate a half-million acres." She peered closely at her daughter. She found a tired look to go with the deathly pale face. "Now tell me, what did I say that made you react like you did?"

Catherine had had no intention of telling her mother about a couple of bad dreams. She pulled her shoulders back. "It's nothing mother, just a couple of bad dreams that didn't set well." Catherine tried to shrug it off, but the last, fearful premonition remained. The anguish showed.

"Don't tell me it's nothing." Sarah snapped. "You're a capable, determined young woman. If something makes you cringe, even a little, it's must be daunting." She reached out and pulled her daughter close. "Now tell me, what you dreamed."

Catherine accepted the consoling embrace, just like she had many times before. She told her mother about the two premonitions. Sarah understood why her daughter was frightened. Just listening to her daughter description scared her.

⁓

In early evening the yellow Piper Cub flew low into the Grand Coulee with its wings waggling. Tim had unexpectedly caught Sarah and Catherine driving north on the old graveled road which hugged the western side of the coulee. He assumed they were inspecting sheep and maybe the road to see if he could safely land on it? What else could there be?

The three men he had spied walking three miles south of the Sumertun sheep were a surprise. Tim observed heat waves rising from the rocks. Between the cliffs on a sizzling July day was not a good place to be on foot. The coulee didn't attract miners, so why were they there?

He'd heard enough from Sarah on their flight to Prentiss to know some jerk named Art Wheeler had threatened her daughter at Soap Lake. Could it be possible the three men were there to cause trouble? Tim looked back. They were walking south to Coulee City. Then he pushed the stick left, kicked the left rudder pedal and circled back toward Sarah and Catherine and the sheep wagons before he banked left and headed toward Electric City. Everything seemed peaceful. He remembered the old saying: *An ounce of prevention is worth a pound of cure.* Tim chuckled at his nosiness, but he felt better.

⁓

Early construction on the Grand Coulee Dam made it apparent the small municipal airport at Electric City couldn't handle the increased air traffic. The federal government financed new wider, longer runways plus several buildings that served as hangars for aircraft or storage units. Tim was relieved to find there was still one service pickup available for use. He unloaded his bedroll from the plane and threw it into the back of the pickup. Sleeping under the stars was much better than inside a closed hangar. Tim enjoyed the leisurely drive on the new highway on his way to the Sumertun camps. Once off the highway any trail to the three camps became an adventure.

The drive down had given him time think of the changes the Grand Coulee Dam might bring. The coulee would be filled with thirty miles of water, some of which would irrigate the land around Othello. That bode well for his father's store, and possibly him. He stopped for a moment to say hello to Virgil and Rusty as he drove carefully through the brush toward the shepherdess wagon. That name evoked amusement, but that was Catherine.

She was the most headstrong woman he had ever met. She grabbed life with a zest which made it interesting. She took to flying with avid interest and determination. That made tomorrow something to look forward to. His musing stopped when the pickup bounced into camp and a warm welcome. This time he didn't have to ask to be hugged.

༄

The ice cold beer and Cokes and the simmering aroma of cooking hamburgers relaxed everyone. Even Virgil got on a talking jag. Tim learned that Flo, the woman attendant from Soap Lake had become a frequent visitor. Rusty just sat and grinned when teased. He finally informed them, "You know she will be here for Catherine's birthday, don't you? The more the merrier is my motto, and she helps."

Tim watched Rusty blush at this admission. They joked, they laughed, but Catherine seemed less jovial and a little tense. There was a subtle difference. What would cause this? Should he ask her? Was it any of his business? Tim admitted to himself that he had come to care about these people. He looked forward to seeing them. Maybe if he had been on the trail for three months he might be a little tired and tense too. A birthday party was just what everyone needed. He forgot the three men.

Afterward the cookout Rusty made it a point to find Tim before he and Virgil headed for their camps. He informed him. "Tim, I'm glad to see you here. Catherine needs a bit of cheering up. You and flying will help."

"I thought there was something in the air, but why does she need cheering up?"

"Ask her if you get a chance." Rusty hesitated before volunteering, "If she needs help let us know. Virgil and I will do almost anything for the Boss Lady. She has become a special young woman."

Tim watched them ride east toward their camps until the slight swishing of horses pushing through brush was all he heard.

༄

The surrounding cliffs shrouded the coulee floor in an eerie stillness as the long summer day slowly shut down. The contented bleating of the sheep was music to their herders. It was a time of peace. In the fading twilight Tim bid Sarah and Catherine good night, took his homemade bedroll from the pickup and found a suitable patch of grass. He folded a couple of old quilts to use as a mattress. Tim stretched out under the deepening darkness of evening and drifted off.

Muffled, mumbled voices woke him. Still drowsy Tim sat up in his bedroll to locate the voices. Someone lit the Coleman lantern in the Shepherdess wagon. The light silhouetted Catherine on the wagon's canvas covering. Tim smiled. The other voice had to be Sarah's. He shook his head to clear the cobwebs, but he still couldn't understand the mumbled jargon. Then the lamp was turned off.

Tim had no idea what caused the stir. He was interested, but it was probably none of his business. Sleep didn't come as quickly after this. He became conscious of movement outside the wagon and heard the icebox on the underside of the wagon open. This was followed by the distinct fizz sound of a soda cap being popped off. In the dim light of a crescent moon he watched Catherine sit on the back step of the wagon and sip her drink.

It was her heavy sigh that prompted him to quietly ask, "Catherine, are you okay?"

"Tim?"

He watched her scan the area until she located him. She came down from the top step and walked toward him. It wasn't the same silhouette as in the wagon. This shape wore pants and a shirt.

"Why aren't you asleep?"

"I was, but I half-heard you and your mother talking." He held his hand up and invited her to sit down.

Catherine apologized for waking him, but hesitated to accept his hand.

Tim pleasantly acknowledged her hesitancy. "It's okay. Why don't you sit and tell me why you're wide awake in the middle of the night." He laughed, "You're safe. I'm tucked into my bedroll and you're outside."

Catherine knew she was safe. How different was this from the time alone with Hank at Vernita. This was quiet and concerned. That was urgent and wanting. This was safe. That was dangerous. That was heated emotion. She didn't know what this was, but she settled for being caring and concerned.

She walked back to the wagon, and returned with an open bottle of pop and sat down. She noticed Tim's bedroll was two blankets, a cotton sheet and a beat up pillow. "Do you always pack a bedroll like this with you?"

"It's always in the plane. My mom insists. "

They touched bottle tops, drank and talked. Maybe a friend was easier to talk to than a   mother. She unloaded the story of her struggle with Rat Face at Soap Lake, his avowed revenge and finally her scary premonitions. She left out nothing. She felt relaxed and much better after she had completely confided in Tim. Someone to share her concerns helped.

"Wow, Catherine that's some story. No wonder you didn't sleep well. I think you can handle Rat Face, but your premonition is a different matter. You keep seeing it as a fire. Any reason why?"

"When I think of Art Wheeler I think of fire. That's probably the connection to my awful premonition. I don't think he has the nerve to avenge his resentment by a direct attack. Fire is an indirect way to fight and that suits him. I have nothing definite; just a feeling. I think he wanted a fire when he smoked at the lambing sheds. He didn't know me then, but after that I've became the target for his resentment. He probably used fire and fireworks at Prentiss as a personal vendetta.

"Trying to free the sheep at the Prentiss corrals was his only senseless act. It's the fire in my dream that scares me. Look around you. July's heat is drying out the grass. A fire in the coulee would be the worst situation for the sheep. That part of the premonition is clear."

She peered at Tim, without really seeing him. "That may be why the premonition of fire in the coulee makes sense. Art Wheeler wants to get even, but now it's personal. Trying to disrupt or destroy the sheep drive is one thing, except now he wants revenge on me. If someone is pushing him and doing the planning they'll want devastating results." She smiled wistfully at this thought, "That also means I don't think Art is smart enough or brave enough to do this on his own."

Tim cautioned her. "Don't ever underestimate your enemy, Catherine."

She agreed with this old adage, but more serious questions roamed around in her head. Who could possibly want to hurt the Sumertun Ranch enough to plan attacks on the sheep. What would these attacks accomplish? There was a time when loan payments relied on selling the lambs, ewes and selected rams at the end of the trek, but not now. The price of wool had been steadily rising since the war in Europe. It had to be someone who could guarantee that Art wouldn't be fired. Someone who would protect him and make sure he would be around to follow instructions. Maybe someone who was no longer around?

She knew only one person who fit this description. Corwin! His income had been jerked out from under him and his life changed. Even hope of a settlement vanished. Sarah didn't own the ranch. The Sumertun Trust did. Art Wheeler could no longer be protected, but why was that important? It didn't connect to the sheep. There were too many questions without answers. It looked like another restless night. She laid back on Tim's bedroll.

⁓

Sarah's eyes popped open at her customary 6:30 a.m. She looked across the wagon at Catherine's empty bed. Malovich and Gilrakis were also gone. It pleased her to know Catherine must be out doing her morning chores. She rolled out of her sleeping bag, washed her face, dressed and put on the coffee. When Sarah stepped outside to enjoy the cool July morning there was still no Catherine. She walked around the wagon to check on Tim. She strolled slowly toward his pickup. She stopped, and stared. There were two lumps in Tim's bedroll. Her harsh condemnation followed. "Damn it Catherine, don't you have any sense?"

At least they weren't still grabbing each other. Sarah had no intention of letting this type of behavior go on. Anger stirred at this total lack of control. My own daughter and this! What about Hank? She knew the two had some misunderstanding, but this was not only unexpected, it was right under her nose. Her stride became longer. Her face became redder. He blue eyes blazed. Total amazement stopped her dead in her tracks.

Gilrakis rose up from between the two sleeping bodies to check this first sound of the new day. Without a clue of what was happening he stretched and yawned. Sarah thought the dog looked very sheepish at being discovered. That pun softened her anger. When Malovich rose to see for himself what caused the disturbance, Sarah's anger disappeared. A wide, happy smile replaced all the hostility.

She knew as long as those two dogs were around, there was no need to worry.

As one, the two bounded over Catherine to greet Sarah. They had no idea what they had done, but they eagerly accepted her loving strokes.

It took no effort for her to wake the two sleeping beauties. She gleefully chortled loud enough to wake the two sleepers, "Come on you two. It's time to start the day." To make sure she turned to Malovich and Gilrakis. "Go get 'em."

&

Catherine escaped further harassment by cooking breakfast. Her mother didn't have to say anything. Her daughter just kept explaining, "It was really nothing Mother. I went outside to get a cold drink because I couldn't sleep. Tim saw me, so I took him a soda and sat down. He asked what was wrong and I told him about Soap Lake and about my scary dreams. Tim is a good listener. It's very easy to talk to him." She kept trying to make her mother understand. "He didn't judge. He didn't expect anything. He just listened and asked questions."

Breakfast continued as a series of embarrassed apologies and explanations. Finally Sarah could stand no more. She held up her hands in mock surrender. "Enough, already! I know nothing happened. I have eyes. I can see." She couldn't resist one final zinger. "I saw the bedroll. There was a blanket and two dogs between you and Tim. No man wants to fight off two dogs. "

Tim reached for two slices of bacon and another spoonful of scrambled eggs. The mischievous glint in his eye gave him away. Sarah knew something was coming. He looked like the cat that swallowed the canary. He quietly teased, "Actually Sarah, it was quite enjoyable. Maybe we can do it again, if it's okay with Catherine." He easily caught the biscuit Catherine threw at him.

He quickly changed the subject. "After listening to Catherine last night there is something I need to say." There was no humor in his voice now. "I saw you driving on the old road yesterday, and assumed you were checking the road to see if it was fit for landing. Last night Catherine told me about Art Wheeler's dunk in Soap Lake." He sighed and carefully folded the dishtowel he had used as a napkin. His news would only make things worse. "Catherine said you were out looking for any sign of trouble."

He noticed their solemn nods. Tim quietly stated. "The reason you didn't see anyone was because you didn't go far enough." He heard the sudden gasps, but he continued. "About three miles south of where you turned around I saw three men on foot in an area where there were no sheep. There must have been a car or pickup somewhere, but I missed it. I couldn't identify anyone from the plane. They were just three men in the coulee who had no reason to be out there.

"Coincidence? Maybe? My dad fishes and hunts with the deputy at Othello, the one you two met at the Crab Creek Coulee. He says there is no such thing as coincidence. Things happen for a reason." He hunched forward, his face stern. "You have the sheep here, Catherine is here, her premonition happens here, and there were three men in the coulee. That's enough reasons to be extra careful."

41
A Fire Escape

Catherine slowly drove Tim north on the old gravel road while he inspected the road closest to the campsite. He wanted to make sure he could land and take off safely and she didn't want to drive too fast and stir up an extra dust. They laughed as they shared the morning of explaining to her mother. Tim wanted to keep Catherine relaxed, happy and talking. "Catherine, I really enjoyed last night. I never thanked you for sharing your concerns. Did I understand it right? Did your mother say Rusty had a much better version of how Art wound up in the lake?"

It pleased him to watch Catherine's face redden.

"Maybe we could get Rusty to tell everyone about our waking up together this morning? I bet he could run with that yarn."

Catherine hit his arm in mock anger.

Tim needed a little more time. His voice softened. "Catherine, do you have any idea of how beautiful you looked in the moonlight last night, or how much better you look up close?" He wanted to keep her listening. A surprising thought surfaced.

She really was beautiful. Hollowness developed in the pit of his stomach before he laughed.

"What was that laugh all about? You tell me I'm beautiful and then you laugh. That's not very good, Tim."

"I was just thinking I should have said that last night, not out here on a dusty road in the middle of nowhere."

"That's much better. I enjoyed last night too. Why are you so shy now?"

He looked north to the tall cliffs to gather his thoughts. Did he dare confess another observation from last night? He decided to chance it. "I learned another thing about you last night."

"And what was that."

"Your silhouette against the lantern in the wagon was more revealing and beautiful than the silhouette outside in the moonlight when you were dressed."

She turned toward him, her eyes wider.

He braced himself for another hit. He sneaked a glance at her. There was only the half-hidden smile of a coquette. Warmth filled his earlier hollowness.

In that instant Catherine looked past Tim to the tall spire of rocks that rose parallel to the cliffs. The relaxed bantering stopped. The pleasant warmth of the moment disappeared. Her eyes opened wide. Fear replaced warmth.

Tim slowed the pickup to a crawl, stopped, put his right arm on her shoulders and pulled her close. Then he looked at the scene before them. "That rock is The Needle. Is that what you saw in your dreams?"

Catherine liked the warm assurance and stayed close. She nodded.

"How long before the sheep will be here?"

"Three or four days, why?" Tim barely heard her whispered answer.

His upbeat voice betrayed none of his anxiety. "That gives us some time. This is the narrowest place in the coulee. The

Missoula floods left nothing but gravel, sand and the Needle. Grass grows fast in the sand and dies quicker. The area will be drier in this July heat. It's the perfect place for your premonition to come true." He rested his cheek against her forehead and smiled. "That gives us a few days to prepare.

"Tim, it's just a pipe dream." Catherine protested. "Who will listen to a vision of danger that some young woman dreamed up?"

"I listened and I believe. So will your mother. So will Rusty and Virgil. Your brother and Hank will be here for your birthday. That's six people who will help without question."

Still stunned silent by her first view of the tall, thin rock spire and what it meant, she mutely nodded.

"Come on, Catherine. Let's get out and take a gander at this place just to see what we're up against." He opened the passenger door. She took his hand, and slid willingly into his arms. She seemed content to stay there. He comforted her for a few minutes before he warned her, "Its okay to be scared, but to do nothing makes you like one of your sheep."

The strong-willed Catherine started to protest, but preferred the reassurance. She made no effort to move away from the warmth his arms gave her.

Tim reminded her of her sheep facts. "I can't remember it word for word, but doesn't the 'Sheep Facts' hanging inside your wagon say that terrified sheep will stand there and wait until the predator kills them." In a low voice he coaxed her. "Catherine, you aren't a sheep. You're the leader of this drive. You must look out for yourself, the others and the sheep. Come. Let's scout this area. You'll think of something to win this fight."

They searched the area hoping for some answers. It was the blind leading the blind, but stubbornness slowly returned to Catherine. The determined jut of her jaw returned. The two of them spent an hour walking around and looking at The Needle.

Finally Catherine protested, "Tim, it's just another, large Tsmee-too."

Tim smiled. "Yeah, it is, but it might give us some answers."

The narrow, solid, basalt spire soared almost as high as the cliffs of the coulee. It rose from a large, three story high elliptical shaped lava base. Its foundation ran almost half a mile in length. A few huge rocks lay strewn around the south end of the Tsmee-too where the vortex of the flood had eddied. Little grass or sagebrush grew in the rock and gravel strewn gap between the Needle and the western wall. Other large boulders had been scattered south toward Dry Falls. The retreat of the ancient glaciers had saved the Needle. Catherine thought one more flood would have toppled the thin needle-like formation.

Back at the pickup Tim asked, "Well, did you learn anything?"

"Not really, but then I don't know what's going to happen. If Rat Face and his revenge happen here, at least I'll know the lay of the land." She scanned the area once more. An idea grew. "You know the days are getting hotter and the grass drier. Give it four or five days and the coulee is the perfect place for a fire, isn't it?"

Tim nodded.

"But, isn't the danger from the fire less in this gap where the grass cover is really thin?"

A great weight had been lifted from Tim's shoulders. Catherine was getting ready to fight. He glanced at the curious smile forming on her grim face. He asked, "Why the smile?"

"Buildings need a fire escape. Right?"

His answer came slowly. "Yeah."

"Isn't the empty corridor between the needle and the western wall what we're looking for?"

ॐ

Once in the air from the Electric City airport for the return trip to the sheep camps Tim told Catherine to take the controls. She calmly accepted her automatic response as natural. Flying was fun, and it no longer intimidated her. She circled the Needle area three times while she probed for any clue of why it was in her dreams. She'd never seen the rock formation before this trip. Her mind thought back to the Wahatis, the much smaller Tsmee-too in the Crab Creek Coulee. Did that image make the connection? Maybe? It didn't really matter. The premonition had come and she had to deal with it.

What did matter was her attitude. Tim had done the impossible. She no longer felt the overpowering fear. She became stubborn. She would not stand there petrified and unable to act. The danger, whether known or unknown, no longer scared her. She refused to be the terrified sheep described in her Sheep Facts. If the premonition came true the real danger was fire and Tim showed her the most likely place to keep fire away from her sheep. Three or four days gave her plenty of time to prepare; for something.

Right now flying demanded her attention. The landing pattern and doing everything but the actual landing waited. She laughed and spoke to herself, "I'm ready even if I don't really know what to prepare for."

❧

The moment Sarah had seen the dust from Tim's pickup leaving on the old road she saddled Jiggles and rode east to see Rusty and Virgil. She told them about her daughter's premonition. She asked them to think about suggestions on how to protect Catherine and keep the sheep moving. Rusty suggested killing the bastard, but didn't think he could do it until after the trek. Everyone relaxed at that.

Virgil thought night patrols were the answer. "That's what the large cattle ranchers used to do. Whenever there was a threat of rustling, someone stayed with the herd all night. It was effective." He wiped his chin with a large dirty hand and reminded

Rusty, "Today's rustler is a little quicker and harder to catch. They find a herd alone, then they park a cattle trailer close by and quickly steal about ten head. If it works they will come back again. Of course a few years back cattle rustling was a shooting or a hanging offense. Today the law might get mad if you shot one of the thieves."

Then he shocked everyone. "Shooting some nut to save Catherine is worth it!"

42
Twenty One

As usual, Sarah woke up early to greet the cool July morning. The rising sun would make sure it didn't stay cool long. The canvas that sheltered the top half of the wagon had been rolled up a few feet to allow any breeze to blow through the wagon. She smiled and rested her eyes on her sleeping daughter across the wagon from her. It wasn't a troubled face of yesterday. For that she was happy.

Whatever Tim had said or done yesterday had changed her daughter's attitude. Her normal, cheerful optimistic manner had resurfaced. Had Catherine forgotten the worrisome dream? Sarah doubted that.

When she had prodded her daughter for more information Catherine had just said, "There wasn't that much to see. The Needle is very a tall Tsmee-too. We didn't do much, but Tim listened, and took me seriously. Most of all he didn't laugh. We actually stopped and walked around the base of the Needle on the drive to Electric City. That's when he told me not to be like one of the sheep in Sheep Facts." Catherine noticed her mother's surprised face. "Maybe you should read the Sheep Facts paper which is hanging at the front of the wagon."

Sarah opened her sleeping bag, forcing Gilrakis to drop to the floor and stretch. That got Malovich's attention, so she opened the back door for the two dogs. Sarah poked her daughter and cheerfully sang the old ritual song, "Happy Birthday Dear Catherine." When her daughter sat up to welcome the special day, Sarah embraced her happily. She softly said, "Happy Birthday little one. Today you're 21. You are now, legally an adult woman. You're much more than that to me. Now let's get the day started. Do you want to wake Tim?"

An impish grin appeared on her daughter's face. "Let's get the dogs to do it."

~

It had been a good day for both women. Morning had been Sarah's time to fly. Under Tim's watchful eye she did everything but take off and land the aircraft. Afterwards she shopped for an hour in Electric City for fresh fruit and vegetables and a cutesy woman to woman birthday gift. She also picked up a gift certificate from Grand Coulee Photography. It wouldn't be a surprise but it was the one gift Catherine had said she really wanted. A photo of the Sumertun's three camp wagons and 4,500 sheep crossing the Columbia River on the Grand Coulee Dam would be her prize to hang on the wall at home.

On the way she flew around the Needle much like her daughter had. She listened to what Tim had to say about the disturbing dreams. "I figure there is something inside her that connects this and the past with Rat Face, excuse me, Sarah, Art Wheeler. Your daughter is not a fly-by-night woman. She doesn't act on whimsy. When she connects something up, it's time to listen. My personal opinion is that the premonition was a connection, albeit one we may not understand, but a connection we should take seriously." He paused to look back to see if Sarah was listening. "We both know whatever scared her may not happen, but wouldn't you rather have her ready to face a problem, especially one that could be as devastating as the ones in her dreams?"

Sarah wondered how one so young got so smart. She replied, "Talking up here while circling this area, it all makes perfect sense to me." She wondered if Tim could hear anything above the engine noise. She did her best to get Tim to turn around and talk, but he kept his attention on flying. That didn't stop Sarah. She just talked a little louder. "You did her a great service: you let her get her confidence back. I can't ever thank you enough, Tim."

She couldn't hear his mumbled reply above the engine noise. She decided maybe there was more to Tim other than a happy-go-lucky, twenty year old aviator.

෨

Catherine was ready to go flying as soon as they finished lunch, but Sarah wanted to see Rusty before Tim flew off with her daughter. Finally at 2:30 in the afternoon Tim taxied the short distance to the road. After a long run on the county road they lifted off. Catherine waited until Tim leveled the flight at 4000 feet before she asked, "Why are you and my mother stalling for time? You do know there's a party this evening, don't you?"

"The truth?"

"Yes, the truth."

"You get your first birthday surprise when we land. It couldn't be arranged any sooner."

"What surprise?"

"You have to wait until we land, but you'll love what's waiting for you."

Tim landed, taxied to the black top in front of the hangar, cut the engine, and left Catherine sitting in the front seat. She watched a tall, angular, blond man, probably in his early forties, ambling out in long, disjointed strides.

He met Tim halfway and they shook hands. Tim laughed, pointed to Catherine sitting in the cockpit and then left to go to the office.

The slender man stood over six feet, but couldn't weigh more than 160 pounds. A stiff breeze would blow him over. A shock of salt and pepper hair stuck out from under his flying cap. Catherine loved his smile, but what the heck was he going to do?

"Tim tells me you have been flying with him, but you need to learn to land and take off. Correct?"

Catherine nodded.

He reached into his shirt pocket and pulled out a small piece of paper. "This birthday gift certificate for flying lessons is from Tim and your mother." His smile widened as he said, "Happy Birthday, Catherine."

He introduced himself, "My name is William J. Foster. Most people call me Bill. I'm a certified flight instructor and I'm here to instruct you in the art of taking off and landing." He pointed to the office window where the smiling Tim stood and waved. There was an underlying good humor to his voice. "I told Tim I would find out if he had been a good moonlighting flight instructor. I know he's a good pilot."

She deadpanned, "Tell me, if most of the people call you Bill, what the rest of them call you?"

He laughed, "Just because you're twenty one is no reason you should learn bad words. You can call me Bill. Other names will come naturally if I can't teach you to land and take off." He gave her his hand to help her out of the plane. "First you must learn the preflight routine. Tim said he hasn't done this." He turned serious. "This is something you must do before every flight. It's the ounce of prevention that's worth many pounds of cure."

They spent a good twenty minutes going over the preflight check list. The list was common sense. Check the tires. A low tire that blows out on landing is disaster. Move the ailerons and the flaps with your hands. Check to see if the rudder pedals move the tail. Check the altimeter reading. The list even included checking the engine oil. There was a star by this important chore. "This may seem like trivia Catherine, but when you're in the air you can't get out of the plane to see what's wrong. This preflight must be done every time you fly. Don't get careless."

Back in the plane Catherine followed Bill's instructions and used the brake pedals to taxi the plane to the end of the runway and turn the nose back upwind. Bill explained, "This is the easier of the two operations. It's kind of like flying, but it's on the ground. Remember, you steer with the brake pedals until the tail rises off the ground. The stick is not a steering wheel on the ground. Ready?"

Catherine nodded.

Bill pushed in the throttle, and soon the little yellow plane was speeding along the runway. He instructed Catherine to watch the airspeed dial. "When the plane gets to a ground speed of seventy five miles an hour enough lift is created to leave the runway. You do this by pulling back on the stick. Feel my lead." Catherine felt Bill pulling back on the stick. The nose lifted. Free of the ground the air speed increased. The magic carpet ride began.

Catherine easily followed Bill's firm hand through the standard landing pattern. Tim had let her do this. They circled the airport and Bill directed her to fly the landing pattern. She entered the downwind leg parallel to the runway at 800 feet, nervously judged her distance past the end of the runway, banked left once until she was ready to turn upwind into the runway. This was as far as she had ever gone.

"Good job, Catherine. I can see Tim has taught you well. Now keep the control firmly in your hand, but allow me to do the flying." Catherine nodded. He cut the throttle to glide speed and lowered the flaps. The altitude faded downward and the air speed decreased. The plane descended toward the runway. Just above the landing area Bill cut the throttle. Catherine felt him pull back on the stick. The nose went up. The plane descended to the runway in a flared position. She felt the tires bump down on the runway and then they were rolling down the runway. Bill used the brakes to steer the plane into the taxi area before they re-entered the runway at the top end. Together they took off again.

Catherine flew the plane through the second go-round until the final approach. Then she felt Bill's firm hand take control of the stick. He complimented her, "Nice touch, Catherine." Her confidence rose. "Now follow me through the landing again." In a calm, assured voice he guided her through the landing. They practiced the take-off, the landing pattern, the approach and the landing for thirty minutes.

The afternoon temperature was July hot and a sultry 96 degrees. Catherine found out why she had to pay attention to the heat. Colder air is denser than warm air. Cold air meant lift came at a shorter distance. Hotter air meant it took the propeller longer to pull the plane to the necessary air speed for lift-off. Bill reminded her, "If you try to take off on a short runway in heat like today, you're in a lot of trouble. Remember the temperature when you go through your check list.

Catherine wiped the perspiration from her forehead. Another take-off and landing awaited her. She sensed a change and she was right. Bill informed her, "This time it's all yours Catherine. You have the controls." He reassured her, "My hand will be there to help, but somehow I think that won't be needed. Good luck."

She taxied onto the runway and pointed the aircraft down the runway. She waited as she tried to remember every little facet of taking-off.

"You okay, Catherine? I know you are a little nervous, but I'm here to help. Let's get going. Concentrate on the end of the runway and aim toward it. If you don't, you'll over correct." The interruption jarred her into action. She slowly pushed the throttle in and the plane started rolling down the runway. She kept in touch with her brake pedal until the tail lifted, and the floating sensation followed. The air speed climbed to 50-60-65. The plane felt like a puppy straining to get off the leash. When the air speed reached 75 and climbing she pulled back gently on the stick and the magic came. She was airborne.

When she had made her final approach to the runway, she cut the throttle to gently glide before she pulled back on the stick. She could feel resisting pressure. For an instant she felt a knot in her stomach much like her first drop in the elevator in Seattle. Then the bump of the tires on the runway buoyed her spirits. The tail settled down. She was safely on the runway. Catherine heard the pleasure in Bill's voice. "Good job, Catherine." When they came to a stop she heard his soft laugh. "Remember you're on the ground. The stick is useless as a steering wheel. You use your brake pedals. Now let go of the stick, push in the throttle enough to get moving and taxi back to the top of the runway. We'll do this one more time and then we'll do it again in two days. Okay?" Catherine mutely nodded.

⁓

Tim had watched the last "touch and go" with keen interest. Like a proud father he knew what should happen next, but he was nervous. His protégé would be flying.

After her second successful landing his breathing returned to normal. A perpetual smile creased his face. When she taxied to the hangar and cut the engine. Tim stepped outside to greet the victorious Catherine. He watched Bill help her out of the plane and onto the blacktop. Her smile, her facial expression, her jaunty walk all said the same thing, "I did it!" Tim knew the moment she spotted him. An enthusiastic wave followed.

Bill congratulated Tim when they met. "You've done a good job with her. And thanks for being smart enough not to teach her to take off and land or try to solo. The FAA appreciates pilots who do things the right way. Before she crosses the dam, we'll make sure she solos." Again he wished her, "Happy Birthday, Catherine.

Catherine's attention turned to Bill. Her spirits bubbled over. Her thank you was a flirtatious wink and a smile as big as the Grand Coulee. "Bill is what I'll call you. I can't think of any bad words after today."

Then she put her arm through the surprised Tim's arm, pulled him close and kissed him on the cheek. "That's for the great surprise. Thank you."

During the uneventful return flight Tim thought again that Hank was a lucky guy. He circled her camp to announce their return and noticed an unfamiliar pick-up. Tim made his approach, sat the plane down on the dusty road and taxied to the little clearing where he parked and cut the engine.

Catherine told him it was Pete's pickup they had seen. Tim pulled his tie-downs from the plane and she helped him secure his plane. Finally they wedged the triangular wooden chucks under the tires. She brushed her hands together when they had secured the plane and then pulled a small white handkerchief from her jean pocket.

"Thanks for everything Tim." She coyly flattered him, "If it wasn't for you I would have never known how to fly. You've been very good to me. By the way, Bill said you were a good pilot. That's big coming from him."

He noticed the laughter building in those teasing dark blue eyes. "What?"

Catherine took her handkerchief and moistened it a little with spit. "I don't think you want to have lipstick on your cheek when you meet Pete and Alex."

She thought; and maybe Hank.

43
Happy Birthday

While Catherine was away for her surprise flying lesson Sarah drove the short distance into Coulee City to purchase cold drinks, ice, fresh vegetables, buns and plenty of hamburger for the evening's party Her daughter's 21st birthday marked her as a legal adult. Her evolution from a carefree student leaving Western to come home to care for her to the present unknown result of her premonition was like watching a movie plot unfold.

Burke used to tell her, "People have to be fire tested before you see their real abilities."

Her daughter had passed every test since the day she came home, including the difficult saying no to Hank at Vernita, but here in the Grand Coulee she faced a different kind of test, a test against the unknown. She hoped it would be forgotten during the birthday celebration.

❧

Pete had been to these gatherings before. Along with supplies and Mrs. Andreason's two-tiered birthday cake, he brought enough battered, but substantial folding chairs for the group. The wooden canopy over the pickup bed also contained extra sleeping bags.

He waited patiently for the time when Sarah would explain the subtle tenseness that hung around the camp. He guessed maybe Hank was the reason. This would be the first Catherine-Hank reunion since Vernita. The approach of Tim's plane got everyone's attention. They watched the plane set down, bounce along the old road, and taxi to the off-road clearing. Then Catherine helped him secure the plane and laughed. With her handkerchief she wiped Tim's cheek. No one could foresee the result of this casual precaution.

Pete's gaze fell on Hank watching the same scene. The set of his jaw spoke volumes.

Pete directed his attention to Alex, who led the charge toward his sister. The two were obviously glad to see each other. After a brotherly hug and much laughing, Alex shook hands with Tim. Catherine walked in the middle, arm-in-arm with Tim and Alex toward the cooking hamburgers.

Pete stole another glance at Hank. The gray cloud of anger got darker.

Still elated from her great flying lesson, Catherine skipped into her mother's arms. "Thank you for the surprise. It was wonderful. Now I can take off, fly and land. Bill Foster said I would officially solo before we cross over the Grand Coulee Dam." She gushed on, "I never even thought about flying until Tim came from Othello with supplies. Now I can get my student's pilot license." She gave Tim another enthusiastic hug. Over Tim's shoulder Hank lurked in the background.

Catherine's enthusiasm carried over. "Hank, I'm glad you could come up for my birthday. Thank you." She walked around Tim and put her arms around Hank and lightly kissed him. It wasn't an "am-I-ever-glad-to-see-you" kiss, but not a peck on the cheek either. Pete saw Hank's reluctance from where he stood.

He watched his arms come up slowly and around Catherine. Pete knew everyone could see the same thing. He hoped Hank wouldn't be a damn fool and kick it all away.

Hank said something to her. Catherine stiffened. Her face tinged pink with embarrassment, maybe anger. Her smile faded. She quickly stepped around Hank and left him standing there, put on a happy face, took two steps, and hugged the pleased Pete.

"Happy Birthday, Catherine."

"Thank you Pete, and thanks for coming up." She reached up and kissed her favorite sheep man on the cheek. "You've seen every birthday, but you still make this day special." She looked around and said, "It looks like it's going to be quite a crowd."

She asked Pete, "Did you meet Tim when he flew my mother to the ranch?"

"No. I knew he had flown your mother to Prentiss, but I never met him."

Catherine made the introduction and the two shook hands. Now came the hard part. She returned back to Hank. "Hank, I want you to meet Tim Odets. His father has been one of our suppliers for quite a few years, and Tim is teaching me to fly."

His stony stare didn't soften, as Catherine made the introduction, "Tim, this is Hank."

"I'm glad to meet you Hank. I've heard a lot about you." Tim stuck out his hand.

Hank ignored the offered handshake, turned away and walked to the ice tub. He mumbled loud enough for everyone to hear. "I need a beer." Stunned silence followed. Pete couldn't believe what he witnessed. He felt a presence and turned to see the interested Sarah standing by his side. "This should be interesting."

They watched Hank pull a cold beer out of the ice tub. Watched him pull up the string that held the bottle opener, open the bottle, and watched him straighten up and turn around to face an angry Catherine.

It took no effort to hear her, "What the hell is the matter with you, Hank Hirsch? You've been like a bear with a sore paw from the time we landed. How dare you come up here and insult me and then Tim. Your behavior has been just plain rude, crude and unacceptable." If Catherine had been a fire breathing dragon, Hank would be burnt to a crisp.

Pete looked at Sarah. There was a trace of a smile and mischief in her eyes. This was a Catherine they hadn't seen before.

Hank didn't back away from this fire eater. "What the hell do you expect? The first thing I see after you land is my girl wiping lipstick--

"Your girl!" Catherine shrieked. She stuck her finger close to his face. "Get this straight Mr. Hirsch. I am not a possession. I'm not your girl. I'm nobody's girl. I'm twenty one and my own woman"

Sarah almost laughed at the stark amazement in his eyes.

Pete thought the loud, angry voice echoed in the coulee. He smiled. It should have.

But Catherine's anger remained. "My birthday has nothing to do with what I feel, but today I'm twenty one. I'll say it again. I'm my own woman. I make my own decisions. For your information I kissed Tim on the cheek at the airport when I was giddy with happiness. I just finished a great flying lesson, one that says I will solo and get my student license. I wiped off the lipstick to protect Tim. That kiss did not take one thing away from my wishing to see you again. Now I'm not so sure." She continued the onslaught with an ultimatum. "If you want to act like a horse's hind end; then-you should leave."

She stormed into her wagon and slammed the back door so hard it popped open. It stayed open. Pete heard muffled crying. Malovich followed Gilrakis through the open door. Pete heard soft keening from the dogs.

Sarah told Pete, "Those two dogs understand Catherine's every mood. I bet she's petting them and talking to them right now." She twisted her mouth a little as she remembered. "Pete, do you still carry that pint of whiskey in the pickup?

"Sure do, Sarah, and this seems like a good time for a real drink." He couldn't remember a day as bizarre as this had been. Somehow he knew there would be more to come.

⌐

Enjoying a drink the group heard Flo's car came bouncing through the open alleyways in the sagebrush. It was a welcome sight, and the eager Rusty made sure he was there to open her door when the car rolled to a stop. Flo stepped out of the car and into a hearty welcome kiss. She couldn't have come at a better time. The steaks were on. The big tossed salad was ready. They wondered what would happen while they relaxed on Pete's sturdy chairs. Virgil nudged Alex. In his quiet way he informed him, "If he isn't careful that Rusty won't be a bachelor much longer."

After watching Rusty and Flo walk arm-in-arm to the tub full of iced drinks, watching Rusty pull out two cold Cokes while barely taking his eyes off Flo, Alex informed Virgil, "I don't think Rusty wants to be careful."

"Amen to that, Alex."

⌐

Catherine washed her face with cold water and gave herself some time to cool down before returning to the group. She calmly asked her mother if food and celebration brought the sulking Hank from Pete's pickup.

"Not yet."

Catherine compared him to a coin standing on its edge. He could fall one way or the other. She longed for the warm loving Hank she wanted to touch and kiss, but right now anger simmered just below the surface. Would Hank apologize for his fit of jealous anger or did he expect her to come crawling back to him after her tirade? He should know better.

The glaring truth became another grating realization. She hadn't been any better than he had been, but his jealous, possessive "my girl" still stuck in her throat.

At 7:00 o'clock Flo gave Rusty the signal. He quickly moved to the head of the line when she announced, "Come and get it. It's time to eat." She stacked food high on his plate.

Alex poked Virgil in the ribs. "What did I tell you? Did you see that?"

࿖

Hank dreaded leaving Pete's pickup. He likened the call to eat, drink and celebrate Catherine's birthday like walking into the lion's den. He knew Pete and Sarah were upset with his actions. Catherine had left no doubt how she felt.

Today was the first time he had seen Catherine since Vernita. And what was she doing? She was wiping lipstick from Tim's cheek. Lipstick meant she had kissed him. Who wouldn't be upset? And what the hell was Tim doing that she wanted to kiss him. She said he was teaching her to fly. What else was he teaching her? He carefully watched Catherine as she helped serve the food and drink. Not once did she look at him. Forgotten was his expressed desire not to let anything interfere with his becoming a veterinarian. Forgotten was the fact they had agreed to be friends. Hank knew an apology was expected.

He didn't think he's done anything wrong when he called Catherine "my girl." Despite their departure at Vernita as friends that's how he thought of her. Hank sauntered confidently toward the call of food, cold beer from the iced tub and the birthday celebration.

He heard Rusty's hearty congratulation. "Happy Birthday, Boss Lady. May you have many, many more?" His "Happy Birthday" was a normal greeting. His term, "Boss Lady" wasn't. It seemed the most natural term in the world for Rusty to use.

He looked around at every happy face. All eyes shifted from Catherine to him. They left him no choice. He simply said, "Happy Birthday, Catherine."

"Thank you, Hank." She sipped her Coke. Neither knew how to react. Hank reached to hug her. Catherine reached up to kiss him. The duty kiss was Vernita all over again.

All eyes were still centered on them. Good or bad, he apologized for all to hear. "I'm sorry for whatever caused you to get so angry." That was the shallowest apology he had ever given, or heard. Would she even pay any attention to it?

Catherine replied, "Me too, Hank." She sounded as insincere and hollow as he had.

The warmth of their cheek to cheek embrace did linger. Maybe that was a start to the way back. He became cautiously optimistic.

He heard Flo's congratulatory "Happy Birthday" wish, but the information she passed on drew his attention. "Catherine you'll be happy to know Art Wheeler won't be bothering you for awhile, so enjoy today"

The relief was obvious. "That's great news, but what do you know that I don't?"

"He registered at the hotel yesterday like someone important. He soaked in the hotel's pool and wallowed in the hotel's mud area. Someone's paying for it. He's flashed more money today than the entire week before. He made sure I knew he would be a guest for a few days.

Hank noticed Catherine relax. Why should that news affect her? Why was everyone so worried about Art Wheeler?" He noticed every anxious face. Then he found Rusty. All eyes focused on Rusty.

They waited. Finally Rusty said, "Hank, I can see there's a lot you don't know. Let me spin you a yarn about Catherine, Art and Soap Lake. It started when I fell in those darn roses and a zillion bees stung me." Sarah and Flo waited for Rusty's entertaining version. The story kept getting a little better each time Rusty told it.

Hank listened intently while Rusty finished his gussied up version of Catherine tossing Art Wheeler into the lake and his "I'll get you for this" promise of revenge. His tale finished to a smattering of applause.

Hank told the gathering. "I agree with you, Rusty. That's quite a yarn, but that was two weeks ago. Nothing's happened since then, so why the worried faces? Besides, all of you know Art is full of beans. He won't do anything."

Sarah announced, "I hate to break this up, but it's time to eat. So far only Rusty has any food. Remember to leave room for birthday cake afterward."

Hank accepted his king sized hamburger from Catherine. The rest of his plate was heaped up with an ember baked potato, green salad and green beans. He found an open chair next to Rusty and settled in to eat and watch the party unfold. It was a happy, chatty group, but the underlying mystery didn't leave. He understood why Catherine would be anxious after her tussle with Art, but he didn't accept that it should still bother her. It must be something else, but what?

Rusty got along with everyone. Finally he asked him the question that had gnawed at him since his arrival. "Hank, I notice you and Virgil often refer to Catherine as 'Boss Lady.' I never heard you call her that before today. Why now?"

"Because that's what she is. She makes good decisions, decisions that Virgil and I have come to recognize as sound. It actually started after ... er..."

Hank understood the pause. Rusty didn't want to be put on the spot about the decision at Othello to let Catherine stay on as shepherdess. It was no secret that Sarah had asked Rusty for his opinion on whether Catherine could handle the job.

"It's okay Rusty. I know the final decision was Sarah's. I just wondered how the term 'Boss Lady' came about. It wasn't there at Vernita."

A relieved Rusty told him about the Ostlermann battle over sheep passing on the open range. He finished by saying, "The rancher is a perfect example. He changed from a belligerent enemy itching for a fight to a willing friend. The name fit after that."

Hank sensed some hesitancy in his friend. He was amused by Rusty's drumming fingers on his chair arm. He waited patiently until Rusty said, "Look Hank, I know you were probably unhappy with Sarah's decision, but the title has been earned, not given, and it didn't come because she is Sarah's daughter."

Rusty had more to say. "Hank, I know you and Catherine were very close at Vernita. I can see the situation is different now, but you're dead wrong about Catherine and Tim."

Hank sarcastically said, "Lipstick didn't just jump onto his cheek."

"They've become good friends, but there has never been any indication of more. He loves flying and is teaching her to how fly. She told you why she kissed him. Take her at her word. Don't lose out because you can't control your temper. Something unusual has scared Catherine, so show a little understanding. You can kiss Catherine good-bye if you keep on acting like a rampaging bull. Okay?"

He reluctantly replied, "I'll try to be a little nicer. Okay?"

"That's not much of an answer. I don't hear any regret in your voice."

"It seems to me that whatever is bothering her is affecting everyone? What is it?"

"Why don't you ask Catherine? Then maybe you'll understand."

❧

Sarah tapped her Coke bottle with a spoon until she had everyone's attention. She announced, "Now comes the good stuff. Thanks to Pete and Mrs. Andreason, Catherine has her favorite cake, a bona fide homemade, chocolate and vanilla, two layer marble cake. There are twenty-one candles just waiting to be lit.

"This celebration in the middle of the Grand Coulee isn't the fanciest, but Catherine, you'll never find one where there's more love. Today you are twenty one. You are now legally an adult, and a blood line heir to the Sumertun land and in charge of your own destiny." She laughed, "And mine until you get the sheep to the railhead. What really matters is you've become quite a woman. One I'm proud to call my daughter."

Rusty jumped up. "And one Virgil and I are proud to call Boss Lady."

Sarah didn't know where that came from, but suspected it was meant for Hank. She nodded to Flo, who brought the cake out from Catherine's wagon. Flo helped Sarah place the twenty one candles on the cake and light them. She motioned for her teary-eyed daughter to blow them out and make a wish.

Alex chimed in, "We have to sing before anyone eats."

"You're right, son." Sarah raised her arm and looked around. "Ready, everyone?" She dropped her arm and led by Rusty's robust, quavering, voice they sang "Happy Birthday" to the smiling Catherine. Amidst her cheering friends and family it took her two mighty tries to blow out all the candles.

Sarah and Flo passed out generous pieces of cake and made sure all of them had a cold drink. Sarah's pride shone like a star on a clear, cloudless, night.

ে৹

Hank had watched Catherine's cheeks expand like a glass blower's. It took two mighty efforts with all the wind she possessed to blow out the candles.

"I guess my wish won't come true." Hank heard the pathos in Catherine's wishful teasing. He watched the haunted look resurface and heard the whisper to her mother. "That's the way this week has been going, isn't it? When will it end?"

Hank had no idea what was bothering her? Whatever it was, everyone shared it, everyone but him. Not blowing out all the candles in one breath shouldn't bother her. He didn't want anything to happen to this woman who once meant so much to him. For a brief moment their eyes found each other. Some of the old warmth returned. They exchanged tentative smiles.

⁓

Catherine loved the momentary sense of assurance. The eye contact and Hank's smile had been the best part of her evening, but now every nerve tingled. Hank had been talking earnestly to Rusty. What had Rusty told him? After that little chat Hank had been very quiet, like a hawk soaring high and watching and waiting for a prey to appear. Now he sauntered toward her. A little gasp escaped. The last time they talked Hank was jealous and very angry, and she had countered with her own harsh angry words.

An electric tenseness hung in the air. All eyes focused on the two.

Hank casually congratulated her. "Happy Birthday, Catherine. I apologize for my earlier actions. I had no right to think like I did. Rusty explained that I needed to understand what had happened. He told me there could consequences for acting the fool like I did. I'm sorry, Catherine."

Catherine swore she heard a collective sigh of relief. She put her arms around Hank's shoulders and kissed him softly on the cheek and then sneaked down to his mouth. It was a gentle kiss that was more than an apology. "I'm sorry too, Hank."

It seemed to Sarah everyone had waited for this moment. Immediately the party loosened up. Everyone started talking.

Bottles of soda and Olympia and Rainier beer were lifted. The last remnants of the birthday cake were finished. They all wanted the fight to end.

Rusty sidled quietly up to Hank, clamped his hand on his shoulder and told him, "That was right thing to do; it was wonderful. Thanks a lot. You came a long way today. You two shouldn't ever fight."

"That's true, but there seems to be a major obstacle. I need some answers."

&

That singular remark slowed the celebration.

Catherine felt the hush and apprehension invade the pleasant aura that had followed his apology. He made his barbed observation, "Boss Lady, I have noticed something that puzzles me." His sarcastic use of Boss Lady permeated the air. The pleasure of the kiss vanished. Catherine asked, "And what is that, Hank?"

"A few minutes ago I asked Rusty why everyone is so anxious. He told me to ask you; so I'm asking you. Why are you still scared? I heard Rusty's version of you throwing Art into Soap Lake, and his snarled revenge, but nothing has happened since then. Today while I was sulking, I heard rejoicing when Flo said Art would be Soap Lake for three more days."

He paused and looked invitingly at each person. No one replied. "Well, it all comes back to you Catherine. Today you're an adult and you obviously have the support of everyone here. So what gives?"

Catherine sucked in every bit of air she could. It wasn't a subject she wanted to discuss,

But everyone here had shown support. She sighed, exhaled deeply and told her story.

When she revealed the secret they all shared, all eyes turned toward Hank. Catherine wanted the warmth and hope his apology had given her. Everyone waited for the endearing hug and encouragement to come.

They were dead wrong.

Catherine was helpless to stop his small laugh that started, helpless to keep it from growing into a sadistic laugh and helpless to stop the tirade that followed.

Hank stepped away from Catherine and looked at the high cliffs that surrounded the coulee. How ridiculous could this whole thing be? He faced the group, who had clustered together following his harsh, grating laugh. "Let me get this straight. Art has caused a lot of trouble. There's no doubt about that, but he has always shown he's not the brightest star in the sky. He just happened to be at Soap Lake when Rusty needed the healing powers of the mud and the lake. Then his tussle with Catherine ended again in humiliation and Art promised revenge." He glanced at everyone in the circle. He saw nodding heads.

Catherine retreated a step from his piercing glare.

"Two weeks later you have a bad dream, one where fire is everywhere. It scared you as a nightmare often does. Two nights later the dream comes again. You tell flyboy here and he sympathizes with you. That gives you the courage to drop your fantasy on Rusty and Virgil. They know which side their bread is buttered on. They give you a little sympathy and agree to help. All of you will drive the sheep into the barren area between the western cliff and the Needle. There you can wait out the fire; if there is a fire." He watched everyone for some reaction.

They stood there like gargoyles guarding the museum. Hank thoughtfully rubbed his chin and lower lip. He quietly said, "That's the dumbest thing I've ever heard."

He looked at the ashen faced Sarah. Her hands were wound into tight fists. "You would have fired me on the spot if I had wilted under these circumstances. You wouldn't have a man working for you who chickened out when your livelihood was threatened; especially when action came from, what was it, oh yeah, a premonition."

He heard the angry protestation before he turned to Rusty. "You and I have been friends. You've always helped me. I thank you for that, but you've misplaced your trust. "Boss Lady" does not fit this illusion. Your misplaced faith in her almost fooled me."

His angry laugh carried in the night air of the coulee. It bounced off the closer western wall and echoed north. "Dream away, Catherine. Follow your Sheep Facts sheet and I'm sure you will get the sheep to Montana, but I don't know when. You should go back to college and plan on marrying some poor jerk like Tim."

Catherine steeled herself with each verbal blast.

Good! He had meant the last verbal salvo to demean. He could see it didn't. She should be crying, but she wasn't. Instead she tried to control her rising temper.

&

The tensions heightened. Hank stood in the middle of quiet shock. No sympathy came from any direction. People were aghast at Hank's irrational attack on Catherine. The result of the tirade was predictable. The Queen of the Sumertun Ranch, as the mother of the maligned rose to stand beside Catherine, her daughter.

Hank had to know what would happen.

"You've passed the boundaries of decency, Hank. I can understand you resenting Catherine when I named her to finish the summer drive and maybe some anger on seeing Catherine wipe lipstick from Tim's cheek, but there's no acceptable explanation for your outburst about her fears. They may not happen, but for Catherine's sake everyone has expressed a willingness to help; that is everyone but you!

"No one should do what you just did. If we're as bad and gullible as you say, then I think you shouldn't want to be around us anymore." Catherine had heard the same deadly, quiet tone before. "Pete, will take you into town to get a hotel room for tonight and he'll pick you up tomorrow on the way home. I won't leave you stranded, although you damn well should be." She looked directly at Pete and saw his nod.

Hank stood quiet and angry. He finally understood he had alienated everyone and that he no longer had a job. For a few seconds he stood quiet and ashen faced, and then he turned on his heels and strode quickly into the night.

Catherine heard Pete's pickup door open and slam shut. She imagined Hank sitting in the pickup waiting for Pete. Soon after Pete left she heard the ignition turn over the engine until it fired and continued running. The clutch pedal was pushed and the gears shifted into low. Soon the taillights let her see Hank's departure. Bittersweet thoughts remained. She had hoped for some revival of the spark that once threatened to burst into open love, but now the romance seemed dead. She felt like a good cry.

Malovich and Gilrakis stood guard in the quiet, loneliness of the sagebrush while Catherine tried to wash away the sorrow and the anger with a good five minute cry. She willed herself to stand erect and square her shoulders. Then she dried her tears, reached down to pet her two protectors and walked dejectedly back to what remained of the birthday party.

Hank's wild outburst was the last thing she had expected. A slight smile graced her face. His sarcastic anger included everyone. She couldn't accuse him of doing things halfway. Catherine walked into loving arms and kind words. They all wanted to help her through this crisis, real or imagined.

⁓

When Pete returned Sarah caught his eye. He nodded and she followed him again to his pickup for the promised drink of the good stuff. Catherine followed. She could also use a rare shot of that hard stuff.

44
A New Thought

The scorching July weather climbed to 85 degrees by 9:30 a.m. It was headed higher. Catherine appreciated the escape aviation offered. She looked forward to her second hour with Bill Foster. After Hank's outburst destroyed her birthday party she welcomed any form of release. He left her with nothing to hold onto. Maybe the cut clean, cut deep way was best, but it left scars, big scars.

This was the start of a new day. Perhaps this was the best way to look at life, rather than worry what an unknown fear would bring. With that mindset she left for her final flying lesson at Electric City.

༄

Bill Foster walked around the Piper Cub with her, read the pre-flight check list and watched her perform the tasks. When they taxied out to the runway, Catherine cheerfully reminded him, "Remember, the hot temperature means we need a longer take-off."

He flashed a familiar "thumbs up" signal.

Catherine's second lesson thrilled and delighted her as much as the first one. Her hand on the student's joy stick followed Bill Foster's hand in the front through the first take-off and landing. Then she did four "touch and goes" on her own before she was instructed to climb to 3,000 feet and follow the Columbia River east for five minutes. It was a vista she had never seen. The river was still a dividing line. High desert and sagebrush lay south and east of the river. Rising mountains, beginning forests and alpine meadows lay north and west of the river. She would reach the greenery when she crossed the Columbia on the dam.

Up here it was so easy to forget her premonition. Maybe that was best. Crossing the dam was fact; the feared fire, imaginary. Hank's vehement rejection remained. Was he right? Probably? Would that stop his plans to become a veterinarian? Probably not! Catherine laughed loud enough that Bill looked back at her.

She followed his instructions to get into the landing pattern and land. She did so with the greatest of ease. Her confidence was visible as she taxied the plane back to the hanger and cut the engine. Bill stuck out his hand and congratulated her as soon as her feet hit the pavement. He said, "Great job, Catherine. You're handling the plane really well and with confidence. The only thing left is to solo. Can you come again in two or three days?"

"I'll let you know. I want to, but the next two or three days will decide a lot. After that things may not be so hellish. How about if I let Tim know, and then he'll let you know?

"That's okay. He held up his hand, leaving a tiny space between his thumb and forefinger. "You're this close to getting your student license. I'd hate to see you not do it."

Catherine thanked him again and walked the short distance back to Tim's plane.

Tim caught up to her and they climbed into the Piper Cub, cheerfully waved good-bye to Bill as they taxied to the runway. Heading south toward camp Catherine looked down on the dominant Steamboat Rock. A few minutes later they circled The Needle area several times looking for any clue that might cause trouble. This might or might not be the spot for the hellish sequence she saw in her dreams. Would she be free to fly or would the premonition stop that? She grimly thought her life was dominated by ifs.

❧

Tim dropped the airplane down to a thousand feet to watch the dust trail being thrown up by an old pickup traveling south on the old road along the western side of the Grand Coulee. Why would anybody be out there? Catherine looked through her binoculars to ferret out any details, but it seemed to be someone driving leisurely south to join the State Highway. Tim flew past the pickup to Coulee City and then came back over the same road. The pickup had never stopped. It had continued south past the three herds of sheep before it left the old county road and drove toward Soap Lake. By ten o'clock the next morning the three bands of sheep browsed near the Needle. Time passed slowly. The ninety five degrees of sweltering heat affected everything. On a normal day the sheep would be allowed to set their own pace. Today it took a constant effort by Catherine, Rusty and Virgil and their dogs to keep them moving. The sheep stopped at every chance, nibbled a little on the browning grass and tried to rest. Catherine looked forward to some relief from the characteristic afternoon breeze, which usually blew down the eastern slope of the Cascade Mountains. Catherine peered at the white puffs in the sky, sighed and wiped her brow with a small terrycloth towel.

She asked Rusty, "See any relief from this?"

He turned in his saddle to look west toward the mountains. A few slow moving clouds drifted toward them. "Those clouds have to be a lot darker before they drop anything. We need a little more heat if more clouds are to rise and cool.

"You can stop worrying, Catherine. We'll be in that protected area by nightfall and we can stay there a couple of days if we need to. Whether there is a fire or not, both Virgil and I agree that it much wiser to protect yourself than to ignore what you must feel. Don't worry you're doing the right thing." His use of her given name surprised her.

Catherine was touched. She stretched over from Jiggles to Rusty to hug him. The horses were too far apart, so she settled for several pats on his shoulder. "Thanks Rusty. It means a lot to know you think I'm not crazy.'

"I didn't say that. I just said we thought you were doing the right thing."

Catherine poked him on the shoulder and laughed. She felt better.

༄

Virgil had planted the seed. His idea of night patrols were enacted the first night the sheep were in the area of the Needle and the western cliffs. They would give the sheep two more nights of protection in the area inside the Needle and one more night when the sheep moved on.

Catherine felt like an idiot. That meant three nights of night patrols. The patrols had been set up to protect the sheep, but against what? Her premonition fire was the only danger, if it came true. If no danger came during this time, how long should the night patrols continue? Her mother had also contacted the Sheriff's office about the possible danger, and he promised to keep his eyes open. What a colossal fool she would be if nothing happened.

༄

Hank spent most of the long quiet ride from Coulee City to the Sumertun ranch looking quietly out the window. He spelled Pete once to drive an hour and a half stint, but the ride home stayed quiet. At the ranch he packed his few belonging in a duffel bag and waited until it was time to get his check. He would miss the check. Who was he kidding? Even before Catherine entered his life working on the ranch had been a pleasant time for Hank; one he would miss. It represented some softness. His father had represented nothing but hardness.

The awkward moment of goodbye arrived when Hank went to Pete's office to get his last paycheck. The two had shared more than a boss-employee bond. They had become friends. Pete handed Hank his paycheck. He reached out to shake hands. "I'm sorry it turned out like this, Hank. I wish you luck."

Hank knew Pete meant it. That hurt. He muttered, "Thanks Pete. I'm sorry it turned out like it did. My emotions just get away. That's no excuse for acting like I did.

They held the handshake longer than necessary, before Pete broke the spell. "Damn it Hank, why did you cause such a ruckus? Those two women really liked you, but you cut them no slack. You left them nothing. No mother will stand still and let you treat her daughter like you did Catherine. You dug your own grave. You're a good hand and I hate to lose you, but I have no choice."

Hank had no bravado left. "Pete, I'd apologize again and again, if I thought it would do any good, but I really was a horse's ass, wasn't I?"

Pete grinned and admitted, "Yeah, that's a fair description. You might get back in their good graces if you were a super hero and helped them solve their problem; if there is one."

Hank thought about the situation. Sarah and Alex were still with Catherine. That meant Pete would be going back to the Grand Coulee also. They would help Catherine ride out the premonition, if it came. That left him a couple of days to find Art Wheeler. Maybe, just maybe.

‿

Ant Tom complained, "That ain't enough money to do what you want."

"You bastards! You know I ain't rich."

"Somehow you got enough money to pay a lawyer and bail us out of jail at Soap Lake. Me and Sam have agreed that the price is not enough. It should be doubled."

"What?" Art Wheeler jumped away from the table in the Dry Falls Bar and snarled, "I already paid you a fortune. I can't get more. "

"So you gave us $250." He slyly smiled and said, "The rest don't have to be right now. We'll take it when we all get out of here, but before you leave Soap Lake. Ant Tom looked across the table at his younger brother, Sam, who nodded.

"Tell you what we will do, Art."

"What will you do?"

His grin reminded Art of a cat teasing a mouse. "We'll buy you another beer."

He wanted to reach out and strangle the cheating son of a bitch.

Ant walked unsteadily to the bar, peeled off enough money for three beers and a generous tip.

Stanton Williams knew it was time to stop serving. "Okay, but this is your last round. It's late and you've had enough."

Ant looked around the room. His brother and the angry Art were the only other ones there. He looked at the clock again. It read 11:55 pm. "Yeah, I guess you're right." He watched the barkeep fill their glasses and deliver their beers.

He proposed a toast. "Here's to a successful night for you, Art. Sam and I will not be there, and you get no money back." He gleefully exclaimed, "If you want to report us, you can tell the sheriff why you paid us.

Art threw his beer in Ant's face. The beer drenched Ant's face and shoulders. Art glared at him. "Drink that and tell me how it tastes! He was ready to yell at Sam Tom, but Sam looked ready to fight, so Art stormed outside into the warm July night. He circled the pickup twice to check the equipment. Tonight the three of them had planned to set the fires. Corwin had blamed him for not getting the fire started at the lambing shed. More harm or shame came when the fireworks at Prentiss failed. He quickly checked the pickup bed again. Everything was there. That damn Catherine had killed every fire he had started, but not this time. Tonight he'd show 'em all. He stepped into the cab, started the engine, and drove north into the Grand Coulee. He giggled at the exhilarating thought of revenge.

⤮

The sheep were settled in the area between the Needle and the western wall of the coulee. Alex took the ten to midnight watch. He sat perched on a wide ledge fifty feet above the coulee floor and leaned back against the Needle. That they considered him worthy to help filled him with pride. His used Catherine's binoculars to watch everything from the Needle to the highway. His first two sweeps were twenty minutes apart. Each sweep ended watching Flo and Rusty. Alex laughed. It looked like kissing was the most action he would see tonight. Who would have thought Rusty was such a romantic cuss.

It had been pleasant duty. He hated to see it end. He doubted Art Wheeler was really dangerous. His experience told him Art did things on the spur of the moment or in anger. If it required planning and determination, he couldn't do it. He reluctantly came down to the coulee floor when he heard his mother yell, "Your sister and I are here to relieve you."

"Okay, but I have to tell you I didn't notice anything unusual." As an afterthought he asked, "Are there any sandwiches?"

The little breeze had shifted. The welcome night coolness came down the eastern slopes of the Cascades. On gossamer wings the darkening clouds whisked in front of the quarter moon.

Catherine sighed. "Isn't it a beautiful night? I hope it cools down some by tomorrow.

Seems a shame to be worrying about what might happen, when we could be sleeping outside and enjoying the night."

"A lot of people believe in you. Don't knock it. You're a fortunate woman."

"Yeah, I am, but it makes you wonder if a premonition is worth all the trouble."

"Don't even think like that!" Her mother protested, "Outside of Hank I've haven't heard anything except a willingness to help. Even the sheriff is giving you some time. That says a lot." She turned in the saddle to face her daughter. "Let's split up. Why don't you ride north past The Needle and then turn east toward the highway. I'll head southeast and then turn toward the railroad track. When we meet we'll decide what to do next. Night patrol is tedious, but at least we will know we have done our share."

She leaned over from her horse and put her arm around her daughter's shoulder. "Let's not hear any more talk about whether you're worth the trouble. You are."

Only the gentle breeze and a couple of howling coyotes interrupted the lonely patrol. The quiet gave Catherine time to think about Hank's unlikely outburst. Evidently letting her keep the job as Shepherdess and the innocent kiss really upset him. Harvest would start about the time the sheep crossed the Grand Coulee Dam. Where would Hank be? If she hadn't been so intrigued by her premonition, would any of this be happening? The support she received was manna to her soul, but her inability to cope with Art Wheeler caused of all this. Catherine sighed. She stood between a rock and hard place. Only the imagined fire justified all this attention and she didn't want the fire to happen.

Two circuits around the area revealed nothing. Catherine and her mother checked in at her wagon for some coffee. Virgil would spell them at three o'clock.

45
A Fiery Night

After he stormed out of the Dry Falls Bar there really wasn't much for Art to do. It was time to put up or shut up. He checked the bed of his old Dodge pick-up again. The twelve, long wood shafted arrows were still in the back of the pickup. Conventional feathers adorned the back of the arrows. These would guide the launched arrows to their target. His target was the flat, dry grassland in the coulee. He laughed his high cackle. It was so big he couldn't miss it.

The large arrowhead at the tip of the arrow was wrapped in burlap and thoroughly soaked with lightweight oil. He planned to use the five gallon can of gasoline to saturate the burlap. The gas was the starter for the oil which in turn would stay burning on its sudden leap from the bow until the arrow punched into the ground. It would burn long enough to ignite the grasses and sagebrush where it lit. Twelve arrows meant twelve fires. Not bad!

He knew the Sumertun sheep had been pushed toward the Needle. So what? Dumb sheep would be scared of the blaze. The closer it came to them the more they would panic. Many would die. There was no place to hide in the coulee. That would teach that snooty witch she couldn't throw him in the lake and get away with it. This would show her. Someday he would make sure she knew just how he had ruined her. His giggle became a cackle again. And I don't need those double-dealing Tom brothers either.

At 2:30 p.m. he doused his lights and pulled off of the state highway and onto the dirt road that led him across the railroad tracks toward the sheep. From there it was all sagebrush, dry bunchgrass and shriveled desert grass. Even the darkening skies were on his side. Only twelve arrows and he would be back on the highway before the fires was discovered. Perfect.

༄

Hank left the police station at Soap Lake with one slim lead. Art had left Soap Lake that afternoon with the two Tom brothers. After hearing about the possibility of fire, the deputy had called Coulee City, but they had heard nothing.

Frustrated Hank went to the Soap Lake Café to eat supper. He checked in with the police one more time to inform them he planned on staying at the Lakeside Modern Motel at the northern end of the lake in hopes they would tell him if they found anything of interest. It was after one o'clock when the deputy called to inform him Art and the Tom's brothers had been drinking heavily at the Dry Falls Bar and had been asked to leave. Hank didn't wait any longer.

༄

Art poured gasoline into the large open pan he bought at the hardware store in Soap Lake. He laid the oil soaked burlap, covered arrowheads into the pan to soak up the gas, and then he waited. He lifted one out of the pan and put a match to the arrowhead. His eyes gleamed at the lighted torch. He fitted the notch at the back of the shaft onto the bowstring. With two fingers of his right hand he held the arrow in place and pulled the bowstring back. He smiled with anticipation as he released the arrow and followed the flaming arrow's arc. The grass started crackling as soon as it landed.

He left the other eleven arrows soaking in the gasoline to return to the cab. He pulled out the throttle so the engine would run at a slow, even speed. The throttle held its position. He jumped back into the bed and braced himself against the cab. He grabbed the second arrow, lit the gasoline soaked arrowhead and shot the arrow into the parched land. The flaming arrow hit the ground and broke into flame. The pickup kept chugging along toward The Needle. Three more gasoline soaked arrows were launched. The pickup went wherever the clods, ruts, or sagebrush mounds sent it. He held on for dear life as the pickup bounced through the sagebrush.

Panic grabbed him when he fell out of the pickup bed on the most violent lurch. As he scrambled up and ran after the pickup he noticed all five arrows left fires. Frantically, he grabbed the top of the pickup bed and leaped into the back. Most of the gas had slopped out of the flat pan and sloshed over the wooden pickup bed. Gas fumes filled the bed.

Art was driven to finish what he started. He grabbed the nearly empty can and poured gasoline over the remaining arrows. He fired two more arrows before the pickup lurched violently again to one side. He lit another wooden match. During his fight to regain his balance and finish his revenge he dropped a lighted match on the wooden pickup bed reeking of gas.

Then he remembered what the Ant Tom had repeatedly told him. "You can light the liquid gasoline, but the fumes will explode."

~

Catherine and her mother mounted up to continue their patrol. The moon drifted behind darker fluffy clouds. The scene reminded her of Halloween. If a witch on a broom skirted across the face of the moon it would be perfect. They rounded the northern end of The Needle. Catherine screeched, "Oh, my God." She pointed to the wild scene in front of them. One after another, five gleaming fire balls were arching through the air. Five grass fires erupted where the arrows hit the ground. There was a lull, but soon three more fireballs were flying and causing three more fires. The flames grew in sudden spurts. The coulee floor became alive with spreading flames.

Catherine spurred Jiggles. Sarah followed. There were no more fireballs. They abruptly reined their horses to a stop as a small explosion briefly outlined a pickup. Through her binoculars Catherine saw the outline of a pickup being engulfed by flames. She jabbed the binoculars toward her mother. "Look at this, Mother."

Sarah didn't need the glasses to understand what happened next. Both sat speechless in their saddles and watched flames scatter everywhere. A second, much larger explosion split the air seconds before more circlets of fire were sent flying from the pickup. The large fiery explosion tossed the pickup into the air. It bounced twice before it settled back on the earth and burned. Every fire in the coulee continued to fiercely burn. Fueled by the dry grass the flames were eating up the sagebrush and bunch grass in large chunks. Several anguished screams rent the night air.

A deathly pall followed. Sarah whispered the obvious. "Someone was in that pickup. Do you suppose- ? Catherine covered her face at the grisly thought.

e⌐

The first small blast woke the camp. No one remained sleeping after the next larger explosion. They all came on the double, scrambling to pull up their pants and tucking in their shirt tails as they ran toward the northern end of The Needle.

They stopped as one to see the coulee alive with spreading flames. The flames stretched for the sky. Rusty stood awe struck with his mouth agape. He kept mumbling, "I'll be damned! I'll be dammed!"

He stared at Catherine. "It's exactly like you told us. I swear if you dreamt you were taking the sheep across the Columbia by walking across on the water, I'd believe you."

⁓

Catherine almost laughed at the comparison, but serious matters remained. Her command, which matched the intensity of the fire, broke the tension. "Rusty, Virgil, Pete, we must keep the sheep behind The Needle. Come on Mother. We're already saddled up so we can get to the south end." She checked Malovich and Gilrakis. "Come on you two, you have a big job to do."

No one noticed the headlights coming toward the Needle on the old county road.

Catherine found her brother completely stunned and engrossed by the galloping flames. Nothing could have prepared him for this. Loud and clear Catherine yelled, "Hop to it, little brother, there's work to do." His sister's loud yell snapped Alex from his trance. He gave a quick look to his sister. She nodded. He put his foot in the stirrup and swung onto the saddle to ride double to the south end of the Needle.

⁓

"Could you use an extra hand, Catherine? I'll do anything you want me to do."

It wasn't possible. Catherine located the voice. Hank stood waiting for her. She wanted to crush him with her arms, there wasn't time for anything. Catherine yelled loud to be heard above the roar of the fire and the confusion of the sheep. "We're going to the south end. Meet us there!"

Hank ran at an easy lope behind them.

Once there Malovich and Gilrakis received their first "Cast" command. The dogs shot off on either side of the milling sheep to move them into one big bunch between The Needle and the western wall of the coulee. Hank took the western side, Alex the area closest to The Needle, and Catherine and her mother the middle. Catherine commanded, "Keep the sheep between the Needle and the coulee wall." Four herders and two dogs worked desperately to keep the sheep from scattering and running outside the area into the inferno.

At the other end of the Needle she knew Pete, Virgil and Rusty were giving the same command to their dogs. That meant six dogs were casting their flocks toward the center of the protective area she and Tim had scouted. Would it be enough?

When Catherine was satisfied she left her mother, brother and Hank to watch the south end. She rode through the huddled sheep and was pleased to notice the smell of fire caused no panic, only wariness. Catherine spotted several of her leaders. She stopped long enough to pet, soothe and reassure them. Blackie wasn't about to be left out. He came running for his share.

She stayed on the north end while Rusty, Virgil and Peter walked back to camp to get their horses. Both ends of the protective area were blocked by men, women, horses and dogs. The sheep would be safe, if the fire didn't become a holocaust moving west. Her watch read 4:30 am. In a half hour the sun would inch above the inferno. What would they see?

The fire had pushed menacingly to within a half-mile of the Needle. The heat surged upward and outward. Did that mean the normal morning calm would replace the easterly wind which was moving the fire toward them? Catherine certainly hoped so. That's when she nudged Pete. "Look at the moon. Which way are the clouds moving?"

Pete studied them for a moment. "You may be right." He chuckled, "Not only did you make the right call on the fire; you may be getting a miracle to help put it out." He checked again to make sure. "The wooly, fleecy clouds are getting darker and taller. They could turn into something good." He rubbed his chin and mulled over what it could mean. "Right now everything is going straight up. It's possible the wind is shifting. It all depends on the heat. Pray for more sultry hot weather. By nine or ten o'clock we may have the answer." Pete knew a hotter fire would be more dangerous. The direction of the wind was critical.

A load of fifteen firefighters arrived at seven o'clock. They went right to work setting backfires. They used their shovels to extinguish any embers left by tossing dirt on them until they were extinguished. Two large water trucks arrived thirty minutes later. No one wanted live sparks flying outside the backfire area to set another fire.

The sultry July temperature rose. The clouds got darker, bigger and taller. Heat from the fire caused them to rise. Colder air came rolling down the slopes of the Cascades. The temperature dropped. Hot sultry air made hotter by the fire rose even faster. The miracle of squeezing moisture from the clouds as they rose and cooled continued. Everyone gazed at the sky for the answer.

The first rumbles of thunder were heard at nine. Every herder and firefighter smiled and hoped. The tall dark clouds kept getting darker. The first lightning bolt crashed from a cloud to earth at five minutes after ten. The noise was deafening. Despite the thunder and lightening strikes the edgy dogs still worked incessantly to keep the increasingly anxious sheep under control. The lightning started new fires in the coulee. Dante's Inferno had come alive.

Pete kept his eyes constantly on the dark angry sky and Mother Nature's continuing barrage. He wanted more.

He got it. The first rain drop hit him at nine, forty three a.m. At first it meant only a few welcome drops. The winds coming down the slopes of the Cascades became cooler. The few drops turned into pelting rain. The full fledged thunderstorm became the hero.

Catherine casually sneaked a peek at everyone at ten fifteen. They were all smiles.

Pete stood in the rain, took off his hat and begged it to drench him. He watched the ecstatic Catherine receive the rain with open arms. She made no attempt to escape. Her soaked clothes clung to her body while she laughed.

Pete heard the laughter and joined her. He put on his hat and made one short comment to Catherine. "Come on, 'Miracle Girl' let's go to your wagon and get some coffee."

The wondrous rain remained over the coulee for a half hour as the west wind pushed every storm cloud eastward over them. The wind moved the clouds eastward on the Columbia Plateau. Catherine watched the storm move. Somewhere on the plateau it would dissipate. She could appreciate the coolness that followed the storm, but she knew tomorrow the heat would return. It always did in July and August. She rode with Pete to camp.

After the storm passed everyone rode to the north end of the Needle. The view was soul satisfying. The firefighters, the west wind and the rain had stopped the flames a scant quarter-half mile from the sheep. A few puffs of smoke still rose from the burnt coulee floor. The fire crews continued snuffing out any smoking ashes. The rain had filled any low spot. Rivulets randomly flowed toward other lower areas. It would take some time, but the coulee floor would absorb any standing water.

The sheep sensed the worst was over. They slowly moved north from their haven toward the wet, revitalized grass. They stopped to drink at every little collection of water. They spread out and the dogs allowed them to.

Catherine and her sopping wet mother stepped close and put their arms around each other. It was a moment of mutual appreciation which was obvious to all. Everyone was smiling and happy to have passed through the ordeal. They had pulled together with shared faith to over come skepticism and had seen what this conflict caused. They had seen and faced the havoc of the fire, faced the anxiety from the thunderstorm together, and emerged happy and whole.

Hank stood off to one side and witnessed another miracle.

After the first moments of gratefulness everyone came to Catherine and Sarah. They formed a tight circle with their arms around each other and stood unabashedly thankful. Catherine swore there were tears in Virgil's eyes. That was okay, there were tears in her eyes.

The pent up emotions gave way to big smiles and relaxation in the form of sitting down and having a cold soda or a beer. The babbling sound of happy people filled the area.

Catherine sensed the anxiety in her mother. She put her arm around her shoulders, hugged her and whispered, "Makes you feel pretty lucky and very small doesn't it?"

Sarah nodded. "It also makes you wonder why Hank came back." She approached the lone figure and stood before him. "I don't know why you're here, but we all thank you for helping." She put her hands on her hips. The Queen of the Sumertun Ranch demanded, "When you left no one here cared if you ever came back, sooo why did you come back?

The jubilant group behind her became silent. No one moved, no one whispered.

A single tear rolled down Hank's cheek. He flicked it off. He had lost it all, so why should he tell them anything? On the other hand what did he have to lose? It was already lost.

"I was selfish. I have no other motive. I was a fool at the birthday party. I told Pete I would apologize over and over again if it would do any good. I came up here looking for Art Wheeler to put a stop to this revenge nonsense. Instead I found the two half-drunk Tom brothers standing on the side of the road looking for a ride. I recognized them from the description the deputy at Soap Lake gave me because they were with Art at Soap Lake. What they told me scared me to death. They told me Art intended to start fires in the coulee. I told the deputy at Coulee City and drove out here on that county road in time to see the fires.

"If I had been an hour earlier there wouldn't have been any fires." He stopped to take a deep breath to stop his emotions from boiling over. He mumbled, "But I wouldn't have seen the miracle."

Sarah took a step forward. Hank couldn't read her, but he bet she wanted him gone.

He held up his hand. "No, Sarah, let me finish, while I can. To get here in time to stop any fire was my first motive. My other motive is simple and selfish." Hank gulped in another long breath, stood militarily erect, and bluntly stated, "If anything happened to Catherine because I didn't put out any effort to help ... well I couldn't live with myself. The fire gave me a chance to help and let her know I supported her.

"If there had been no fire I probably would have driven away. After all she was safe.

The fire caused all sorts of trouble, but I'd say Catherine is a very lucky person to have so many friends who believe in her, regardless of what I thought sounded stupid."

He added, "I also want to thank all of you. You've made my stay at the Sumertun Ranch pleasant, and you all had the great faith that was paramount when it was needed."

Catherine watched her mother step forward. Now what? Everyone waited. She said, "The harvest is less than a week away. There'll be work at the ranch until you leave for Washington State. You'll be a good veterinarian."

Everyone had witnessed another miracle; forgiveness. Sarah embraced the surprised man. Rusty called out, "You better have some grub and a beer before you go back."

There was guarded acceptance but that was a giant step from three days ago. Catherine became the awkward symbol of acceptance. Hank knew he would have to face her before he left. Would she follow her mother's forgiveness? He sat on a wagon step to nibble at his food. He didn't look up, but he knew when Catherine approached. He had cut her no slack and personally attacked her. Why would she even speak to him again? He waited.

"Hello Hank." It was a very timid beginning from a woman who wasn't timid.

"Hello, Catherine. I'd say you have been through hell since your birthday. I apologize for my share of it. You didn't deserve all the crap I dished out." He took another deep breath. "I can't begin to tell you how happy I am you survived Art's intentions." He bowed he head before speaking. "Ironically I'm glad the fire happened."

"Why on earth would you say that, Hank?"

"Because I got to help! Being here and helping says a lot more than an apology does."

"Then I'm glad it did. Thanks for the support."

One question still bothered him more than he would admit. "Can you forgive me for my part in all of this? I was so wrong. Are we still friends."

Catherine wanted far more, but would not take that step. It was too easy. "I can forgive you, but the scars will take a long time to heal. I can offer friendship, but no more."

He smiled. "Still bluntly honest, aren't you? I can and will accept that. Thank you."

Catherine reached out and lightly touched her hand to his cheek. "It could have so much more. Take care of yourself. " She turned and walked toward her mother.

He was thoughtfully munching on his roast beef sandwich when Pete came forward in the same purposeful stride Hank recognized. "What can I do for you Pete?"

Pete reached out to shake his hand. "I said you had to become a super hero to be accepted again and you did it. I'm proud of you. It will take some time and the result may not be what you want, but you are accepted. Nice work. See you in two days."

No one walked with Hank the short distance to his old black Ford.

46
Identification and Philosophy

The celebration was over. Who shot those arrows was the unanswered question. Thinking out loud Sarah said, "Hank had come up to Coulee City looking for Art Wheeler and the Tom brothers told Hank he was going to set a fire in the coulee." She looked at Catherine and asked, "I wonder what happened to whoever shot those damned arrows. Are you thinking the same thing I am?"

"I think so."

"You don't suppose -? It came out as an answer not a question.

In the quiet, late morning warmth Sarah, Catherine, Pete, and Rusty rode through the blackened coulee toward the charred pick-up. Scattered firefighters were shoveling dirt on any remaining embers.

Sarah noticed the sheriff's pickup leave the highway to follow the dirt road over the railroad tracks and head for the pickup's blackened skeleton. They dismounted at the burnt carcass of the pickup in time to greet the sheriff. Rusty happily joked. "We'll soon find the answer to our burning question."

Sarah shook her head, "That's awful, Rusty!"

Catherine slid her hand over her mouth to hide a smile.

Rusty slyly grinned over his groaner pun.

Sarah quickly turned away to hide her smile before she greeted the lawman. "Good morning Sheriff. We're glad to see you out here. It's been an exciting night."

"Good morning, Sarah." He extended his greetings to the other three. "It looks like there was quite a party out here. Can any of you tell me what happened?"

Sarah explained in detail what they saw from the time they spotted the first ball of fire flying through the air until the final explosive blast which sent the pickup, engulfed in flame, several feet in the air. "After that the damn fire spread in every direction until the firefighters arrived, but it wasn't out until the rains came. I guess you understand there was a lot going on here besides the fire."

The sheriff nodded.

Sarah proudly looked at Catherine. "Thanks to Catherine's hiding them behind the Needle we didn't lose one sheep to the fire. This is our first chance to investigate."

The four of them walked with the sheriff to the burnt pickup. It stood desolate and lonely on wheels bereft of tires which had added to the intense heat. The sheriff carefully surveyed the burned area. He pointed to the demolished gasoline can lying on the ground a good thirty yards from the truck. "Looks like it was blown quite a ways."

Rusty poked his head through the glassless window on the passenger side. "Hey Sheriff, look at this. The throttle is still out. It looks like someone pulled it out to keep the motor running and the pickup moving. Why would anyone do that?"

Catherine remembered the balls of fire were launched from different places. "Maybe someone stood in the moving pickup bed to launch the fire balls."

The sheriff's tone was sharp. "Why would you say that?"

Shocked at the tone, she mumbled, "It was just a thought. The arrows had to be shot from different locations to set the fires like they did!"

His voice became milder and less accusative. "Maybe I can help. About twelve-thirty this morning Stanton Williams, the bartender at the Dry Falls Bar, called the deputy on duty and told him he had refused to serve any more liquor to Art Wheeler and the two Tom brothers. An angry Art Wheeler left, but the brothers left a half hour later half drunk, laughing and flashing a lot of money. Stanton figured Ant and Sam got the money from Art."

He noticed their startled expressions so he explained. "Ant's real name is Anthony, but Ant is the name he uses. We didn't know why Art was angry until this morning when we picked up the brothers hitchhiking back to Soap Lake. It seems one of your hands, Hank Hirsch, had found them and talked to them. They've been in trouble before. It wasn't hard to get them to tell us more about Art and why he gave them the money."

He looked at Sarah. "Thanks to Sarah and the deputies at Soap Lake we knew about his threat after Catherine threw him in the lake." He asked Catherine about Prentiss. "He fired Roman candles from the old barn in Prentiss, didn't he?"

Pete, Sarah and Catherine nodded.

"Ant and Sam Tom told us Art had twelve, long shafted arrows with the arrowheads in the back of the pickup. Ant claimed they refused to help him start the fires, even when he offered them more money. My personal opinion is Art paid them for the arrows plus help to set the fires. Stanton heard Art demand his money back, but the brothers just laughed at him. That's when he stormed out of the saloon."

He asked them point blank, "Do you believe it was Art who shot flaming arrows into the coulee to start the fire?"

Catherine nodded. Sarah said, "Yes. We both thought of Art when we heard the scream."

Rusty interrupted again. "That throttle is the answer. If the two brothers weren't there to help, there was no one to drive. The pickup had to be kept moving because both Sarah and Catherine saw the flames coming from different places. That means Art was trying to stand up in the moving pickup, pour gasoline on the burlap, light and shoot arrows while the pickup moved." He had captured everyone's attention. "Does this make sense?"

"Maybe," the sheriff thoughtfully conceded. "That's a lot of ifs. If the gas can was open and spilled; If the open pan spilled; If the wooden floors soaked up the gas and left fumes; If a match were dropped when Art lit the arrows. Any flame would cause the fumes in the pickup bed to explode. If that happened all hell would break loose. The first explosion probably caused the gas tank to explode. It's a good theory, but we need evidence."

Rusty laughed, "It really makes no difference. Whoever did this has paid the price."

The sheriff told them he would radio in for two off-duty deputies to come out and help scour the area." He added, "I'm not trying to insult you, but they're trained to this sort of thing and you aren't. Please go back to your sheep and relax. We'll let you know as soon as we find the body, if there is one."

The deputies found the body within the half-hour. The sheriff walked slowly through the burnt grassland and sagebrush stumps to the campsites. He would report their find to the Sarah, but he needed more. "We think we know who it should be, but I need a positive identification." He searched their faces. "Any volunteers?"

The sheriff had reopened the dreaded morning memories. The two women had heard the early morning scream. Shivers ran up Catherine's spine. She glanced at her mother, who was hugging herself. They looked hesitantly at each other. Neither spoke a word.

Rusty understood. He silently nodded to Pete.

The victim had almost made it back to State Highway 155. Pete and Rusty were solemn as they scanned the body. The size was about the same. The clothes were charred pieces. The body smelled of burning flesh. The hair and eyebrows were singed; one ear was badly burnt, but the damaged face left no doubt. The sheriff unfolded a canvass tarp and asked the two men help him roll the body onto it. He carefully extracted the wallet from what was left of the back pocket. The outside had been singed, but the tightly packed inside remained unscathed. The driver's license was the final proof. Sheriff O'Connell wondered why Arthur Wheeler had an Oregon driver's license.

Pete and the sheriff lifted the tarp with the body onto the sheriff's pickup bed. Pete looked down at the tarp and made his salient observation. "Finally Catherine is free of Art Wheeler." Corwin slipped into his mind.

◦◦

The hot, sultry days of July returned the next day. Relaxed good spirits replaced the tension and the terror caused by the fire. At the Sumertun ranch harvest time approached right on schedule, two weeks after Catherine's birthday. Rusty, Virgil and Catherine waved goodbye to the home guard and returned to guiding their bands of sheep through the coulee. That evening the solid lava walls of the coulee were giving up their absorbed heat ever so slowly. Rusty mopped his head and neck with a large red-black bandana as he gazed at the cloudless sky. "Don't believe there'll be any rain for a while."

Virgil quietly observed. "No, but what we got came at the right time." Rusty smiled at his friend of many years. Virgil wasn't one to waste words. They had pulled their wagons to new campsites ahead of the sheep, and were riding back to move Catherine's wagon.

"It was a miracle, wasn't it, Virgil?"

"What was a miracle?"

Rusty pointed to the three bands of unconcerned sheep grazing north in the coulee. "If that fire had caught the sheep unprotected in the middle of the coulee, only God knows how many sheep we would have lost. Do you realize we didn't lose one animal?" He reached over to playfully slap his friend on the shoulder.

Virgil smiled as he reined his horse to the side, just out of reach. Rusty replied, "You know me too well, my friend, but my point is still true." While he had Virgil's attention he asked, "I've been wondering about Catherine's premonition. Can you tell me why on earth grown men would accept a young woman's premonition of hell's fire and brimstone, and never question it? It's laughable. Hank was right. It made no sense." He swept his arm around to the scene in front of him. "Think of what could have happened if we acted like Hank?"

"That's easy. We would've destroyed Catherine and sent her back to Western." The sagebrush philosopher reached down from his saddle to grab a slender spear of bunch grass and stuck it in his mouth to chew. "Couldn't let that happen."

"Why you old softie."

Virgil nodded, "S'pose so."

"Catherine told me it was destiny that brought her home when Sarah took sick so she could be ready when Hank broke his leg. That makes about as much sense to me as her premonition, but it happened. That's scary Virgil." He paused to see what Virgil thought of this nonsense.

He just listened and waited for Rusty to say more.

"She also confessed to me one day when we were bringing in the sheep from the river range that she feared she would never get the chance to do the summer sheep trek." Rusty shrugged his shoulders and looked questionably at Virgil. "Think she's right?"

Virgil chewed on the bunch grass stem another moment. "Don't know about that, but I do think she was a mighty proud when she left the ranch as the Shepherdess."

"She was good from the start."

Virgil nodded. "Her first concern was always for the herders and the sheep. That has never wavered. You couldn't help but see it. She was never a young woman on a lark. Even the premonition didn't change that."

Rusty smiled. "That's true, but she never really blossomed until Othello when Sarah told her it was her job. Why do you think that was?"

"Faith. You gotta have faith in people you love and trust."

"That's all?"

"Well, Rusty you're the story teller. You got anything better?"

Rusty turned in his saddle and looked at the blackened area were leaving. "Not really. You make it sound so simple. You say love and having faith will do it, huh?

The sagebrush sage nodded again.

The teller-of-yarns finished their scholarly discussion. "Tim deserves a lot of the credit for getting her back on track. He got her to think sheep first and premonition second. Right now she is sitting on top of the world. I'm not sure any of us really understands what happened or why. I guess we should be thankful we're all alive and we didn't lose any sheep. It's like Pete said 'It's a miracle'."

The contented Virgil smiled, nodded and then added. "It seems to me Hank was the only one without enough love to foster faith."

It was Rusty's turn to nod.

Virgil responded to the nod. "Guess we have to give Hank some credit for coming back. When I first saw him that night by the Needle I thought he just wanted to get back in the good graces of the women, but I believed him when he said he couldn't live with not helping Catherine. Helping with the fire and the sheep said it all."

"Okay, answer this question. Will Catherine and Hank ever be close again?"

"It will take a powerful lot of forgetting and forgiving. Forgiving will be much easier than forgetting. Catherine will have some great memories of this sheep drive. Hank's memories aren't that great." He spit tobacco juice off to the side. "Hank and Catherine might be friends; maybe?"

Rusty had one more question. "Do you think Art acted alone? Sarah thinks someone was pushing him."

"I don't think Art could cause as much trouble as he has by himself. I think there is still one person who is unaccounted for. That might mean more trouble" Little did he know how true his prophecy would be.

47
Dream Crossing

C atherine's spirit had started healing the minute she stood with Pete at the northern end of The Needle, heard the thunder echoing through the Grand Coulee, and felt the first light rain touch her face. The journey from The Needle to Electric City became as pleasant as it could get. Catherine was back in her comfort zone with Rusty and Virgil, and three bands of sheep. The tension was gone. The rain had left drinking water for the sheep and revitalized the grass. Songbirds returned until the water evaporated. Malovich and Gilrakis made the drive through the coulee easy. Blackie was even spotted cavorting at the front of the flock.

Catherine cast her eyes skyward to the drifting clouds, but no yellow Piper Cub appeared. Two days ago she had proudly accepted the certificate signifying she had soloed. Now she waited for the student license to reach her.

She often caught herself singing. It didn't matter if she was good or not. Nobody was there to put a damper on her carefree spirit.

ᥱᴏ

Catherine could hardly believe what lay ahead. Anticipation gave her a feeling of floating about two inches above the saddle. She flashed a happy smile at Alex driving her wagon as he led the sheep on State Highway 155 through Electric City. Her smile broadened as she and Jiggles fell back opposite her mother on the other side of the flock.

She flashed her daughter the same happy smile. Behind them Rusty, Virgil were moving their sheep along. The ewes that had made this trek before and led the way. The patrolling dogs made sure none disappeared at street intersections guarded by local volunteers and merchants. Flo and Pete followed the procession with the last two wagons.

Glenn Simons was the surprise. He had come to see Catherine's first crossing, but she had no doubt it was Sarah he came to see. He confessed it was also his first time to see this spectacle. Still, he had been attentive and excited. He drove his pickup into Electric City ahead of the parade, parked in a city parking lot, and took photographs of Alex driving the Shepherdess wagon, and the sheep and riders as they approached and then passed him. Then he hustled on a back street to get to the top of the hill to take some more pictures.

The clip-clop of the horseshoes on the pavement, the shouting riders, the curious crowd, the barking dogs and bleating sheep was music like no other. Catherine couldn't imagine life being any better. She didn't have to look back over her shoulder and worry. The last ten days had been some of the happiest of her life.

೬⌐

The anticipation, which started as they left their camp on the outskirts of Electric City, turned into exhilaration at the top of the hill. A mile of curved road would carry the procession 300 feet down to the largest concrete dam in the world. She cast her gaze east to the wide blue ribbon of water flowing west in a powerful, but unspectacular, current toward the huge cement dam which controlled it.

Grand Coulee Dam's hydraulic height was twice that of Niagara Falls. The crossing highway was almost a mile long. The strong even current from the east changed to roaring visible, violent foam and spray as it dropped 380 feet down the 1659 foot wide spillway to its river bed. The breathtaking roar overpowered them.

On State Highway 155 the sheep would cross the Columbia River above the spillway. The noise permeated every corner of the canyon. Catherine quietly scanned the entire entourage. She smiled. They were just as mesmerized as she was.

While the sheep passed above the spillways a rainbow formed through the constant mist at the bottom of the spillway. It would be noon before they were safely across the dam. Catherine could not describe her feelings. She caught her mother's wide grin and matched it.

The image of the dam large enough to control the drainage of an area larger than France and convert it into electricity and irrigation defied all reasoning. The construction of the planned power houses on the either side of the spill way was under way. If war came, they would furnish much needed electricity. After passing through the Engineers Village and the little town of Elmer on the north side they would leave the canyon and head north into the Colville Indian Reservation and the forest land.

⤳

The whole procession came to a standstill at the top of the hill. This was supposed to be work, but today it was unimaginable pleasure. Catherine's heart pumped wildly. Somehow she gave the "Western Ho" hand signal which started the procession down the hill. Her loud "Yahoo" shout startled everyone, but not the sheep.

On the southern hillside the construction had begun on the huge conduits that would carry pumped water up 280 feet from the Columbia to the proposed Banks Lake. When the irrigation part of the project was finished, the thirty mile Grand Coulee, through which the sheep had just passed, would be under water. Unimaginable! Who possessed such ability to look at all of this and see the possibilities? She just couldn't contain the thrill, enjoyment and a few tears that came as she led the procession down the hill.

At one time the sheep crossed the river on a ferry downriver from the unfinished dam. Later they crossed on the state bridge. Now they walked freely across the dam on a paved highway. The Sumertun Ranch was just one of several ranches whose sheep or cattle crossed over the dam. Most of the car's passengers and drivers were interested in watching the unusual sight. It was one to be enjoyed, and one to remember.

High above Tim's yellow Piper Cub circled the crossing several times and wangled his wings before heading for the airport. Catherine wondered what the devil he was up to.

Catherine felt crossing the river on the dam was the absolute epitome of the drive. She felt selfish as she and her mother led the way half way across the dam. Then they dropped back to check on the others and left the lead to Alex in the Catherine's Shepherdess wagon.

The total feeling of ecstasy was complete when Catherine spotted the photographer, high on the northern hill, taking pictures as they came across. It was taken from the same spot as the photo which hung in her wagon. Now she would have her own.

This was the part of the trek that had fired Catherine's imagination since she left Othello as the shepherdess. No wonder her mother reveled in the title, "Queen of the Sumertun" and the prestige that went with it. She felt like one herself while crossing high above the river.

The turmoil which had started at Soap Lake had given way to contentment and pride.

Once over the dam her personal elation gave way to the business of getting the sheep up the steep slope on the north side of the river. The sheep were pushed off the highway and guided northeast onto the long, grassy slope amidst the first small clusters of pine trees. The steep canyon forced the wagons to stay on the road until the top of the canyon.

The wagons left the highway when they passed the crest of the slope and pulled into a grassy meadow designated in Ricardo Urritia's log book. When the sheep joined them they sensed there would be no further pushing. They plopped down and rested or munched leisurely on the green grass, so different from the brownish grass of the arid, hot Grand Coulee. The dogs pulled back and let them browse. The long, grassy glade, amidst scattered pine trees, was still partially green in late July. The meadow marked the end of the first two thirds of the summer's journey.

Catherine sat atop Jiggles with one leg wrapped around the saddle horn and surveyed the peaceful scene. The day had been exciting, invigorating and fulfilling. She thought crossing the dam should be the grand finale. Nothing could be better than what had occurred.

48
Buffalo Meadows

In the protected meadow of good grass and surrounding pine trees the celebration aura faded into tiredness. It had been a long day filled with incredible memories. At the foot of the meadow the wagons had halted close to an old fire pit. The thirsty horses were unhitched, unharnessed or unsaddled before Virgil, Rusty and Alex led them to a small creek which frolicked through the meadow. After drinking their fill the horses were staked out on long ropes close to the wagons and in good grass. The horses found soft patches of open ground. Each of them rolled and rolled stirring up dust. Then they stayed on their backs and pawed at the sky. Their joy was apparent.

An easy smile graced every face. The message was simple; the work day was over.

Everyone took advantage of the three large logs embedded in the ground around the fire pit. In an idyllic setting of mountains, green meadows and contented sheep they sat down and relaxed. Catherine leaned back against her log to enjoy a cold Coke in this new setting.

Then she spied Alex. After the horses were tended to, he'd found the closest camp log and plopped down. He was beat. His first cold soda almost disappeared in one, long gulp. A tinge of guilt assailed her. Sometimes she became so concerned with the drive that the obvious was neglected. This was also Alex's first time across the dam. Catherine had to cover her mouth to keep from laughing when he dozed off and almost fell off the log. She quietly rose and sneaked up behind him and pushed her cold bottle of Coke against the back of his neck.

Startled he jerked away and discovered her concerned face. "Sis, what the devil?"

"I didn't want you to fall off of the log. Scoot over, little brother, and share this with me." She wriggled as much of her bottom as possible onto the log and wrapped a warm arm around Alex's shoulder to make sure she didn't fall off. "Well, little brother, what did you think of our first crossing? You looked pretty good driving that lead wagon over the dam."

He stood to stretch causing his sister to almost topple over the back of the log. The amused Alex grabbed his sister to pull her back. Then he asked, "Sis, did they have 'Show and Tell' when you were in grade school?"

She held on to his arm until he was securely perched on the log again. She answered. "Don't be an idiot. Of course they did. Why?"

"I want to tell the world what I saw today. That's how I feel. Whatta day! From the top of the hill to this meadow is a day I'll never forget. If taking sheep over that Goliath of a dam doesn't impress you, nothing will." His voice became a near whisper. "Amazing!" He became silent.

Catherine waited and let him enjoy his moment.

"Sis, there's just no other way to describe it." Alex put his arm around his sister and hugged her. "It was a little slice of heaven. Thanks for letting me lead the way for half the drive across the dam. Those spillways were loud."

"You're more than welcome, Alex. You were a rock back at the Needle, a cool head at a time when a cool head was needed. You deserved to lead us over the dam." A small chuckle escaped, "And don't forget I led part of the way. Great, wasn't it?"

"Amen to that."

They turned and watched their mother approach with open arms. "Well, little ones, you've had quite a day."

They nodded, accepted her infectious embraces and hugged her back. Alex told his mother, "I was telling Catherine I would like to describe to the world what I saw today. It was great." He teased, "Harvest will be dull and dirty compared to this, don't you agree?"

"Yes," laughed his mother, "but that's the other half of the ranch, so tomorrow you go back with Pete to the irritating dust and wheat chaff and the long hours that's harvest. The fields are golden ripe." She playfully teased, "Don't worry; you'll come back to the tall pines when it's time to sell the lambs and load everything on railroad cars to bring home."

From behind Sarah Glenn Simmons stepped forward and reached out to shake Alex's hand. "That was one great spectacle, one which everyone should see. I've built grain elevators all over Washington, Idaho and Oregon and I've never given a thought to what I saw today. You're right, Alex, it would be a great show-and-tell."

Alex grinned and gave his "aw shucks" impersonation.

Glenn quickly added, "You too, Catherine. Your mother told me all about your ordeal of fire, how it came about, and the result. You've proven that you are a very capable young woman. What did Rusty call you? Oh yeah, Boss Lady. He's right. I watched you very carefully today and I'd say you're a dangerous combination; beautiful, and determined."

Catherine dryly commented, "Nice to see you again Glenn, but aren't you laying it on a little thick?"

Glenn had the good grace to blush. "Maybe. But only a little. I run a construction company and I know a good foreman when I see him, excuse me, her. You may not know construction, but you would get things done. You don't easily accept compliments, even those that are true. I kind of like that." He reached down to pet Malovich. Gilrakis moved closer for his share.

She thought two grinning, tail wagging dogs were a great endorsement. She thought he was a handsome devil, and her mother had better be careful. He isn't some wimpy man she can boss around. As smoothly as possible she peeked at her mother standing beside Glenn. That picture jolted her. That wasn't two people standing apart. They were two people who were together.

She slyly observed Sarah's sun bronzed face, sun streaked hair, fairly youthful figure and shining eyes—that's was it. Blue eyes that shined posed a definite problem. She knew her mother thought she was in control, but Catherine had her doubts.

꩜

"It's about time." Rusty shouted.

They turned all attention to the tan, GMC pickup that followed the meadow road toward the campsite. They heard the horn's high pitched blare and saw an arm fly out the window to wave. The truck stopped close to her wagon and Catherine read Odets General Store, Electric City, Washington on the door. The driver's door opened and Tim stepped out.

Catherine watched him reach into the back and lifted out a large paper sack. Tim looked at Rusty's with a stoic, dead-pan face and innocently pointed and counted the contents. "I don't know if there are enough steaks here." He smiled to Sarah, "Maybe you didn't order enough. It looks like Rusty may have to settle for bacon."

"It won't be Rusty that eats bacon. Maybe you had better hustle back to Odets and find something to eat for yourself."

Tim feigned an earnest search into the sack. "Looks like you're safe, Rusty. Guess I miscounted."

"That figures. You should never trust something as valuable as steaks to someone that's not dry behind the ears. Gimme that sack!"

Tim pulled the sack away. "Only for a cold Cola. Deal?"

"Deal." Rusty's eyes still sparkled when he returned with Tim's cold drink. He thought that Tim was all right. He had showed some real smarts back at The Needle at a time when Catherine needed a calm influence.

❧

Supper became the main interest. The fire pit hosted a blazing fire. Tim and Rusty unstrapped the large iron grill from the side of Catherine's wagon and sat it on several rocks outside the open pit. Sarah directed the placement of the giant skillet on the grill. Then Flo and Glenn carefully dumped sliced potatoes and onions into the hot bacon grease. Soon the sizzling pan sent its aromas wafting around the camp arousing hungry appetites. Everyone tossed their steaks on the grill. At the right time Sarah cracked a dozen eggs into the potatoes, and turned them several times so the yolks and whites settled into the mixture.

Eating at the end of the trail became serious business. The steak, fried potatoes with onions with eggs washed down with water, beer or pop required their full attention. The fresh tomatoes were the unexpected treat. Virgil exclaimed, "Life doesn't get any better."

Glenn chimed in, "I'll second that! Sarah where in the devil did you come up with that eggs in the potatoes bit? That's wonderful."

Catherine noticed her mother's eyes were shining again.

❧

The group scattered some after supper, but Catherine never forgot the sheep. About an hour after everyone ate their fill, she exclaimed, "Okay everybody, up and at 'em.' It's time to check on the sheep."

It didn't work out the way she planned. The "Queen of the Sumertun Ranch" told Catherine, "Let me take Jiggles so Glenn can ride Mr. Gray. I think he'd like to ride out with me to check on the sheep." She tactfully gave her daughter an easy out. "You've had a long hard day in the saddle, so why don't you stay here with Tim and relax."

Catherine knew who wanted the evening ride and with whom. She laughed, "Okay mother. Just make sure you get back before dark. I don't want to worry about you."

Glenn understood. In a stern baritone voice he said, "Don't worry Catherine. I'll make sure your mother is safe."

"It's not my mother I'm worried about. It's you."

Catherine enjoyed her mother's warning look. She told Catherine, "Why don't you and Tim take the dishes to the creek and wash them while we're gone."

Only Virgil, as the elder statesman stayed behind. He filled his coffee cup before he returned to his nearby wagon. He casually advised Catherine, "I'd better enjoy this while I can. Tomorrow everyone will leave. You, Rusty and me will be alone again." Catherine heard the teasing in his voice as he left. "If you and Tim need any help with those dishes, be sure and let me know."

Catherine stacked the tin plates, tables knives, forks and spoons and tin cups back into the cardboard box that once contained supplies. Tim grabbed the large camp skillet and a large scouring pad and they headed for the creek. In a small eddy the huge frying pan was scoured with sand, steel wool and soap until it shined. Then Catherine filled it with soap and water to wash the rest. Making conversation at the creek, she asked Tim, "That was you circling overhead today, wasn't it? "It was."

"Why?"

"I know it's a spectacle from the ground, but from up there you can see the entire panorama. Now I have a surprise for you."

"Another surprise? What is it?"

"I'll tell you back at camp."

After putting the dishes, utensils and frying pan in their places in the wagon she reminded Tim of his promise. "What's the surprise?"

"Actually, I have two. One is for now and one for the future. How about a cold bottle of pop first?"

"Stop teasing me."

"Get me a cold pop. I'll even share it with you."

Catherine hustled to the cold chest under the wagon and returned with two uncapped bottles of Coca Cola. Together they tapped their bottle tops together, tipped the bottles to their lips, and took a refreshing first cold swallow. "Now," she demanded, "tell me why you were circling around the dam and the sheep."

"Do you remember Bill Foster?"

"Of course I do. Just tell me the surprise, and no more stalling."

"Did you know his hobby is aerial photography? He's very good. In fact he does quite a lot of work for the government." Tim watched her expressive face brighten. "That's right. Your first surprise is an aerial photo of the sheep crossing the Grand Coulee Dam. You probably won't see the developed photo until you cross the Columbia again at Inchelium."

Catherine put her arms around Tim's neck, pulled him close and kissed him on the cheek. "That's a marvelous surprise. How can I ever thank you enough?"

His casual request surprised her again. "Just slide your kiss down my cheek a little further."

She pulled back. They stood face to face. Their eyes met. She saw tenderness, not lust.

His firm, strong body felt so good. She laid her cheek back against his, held it there for a few seconds and whispered. "Not yet, Tim. I'm not ready; not yet."

She laid her head back on his shoulder. In the distance Catherine spied her mother, Glenn and Alex riding back toward camp. She wondered if they saw the clinch. She thought it wouldn't make much difference if they did. *I didn't see it coming.* She giggled. It was no wonder her love life was at a standstill.

Tim continued to hold her for a few moments. Softly he said. "I'm sorry Catherine."

"There's no need to apologize. You did nothing wrong Tim In fact it was quite nice."

Catherine hurried to change the subject. "What was the second surprise?"

He abruptly turned and walked to his uncle's pickup, reached inside and came back with a newspaper. He told her to read the headline. Bold letters proclaimed, "AMERICA ACTIVATES GENERAL HEADQUARTERS."

It was a scary headline. Catherine asked, "What does that mean?"

"You've been out here away from the world all summer. It means the United States can prepare for war by training armed forces within the continental United States. It means Congress will probably institute a draft sometime soon. They're already talking about it. For me it means I should enlist in the Army Air Corps and not wait to be drafted. I've talked to my dad and mom and they agree with me about choosing. I've talked to the recruiters at Geiger Field in Spokane. Right now, it's just a matter of time."

Catherine mutely stood in a state of shock. Tim reached out and embraced her. They clung to each other until the sound of the horses came close.

☙

The report was the same from everyone. The sheep were full, contented and resting. The evening finished as the half moon rose in the sky. This time it was silhouetted against tall pines instead of wondrous cliffs of the Grand Coulee. This time the evening cooled instead of the heat staying absorbed in the rocks. The excitement of the day gave way to sleepiness and getting ready for tomorrow's departures.

Catherine sat on the log closest to the fire and stared into the dying embers. Soon she had to get up and dowse the embers to make sure they were out. She had hated to see Tim go back to town and a warm bed at his uncle's house. Tonight she wanted to sleep close to him. She laughed. Her mother wouldn't mind if the dogs were there. Tomorrow morning Tim would be back with the last of the supplies. What would the future hold for him? That newspaper headline scared her to death.

She knew that the possibility of war existed, but it had always seemed so far away. Now the dreaded fingers of danger and death had spread to threaten those around her. She shivered at the possibilities. Tim and the Army Air Corps would surely be involved. Her thoughts drifted to Hank. Would he be drafted or be allowed to finished school?

She felt her mother's hand on her shoulder. In a soft, caring voice she asked, "Why such a long face, Catherine?"

She took the folded newspaper from her lap and handed it to her mother. "Read that hummer. It means Tim is joining the Army Air Force. It means Congress is authorizing army training. It means both Germany and Japan are causing big problems on each side of us. It even means Hank may not become a veterinarian. It means...," she buried her head in her hands, "Oh hell, I really don't know what it means."

She reached down and petted Malovich and Gilrakis.

Sarah smiled at the sight before sitting down beside her daughter. The two talked quietly until the last glowing ember disappeared, and Catherine threw water on the ashes.

49
Fish and Bears

The morning after the mesmerizing crossing above the Columbia River on the dam, everyone prepared to break camp and go their different ways. They waited for the last of their supplies from Odets Mercantile, so they could get started. When Tim arrived the eager group moved as one toward the pickup to distribute the last of the supplies. Within the hour the campsite would be deserted.

Catherine met Tim at the pickup ahead of everyone, and hugged him. Her pert "Good morning, Tim" should have warned him. She pulled him close. She felt the warmth of his cheeks, as she slid down his cheek for a quick peck. She asked, "Is that better"

"Way to go, Tim," chortled the delighted Rusty.

She teased. "There's no time for more, Tim. There's work to do."

Rusty laughed and wrapped his arm around Tim's shoulders. "After that big kiss you had better rest, fella!" He grabbed a box loaded with supplies and took them to the large table. Then everyone pitched in and soon the table was full of supplies.

When they were distributed to the three wagons the party broke up. There was nothing left but good-byes.

↬

The three bands often merged in the narrower confines of the mountain meadows. The sheep weren't allowed to linger too long in good grass as they had in the open spaces of the Columbia Plateau and the Grand Coulee. Catherine could almost see the lambs grow bigger and stronger. The higher, cooler elevations and the abundance of good meadow grass and water let Catherine keep the sheep moving without the worry of summer heat. Catherine looked forward to Inchelium, not because it marked another milestone in their journey, but to see Bill Foster's aerial photos of the sheep crossing the Grand Coulee Dam. Thanks to Ricardo Urritia's dog-eared journal and Rusty's and Virgil's experience the route north from the Grand Coulee Dam was well defined. The narrow valley and the surrounding mountains were entirely different than the slight slopes of the Columbia Plateau. The Sumertun sheep would travel north for about eighteen miles. A dirt road running close to the western side of the Kettle Mountains guided them through good grass, plenty of water, and her first ever bear sighting.

↬

She and Virgil were fishing in a creek sized tributary of the Nespelem River. Virgil selected a long, slow moving stretch of water fed by a faster moving riffle. They soon caught enough eight to ten inch rainbow trout for supper and for breakfast the next day. Fishing had been great, but there was no use catching more than they could eat. Virgil had told her fishing would be good the rest of the journey.

Relaxed and content, Catherine enjoyed the beauty of the creek running by the edge of the forest. She noticed Virgil switch from using grasshoppers as bait to a bright silver spoon.

"How come you're switching to a lure?"

He pointed upstream to the white water entering deeper water. "That pool is bigger and deeper. The spoon might attract a bigger fish." Virgil walked thirty yards upstream to flip his spoon upstream into the main current and let it work its magic on the edge of the strong current as it entered the quieter water.

Catherine was content to enjoy the alpine scene and watch him fish. Her reverie was interrupted by Virgil's loud yell. He motioned for her to come on the run. The fish fought to get back into the swifter water. Virgil kept the pole's tip up and tried to keep his balance as he stepped on mossy slick rocks. He had to be careful. The lighter line didn't allow him to muscle his fish to shore. His rod vibrated and flexed almost double under the weight.

Catherine was intrigued. That had to be one big fish.

Virgil had all he could handle to keep the fish from getting to the faster moving water. He nodded toward the bank and yelled, "Get the net."

Catherine grabbed the net from the grassy bank and waded out into the shallower current toward the end of the pool. Virgil's rod still vibrated violently. He was embroiled in a tense give and take battle. Gradually the fish tired. Virgil inched it into shallower water and toward the excited Catherine.

He yelled, "Net it!"

She reached out to push the net down on the fish. The line got in the way. The mouth of the net bounced away and the fish headed back to the protection of faster, deeper water. The brightly colored fish jumped out of the water. It shook its head violently to shake the hook. She gasped at the size of the fish. She thought of the big fish that came up the Columbia River and yelled, "That's a salmon Virgil. That's a salmon." He was too busy trying not to lose the fish to answer. Virgil just grinned. The fight was on again. Once more he brought the tiring fighter closer to shore.

She had some doubts if she could ever get the net over it?

"Net it from downstream, Catherine, so you won't hit the line."

She carefully took two steps downstream over the slippery rocks and held the net open. Virgil steered the fish into the mouth of the net and let the current take the fish into the net. Catherine triumphantly lifted the net high as the fish slipped deeper inside the net.

Virgil commanded, "Keep that net high, Catherine."

She couldn't believe the size of that fish. Her eyes focused on the prize. The wide red stripe ran the length of the fish. Black random freckles decorated the dark-moss colored dorsal view. She lost her concentration for just a moment to excitedly yell again, "Virgil, that's the biggest fish I've ever seen!"

The current's pressure against her feet didn't let up. She carefully slid her foot to get a better position. It became a struggle to keep the net high. Her foot hit a flat, slick, moss covered rock. She floundered about kicking and splashing water everywhere. Unable to keep her balance her feet shot up high in the air and her rear end went down. Kerplop! She sat down half submerged in two feet of fast water. She still held the net high and triumphantly gasped, "I still got him, Virgil."

"You sure do Catherine" Virgil splashed into the river to help her stand. "You just netted the biggest fish I've ever caught."

They waded ashore holding the big trout securely in the net. Catherine was soaked from head to foot, but she didn't care. She shook her head. Water flew in all directions. Like a clear bell her laugh echoed through the meadow.

Virgil proudly held the flopping prize high. Its silvery lower scales reflected light like a diamond. He proudly proclaimed, "Looks to be about eighteen inches long, probably six inches deep, and maybe eight pounds. That's one big fish." Virgil stepped back into the river and lowered the fish into the current. The moving water flowed through the mouth and out the gills.

Virgil held it the big fish by the tail and head while it recovered. Then he released it and the big rainbow slowly swam upstream like nothing had ever happened.

Catherine stammered, "What on earth! Why are you letting it go?"

"We have all the fish we'll need." In the clear mountain stream Virgil could still see the dark shadow moving away. He chuckled with admiration at the sight. It took one quick flip of the tail for the fish to disappear. "Besides he has the right to live the rest of his life here. It takes several years to get that big."

This was a side of Virgil she had never seen. Maybe he was right. To give back and not just take was something to think about. They used a few minutes to clean the remaining fish before leaving the creek. They still had plenty of fish for dinner and breakfast.

Catherine posed a question that had been bothering her. "When I first saw that huge rainbow, I thought it was a salmon. Isn't that why you switched to a spoon?"

He shook his head. "When I told you I wanted to catch a bigger fish I meant a big trout. There's no salmon in this stream. They couldn't get here from the Columbia. The canyon walls are too steep."

Before she could pursue this subject any further she saw Virgil straighten up and look intently into the forest. She followed his eyes fifty yards left where the bend in the creek stayed close to the forest. She saw nothing. He warned her, "Just slosh quietly toward Jiggles and mount up. There's no reason to be scared. I believe in just being cautious, especially with bears."

They pushed their telescope rods back to their 2 foot lengths. Catherine took them and the net to her horse. Virgil slid the cleaned fish into a gunny sack and tied it to the back of his saddle.

Virgil returned his gaze back upriver and the forest.

"What do you see, Virgil?"

He pointed upstream to the edge of the shade where the water and forest blended.

Catherine saw nothing. Then she exclaimed, "Something moved and it's coming from the shadows to the river." She gasped, "It's a bear."

"It's a mama black bear. Let's wait quietly a few minutes and see if there are cubs."

They watched the bear stand up and raise its head to sniff the air. When she was satisfied that no danger lurked she ambled into the river, and plowed upriver to the head of the rapids.

"Why is she going there, Virgil?"

"Use your head, Catherine. Where did I cast my spoon?"

"Upstream." She admitted, "I guess that was a dumb question. Here's another dumb one. Is the bear just waiting for the fish to swim right into its jaws?

"The bear is a lazy fisherman. She'll wait until supper comes to her." He shrugged his shoulders. "If supper doesn't come to the bear she'll move to the quieter, shallow water and use her claws to swipe a fish out to the shore or she'll dive in with its mouth to catch dinner." He warned the curious Catherine, "Its best not to irritate her, especially if there are cubs. That's what I was hoping see. Maybe another day?"

The y didn't have to wait for another day. "Look!" cried Catherine. Virgil looked back and chuckled. Without a care in the world twin cubs ambled out of the shadows. They jumped into the water and splashed, looked around and then splashed some more. The mother cuffed one of them. They immediately climbed out of the river to sit and watch their mother fish.

Catherine found herself wishing the black bear would catch a trout while they were looking, but it didn't happen. The mama bear had other problems. Catherine's attention was drawn back to the cubs. She couldn't help laughing. One had playfully pushed the other. Like two small children it was impossible for them to sit very long. Unaware of anything they frolicked like two fur balls on the grassy slope. The fun stopped when the cubs rolled into the river. Like any mother, who had enough, she left her fishing to discipline her charges. This time the subdued cubs stayed out of trouble while their mother fished.

᭳

Back in camp, after a short afternoon reconnaissance ride, Catherine watched Virgil use his small camp shovel to push the dying embers aside revealing the top of the cast iron Dutch oven. He poked around with the shovel to locate the bail and get it upright. Then he used a heavy padded mitt to lift the heavy pot out of the fire pit and set it aside to cool.

Later when Virgil used the padded mitt to lift the lid oohs and aahs filled the area. All they saw were packages wrapped in tinfoil, but the aroma...ooh-la-la. Impatiently Rusty asked, "Is it ready yet? I can't wait to taste whatever it is."

Virgil barked, "You're worse than coyotes. Step aside." He carefully removed one of the packages and put it on a plate so he could open the heavy layered tinfoil. Carrots, onions, potatoes and fish had been roasted together. He eyed Rusty, "Go ahead and take some. I'm afraid if you don't you'll drool on everything."

Catherine followed Rusty. She cautiously sampled the trout. Her eyes opened wide in amazement. The breath taking taste backed up the aroma. She had to know. "Where in the world did you learn to cook fish like this, Virgil? It tastes even better than it smells."

"Sheepherders who don't become decent cooks do one of two things; they get really skinny or they get disgusted and quit. Out here you have time to experiment a little."

Rusty's hearty laugh interrupted, "It looks like you had enough time to become a good cook. You sure ain't skinny."

Virgil smiled and invited them to dig in. As everyone filled their plates, he quietly chided Rusty, "You know what they say. Never trust a skinny cook."

Catherine smiled. She felt so comfortable around these two men who had stuck by her in her time of need. She quietly sipped her after dinner cup of hot tea before she told them, "You two relax and enjoy the evening. I'll ride out for the evening round. It's so easy to enjoy the sights here. It's the exact opposite of the earlier, arid scabland south of the river."

Rusty made her sit up and pay attention, "I'll go with you. You and Virgil seeing that black bear and her cubs this afternoon made me realize we are getting into bear country."

This surprised Catherine, so she asked, "Are bears really that dangerous, Rusty?"

"Not really, but it pays to be careful. That black bear you saw today seemed only interested in fishing, but if you bother her cubs there's hell to pay. Black bears are pretty casual." His tone became serious. "The closer we get to Montana the closer we get to grizzly bears. You never bother them; period. They were heading south of Grizzly Mountain on their way through the Kettle River Mountain Range. Catherine felt a quiet shudder. She hoped this wasn't an omen.

❧

The three wagons moved east using the bridge to cross the Sanpoil River. Catherine, Rusty and Virgil set up camps a mile or so past the bridge. The three herders rode back to the three bands to bring them over the bridge. With their natural zest Malovich and Gilrakis and their cohorts warmed to the task of turning Catherine's band east onto the narrow bridge. There was only one traffic delay of a few minutes on the seldom used road. By late afternoon all three bands were all across the bridge, in separate lanes, and feeding peacefully.

Under the hot embers Virgil's Dutch oven neared the time to be pulled up, allowed to cool down and served. Catherine had often thought about salmon since Virgil's large trout on the east fork of the Nespelem. While they were waiting for it was time to say something. "Virgil."

"Yes, Catherine. What can I do for you?"

"You can take me fishing for salmon. I've never caught one. The Sanpoil River is close so the sheep won't be neglected." She waited for Virgil's okay.

"You'll never catch salmon in the Sanpoil."

"How can you say that, Virgil? The canyon is not too steep and the stream is bigger than the Nespelem where you caught that huge trout. There should be salmon here."

"You'll catch plenty of trout, but there will be no salmon. Think about it, Catherine. How did we get across the Columbia River?"

"On the Grand Coulee Dam." Comprehension came. "Oh! You're saying fish don't get past the Grand Coulee Dam. The Bonneville Dam in the Columbia Gorge has fish ladders. I saw them from the train window when I came home. Why didn't they do that here?"

"They couldn't. The Grand Coulee Dam is the tallest dam in the world. They couldn't build enough fish ladders in the narrow canyon to overcome that height. The engineers tried to figure out an elevator system to lift fish to the upper lake, but it was discarded as impractical. The Sanpoil empties into the Columbia east of the dam. Guess what Catherine? There are no salmon east of the Grand Coulee Dam."

Catherine sat stunned. She tried to think this through. What was the impact on those who had depended on salmon all their lives? From college she knew The Grand Coulee and the Bonneville dams were hyped for flood control and electricity. The Grand Coulee, via the Banks Lake in the coulee, would irrigate many thousand of acres in the Columbia Basin. Most of all, coveted jobs were delivered. This was a huge selling point during the Depression years. She had never heard any great debate about the loss of salmon.

She summed up her amazement. "It seems impossible, Virgil. You can't catch a salmon in the Sanpoil or any river above the Grand Coulee Dam. What about the Indian tribes that depended on the salmon?"

The philosophic Virgil replied, "I bet they don't believe the dams are so glorious, but what's done is done. A great many people will benefit; some won't. That's how the dams were sold to Congress."

50
Bait

"It looks like we got company, Catherine." The traditional Forest Service green pickup pulling of the main road got their attention. Virgil explained, "Don't worry, Catherine. The rangers check every band of sheep or herd of cattle that trail through the area." A grin creased Virgil's weather-beaten face. "I bet I know the ranger." The medium tall, heavy-set forest ranger stepped out of the pickup and donned the traditional tri-creased Stetson hat. Virgil warmly greeted him. "I thought you'd be retired by now, Vic."

The man dressed in dark forest green pants and a light green summer shirt stuck out his hand. "Good to see you again, Virgil. How many summers have we been doing this?"

"Quite a few, quite a few."

The ranger's eyes speculated on the young, good looking woman standing beside his friend. "Don't tell me that--."

Virgil held up his hand to stop the ogling. "Life out here must make you lecherous, Vic. Let me introduce you to Catherine

Sumertun. She's our Boss Lady and she's a damn sight better shepherd that most men you meet out here."

Pleased, but surprised, Catherine stepped forward. "Hi, I'm glad to meet you. I'm Catherine Sumertun." Curiosity prompted her, "If you meet every livestock group that comes through here, maybe you know my mother."

"I do for a fact, and I also knew your father." He smiled. He wasn't going to miss a chance to kid Virgil. "My old friend here didn't finish his introduction. My name is Flynn, Victor Flynn. Call me Vic. I'm here to offer any assistance that you may need, or to warn you of any problems." He turned to Virgil, put his arm around his shoulder and confidentially said, "The Sumertun name makes her presence here understandable."

He asked Catherine, "Do have a good cold drink of water?"

"We can do that, but we also have cold beer and cold soda. Take your choice."

"Water's fine."

Virgil watched until Vic drank his fill from the two-gallon water bag. "Vic, I know you check the routes of cattle and sheep that come this way. Is there's a problem with our permits?"

"Oh no, Virgil. As usual Sarah and Pete have everything in order. No problems there, but I need to warn you that someone is hanging baits in this area. So far we've found two, but no evidence that they were successful. One was a little northeast of here and the other was south of the state road." He walked to his pickup and retrieved a map. He pointed to the long valley which ran from west to northeast and crossed through the range over a low saddle pass before dropping down to Inchelium. "Is this where you plan to cross the Kettle River Range?"

She handed him Ricardo's journal with his marked trail. She ran her finger over the trail and compared the maps. "Yes. This is the way Virgil, Rusty and I will travel with the three bands." She paused and hesitantly asked, "Is it as brushy as Ricardo wrote?"

Vic nodded. "It's pretty brushy. It will be slower than you're used to, but you've got six good dogs plus Rusty and Virgil. The area is a web of dirt roads used by the stockmen who bring sheep and cattle through here. The twenty one miles to Inchelium will be slower, but you should be there by September. I know which way you're going, so I'll stop by and see how you're faring. He casually added, "There is an unconfirmed report of a bait close to the last low saddle area on the way out of the Kettle Mountains. I plan on checking it out today."

Catherine wasn't ready for him to leave. "I don't understand the term 'bait' and how it might affect us. Before you leave I want to know what it means."

She noticed the hesitancy, but Vic gathered his thoughts enough to elaborate. "Baiting is something poachers do when they want a trophy bear for their game room. The poachers hang large chunks of meat from a tree to attract bears. This time of year the bears are ravenous. They'll eat anything to put on protective fat that will see them through hibernation. Baiting violates all game laws and is strictly forbidden.

"The poacher hangs his bait high enough so that the bear has to stand up to reach the bait. In this position it is vulnerable to a high powered rifle. If the bear isn't what the poacher wants he doesn't shoot and the bear has a free meal." He added, "These two baits have been hung high enough that a black bear couldn't reach them."

Catherine's remained curious. "What can reach them?"

"Grizzlies."

Catherine reacted with stunned amazement. "You mean poachers actually hunt the grizzly bear that way?"

Vic looked at Virgil and both of them nodded.

Catherine wondered how much of a threat this was to the sheep. "What do you want us to do if we happen to see bait hanging from a tree or see a grizzly?"

"You can cut down the bait and notify me or the game warden." He paused to switch subjects. "Deer season is coming. There are a lot of locals who believe hunting deer any time is their right. They also think they don't need a license, so the game wardens will be busy. If you happen to run across a grizzly don't shoot. It's illegal to hunt them. Just silently move away. Try and avoid any aggressive action. They're tough to kill and meaner than hell if wounded or disturbed."

"What happens if the bear becomes a threat to the sheep?"

Vic visibly cringed at this hated question. He sighed in resignation, "Then you'll have to shoot it. Just don't go looking for trouble."

Catherine sensed Vic wasn't telling her everything. She excused herself to go get a cold pop and to think about why the ranger was holding back.

When she disappeared Vic Flynn made his observation. "I can see why she's the Boss lady. She grabs a hold of idea and wants to know everything." He chuckled, "I'd hate to be the bear that crosses her."

Virgil warned his friend. "Don't patronize her, Vic. She really is a nice, smart young woman. You've no idea how much she's had to learn and overcome. Rusty coined the term Boss Lady and it fits. Tell her why the grizzly can be so much trouble, and do it before you leave."

Catherine sensed the different attitude when she returned. She didn't have to ask any questions. Vic put forth his worry while she sipped her Coke. "I knew you were upset when I told you about baiting. You have a right to be worried, and a right to protect your interests." He didn't hedge. "This hasn't happened to Sumertun sheep yet, but in the last three years there have been two very serious grizzly attacks on sheep. One attack was by an injured bear. It was hungry and mad as only grizzlies can get. It waded into a band and killed fifty-six sheep before it was satisfied. It was last seen carrying a lamb away."

Despite Catherine's horrified expression, Vic ploughed dog-gedly ahead. "The second incident was a direct result of a lamb being the bait. Evidently the bear liked it. The healthy grizzly proceeded to mutilate or kill twenty six sheep just for the fun of it." He sighed. "Now you know why I'm worried about the two baits we found."

Catherine countered, "And the unconfirmed report?"

"Like I said, the game warden and I will check it out. Just be careful when you go through that low pass. I'll try to keep you informed."

"What do you mean, you'll try?"

"This is a big country, Catherine. I mean what I said. We will do our best." He pointed to the rifle scabbard, propped up against her saddle. "Can you use that?"

"Want to check me out?"

51
Ursus Arctos Horribilis

Catherine never realized how easy the earlier sheep routes had been until now. The brush covered slopes, towering pine covered mountains and small, narrow meadows northwest of the Columbia were a stark contrast to the wide desert meadows and the gentle sagebrush covered slopes the sheep had easily passed through.

The six dogs followed their instincts and the familiar directions from their herders. It took a constant effort to keep the sheep moving through the brushy terrain. The weather was cooler and the grass good. The sheep didn't share Catherine's concern about moving. They took their own sweet time to reach the saddle south of Grizzly Mountain.

Only Vic Flynn's two visits broke the hard working, peaceful progress. His visits were relaxed and reassuring. Neither he nor the game warden had reports of any new baits. His occasional glance north to the 6,300 foot Grizzly Mountain served as a reminder. Vic seemed happy to report any worthwhile news about the possibility of poaching.

Catherine had to smile. He talked to her first and then he stayed to visit with Virgil.

෴

The wide saddle, which loomed ahead, was the gateway to an easier descent into Inchelium, a small village of 746 inhabitants. The sheep would ferry across the Columbia for the last time there. Catherine leisurely patrolled the northside of the meadow. Malovich and Gilrakis made sure the sheep didn't stray into the wooded areas. Virgil was visible driving his wagon toward the saddle. His horse trailed the wagon. His job was to bring all three wagons to a camp site. Rusty and his dogs patrolled the south side of the flock. The peaceful aura was broken only by Rusty's plaintiff singing, floating across the small lea.

Two loud rifle shots pierced the morning quiet. Catherine cursed. The shots had come ahead and to her left. Was a poacher at work? Did the shots mean a grizzly had been attracted to a bait and shot? A dead bear meant the poacher had to work fast to remove the pelt and the head for the taxidermist. Anyone who poached a trophy bear didn't want to be caught.

A wounded bear meant real danger to her charges. Vic's tale of sheep being slaughtered by an angry grizzly had jolted her. She automatically reached down to her scabbard and withdrew her rifle. She pumped a shell into the chamber to make sure the gun worked. Then she rejected the shell and put it back into the magazine. Eight quick shots were ready if needed.

What the devil was she thinking? She had never shot at anything bigger than a coyote. Never had she shot at a bear. Could she?

She set her jaw. *Damn right I can if it was killing my sheep.* She slipped the rifle back in the scabbard and cautiously rode ahead. Her dogs' ears were up. They growled and looked to Catherine. They waited for a command, perhaps sensing some danger. With her binoculars she swept the area north of her trail, but saw nothing out of the ordinary.

Catherine reined Jiggles further inside the forest on a trail which ran parallel to the meadow. She stayed on the trail as it circled east around the knoll. Nothing!

Malovich growled and looked intently at the rise ahead. Gilrakis barked. The hackles on their necks stiffened. Catherine followed their intense interest to the trees ahead. Among the pines a lone mountain rowan tree stood. One branch bent toward the ground. A muted shriek escaped before Catherine slammed her hands to her mouth. Twenty-five yards ahead she had spotted the lamb held by a small rope dangling from the branch.

Catherine dismounted and pulled her rifle from the scabbard. She called to her protectors. "Come on, you two." She cautiously walked toward the lamb. She noticed blood on the fleece. Some rotten poacher had killed one of her lambs and hung it from the tree so he could get a trophy for his den. Her temperature rose. There was no doubt what the poacher wanted. Only a trophy sized grizzly capable of reaching eight and a half feet could slash the lamb loose from the limb. The lamb was hung too high for her to cut down.

Catherine tied Jiggles' reins to a nearby Aspen sapling and circled the lamb to get a shot where the rope's knot was exposed. For steadiness she laid the rifle's barrel inside the fork of another tree and sighted in on the knot. She squeezed off a shot. The bullet tore out a chunk of wood, but the lamb didn't fall.

She wondered if Virgil heard the shot. She looked down into the meadow. Sure enough Virgil had stopped and was walking back to his horse. Catherine smiled. It gave her a warm feeling to know help was close. She aimed again, exhaled and held herself very still to squeeze off another shot.

The bullet blew the knot away. The rope fell away. The limb snapped back. The lamb dropped like a stone and lay crumpled on the ground. Her anger boiled over as she pumped another shell into the chamber and strode to the fallen lamb. She knelt and rubbed the lifeless fleece. Malovich growled again. She wanted to cry. Instead she cooed, "Poor little lamb. You never hurt a soul. You deserved better than being used to bait a grizzly." She pushed the butt of the rifle into the ground to help her stand from her crouch. She declared, "I'll make sure you aren't used for that."

～

"The lamb wasn't meant to bait bear, Catherine. It served its purpose. It baited you."

She slowly stepped away from the lamb and tried to locate the familiar voice.

Higher on the knoll and to her left she spied the seedy looking, unshaven man who stepped from behind the protective pine tree. Catherine thought back to the first time she had seen him. The beard and shabby clothes didn't change a thing. He still looked like the man who came to the door asking for a job.

"Corwin?"

He acknowledged her.

Then she noticed the rifle pointed at her. She blurted out, "You set up this bait? What the hell for? Grizzlies are tough and mean to kill. Why?"

"That means nothing has changed. I told you, but you didn't listen. Nobody ever listened. I didn't bait for a grizzly." His voice was soft, cold ... lethal. "A Sumertun, not a grizzly is what I wanted. It wasn't planned this way. I had to use the two shots this morning to scare a grizzly away, but then I thought the shots might lure you here. You always had to know everything. Now you know, and now I get my revenge."

Hatred stared directly at her. How different was this? Eye to eye wasn't Corwin's style. A chill ran down her spine. His vow of revenge scared Catherine "You want revenge on me? Why? I've never done anything to you!" She wondered if Virgil was coming.

"Look at me." He commanded. "You think I'm nothing. So did your mother."

"My God, Corwin she married you. That's not nothing!"

"Yes, it was." His angry voice rose. "I never understood why she married me, convenience I guess. All marriage did for me was to make it respectable for her to boss me. I was married to the 'Queen of the Sumertun Ranch' and she never let me to forget it. I was never more than a hired hand she married to do her bidding. I had a title, but she never considered me capable of doing anything. Pete ignored me and she backed him. She and Carter made every decision on the ranch. Did I have a say in anything? No! You were there the night she made it clear where my place was."

Catherine vividly remembered the night when Corwin left. His bitter voice abruptly pulled her back to the present. "I made my first mistake when I asked you to come home to take care of your mother. She was at death's door. A couple more days with no pills and she might have died."

Catherine gasped at the sudden realization of what Corwin had said. "You son of a bitch! You deliberately forgot to give her the sulfa pills, didn't you?" She stepped toward him.

The chilling voice reached her. "Just back up a step, Catherine. Any more moves like that and I'll shoot." He seemed to enjoy admitting that he would have let her mother die.

She tossed out an idea. "Did you think no one would blame you for not giving her the correct dosage because you can't read?"

"How in the world did you know that?"

"Alex told me. He had figured it out. How did you know about the correct dosage for the sulfa if you couldn't read?"

"See! You're just like Sarah. You always did think I was too dumb to listen. You both should be more like Alex. He always treated me with respect." He thought for a moment. "How did he find out?"

She told him how Alex figured out he couldn't read, and how he made sure Corwin wasn't embarrassed. She wanted to keep him talking and give Virgil and Rusty some time. "He told me the morning we had our big argument over the medicine. How many other attempts did you make on my mother's life?"

"None! That one time was just a twist of fate. When you came home to take care of your mother you started making life a living hell for me and especially for Art. He didn't deserve what you did to him."

"What I did to him? I did nothing but throw water in his face for smoking around straw. He deserved that."

"Maybe, but that humiliated him. His shooting along the river to move the sheep was a dumb act, but shooting Mr. Gray was an accident. Even Hank turned against him after his leg was broken. Hank became a hero and Art was fired. Even his bad burns from the barn fire were accidental. All he ever wanted was to get even with you, and I don't blame him." His eyes glared with animated anger. "He did some jail time because of you."

Catherine couldn't believe what she was hearing. She stoutly protested, "I'm not to blame for him starting the fire in the barn. He did that himself."

"When he went to Soap Lake for his burns, you totally humiliated him again."

"I went to Soap Lake because Rusty needed the waters to heal his bee stings. I didn't know Art was there, until he made sure I did." Another unanswered question popped out. "Did you send money to the attorney in Soap Lake to get him out of jail?"

Corwin was slow to nod. "Yes, I got the money for him." Then he hissed, "Then I had to claim his body because of that fire in the Grand Coulee." He silently shook his head. Catherine could only imagine the torture he felt.

The new menacing, intensity in his voice startled her. "He was there because of you. Now Sarah will feel what I felt."

Catherine grasped at this straw of a clue. She asked, "Why did you have to come and get Art Wheeler's body. What was he to you?"

His voice was defiant, yet sad. "He was my stepson."

Somehow that didn't surprise Catherine. Somebody had given him the confidence that he would never be fired. "Did you tell Pete he couldn't fire Art?"

"Yes, and he agreed. He went back on his word after Hank broke his leg."

"Don't you think that Art should have been fired after the shooting? Wouldn't you have fired him?"

"What I would do doesn't matter. You heard your mother. She told me to stay on the wheat part of the ranch. That meant I was never more than just a hired hand." He bitterly continued, "When your mother threw me out she also threw out any future for Art."

"Did I missed something? I don't remember her throwing you out. I do remember you being drunk, angrily slamming doors and leaving."

"What would you have done if your mother slammed the door on your future like she did on mine?"

Catherine sat silently. He had a point.

"Not being wanted hurts, but that was nothing compared to losing Art. I hope it hurts Sarah as bad to lose a daughter. Now, she will."

"What do you mean Art's future was thrown out? I never heard anything like that."

"Your mother's attorney letter told me about the blood descendent clause of the Sumertun Trust when he sent me the divorce papers from Sarah. The divorce left both Art and me out in the cold. I deserved a settlement of some kind, but now there is nothing. Nothing was my pay for years of servitude and humiliation." He angrily pulled himself erect. "Enough of this! The moment I've dreamed for is here." He raised his rifle to his shoulder.

Catherine quickly whispered, "Malovich—right. Gilrakis—left—sic em". The dogs split and raced toward Corwin from either side.

Corwin shot once at Gilrakis but he was too slow. He immediately swung the rifle barrel back to Catherine, who had dived for the protection of a pine tree. He saw the flash from her gun barrel as he fired in desperation. He fell to the ground under the fearful assault of the two dogs.

He felt the comic relief of another failure when he heard the familiar command, "Malovich, Gilrakis, come." It was repeated until the two dogs left him.

Painfully Corwin rolled up to his knees and faced Virgil. The two dogs sat sedately on either side of Catherine like nothing had ever happened. Virgil's eyes blazed at him through the front sight of the rifle.

The gentle man commanded, "Now Corwin, push the rifle aside and stand up."

Corwin had no doubt that Virgil meant to shoot him, but he doubted the gentle man actually do it? He carefully pushed his gun aside and stood. His shoulder hurt like sin. He looked in horror at his blood soaked coat. Catherine's bullet had gone though the left shoulder muscles. He felt his shoulder. It throbbed with every move. He whined, "I need help."

Another voice threatened him. "Who gives a damn? Right now we're concerned about Catherine!"

Corwin searched the area behind Virgil and located Rusty bent over the fallen Catherine. He couldn't believe what he had done. Revenge didn't feel sweet. It hurt. He sank to the ground and moaned. He moved his right hand and put pressure on his bleeding wound.

The move brought none of the threatened shots. Both men were interested in Catherine." A plan surfaced. If they pay enough attention to Catherine maybe they will forget about him. A relieved Corwin asked, "How bad is she?"

"It's a flesh wound on the inside of the right thigh. She won't be walking pert and full of it for a while, but that's it. You're lucky she wasn't really hurt, or you'd be dead right now." Rusty had an unanswered question that needed an answer. "Tell me what the two early morning shots meant and when did you kill the lamb."

"I caught the lamb last night and killed it this morning. I barely got the lamb tied to the limb this morning when this huge grizzly came lumbering into view. He must have caught the scent of blood and came looking for a meal. I shot at his feet as a warning. He scurried off, but soon he came back. My second shot hit him and he left in a hurry."

"Did you kill him?"

"I doubt it. What difference does it make? He won't be any trouble. Now are you going to help me or not?"

Rusty spat out his answer. "You don't deserve any attention. Virgil will let the dogs guard you. That thought seemed to amuse Rusty. "I know you can't outrun them."

Virgil commanded the dogs. "Stay. Sit. If that bastard moves "sic em,'"

Rusty walked to Jiggles and took the canteen from the saddlebag. Virgil opened his pocketknife and cut one sleeve from Rusty's shirt. Then Rusty poured water on the cloth and carefully washed the blood from around Catherine's wound. Then he folded the sleeve into a compress. "Hold that tightly against the wound Catherine." When finished he asked, "Can you ride the short distance to your wagon?"

She gritted her teeth and nodded.

"Good. Virgil and I will put you in the saddle. Then keep this cloth pressed against the wound. We'll follow with this worthless piece of scum."

The two men made by a seat by interlocking their hands and arms. They gently lifted her and carried her to Jiggles. Blood seeped from her wound. Catherine pushed harder against the homemade compress. Then she grabbed the saddle horn. She gritted her teeth and struggled to pull herself up, then survived Rusty's final push into the saddle. She smiled her thanks through gritted teeth. She looked down at Malovich and Gilrakis and their two alert faces. This is the first time Catherine had known them to disobey a command.

&

When the dogs left to go to Catherine, Corwin saw opportunity. Virgil and Rusty wouldn't leave Catherine and the two dogs had just shown where they wanted to be. He quietly rose to sneak away.

Virgil heard the movement, but couldn't do anything until Catherine was safely in the saddle. Then he hustled to his propped up rifle. He saw the triumphant Corwin holding his shoulder and jogging into the forest. He wanted to shoot, but he couldn't. He cursed himself for being such a weak fool. He was even more helpless to stop the next event.

Virgil knew *Ursus arctos horribilis* as the Latin name for the huge grizzly bear. The *horribilis* subspecies label certainly fit the enraged animal that emerged from the forest. The wounded grizzly had returned as the hunter. The grizzly stood to a full height of over eight feet. Its front legs spread wide to attack. Virgil saw the blood stained right shoulder where Corwin had shot him.

He screamed as loud as possible, "Stop, Corwin, for God's sake—STOP!"

Virgil heard Corwin's derisive laugh and triumphant yell. "Ha! You won't shoot me. I'll be back." He turned to continue into the forest. Virgil saw him freeze in front of the dark brown monster towering above him. Corwin tried to stop, but couldn't. He tottered into certain death. His amused dismissal to Virgil became a terrifying scream.

Virgil's eyes widened with horror. His last thought came from left field. Corwin had wounded the grizzly this morning. The saying that had been around since the first trappers came to the Rockies flashed through his mind. "Nothing is as dangerous as a wounded grizzly." The bear's angry, terrifying snarl reaffirmed this wisdom. The bear's louder roar and Corwin's scream echoed over the knoll. Then only the roar remained.

Virgil would never forget what he witnessed. The four to five inch claws of the grizzly are used to mark trees by tearing off the bark. They dig roots and varmints from rocky soil. They are sharp, terrible fighting weapons. The enraged bear's first swipe with its left paw powered by the characteristic large muscular hump across the shoulders tore Corwin's midsection apart.

Corwin instinctively clutched at his belly.

Virgil wanted to throw up.

Part of Corwin's bloody head flew into space after the second swipe. A third swipe tore the falling body apart.

Virgil paled when the frenzied bear looked directly at him. Those eyes bored through him. It scared the hell out of him, but he raised his rifle. It had become either him or the bear.

"We'd better get him while he's standing." By his side Rusty's voice reassured him.

Virgil nodded. Rusty fired the first shot and it hit the grizzly in the left shoulder. Virgil fired a second shot into the muscular chest.

They shot again before the stunned *Ursus arctos horribilis* roared another challenge and dropped down to all four feet.

Virgil knew that meant a charge.

Three shots rang out as the bear took two more menacing steps toward them. The puzzled bear hesitated. Another three shots slammed into him. The bear took two small, tottering steps before it stopped and sat down. Then it slowly rolled over on its side and roared his final defiance. *Ursus arctos horribilis'* killing days were over.

Virgil knew who first shooter was, but who was the third? Malovich and Gilrakis walked cautiously past him toward the fallen beast. Now he knew. The dogs tentatively sniffed around the carcass until they were satisfied. Then they trotted back to Catherine. He turned around to see a grimacing Catherine sitting atop Jiggles with her rifle resting across the saddle. The last wisps of white smoke wafted from the gun barrel.

Virgil sank to one knee, bowed his head and sighed deeply before he wiped the sweat from his forehead. He was exhausted and nauseous. He needed Rusty's helping hand to rise.

"When that grizzly looked at me I knew it was him or me. I've never been so scared in my life." He vividly recalled the scene. "Thanks for being there, Rusty, Catherine. It took all three of us to kill that monster."

Rusty smugly reminded Virgil and Catherine, "Remember I told you to never to irritate a grizzly. They're just plain mean when mad, and a shot to the shoulder will do that!"

"Amen to that, but it was Corwin who wounded the bear." She wondered aloud, "Do you suppose that's why the grizzly came back?"

They all pondered on that, before Catherine said, "It's time to get me to the wagon."

Virgil shot back, "Let's do it. You need to get that wound cleaned and dressed. Do you still have some of that sulfa powder at your wagon?"

Catherine nodded.

"Good. We'll get you fixed up." He grinned at the thought. "I can't wait to tell Vic that you shot a wounded grizzly; after you were already shot. That should convince him that you're one tough cookie."

Catherine didn't feel tough.

౭౬

It didn't take long for Vic Flynn to show up. That many shots echoing through the area didn't go unreported. Vic listened in amazement as Rusty told him a slightly enhanced version what happened. He swore Vic looked at Catherine with a lot more respect.

The ranger wanted Virgil or Rusty to stay with the body. "The body has to be protected until someone from Inchelium comes out. The damn coyotes have probably already picked up the scent of a free meal. If you have a tarp, throw it over the body."

Rusty took one look at the pasty faced Virgil. No way was he going to allow his friend to relive the morning's ghastly killing. He volunteered.

Vic was glad that angle was covered. "Good. Now I'll get Catherine to the Inchelium clinic. I am in charge out here, but shooting is a matter for the police. I'll also contact the coroner about the body."

Rusty picked up Catherine. She clung to him until she was seated in the pickup. After she was made as comfortable as possible they started for Inchelium over the bumpy trail road to the isolated secondary state road to Inchelium. Vic concentrated on making the ride as smooth as possible. "Rusty told me about the grizzly scene." He smiled at his little pun. "I have a good picture of that, but I have one question. Catherine. Did Rusty say the victim was your stepfather?"

Catherine nodded.

"Should I have the coroner contact your mother about the body?"

She smiled at the irony of it. "Yes. After all, technically she is still married to him."

52
The Clinic

Inchelium, Washington, population 759, was lucky. The rambling one story, five bed clinic which served the isolated area, was the result of Dr. Monroe Wattling's long love affair with the region. He had lived in Inchelium all his life. He had wanted to follow in his father's logger footsteps. Two things got in his way, and both were because of his father.

He hadn't planned on going to college but his father insisted on it. Finally Monroe agreed to give college a try. To his surprise the University of Washington opened up new worlds. One of them was science. During his junior year at the University of Washington his interest leaned toward the university's Medical School. His grades were good enough and his dad gratefully approved of this new direction.

Two month's before graduation his father was seriously injured in a logging accident. The men at the lumber camp were well trained in first aid and did the best they could, but by the time they could get him out of the woods to Inchelium, waited for the ferry to cross the Columbia River and got his father thirty miles to the Chewelah hospital it was too late. The lack of medical facilities in the area set the course of Monroe's life.

Monroe vowed the people of the lower Kettle River Mountain Range would have medical attention when they needed it, not when they could get to it. The small village was overjoyed when he announced his intention to hang his shingle in Inchelium; so much that they purchased a rambling frame house and converted it into a small five bed clinic.

At the moment Dr. Wattling stood by the wide, two door front entrance and watched the green Forest Service pickup enter the u-shaped drive to the clinic. He waved to Vic and motioned for his nurse to wheel out the gurney. They waited for the pickup to stop and then efficiently moved their patient from the pickup, onto the gurney and into the clinic.

&

Sarah had been like a caged tiger since Dr. Wattling's call. To learn her daughter had been treated for a gunshot wound and would be in the clinic for another two or three days shocked her. The doctor's young voice had patiently answered every medical question, had assured her that her daughter would fully recover, but he couldn't help her with the who, why or where. He had promised to have Catherine call her the next day.

Her phone rang at 9:00 a.m. the next morning. Sarah didn't wait for the second series of rings on her party line before she snatched the phone from its cradle. Her ragged emotions welled into tears at the first groggy "Hi Mom. Don't worry, I'm okay." The tears turned into scorching cursing when she found out who shot her.

Sarah sobered considerably when she heard how Corwin had died. "What a horrible, horrible way to die, but no more talk of this. Right now I can't take it." She said, "Pete and I are driving up. We should get there in the afternoon."

"That's wonderful, Mother." She thought of Corwin. "I'm surprised you haven't already heard something from the mortuary or the sheriff's department."

"Mortuary! Why the mortuary?"

"I didn't know what else to say when the Forest Ranger asked me about Corwin's body. The divorce wasn't final, so I told them to contact you." Her soft laugh took the sting from this announcement. It took another twenty minutes for Catherine to convince her mother it was time to say goodbye.

⁊

Sarah peered out the window at the tiresome sagebrush and scabland vistas of central Washington. The long drive and lonely view fostered a general discussion of the annual sheep drive; its weaknesses, its strengths, and what they could do to improve it. Sarah summed it up. "The isolation has always been a problem with the summer trek, hasn't it Pete?"

Pete thought about the question. "I know there is little communication, but we can't string telephones lines to the wagons." He smiled at that image. "The long drive still takes care of feeding the sheep for the summer. It's the reason we make money on them."

"I know, but this summer has been a real tester."

"There will always be trials and tests, Sarah. Over the years the men have learned to take care of themselves, just like Catherine has learned. You and I still have to rely on personal visits and supply trips, but I agree. This has been a very unusual summer."

Sarah's eyes questioned him.

"Your daughter has been involved. That has made it different."

Sarah nodded. "It's true. She's made the summer's drive very personal."

Pete laughed. "Catherine has faced dilemmas that were different, but some of it has been very good. You two learned to fly. Tim did manage to make supplying the wagons interesting." His mood sobered. "He was solid granite for Catherine in the Grand Coulee."

Sarah agreed. They lapsed into silence for a few miles, each absorbed in their own thoughts. The scablands and miles of sagebrush, bunchgrass and exposed lava rock affected people that way. Finally Pete broke the spell.

"We both know the real problems were caused by Art Wheeler and Corwin. Did Corwin ever tell you he insisted I take on Art and that he had cleared it with you?"

"No. the first time I heard of Art Wheeler was when Catherine threw water on him for smoking in the sheep pens. She wanted to fire him then, but realized it wasn't hers to do. She also told me on the phone last night that Art was Corwin's stepson. Surprised?"

"Yes." He thoughtfully rubbed his chin. "That answers a lot of questions, doesn't it?"

Further questions were pushed aside when the highway approached the east side of the Columbia River. The panoramic views of the free flowing river coming south through the mountains and grassy slopes would continue as they drove north to the Inchelium ferry.

"Look at the Columbia, Pete. It's beautiful. It's hard to imagine that all of this will soon be under water. Think of it. This highway will have to be moved. This whole country will change when the backwater inundates this area." She sighed audibly. "It seems the whole world is changing. Pete, do you think the wars in Asia and Europe will reach us?"

"It already has. Congress is thinking of a draft. They're allowing military training within our borders. Tim is thinking of enlisting in the Air Corps. I'm afraid the winds of war will reach far." He smiled, "However, the price of wool is getting better." Pete noticed her wistful smile. "Are you thinking it's also time for change?"

She nodded.

"You didn't really love him, did you?"

Sarah smiled. She took no offense at Pete's personal question. They had been together too many years. "Loneliness makes people do strange things. My marriage to Corwin was one of them. Somehow I thought I could make him into another Burke. The illusion of love disappeared long ago, but his death still saddens me. He wasn't a man who thought for himself, so why the sudden urge for revenge?"

"I don't know, but it was probably just what he told Catherine before he tried to kill her. I know getting a divorce was distasteful to you, but he left you with little choice. It sounds callous, but Corwin's death frees you for the first time in a long, long time."

Pete turned philosophic. "Catherine has been tested and shown an inner strength, and Alex is growing into a capable, hard working, young man." He cheerfully patronized this woman he had admired and served for so many years. "It seems to me your cup runneth over. Maybe you should find time to enjoy life." He wondered how this observation had been received. "You forget, I knew 'The Queen of the Sumertun Ranch' when that meant the ranch's survival. You've earned your quiet time."

She reached over and patted Pete's hand. "Thank you. I couldn't have done it without you." Her eyes sparkled, "Yes, maybe I've earned some quiet time."

❧

They riveted their attention to the Inchelium Ferry approaching from the west side of the Columbia. The small, eight car ferry connected the village with eastern Washington. As they joined four other waiting cars to board the ferry, Sarah confided to Pete, "I'm always fascinated by ferry boats. I enjoy watching them come in, riding on them and it's always pleasant to watch the water boiling up around the stern. Silly, huh?"

"Nope. Not silly, just human. At home I enjoy watching the big white pelicans dive into the Columbia like it's their private fishing grounds. Same thing." He turned his attention to driving on and off the ferry. "We'll be there in just a few moments. Are you okay?"

"I'm not sure. My stomach is very nervous, but I'm looking forward to seeing my daughter. I want to run my hands over her just to make sure she's real. I'm sure there will be a lot of talking." She changed the subject. "Do you still plan on staying two days with Rusty and Virgil before we head back?

"Yes. They can use an extra hand. Who is the problem. I should know what to do by the time we leave." He peered directly at Sarah. "We really don't have much choice do we?"

Sarah slowly shook her head. "Not really Pete. You could be spared for a several days until we sell the sheep and put the unsold sheep, horses and the three wagons on the train to bring them home. Catherine will come home now to mend, and I don't want any conflict during that time." She sucked in her breath and reluctantly said, "That leaves Hank as our first answer. Make sure you stress this fact to Rusty and Virgil. They're veterans and they'll understand. If Hank doesn't want to do this," She paused, "We do have Alex as a back-up."

The long journey ended when they entered the U-shaped driveway to the clinic. Sarah was out of the pickup almost before it stopped moving. Smiling, Pete took his time to find a parking spot so the two women would have a few moments together before he made his brief appearance.

⁓

Breathless, Sarah left the nurse's station to rush into the clinic's small solarium. She found her daughter in a wheelchair soaking up the late August sun. Two windows were open for ventilation. Sun beams burst through the remaining windows to reflect through her sun bleached hair. She was half asleep with her head leaning on the palm of one hand. The whole aura spoke of angelic serenity. It was hard for Sarah to believe she had been shot and had faced a berserk grizzly bear yesterday.

She became keenly aware of the razor edge difference between life and death. That thought hit her stomach like a sledge hammer. How could she have faced reality if it was Catherine instead of Corwin that had been killed?

Her presence gradually interrupted Catherine's half-sleep. Sarah quickly covered the distance to the wheelchair and they tenderly held each other for a few minutes. Words couldn't express the thankfulness that existed.

∽

"Good afternoon. I take it you're Catherine's mother. The nurse told me you were here. I wanted to give you a few minutes together before we met. I'm Dr. Wattling."

Sarah no longer wondered why the voice on the telephone had sounded young. The figure clad in a white smock, who stood in the doorway, was young. He couldn't be thirty. The auburn haired Dr. Wattling stood a solid six foot. The affable smile quickly gave confidence. The hazel eyes twinkled as he openly appraised her.

Sarah decided Catherine was in good hands. "Yes, I'm Catherine's mother. Thank you for calling me, Dr. Wattling." She smoothed her hair into place with one hand, smiled and tried to explain her feelings. "Unexpected news is always a surprise. When you hear your daughter has been shot it's not a surprise, it's a helluva shock. I just couldn't comprehend it at first. I really appreciated your patience."

She heard Pete's boots clicking down the hall before he appeared behind the doctor. "And this is Pete Alzola. He takes care of the Sumertun sheep. He has known Catherine since the day she was born." The two men shook hands as Pete thanked him for all he had done. Then he excused himself and carefully embraced Catherine.

Sarah half-demanded, half-asked, "Well, doctor, how is my daughter?"

Dr. Wattling had heard authoritative voices before. They didn't bother him. A slight smile appeared. "Don't worry, Mrs. Turnoch, she'll be fine. The bullet hit her on the inside of the right thigh. It didn't hit an artery, but there was still quite a lot of bleeding. It took eight stitches to close. In a nutshell that's what we did." He reassured her, "She's young, strong and fit. She'll need crutches for a short time, but her recovery will be complete."

"Will there be a scar?"

"Definitely, but it will fade in time. I took special pains to make it a tight seal. The only real danger might have been loss of blood before she could get here. Thanks to Rusty that didn't happen. Back in the wagon after the shooting he washed the wound, put some sulfa on the open area and made a very good compress from a clean towel. I understand he also lost a shirt sleeve after the shooting. Be sure and tell him he did a great job. In this country the injured person is often out in the boonies and first aid is vital."

"Hear that, Pete? Be sure you tell Rusty today and give him my heartfelt thanks."

Her request for the doctor came much softer. "How soon will I be able to take her home? I've planned to take her home in two days. Isn't that what you said on the phone?"

His optimistically replied, "That's what I said, but she's mine until then."

"That's okay." Sarah smiled, "I think she's in good hands." She patted her daughter's shoulder. "Pete has to leave to see Rusty and Virgil, so he'll drop me off at the North Star Hotel. After I settle in and get a bite to eat I'll walk back to stay until they throw me out."

53
Introspection

After a warm shower, a short rest, and a chef's salad at the hotel's restaurant Sarah left for the clinic refreshed. Her idea to phone Tim came while she ate. It had been a productive phone call. She hoped her daughter would be pleased. She enjoyed a carefree amble back to the clinic. It was her first relaxed moment since Dr. Wattling had called yesterday.

On the clinic's tree lined front lawn she sat down and leaned into the back of the comfortable wooden bench and stretched. The nearby Columbia River and the surrounding, forested mountains provided a comfortable, cooling evening. It shocked her to realize how long it had been since she had enjoyed such a carefree, relaxed moment.

Her idea to stay with her daughter when Pete returned to the ranch pleased her. It meant two days of hard driving for Pete before he returned with either Hank or Alex, but what the heck, it was her ranch, her sheep and her daughter. Every day the sheep grazed closer to Inchelium, so it was possible in three or four days the sheep might reach the ferry. It gave Catherine another day to heal. She chided herself for such reasoning. Tim gave her another possibility.

She'd never been satisfied with the abrupt separation between Catherine and Hank. There had been no contact since those bizarre rantings and accusations on her birthday. After Hank had returned to the Needle to make an effort to help Catherine Sarah had softened and took him back to the ranch. He had been contrite and humbled by his actions at the birthday party. He had worked hard and caused no problem. Sarah was sure neither of them had completely forgotten the other. The idea intrigued her. An extra day or two might be worthwhile.

⁓

Sarah stopped at the nurse's station to ask if her daughter was in her room or in the solarium. She looked forward to sharing her thoughts with Catherine. She carefully inched open the door to Room 103. It was ironic. She was in a talking mood, but her daughter was sound asleep. Sarah tip-toed into the room painted in soft warm colors and settled into what looked like the more comfortable of the two chairs. It was comforting to watch her daughter sleep safe and sound in the hospital bed.

In time Catherine slowly sensed a presence in her room. She spied her mother through half-opened eyes and smiled. "Well, well, it didn't take you long to get back."

She watched her mother stand and come to the side of the bed opposite of the wound. They warmly embraced.

"How long have you been sitting there?"

"About an hour."

"Why didn't you wake me? What time is it?"

She looked at the wall clock. "7:46. I'm just a mother watching and waiting. Sleep is a great curative. How are you feeling?"

"I feel okay, but the leg hurts like the devil. Dr. Wattling has prescribed a sleeping pill for tonight." Catherine became philosophic, "I guess a little pain now is much, much better than what could have been. All in all I'd say I was lucky. Did you know that Corwin set the lamb bait for me? The two shots I heard were at the grizzly bear. Corwin told me, 'I knew you were nosy enough to want to find out what the shots were'."

"How would I know that? If you're up to it tell me everything that happened."

They talked until the nurse came with the sleeping pill.

❧

Thirty miles to the east and right on schedule, Tim flew into Chewelah, and collected the needed supplies from the Chewelah IGA for delivery. The store's delivery truck was his to use after the sheep crossed the river on the state ferry. The exact day was the iffy part. The other starting iffy part was Sarah's message. "Catherine is in the Inchelium clinic. Please call." Tim appealed to the store. They gave him limited use of the delivery truck. He phoned the Inchelium Clinic and spoke to Sarah.

He shook his head in disbelief at the news. His mind had one question. How in the devil did Catherine get herself shot? He'd soon find out. Sarah didn't call just to socialize.

❧

The next day Sarah was back at the clinic to share lunch with her daughter. She was cheered to see her daughter looking better. "I take it you had a good night's sleep and you're feeling better."

"I can now say I feel fine, except when I move. You seem to have had a busy morning. Tell me what you've been doing that has kept you so busy."

Sarah confidently out lined her plans. "Today Pete goes home. He'll return tomorrow with either Hank or Alex.The day after tomorrow he and I will go back to the ranch." Sarah saw the question in Catherine's eyes. "Don't worry little one. You'll come home as soon as Dr. Wattling releases you. By the way, Tim will be here today and he'll be around until the supplies are delivered. Then he will fly you home when you're released. She triumphantly declared, "There will be no day-long, jarring ride home for you.

"In the meantime I'll visit the local mortuary and make arrangements for Corwin's body. It isn't a happy feeling. The circumstances of his death caused a damn sight more anger than sorrow, but I'm a realist. Corwin's death solved the divorce problem."

"Does that mean romance and Glen Simons will rise again?"

"Not for a while, but at least I'll be free to try."

"That silly smile says a lot."

"Yes, it does, but not as much as seeing you alive and getting better. That phone call from Dr. Wattling was the scariest bit of news I ever heard. It made me realize how much I love you and how much you mean to me." She squeezed her a little harder with her free arm.

"I love you too, Mother." She returned the squeeze. "Being shot scares you. One second you feel angry, but you're okay, and the next second something someplace hurts like the devil or worse. You look and there's blood. That's scary." She paused as if remembering the entire event. "I don't think that scared me as much as seeing that grizzly charge Rusty and Virgil. Mother, it was the bear or us. Rusty and Virgil saved my life. "All things considered Mother, I'd say we came out of this very good. We're lucky to have each other. We are truly blessed."

Sarah thought back to Pete's earlier comments on the threat of war and its financial effect on the ranch. The sheep drive was in good hands and getting close to the end. Catherine had passed every possible test and emerged as a young, strong, competent adult. It made no real difference if Hank, Tim or someone else became her man of choice. She was free and able to choose. Alex was becoming a happy, reliable young man. Either of them would be capable of taking care of Sumertun business.

Only the cloud of approaching war threatened, but her son was two years away from eighteen. The things that mattered in life were good.

Pete had been right. Her cup, no, their cup runneth over.

9004971R00249

Made in the USA
San Bernardino, CA
05 March 2014